Jesus: The Untold Years

Dale Kueter

Print ISBN: 978-1-959620-98-3
Ebook ISBN: 979-8-88531-833-4

This is a work of historical fiction, based on actual persons and events. The author has taken creative liberty with many details to enhance the reader's experience.

Published by BookLocker.com, Inc., Trenton, Georgia, U.S.A.

Library of Congress Cataloguing in Publication Data
Kueter, Dale
Jesus: The Untold Years by Dale Kueter
Library of Congress Control Number: 2024917998

BookLocker.com, Inc.
2024

DEDICATED TO ALL PEOPLE OF GOOD WILL.

Therefore, the Lord himself will give you a sign: the virgin shall be with child and bear a son, and shall name him Immanuel.

■ **Isaiah 7:14**

About this time there lived Jesus, a wise man, if indeed one ought to call him a man. For he was one who performed surprising deeds and was a teacher of such people as accept the truth gladly. He won over many Jews and many of the Greeks. He was the Christ. And when, upon the accusation of the principal men among us, Pilate had condemned him to a cross, those who had first come to love him did not cease. He appeared to them spending a third day restored to life, for the prophets of God had foretold these things and a thousand other marvels about him. And the tribe of the Christians, so called after him, has still to this day not disappeared.

■ **Flavius Josephus**:
Antiquities of the Jews, Book 18, Chapter 3, 3. First century Jewish/Roman historian.

Introduction

For 20 centuries people have been thinking and talking and writing about an unusual man who grew up in the backwater town of Nazareth, Galilee.

Christians believe he is the incarnate God, the human manifestation of God's great love and mercy for all people. Through his salvation mission the gates of heaven, closed by the disobedience of Adam and Eve, have been reopened and the opportunity for eternal life restored. Christians believe his healing, loving and forgiving ministry is a guide for all as they ponder their own meaning of life during a brief time on Earth.

Jesus.

No human being in history has had such a sustaining impact on the world. His existence is well documented. Through both the prophesy of the Jewish Old Testament and the gospels of the New Testament, there is abundant evidence of his messianic role.

Jesus.

While Gospel accounts inform us of his birth, his family's flight to Egypt, and an abbreviated period about his public ministry, passion and death, and resurrection, most of his life remains unknown. There is a barebones account when he is 12 years old about his encounter with elders in the Temple. His family is in Jerusalem for Passover and, in the process, he becomes immersed in serious discussions with Jewish religious leaders. When the Nazareth contingent heads home, he is reported missing.

Jesus.

His family, the Holy Family of Jesus, Mary and Joseph, has been the subject of unparalleled writing. John's gospel recounts many things

Jesus did, and then simply concludes by saying that if everything were recorded "I do not think the whole world would contain the books that would be written." Members of the Holy Family have been the theme for thousands of musical compositions and depicted in an equal number of paintings. Jesus is the best-known religious figure and perhaps the best-known person in the history of the world.

Jesus.

Some books of fiction have him traveling to far off lands – India, Japan and even China. Some claim he had biological siblings or half-siblings, children of Joseph, his earthly father, from a previous marriage. A recent popular author has Jesus married. There is endless speculation about his life and who he was.

Some historians claim Joseph was a widower and an old man when he married Jesus' mother Mary. In the following story, Joseph is depicted as a young man, nearly 30, at that time. His father was Jacob of the House of David.

This is not a theological or academic effort regarding the unknown life of Jesus. Rather, imagination projects the untold years in the context of the time. The author apologizes for any errors in reflecting historic and cultural matters. So, come along on this journey to visualize what it have been like to live in the first century. Picture the challenge for Mary and Joseph, called on an unimaginable undertaking to be parents of Jesus, the son of God. Imagine Jesus. Imagine his birth. His desires. His friends. His quandaries in life. His happiness. His disappointments.

Imagine when he first pondered his divine nature.

Jesus: The Untold Years is one more attempt to fill in the unknown about Jesus, to contemplate what his life may have been like. This account, too, is conjecture.

Flavius Josephus, the first century Roman-Jewish scholar and historian, mentions Jesus briefly, and there is much speculation in many sources about various people of the time. For example, most identify Mary's parents as Anne and Joachim. Some say Joachim died shortly after Mary's birth and that Anne remarried. In tribute to all grandparents, this account says both lived to see Jesus when the Holy Family returned from Egypt.

This story neither creates new major miracles nor will it downplay Jesus' humanness. Like the great film series, *The Chosen,* it is rooted in the Scripture account, though some recalled events may not be in proper sequence. This narrative strives to fill in the missing years with imaginative happenings, interaction of family and contemporaries and dialogue consistent with what we know about Jesus and the period he spent on Earth.

And then there is the matter of dates. Time itself is measured by Jesus' birth. Historians and religious scholars have disagreed for centuries on the time frame surrounding Jesus and more than likely will continue those debates. Many maintain that Jesus' birth was in 4BC. For this account, it is simply accepted that Jesus was nearing four years of age when Herod the Great, king of Judea, died in Jericho. Jesus, Mary and Joseph fled to Egypt because of Herod's paranoid rage. Herod's death meant it was safe for them to return home.

A great satisfaction for any author is when readers travel along to another time and place, and in the process have their own visions of what may have happened. That's my invitation to you. My hope is that these words will transport you to Jesus' time, help you sense his life and that of contemporaries, and imagine your own scenarios for the Holy Family.

Put yourself in Mary's place. Sure, she knew well the scriptural references to the coming of a Savior, but pregnancy while being engaged to Joseph? In a small-town atmosphere? Why me? Why now? Faith is powerful

Assume the position of Joseph. According to custom the betrothal had been arranged, the usual year-long waiting time before marriage agreed upon, and then this? What's the solution? Break off the engagement? Faith is powerful.

And Jesus. He fled for his life as a baby. How would that affect your growing up? Think teen years are difficult? Imagine an emerging understanding that you are divine as well as human. And later, map a basis for establishing a church, convince people to change, preach the kingdom of God and eternal life and in the process prepare for the salvation episode? That's a full-time job.

It is my sincere hope that many of you will someday be able to visit the Holy Land, see where Jesus walked and talked, feel his climate and culture and sense the enormity of his mission.

Jesus was born at a time when the Great Sea (Mediterranean) was the center of the known geographic universe. The Jewish people were restless under Roman rule and talk of a Messiah was widespread. Rome was the political powerhouse. The Great Pyramid of Giza was 2,500 years old. However, the Roman Coliseum didn't exist. The Second Temple (the first, Solomon's Temple, was destroyed by the Babylonians) was still standing, although it, too, was destroyed in the Jewish revolt of 70AD.

The spoken word was the primary means of communication. Most in Palestine could not read or write. Jesus spoke Aramaic. He was taught to read the Hebrew Scriptures. His mother may have taught him some words in Greek. Galilee was comprised mostly of farmers and meager businesses. However, in broader Palestine there was not only a class order but the system of slavery. Outside the monotheistic Jewish faith, Rome and Greece had many gods.

I read a number of books and Internet articles on Jesus, Galilee, Hebrew culture and history of the time. I want to especially acknowledge as a most helpful source a book by Jean-Pierre Isbouts,

In the Footsteps of Jesus, a treasure of information published by National Geographic. I also thank my family for support in this project.

This story begins with Simon Peter as narrator. In chapter two, Jesus and Mary are visiting at home in Nazareth in about 29AD. The future is heavy on their minds. Joseph has been dead for nearly 10 years. Chapter three travels to Egypt where the Holy Family fled after Jesus was born. Herod has died and they are about to return home. The Jesus-Mary colloquies continue in future chapters, interwoven as his life unfolds. Please note the time and location before each chapter.

Prologue

Matthew 1:1-17

The book of the genealogy of Jesus Christ, the son of David, the son of Abraham.

Abraham was the father of Isaac, and Isaac the father of Jacob, and Jacob the father of Judah and his brothers, and Judah the father of Perez and Zerah by Tamar, and Perez the father of Hezron, and Hezron the father of Ram, and Ram the father of Ammin'adab, and Ammin'adab the father of Nahshon, and Nahshon the father of Salmon, and Salmon the father of Bo'az by Rahab, and Bo'az the father of Obed by Ruth, and Obed the father of Jesse, and Jesse the father of David the king. And David was the father of Solomon by the wife of Uri'ah, and Solomon the father of Rehobo'am, and Rehobo'am the father of Abi'jah, and Abi'jah the father of Asa, and Asa the father of Jehosh'aphat, and Jehosh'aphat the father of Joram, and Joram the father of Uzzi'ah, and Uzzi'ah the father of Jotham, and Jotham the father of Ahaz, and Ahaather of Hezeki'ah, and Hezeki'ah the father of Manas'seh, and Manas'seh the father of Amos, and Amos the father of Josi'ah, and Josi'ah the father of Jechoni'ah and his brothers, at the time of the deportation to Babylon. And after the deportation to Babylon: Jechoni'ah was the father of She-al'ti-el, and She-al'ti-el the father of Zerub'babel, and Zerub'babel the father of Abi'ud, and Abi'ud the father of Eli'akim, and Eli'akim the father of Azor, and Azor the father of Zadok, and Zadok the father of Achim, and Achim the father of Eli'ud, and Eli'ud the father of Elea'zar, and Elea'zar the father of Matthan, and Matthan the father of Jacob, and Jacob the father of Joseph the husband of Mary, of whom Jesus was born, who is called Christ.

So all the generations from Abraham to David were fourteen generations, and from David to the deportation to Babylon fourteen generations, and from the deportation to Babylon to the Christ fourteen generations.

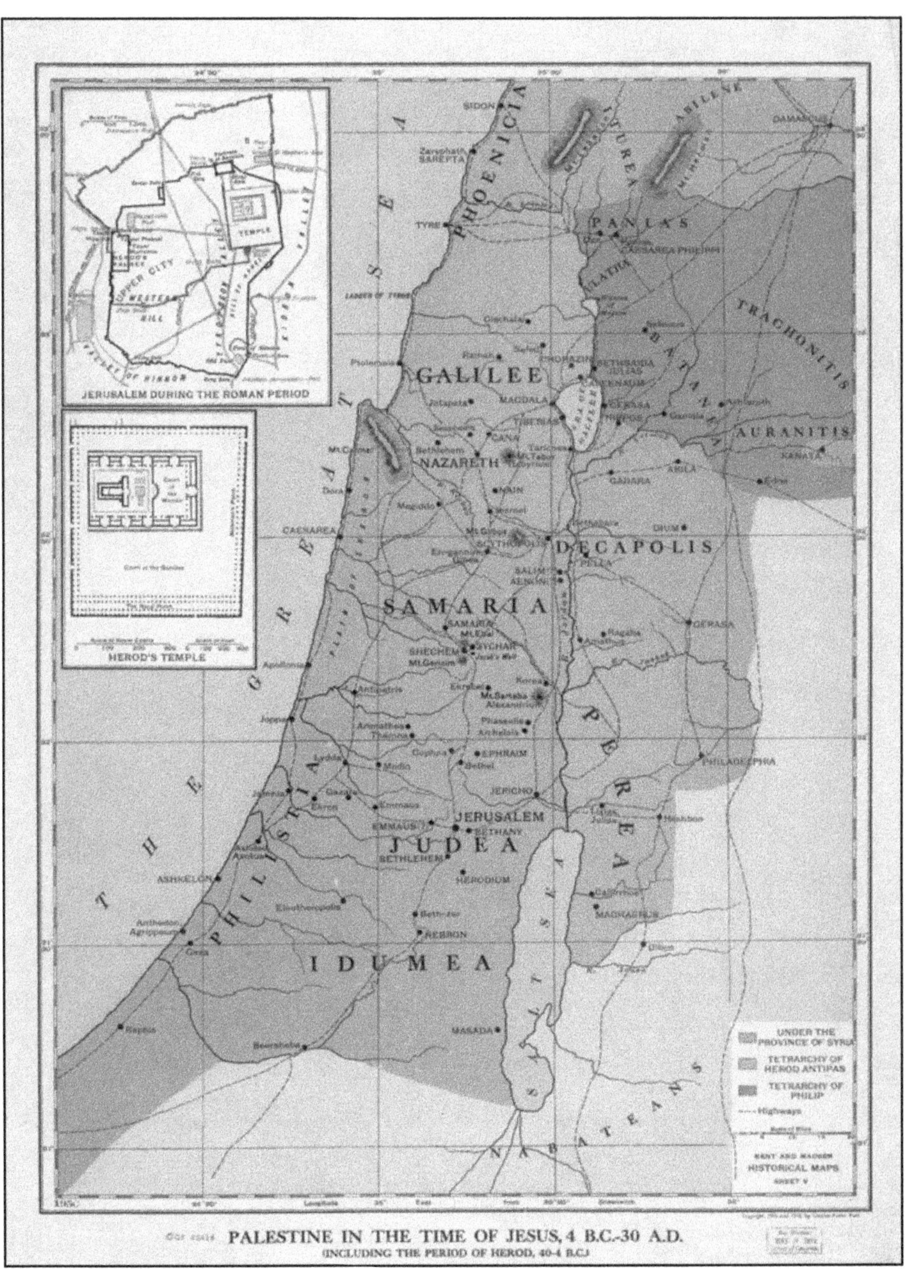

Courtesy of The Library of Congress.

Jesus: The Untold Years

CAPERNAUM, GALILEE, about 29 AD – My name is Simon, although it is formally Shimon.

I don't know how the 'h' was extracted, but my older brother, Andrew, claims my father scared the 'h' out of me years ago when I talked back to our mother. I can believe that. My father Jonah always liked Andrew better.

While I have no formal education, our mother – her name is Joanna – was an excellent teacher. She made sure we knew our letters, understood numbers and could converse intelligently. Still, I have a difficult time reading.

I am a fisherman. The entire family fishes for a living. My father has said he knows the Sea of Galilee like the back of his hand. I've also heard him say he is as familiar with the fishing business as David was with Bathsheba. But he'll deny saying that.

My family fishes mainly in the northern region of the sea and our headquarters are in Bethsaida, a north shore town where I grew up. I now live with my wife Eden and her mother in the nearby town of Capernaum, which is about a two-hour walk west of Bethsaida. Our small house is a stone's throw from the seashore and just across the street from the Capernaum Synagogue.

I must tell you that lower Galilee is the lushest part of all Israel. As the rainy season transforms to drier weather, the valleys and slopes burst forth in spectacular color with honeysuckle, jasmine and other wildflowers and blossoming trees. Grape vines, pomegranates, fig and olive trees get their juices flowing in the pleasant subtropical climate.

In an ambition of nature, as one vintner describes it, plants are forced to coexist in ambient sustenance. The tempered breezes provide cooler air for walnut trees and a mix of hotter winds to nurture palm trees. In a seeming lesson for mankind, vegetation that would compete for space and favorable weather share in harmony. Almonds, apricots, and plums flourish side by side.

On nearby ridges terebinth trees and evergreen oaks share the skimpy soil. In lower lands, people and animals are grateful in hot weather for the shade cast by the soft, silvery leaves of olive trees. Before the Romans came with their high taxes, the farmers and commoners, who make up the vast majority of our citizens, supported their families without worry.

The Hebrew word for the season (spring or April) is Nisan. Under the influence of the Greco-Roman civilization, the Jews divided the year into four seasons. Tishri became October, Tevet became January and Tammuz, July, or summer.

In much of Galilee, especially along the Great Sea (Mediterranean) to the west, there is heavy dew. Moist air drifts eastward during thedry season, and then falls to the ground as the night cools. The dewfall makes a significant contribution to the moisture needs of farming. It also saturates sails, ropes, and other gear of fishermen. That's the situation this morning.

"I swear this confounded wetness delays fishing time more than ordinary rain," I complained to anyone who would listen. I struggled to untangle the nets. "This stuff weighs twice as much as when it's dry. Whoever piled these nets in the corner of the deck should teach knitting lessons to the women and girls. What a mess!"

"Simon, Simon, Simon," father repeated for emphasis. "First off, you shouldn't swear about anything. You know the Commandments. Do you pay attention to the rabbi at Synagogue? Second, how can you be so grumpy on such a beautiful morning? The sun is warm. The sea is glistening. The fish wait to be caught."

Then he showed signs of scoffing mirth. "And thirdly," he said, "It was you who piled up the nets when we finished our last outing."

Father is tolerant and patient. You had to be enduring if you fished for a living with sometimes contrary sons. But we seldom come home without a catch. Sometimes it is just enough for supper, but often there is plenty to sell to neighboring families and the market.

Unlike many men, father pays scant attention to Roman politics. While Capernaum, a major trading town on the Damascus to Jerusalem road, is ruled by Herod Antipas, Bethsaida is under the jurisdiction of his brother, Herod Philip. Both levy heavy taxes on fishermen. On everyone for that matter.

"Andrew, give your brother a hand in sorting out the nets." I confess Andrew is far less impetuous than I and more interested in the business end of fishing. He not only soaks up father's experience at boat operations, but also his fishing knowledge. Andrew is able to read the water for schooling musht, biny, sardine and other species.

Andrew is 28, taller and stronger than me. I just turned 26. We get along in a brotherly fashion, he says largely due to his even-handedness and forbearance. Andrew is such a humble guy. He is the quiet type, doesn't like to stir up the water. His Greek name supposedly means brave, but he's as meek as a fish tip-toeing on the sea floor. I hate it when he gives me the silent treatment.

We both love the sea and fishing. I'm the one with a missing tooth and bird inkings on my upper body. I won't go into detail about the missing tooth other than to say the other fellow didn't fare well either. I admit I'm on the boisterous side and even like being the center of attention. Andrew shuns such behavior and knows twice as much as me about Scripture and Mosaic law.

"How can I help you?" Andrew approached with caution, not wanting to ignite my fuse by any insinuation that I was unraveling my own mess. "I will try to untangle the weights section if you want to work on the upper part of the net," he proposed. "If we free up the weights, the rest will unfold much quicker."

I agreed. We had all the knots and debris removed from the nets in short order. Then we swabbed down the boat, rinsed off the remaining fish blood and waste, and reorganized the other fishing tools – spears, knives, ropes. There was a place for everything on the boat, which is 17 cubits long and eight cubits wide. It sits just under three cubits above the water.

Our vessel is smaller than most commercial crafts on the Sea of Galilee. The sea, also known by the Hebrew name as Lake Kinneret, is shaped like a heart, 28,000 cubits wide and 45,000 cubits long. It is a freshwater lake, 95 cubits deep in places and primarily fed by the Jordan River. (A cubit is the length from the tip of an adult's middle finger to the elbow, about 1.4 feet.)

Father says there are some 200 commercial fishing boats on the lake. It is a demanding, labor-intensive business. He knows the competition and customers. Many operators are gruff, hard living sorts. None are social climbers. Father is a moderate man, savvy about the lake's structure and where fish would likely congregate. Some Sea of Galilee fishermen cull their catch, tossing out oysters, lobster and other shellfish forbidden by Old Testament law. Father sells those to Greek residents and the scaled fish to Jewish families.

"Please make sure the net is in order and folded neatly in the stern," father yells out. "And make sure there are no rents, no holes."

"Yes, father, we know," I replied. "This isn't our first boat ride."

The usual procedure, after scouting an inlet for schools, is for Andrew and me to wade into the shallows, each guiding a section of the net. The weights drag part of the net to the bottom while floats keep the top section on the surface. Father rows the boat in an arc, in hopes of trapping fish, which are ultimately drug ashore or on the boat in a frenzy of flopping.

"All right then," father said. "If everything is ready, we will try our luck this afternoon. Andrew, run up and tell your mother we'll be back by nightfall. The weather looks mild. When you return, we will raise the sail and head down the eastern side."

On hot days, when the sun radiates off the water and boosts the temperature even higher, fishing crews go bare-chested. Only a scant wrap covers their mid-section. In such conditions, they often go out early in the morning or in late afternoon, avoiding the warmest part of the day. Those days are still several weeks away.

By midday, we had drifted into an inlet. Six eyes scan the water for feeder fish and larger ripples. An hour passed with no signs of fish. We hoisted the sail again and drifted into another cove. This time there was success. In the excitement of the catch, we gave little attention to the rising temperature and gathering clouds. Shoreline cypress and red gum trees veiled a developing storm.

"Father, look at the western sky, over the trees!" Andrew shouted from his position in the shallow water. It was a fearsome firmament, red and pinks to the east and fast-moving billows of black and gray approaching quickly from the west. The sail began snapping in the rising wind. Waves rocked the boat, first gently like a mother rocking a baby at bedtime, then with a mounting intensity that fashioned fishermen into drunken sailors.

"I'm going to lower the sail completely," father yelled. "You boys bring in the net and walk toward the shoreline just beyond that large cypress. I will try to maneuver the boat toward the same place. We'll have to wrap things up in a hurry."

The storm's force grew as if being pushed by an angry giant. Streaks of lightening slashed the sky and were accompanied by nearly simultaneous thunder, meaning the tempest had arrived. We were soaked by sheets of rain and our vision was hampered. The only fortunate part of the situation was that we were not caught a distance from shore.

Usually, father is wise to any unexpected weather developments, but this time the elements caught him by surprise. His attention had been occupied by the prospects of a sizeable fish haul. Fishing activity often picks up with an approaching front. Now, however, attention had to be re-directed to the storm.

"The net is too heavy with the catch!" Andrew shouted. "I can barely drag it, and I know Simon will have difficulty."

"Take care of your end, big brother!" I bellowed. "I'll handle my chore." But I stumbled. My haughty determination was dashed by a five-foot wave and mouthful of water. Resolve gave way to reality. I wanted to be as strong as Andrew, and certainly didn't want to disappoint father. Vanity was checked by nature, and father saw me struggling.

"Simon, Andrew," he yelled. "Drop the net. Release the catch. Swim to shore. We will recover the net after the sea settles. It's still anchored to the boat. And don't sit directly beneath the cypress. The tree attracts lightening!"

"But father, these are beautiful fish, enough to keep us in business all week," I responded.

"Do as I say, Simon, or I'll have Andrew drag you to the shoreline."

With that, we released the net and the fish found freedom. We swam and waddled our way to shore. Father strained to beach the boat, manipulated the oars and kept the rudder fixed. As he worked the boat closer to shore, the waves grew higher. A gust sprayed his face, and the accompanying surge nearly swamped the vessel.

Just 10 boat-lengths from shore, he tossed a rope as far as his waning strength could muster. Andrew waded out, grabbed the line and pulled the boat onto the beach. I helped secure it to a nearby tree. Then we all collapsed on the sand, faces battered by the slamming rainfall and the howling wind. Father said a prayer of thanks that we were safe.

The Sea of Galilee is made to order for quick-developing storms. Winds can change in the blink of an eye. Differences in temperature along the seacoast and surrounding mountains are the formula for potential bad weather. Warm, moist sea air is suddenly bombarded by dry, cool mountain air and the clash creates trouble. Small boats further out on the sea are especially in peril.

"We were lucky not to be far out," father said. "Did you boys notice any other fishermen out there? The wind is starting to slacken. Let's walk out on that point and look for other boats. Our trip may turn out to be a rescue mission." We walked 200 cubits but spotted no one on the lake.

"Father, instead of looking for other fishermen we should be looking for our fish, the ones that may still be trapped in the net," I proposed. "Otherwise, we will be eating leftovers from last night instead of fresh fish." Andrew said nothing.

"Simon," father responded, still scanning the sea for any foundering fishing crews, "someday you will understand that it is more rewarding to fish for men than to fish for fish."

I wasn't sure what my father was talking about but it sounded a lot like that preacher who is making the rounds. He has spoken at our Synagogue several times. Pretty good speaker. Knows his Scripture. What I like about him is his relaxed manner. He loves people of all kinds. Even me, a not too pious person who tends to violate the commandment against swearing.

But I don't cuss at home. Eden would kill me. She is a devout person and knows Scripture like this Jesus fellow. He's from Nazareth, a dot on the map southwest of here. I have to admit I usually don't cozy up to rabbis and preachers, but this Jesus is different. I've known him for several months now and he seems like a regular guy.

He tells me he is spreading the kingdom of God, whatever that means, and he needs help. He said he is forming a band of followers and even asked me to join, that sons of Zebedee have already signed on. Maybe he needs to get to know me better. I told him I was a sinner and he said he knew that, and that I could change. I pointed out I am married and have a job, and he said he knew all that, too. He must have spies.

I said I would think about it, talk it over with Eden. He has quite a story. Born near Jerusalem. Spent his early years in Egypt. He's a carpenter, taking over the trade from his deceased father. I'd say he is a couple years older than me. Lately he seems unsettled, like there is something worrisome on his mind. He said he had to talk to his mother about it.

I met her when visiting their Nazareth home a short time ago. I don't think she likes me very much.

The wind eased and waves obeyed in kind. We recovered the net, raised the slightly tattered sail, and returned home to leftovers.

Chapter 2

NAZARETH, GALILEE, about 29AD – "Please close the door, Jesus. You weren't born in a barn."

I was busy darning a torn garment and hadn't even looked up.

"Oh, sorry mother. I had things on my mind." He turned around, shut the door, and walked over and kissed me on the head. "Correct me if I'm wrong," he said, "but I thought you told me I was born in a barn. At least you said there were animals there."

I laughed. "It was a stable. That's akin to a barn, I guess." We hugged each other tightly. My entire being radiated with satisfaction and love.

As I looked at him I pondered how tall he had become. (He was nearly six-foot tall, or about four cubits to use the measurement of the time.) His hair was longer now, brushing his shoulders, but still curly at the back of his neck. Like most men of the region, his skin was olive toned, his face mostly covered by a beard that frequently begged grooming. A beige colored tunic covered a strong body shaped by hard work as a carpenter.

"How did you know it was me at the door?" Jesus asked. "It could have been a thief."

"Mothers just know. I know your walk, your mannerisms, how you breathe. Besides, coming down the path you were humming one of your favorite psalms, though a little off pitch I thought."

"Really?" Jesus replied with an upturned eyebrow. "I never imagined you as a music critic."

"Where have you been the last week? I thought you were going to work on a gate repair job for that farmer."

"I finished that the week before. I was over to Capernaum and Bethsaida."

"What took you over there? That's a long hike."

"I have friends there. And I wanted to check on the fishing."

"I didn't know you liked to fish. Did you bring some home. I don't see any. I guess they weren't biting."

"Mother," he said, grinning. "Sometimes you can be so much like father. He enjoyed grilling me about this and that."

There was a chill in the little house, but it had little to do with the drifting westerly breeze that found its way from the Great Sea over the hills to lower Galilee. Mary, like only a mother can, sensed there was something different going on with Jesus. A big change in his life was emerging, and it was more than his sporadic readings and commentary at area Synagogues.

"Have you eaten supper? I have some chicken soup left over, and I can slice some bread."

"That would be wonderful," he said.

"Did you go back over there to visit that Simon man?" I asked, admittedly with a little edginess in my voice. "When he visited here some months back, he seemed sort of rough, a rather coarse fellow even for a fisherman. He comes, bare chested, with ink drawings all over his body!"

"Yes, that would be Simon," Jesus said. "But under those drawings there is a heart of gold. Maybe a little stubbornness. And, sometimes, fervent pride. Yes. I saw him. You would like his older brother, Andrew. He's more soft-spoken, actually on the meek side. They are sons of Jonah, who runs the family fishing business."

"Well, from that one experience I would say that Simon has never been accused of being soft-spoken. He is certainly no wallflower."

"Mother, I have asked both to be my followers, to help spread the kingdom of God. I intend to ask others, too. I was thinking of that when I walked in the house."

"You asked this Simon? To go around with you preaching the Scriptures? Better ask him to cover up all those drawings on his body or the kingdom will be distracted before it gets started. And isn't he married?"

"He is. And I considered that. His wife is a holy person. She knows Scripture, especially the meaning of Isaiah, and she knows our history and the role of the Hebrew people. After visiting with them, together, they agreed. Simon will give it consideration."

He looked at my questioning eyes. "What? I should exclude married men from doing God's business?"

"No, I guess not," I muttered as I sipped the reheated chicken soup to see if it was hot enough. I placed a soup bowl and spoon on the table.

"Did you say something, mother? I thought I heard you say something."

"I said, maybe you should ask Simon's wife instead to be a disciple."

"Well, that's possible. Right now, she is caring for her sickly mother."

Except for traveling to Jerusalem for the annual Passover celebration, Jesus had confined his travels to the Galilee and Jordan River areas. He had visited the burgeoning city of Sepphoris northwest of Nazareth and regions in Phoenicia, but mostly limited his preaching and carpentry business to the small towns that surrounded the Sea of Galilee.

"Simon and Andrew grew up in Bethsaida," Jesus explained, "but Simon moved to Capernaum after his marriage. The family boat works out of both towns. And, you'll be interested to learn, the two know my distant cousin, John. That's how I met them, through John. John has been preaching up and down the Jordan."

"I heard about John's baptizing people and stirring up the water over at the Jordan," I said. "Mothers don't live in a vacuum. I have to tell you Jesus, to think John, this baby I helped usher into the world, is living like a wilderness man, eating grasshoppers and hair a flying wild. I don't know what his mother, God bless her soul, would say."

"He is enthusiastic," Jesus agreed. "He knows a lot of people in that region, all the way down to Jericho. I just hope he doesn't get caught up in some kind of political confrontation with the Romans. He doesn't mince words, mother. He reminds me a lot of Simon. Fierce in his beliefs."

"This Simon. What kind of fish does he catch? And why does he decorate himself with bird drawings? You'd think he'd have fish drawings."

"I have no idea, mother, why Simon prefers bird inkings. You ask him the next time he visits. As for species, Simon says there are sardines, barbel (carp), and musht or tilapia. They also net catfish, which are not of real economic importance because they are without scales and may not be eaten by Jews. They sell them to non-Jews.

"Most fish, except the sardines, are sold immediately, or as they say in Capernaum, from the sea to the frying pan. Fishing is the main occupation over there."

Talk about fishing diverted the real question that occupied the back of their minds. Mary knew this time would come, that her son's mission would take final form and that all that the Jewish Scriptures had prophesized was about to unfold. After all, she had agreed at Jesus' conception to take a major role in God's great salvation plan. But that awareness didn't ease her anxiety. She suspected there would be painful days ahead. Simon and fishing were her temporary foil.

"Does this mean you are giving up your carpenter and handyman work entirely?" I asked, knowing the answer. "My dear Joseph taught you well. And while you reflect his great patience in working with people, and in many cases not even charging them, I must say he was truly an artisan. And a caring man. I miss him so much."

She paused for several seconds.

"Our lives," I continued, "your effort in fulfilling God's design, are beholden to Joseph's holiness and great understanding." She tasted the reheated soup to see if it was hot enough.

"I know mother. I miss him, too. And I miss your parents and Joseph's father. And I will miss all my brothers and sisters in Galilee, the many friends we have made through the carpentry and masonry business, at the Synagogue and traveling around the region. Yes, I must get on with the reason I was born. Oh, I will finish some odd jobs I promised to neighbors, but everything then turns to fulfillment of God's word."

There. It was out in the open.

Jesus knew it would be a difficult time for his mother, even though it wasn't a surprise to her. But the time had come. His enlistment in the service of the Father had progressed to active duty. While he had gained attention for his unique humanness, his treatment of the poor and sick, concern for ordinary folk and his example of living a holy life, it was time to slowly reveal his divine nature.

"Son of God, son of man," I looked at Jesus as she placed the soup pot on the table that Joseph had built. "How will you tell the people? How do you know they will understand the full dimensions of who you are and your mission? How do you know that some, especially the more rigid thinkers, won't reject you outright and say you are a blasphemer?"

"I can't predict how some people will react, mother," Jesus said as he supped the chicken broth. "Remember, God gives everyone free will."

"Is the soup hot enough?" I asked. "And what will you do if they yell names at you or worse?"

"The soup is delicious, thanks," he nodded. "When that happens, I guess I'll just have to go on to the next place. The other day a mute man came up to me, I think it was on the other side of the Jordan River, and he was agitated by his condition and other matters. I prayed with him and suddenly he began to speak. And he was relieved of other troubles, too. Some saw and believed in the hand of God. Some didn't.

"Mother, could I please have another piece of your delicious barley bread? I smelled it before I opened the door."

"Of course. So, if someone comes up and wants to bash in your head because of your preaching, what then? Will this Simon come to your aid?"

"Maybe," Jesus smiled. "Maybe not."

"Well, why have followers if they are not going to protect you?"

"Mother, you realize as well as I that many, particularly zealots, are looking for a messianic leader who will direct Israel to victory over the Romans. Boot them out of our land. I am not that person. I bring the kingdom of God, God's message of peace and love and forgiveness. Eternal life! And my followers will spread that kingdom to the ends of the Earth."

"And no one gets hurt in the process."

"I didn't say that. Some may lose friends. Some may be imprisoned or worse. Some will find it too difficult to work in the vineyard of the Lord. Take the matter of forgiveness. Not an easy thing. I say we should forgive just as we expect to be forgiven. I befriended a woman the other day – some claim she is unclean and a prostitute – and after I spoke, she asked that her sins be forgiven. I said they were if she truly repents."

"What happened? Do you want the rest of the chicken soup?

"Sure. Well, one would have thought I had suggested that taxes be doubled. Several protested that I shouldn't even be speaking with her. Not speaking? That's a fine way to make progress."

A collision of thoughts ran through Mary's mind. Would her son weather the agony of rejection and possible persecution? How much would he suffer? Would his followers be fair-weather fans or true disciples of God's promise of everlasting life? How would the Romans react to his expanded ministry and growing number of supporters? For that matter, what would be the response of his own people. Her contemplation turned practical. How did he intend to feed himself and his followers?

"Will you leave Nazareth and Galilee for good or return now and then?"

"Mother. I am not abandoning you. I will go wherever the spirit directs me, throughout Galilee for certain, along the Jordan River and probably down to Samaria. Maybe Jericho. But," and he looked at her with a warm smile, "I will come home from time to time for your good cooking."

"Did you get enough to eat? Do you want something besides soup and bread?"

"I've had plenty. Thank you."

"Samaria?" I said with more than a little surprise. "The Samaritans are not our closest friends. You know that."

"Yes, I know. And it may be with good reason. They haven't received the kindest treatment from us. After their assimilation with the Assyrians, we called them dogs and half-breeds. Then there was the matter of worship. Our focus is on Jerusalem and Mount Zion. Samaritans decided to worship God at Mount Gerizim near Shechem. These are our people, but it shows what division and hatred can do.

"Do you know that some local Jews – on their way to Jerusalem – refuse to travel through Samaria? Instead, they cross the Jordan River and go around Samaria. Such stiff-neck attitudes need change."

"And you will change those feelings?"

"I don't know, mother. All I can do is tell them that we worship the same God, and that God loves all people."

After eating, Jesus walked over to the small stone oven, still warm from Mary's baking bread. It was part of a semi-circle of stones that served as the cooking area. The same room contained space for eating and sleeping. He placed his hand on the oven and smiled.

"I remember when father built this," he looked at me. "He was far more than a carpenter and stone mason. He was a designer, a tekton as the Greeks say, a master of all trades. He showed me how to get the most out of the available space. I think his craftsmanship surprised a lot of customers. I know I was amazed at many of his ideas. And greater than all his building skills was his love of people, just doing things that pleased others."

"You are so right. Is it any wonder that you are known throughout the area as the 'carpenter's son'? Joseph was respected as much for his sociability and kindness as he was for his workmanship. He was patient and understanding." She paused to reflect. "I should know."

I remembered my years with Joseph. "He was humble and never lost hope. Most of all, he was loving and faithful to his God and as husband and father. I never saw him angry except that time when you were 12."

"You mean in Jerusalem when I was caught up in Scripture discussions with rabbis and elders in the Temple? Yes, I'd say he was more than a little displeased by my behavior, and my explanation didn't improve matters. But, as much as anything, he was upset because you were upset." He hesitated. "I could have handled that whole thing a lot better."

"Jesus. Are you staying the night?"

"Yes. Will that be OK?"

"Of course."

Mary grabbed an extra mat, several blankets and spread them on the tamped earthen floor away from the entrance. Joseph had deposited lime on the floor to harden the surface and reduce dust.

"I most likely will be up by sunrise," I said. "After prayer, I enjoy some fruit and a piece of bread, and, as you know, I dab some honey on it."

"Usually, it's more than a dab," Jesus laughed. "I prefer, as you know, to pray in that grove just down the road, the one with the single sycamore surrounded by old olive trees and undergrowth. There I can see the splendor of God's early morning, the first light, and hear the overture by a choir of birds proclaiming the dawn of a new day. All of God's people get another chance to serve one another."

"And after you've eaten? What are your plans?"

"I told Mr. Katz' wife that I'd repair a door leading out to her garden. I hope it's not too difficult a job. Father could probably have done it in his sleep, but it will take me most of the day."

"Do you want me to help? You remember Joseph's saying: When measuring to cut a board, two more eyes often save grumbling later."

"I think I can manage, mother."

I wasn't ready to retire for the night. And I didn't want Jesus to go to bed either. Mothers are extraordinarily uneasy when their children are at a crossroads in life. Sometimes it is unnecessary worry. More often it's a combination of defined and unspecified anxieties, disquiet rooted in the present and the past. It is inherent in love.

Where Jesus was headed surpassed any ordinary twists of life. It encompassed all the joy of human interaction and simultaneously encumbered all the disappointments. Mary recognized the world-changing dimension of his life and mission. And she knew that could not happen without both exultation and sorrow, loving acceptance and piercing rejection.

She knew Jesus' reason for entering human life was to save human life, and she also realized the world had ideas of its own. That's where her fear was centered.

"Do you remember anything of our life in Egypt?" she asked tenderly.

"Mostly from what you and father have told me. I do recall the everlasting winds and blowing sand. And the lack of trees. I wonder if people fully understand the significance of a tree," he mused. "It stretches upward in reverence and gratitude to God, grants shelter to humans and creatures, and many even provide food. A tree is a gift of beauty.

"I remember father sawing a piece of lumber one day. He stopped, gently patted the wood and said, 'thank you tree'."

I smiled. "That would be Joseph."

"And I won't ever forget that large man who operated the boat on the Nile River on our trip home from Egypt, what, some 25 years ago? The stories he told!"

"Yes," I laughed. "He surely frightened you. You clung to me like a chick seeks protection under a hen's wing. I'll be honest. He scared me, too."

"Funny," Jesus said. "After we got to know him, he became a different man. So, was it a problem with him or a problem with us?" He paused. "Simon is that way, mother. Once you truly get to know him, he's steadfast as a rock."

Jesus retrieved a couple pieces of cedar wood to toss on the waning fire in the cooking area. He looked up at Joseph's clever venting design that kept the room mostly clear of smoke. "He and the tree still keep us warm," Jesus said.

"How about the time you backed into a cactus? Or, when we ran into that dust storm in the desert? The parade of pack animals and caravan? Remember any of that?"

"Oh, sure. I recall images from that time, particularly a boy my age and his dog." Jesus smiled. "I remember the warning father gave when we first joined that camel train. I was engrossed in all the excitement of soon walking where Moses and our ancestors walked. Everyone was excited about that. Father said one should also be aware of where camels have walked and how messy it would be if I stepped in their deposits."

"Reverent but practical Joseph," I said.

"Mother, would you like a glass of milk? I'd be happy to pour a cup for you."

"No thanks, Jesus. I'm fine." The truth was I thought goat's milk would add to my stomach's churning feeling.

"When I first laid eyes on the Great Sea," Jesus continued, "it took my breath away. We were coming out of the desert, remember, and there it was, gleaming like a massive diamond. I had never seen so much water. It made the Nile and its tributaries seem like a trickle. And later, when I initially saw the Sea of Galilee, it, too, seemed tiny in comparison."

"I had the same feeling. The Great Sea appeared never-ending," I said. My entangled mind of memories and impending events led me in a new direction – toward Jesus' divine nature.

"You don't have to answer this if you don't want to," I said in a loving but cautious manner. "I have often wondered about this, and Joseph did, too, when he was still living, but we never seemed to find the right time to ask you. Or, maybe it's more accurate to say we never had the courage to ask you."

"What is it, mother? Your hesitancy suggests a monumental issue."

"It is."

"Well?"

"Jesus, and I'm not trying to pry or be flippant, but . . ."

"Mother, you can ask me anything."

"OK. I have always known you are the Son of God as well as my son. God's messenger let me know that before you were in my womb. I was, of course, overwhelmed by the thought that I, Mary of Nazareth, a place few people have heard of, would be an instrument of God's salvation. To this day, after three decades, I shudder at all that that implies. I have grown into the role God assigned me. But it still isn't easy."

"Mah," and Jesus resorted to his name for her when he was little, "You are the holiest of women. You were selected to be my mother because of that, because God the Father knew you believed all that Isaiah said. I thank you for all the trials contained in saying 'yes.' But I also know that millions in the future will also thank you and praise you for it."

Silence filled the room as Mary and Jesus gloried in one another. The history of the world was wrapped in their holy presence. It was as if time stood still, but both knew time didn't.

"You forgot your question, mother," he asked tenderly.

"Oh, my son," and I rose, walked to the other side of the table, and embraced him with the deepest of love. "What Joseph and I often wondered, and it may seem silly, but as you grew, when did you first have a feeling that you were more than human."

I bent down and looked into his eyes.

"When did you sense that you were God?"

He drew her to his lap, holding her with his right arm. A tear formed and trickled down her cheek. Jesus cleared his throat.

"Did the two of you come up with an answer?"

"Now stop that, answering a question with a question," I pinched his cheek playfully. "We sort of guessed you had an idea at age 12, when you recited and interpreted Scripture with the brightest of scholars in Jerusalem. The divine factor had to be working there. At the same time, human nature was certainly present when you forgot the scheduled time to leave for home."

"Hmmm. I can tell that's still a little sore spot with you," Jesus said.

"I suppose you are right," he continued. "The divine may have been at work as we talked in the Temple court, but the real question is if I recognized it. OK. So, they marveled at the answers of a boy, a boy whose parents educated him in the Scriptures, relished in telling him stories of ancestors and prayed. To answer your question, I'm not sure. Perhaps it was a gradual thing, as any child learns."

He paused, thinking.

"I believe the strongest feelings about my divine nature came to light when I was in my late teens." He thought back some 10 years. "I liked that girl, and I think she liked me. Mother, you remember Naomi. Her family lives between here and Sepphoris. She is a beautiful and holy person. Never missed Synagogue. She reminded me of you. But I had this profound sense that God was calling me to be me. How does one explain that to a girl?"

"Sure, I remember her," I said softly.

"I wasn't good at explaining things," Jesus continued. "The good news is that she found another fellow, got married, and has three daughters. No sons. Revenge maybe?"

"I don't think it works that way," I counseled, "but then I am no expert on the mystery of conception."

"Mother, I don't intend this to sound like a farewell speech, for surely it isn't, but I need to thank you, praise you, and thank the Holy Spirit for selecting you as my mother. What you have done, from the beginning, trusting in God and the Scriptures, is more than amazing. Lending your womb in God the Father's plan for reconciling heaven and mankind elevates the stature of all women in their unequaled role to nurture the world.

"I thank you for the humiliation of gossip that accompanied your pregnancy, all the stares and threats you suffered on my behalf. To say your reward in everlasting life will be great is begging for exclamation. If my role on Earth is the doorway to heaven, then you hold the key.

"I thank you for the personal care given to me, even now fussing over my nourishment. I thank you for all your sacrifices. It couldn't have been easy to keep my identity quiet all those years while other moms were bragging about their children."

"Yes, there were trying times," I confessed. "Don't forget morning sickness after I went to visit Elizabeth."

They laughed. She hugged him tightly. They talked about many other things before heavy eyelids messaged the time for sleep.

Chapter 3

UPPER NILE VALLEY (about 4AD) – "I can see your mind is made up, Joseph. No use trying to convince you elsewise. The decision is in your face." He looked away, meditating on the endless parade of sand dunes to the west, hoping to find a grain of evidence that would change the inevitable.

"Well, no doubt the entire village will miss you and Mary. And the boy, too."

Abasi Salah peered into the Egyptian distance, his mind perceptively fixed on the impending absence of his good friend and neighbor, Joseph of Galilee. It is amazing, he thought, how close one can become to a fellow who was a newcomer to the region less than a year ago.

Joseph was a likable man, a good neighbor, soft spoken and even tempered, always ready to lend a hand. And he could fix anything. He was a handyman's handyman.

"If you need anything for your trip, food or tools, just name it. Anything we have is yours," Abasi said.

"Appreciate that, Abasi, but my focus is on traveling as light as possible," Joseph replied. "I'm trying to convince Mary to concentrate on packing small, taking useful things, not big pots and pans she won at some bazaar."

The two men laughed.

"Good luck with that," Abasi said.

"We will miss you and Nubia," Joseph said, "and our son will have an empty spot in his heart for your boys. Everyone down here, but especially your family, has been so accepting and kind. We were nomads, and you graciously made us feel welcome."

Joseph paused. He walked up to Abasi and the two embraced. Both men tried to hide emerging tears, knowing that after tomorrow they would likely never see each other again.

"I've been meaning to ask you," Joseph wiped his blinking eyes. "Your parents named you Abasi, a name Nubia once said meant 'stern'. But we have never witnessed that meaning. Are you misnamed?"

"Oh, Joseph," Abasi laughed, "you don't see me all day, every day. I'm afraid I sometimes display a temper, especially when Nubia doesn't understand me. Or, when I hit my finger with a hammer."

"Who doesn't get upset about that?" Joseph rejoined. "I mean when you slam your finger instead of the peg."

It had been almost four years, short and simultaneously long for Joseph and Mary since they left Judea in haste. They drifted for weeks enroute to Egypt, stopping in many towns and hamlets, subsisting and always keeping a watchful eye for the unusual. They moved frequently. Eventually, they settled in a cave far south of Memphis (Cairo) in the Eastern Sahara Desert, not far from the famous Nile River.

Now it was time to go home.

Except for small incidents and misunderstandings, their temporary residency in a foreign land had not been that unusual. Alexandria, the capital of Roman-ruled Egypt, and some other urban centers were still dominated by Hellenistic influence. Most of the countryside and villages remained peasants and tenant farmers.

But make no mistake. The Romans were in charge here, too. Much of the produce from the Nile valley was exported to feed the growing Rome masses.

There was an emerging Jewish population along the Nile outside Alexandria, creating possible clashes with Greek aristocracy. Roman law under Emperor Caesar Augustus (Octavian) superseded Egyptian statutes and culture even though many of the institutions of the old Greek Ptolemaic dynasty survived.

The trysts and drama surrounding Julius Caesar, Mark Antony and Cleopatra were fading into history. Under Augustus' rule, backed by 27,000 troops along the Nile, life was peaceful. And such was the tenure for the displaced, small family from the lower regions of Galilee in Israel. That and bonds with friends and neighbors were now being uprooted.

There was that incident when a Roman consul had wandered outside the Nile Valley to the sparsely populated cave region – largely, most locals believed, to make his presence and power known. He questioned Joseph's heritage and dark skin. He appeared satisfied when

Joseph related that he was a Jew, and that his family was only a temporary resident.

"Who will fix our broken plows?" Abasi petitioned in vain. "Who will repair the busted yoke? Or mend the cracked rock in our homes?"

"Abasi, Abasi," Joseph smiled and waved his arm with dismissal. "You are one of the best hands in repairing harnesses, and I've seen your masonry skills. Have you ever thought of running for political office? You make a good appeal. Maybe you should come with us to Galilee and work in our shop."

"What? And trade our glorious Roman rule for your Roman rule?" Abasi chortled. "That is a sideways move. I'm looking to improve our political posture."

"Maybe then you should run for office," Joseph gave him a sly look.

"I think I will leave good enough alone," Abasi replied. "On a more serious note, you should be aware of possible flooding near the Nile River. We call it the season of Akhet. It is a long river and drains a wide region. There is a reason why the land along the Nile is so fertile. Over the centuries, floods have washed in good soils from the south."

"Thanks for the advice. We hope we are in advance of any flooding problems."

The two men proceeded to exchange awkward glances that carried many thoughts. What would become of them? What would Egypt and the Nile Valley look like in 50 or 100 years, for that matter in 2,000 years? Would the Romans still be in charge? Who, if anyone, would be living in the caves of Asyut Mountain?

Joseph offered words for their contemplation.

"Maybe history will refer to you as Abasi the Great, the venerable and just ruler of the middle Nile. Like Alexander the Great, who ruled the ancient Kingdom of Macedonia."

"Sure. And Joseph, where will history place you? In the Carpenters Hall of Fame?"

"Well then, our futures are settled," Joseph said, and this time the two shook hands in a personal leave-taking that assured them they would never forget each other. "Time for me to do more packing."

"Don't forget," Abasi injected with heartening voice. "We'll see you, Mary and the boy tonight at the farewell gathering."

The desert wind played a solemn and even mournful sound, Joseph thought, as it picked up its afternoon strain. Here, east of its vast emptiness, the air was slightly less arid. Vegetation began to flourish as one approached the river. It was a strange land, with many myths. One legend told of a huge body of water beneath the broad desert.

While sandstorms are common in the heart of the Sahara Desert, they are unusual and less intense over the Nile River valley. But there have been times when the "orange winds" invaded the region, usually in early spring. Another thing for Joseph to worry about.

When he returned to the family's living quarters, he found Mary sitting on one of the chairs he had made from a dead acacia tree. She had fashioned cushions for the seats, and now sat in meditation of their past and future. The trip ahead would not be easy.

"I know you are worried, Mary," he said gently. He tried to deflect her concerns. "But no, you can't take any chairs on the journey. I'll make you new ones when we get back to Nazareth. For now, you must decide who among your friends here will get your chairs. Maybe we could have a drawing, or auction, to raise money for the needy?"

"Joseph. Be serious," Mary replied. "Not only are we leaving good friends, but I must think about food for the next several weeks, medical needs, cleaning materials and who knows what else. When was the last time you planned any menus? And I worry about our son's stamina for such a long journey," she sighed.

"He'll be fine," Joseph assured. "We need to finish packing and then get ready for tonight's farewell gathering. I agree. It won't be easy leaving our neighbors." Their eyes reflected the pending goodbyes. "At least you won't have to cook tonight."

When the three arrived at Singing Sand Park, so named generations before because of the nearly constant desert winds sweeping in from the west, organizers of the farewell had a small fire started. It not only served practical cooking needs and offset the evening chill, but equally symbolized the bond that prevailed in the enclave.

"Ah, Mary," a woman with a tag-along child said with a tap on Mary's shoulder. "We couldn't have wished for a more lovely evening. I'm just sorry it will be the last for you and Joseph, and of course your son, to be with us. I will truly miss you."

Reem El Shamy did not intend to make Mary's departure more traumatic. While Mary attempted to make everyone feel special, she and Reem had a unique closeness. It was Reem and her spouse who were first to welcome them to the area, and first to aid them in getting established. It was a friendship that grew stronger over time.

"Oh, Reem. I will miss you. You have been so kind. And your husband, too. Please know that you will be in our hearts always, wherever our lives may take us." The two women embraced. Tears trickled down their cheeks. Mary wiped her face with her hands as others approached to wish her well.

"Mary!" Aya Fouda exclaimed. "Look at the tables. Have you ever seen so much food? Breads, beans, coriander, falafel and a variety of kochari. And I didn't even check out the sweets. I expect there is baklava and basbousa. And look there. Dates and figs. No one will leave hungry." Some of the food was home grown, some from the Nile River markets.

Anemone and jasmine decorated the tables. The cooling sun, setting in the west, was further subdued by trees and surrounding hills. Some of the children crisscrossed the gathering area, running and squealing as their homemade windmills spun in the docile breeze.

Mary's motherly eyes instinctively scanned the hubbub of playful youngsters, satisfying herself that her son was not testing trouble. That she was inordinately concerned with his well-being was, for her, a matter of assignment. It was the perpetual consequence of her "thy will be done . . ."

Reem spotted Mary's unease and approached her.

"You worry too much about him," Reem counseled. "Boys especially seem to test one's patience. One way or another, at some age, he is bound to anger someone, get into some kind of serious tribulation. Here is a gift," she said, handing Mary a stone with the inscription *Hotep.* "That means 'peace'. I pray that you have it all your life."

Mary was overwhelmed. Hugs and tears were repeated.

"That is so kind of you," Mary said. "I will treasure it. What a wonderful wish. Thank you. Before we leave tomorrow, I would like you to have our son's baby blanket. Something to remember us by. And, you never know, Reem. You may need it."

They giggled and embraced again.

"You, too, may need it, Mary. You are so young. You could have several more children."

"Yes. I suppose so. But only God knows for sure."

Nubia walked toward Mary. They embraced but suddenly were interrupted by a young man who was assigned to distribute drinks.

"Beer, goat's milk or water?" he quizzed the crowd.

The women laughed but declined with a shake of their heads.

Beer was a popular drink for the lower classes, adults and young alike. Most was made from barley and some flavored with honey or ginger. Red wines were expensive to make and reserved almost exclusively for the wealthy. The air quickly was charged with lively conversation.

"You don't like our beer?" Mido Mabrouk asked Joseph before taking a gulp of the brown liquid himself. "It is the nectar of the gods. It is not uncommon," he felt the need to explain, "for laborers to be paid in bread or beer. Certain you don't want a cup of beer?"

Joseph hoisted a goblet of water in tribute to Mabrouk and his beer. "It's not that I don't like beer," he said. "It's just that sometimes after drinking beer I wake up the next morning with a headache. That's the last thing I need tomorrow morning. But I must say beer, with a little honey, is most attractive to the palate.

"Also, after drinking a few beers my hometown language of Aramaic could easily get entangled with your Afroasiatic lingo, so I best stick to water."

That provoked boisterous laughing.

"Joseph. You and Mary have done quite well with our jumble of dialects, much better than we have done with learning Aramaic." A brief quiet entered the group of talkers.

"You plan to depart early tomorrow, then?" Mabrouk asked.

"Well, as early as family procedures and last-minute adjustments allow."

Mabrouk nodded understanding, then acknowledged the approaching Abasi Salah. Salah, too, was carrying a glass of beer.

"Hello, Joseph," Salah said quietly. "And a good evening to you, Mido. What are you two discussing? Beer, religion or politics?"

"Yes," said Mabrouk, and the three guffawed.

"We are an interesting trio," Mabrouk offered. "Abasi and I believe in many gods. Joseph has just one. We as farmers pound the earth for a living. Joseph pounds pegs into round holes and fixes things. Some of us eat pork. Joseph doesn't. But we all get along and wouldn't that be nice if everyone did."

"You forgot another commonality," said Abasi. "We are all ruled by Rome."

Chapter 4

DOWN THE NILE RIVER – I admit that I had become attached to the Asyut cave community. It became home and I hated to leave. Then, too, I was worried about the long trip, worried if Jesus would be okay. As his mother I am forever mindful of his divinity. I know Joseph is more attentive to his human nature. We have had discussions about that.

I emphasized to Joseph just last night that he is a special child, that we must always be aware of that. He says to me, somewhat edgily I thought, "Mary. I'm aware. I've been here from the beginning." Then he says, "He made it down here as a baby. I'm sure he can make it home to Nazareth."

The wind seemed to mimic the sun, rising in intensity as the morning sky brightened. In reality, desert wind was as two-faced as Roman politics. At times, it could whirl like a blast furnace, propelling grains of sand like tiny bullets. On this day it presented its nice side, caressing the new day and its denizens with refreshing gentleness.

The air movement was a welcome tempering of unusually early summer heat. Even so, sweat drizzled down Joseph's face as he led the donkey eastward toward the Nile River.

He had hoped to get an earlier start, but packing the family's meager belongings – clothes, tent shelter, food and tools – took longer than he expected. It was mid-morning by the time the trio left their cave near Qusquam on Asyut Mountain. His plan was to generally follow the route that had brought them to Egypt nearly four years before.

Once at the Nile, he anticipated to again earn passage on a wooden boat that would take them north down the river 230 miles to Memphis. On the trip south, he had plenty of boat work mending leaks in the hull and miscellaneous carpenter work. Modeled after the old papyrus boats, the more modern craft featured wooden planks bound by rope, with spaces calked with a blend of reeds, tree gum and clay.

Joseph chuckled as he tugged the bridle rein of the reluctant pack animal, then looked back at his son. To say the boy was going to be much of a helper in the trek stretched reality. After all, he was just a child. Still, he knew tools, the difference between an awl and chisel. He could fetch a saw or hammer without mistake. And he was learning as he watched his father repair things.

The boy was lagging.

"I'm tired of walking and my toes hurt," the lad informed his parents.

"Joseph, did you pack my cloth bag and darning set?" I asked with some urgency, temporarily overriding Jesus' complaints about sore feet. "It's not like we have the money to buy clothes on the way. Things will have to be patched."

"Yes, Mary. I tucked them inside one of the cooking pots. Can't you hear the needles rattling? Or maybe," Joseph added, "that jingling could be some nails I stuck in your special jar, the one you received as a gift from your cousin, Elizabeth."

"You didn't!"

"I did. We don't have all kinds of space to bundle small things so they will endure travel. We have a few miles to go, you may remember."

"Aba. My feet are sore."

"You better get used to the hot sand, Jesus." Joseph replied. "These roads aren't covered in squishy fiber even though Egypt is a large producer of cotton. We've been traveling less than two hours. Toughen up, son."

"But Aba. I'm tired. When are we going to stop and eat?"

"Ask your mother."

"Immah, when are we going to take a break. My feet are sore and tired. Can't we stop just for a short time? Are there any figs or nuts in the food bag?"

"What does your father say about stopping? And, yes, we have some snacks."

"Aba said to ask you. Who will decide when we stop? It's not like I can read your minds."

"Now, Jesus," I counseled, patting him on the head. "Don't become impatient. This is a long trip, and it's best you set your mind on that."

"Immah, may I take my tunic off? It's hot."

"I don't think that's a good idea," I said. "While your skin is dark, that doesn't mean the desert sun won't burn. You best leave it on."

"Aba. Will you carry me?"

"Joseph," I lobbied, "remember the boy is not yet four. He doesn't have your stamina or blessed with your resolve."

Joseph, already toting a large satchel on his left shoulder, wiped his forehead again. His eyebrows raised in resignation. How many more gray hairs would sprout from his head before they reached Nazareth?

"Come on," Joseph conceded. "I'll carry you a short time in my right arm, but you must take the strap and pull Dynamo. Is that a deal?"

"A deal," Jesus agreed. "He won't balk. I'll see to it."

That lasted awhile before Joseph's arm began to ache. He decided to stop and eat, relieving both his arm and a grumbling stomach. Another incentive was the shade of a lonely acacia tree. His goal was to reach the river before sunset.

"Let's stop here, Mary, for rest and a bite to eat. Jesus, please help your mother. Spread a blanket under the tree. Then find a frond of some kind to chase the flies off Dynamo. He'll hee-haw in gratitude, and it may improve his attitude."

"I don't think so, Aba," Jesus laughed. "Donkeys are just slow and stubborn. They can't help it."

"You mean like little boys who can't help but get their clothes dirty?"

"I guess," Jesus looked at his father with a grin.

"It's hard to believe, Joseph, but we were at Qusquam for 11 months, longer than any other place since we departed Judea some three years ago," I said with a slight tone of reluctance. "We were just getting to know the neighbors." He said nothing. "What roads will we take and are you sure it's safe to return to Nazareth?" I asked.

"There are no guarantees in this life, Mary. All I can say is that I trust in the Lord. He sent a message in a dream, as I told you, that King Herod has died. I think it is best that we return to the place where we grew up in Galilee, where your parents live. It's our home. And remember, your father Joachim gave me my first job. I have some standing as a carpenter in that area."

"You are right, Joseph. It's just that it seems we are always moving."

"Mary, yes. The people in Asyut have been good to us," Joseph agreed. "Shortly after we arrived, they helped us discover a well. I ask you to remember, however, there were some at the river who weren't so friendly. Some chased us with rods and axes. It didn't take us long to leave that place."

"Why did they hate us, father?"

"Well, Jesus. I imagine it's an age-old question. Some are threatened by outsiders, people who don't look and act like them or maybe dress a little differently. Or maybe they just didn't like the looks of Dynamo. He's not the best-looking donkey, what with one ear ripped."

"But that wasn't Dynamo's fault," Jesus defended the pack animal. "Remember? That mean, old camel just came up and bit Dynamo. For no reason at all. I don't like camels. They make this weird, painful moan, as if they have bees in their hump. And none of God's creatures have such bad breath and smell."

Joseph laughed.

"To answer your other question, Mary, I see no reason but to return by a route similar to the one we traveled here. We'll take the Nile down to Memphis, angle up to the Great Sea and take the sea road through Farma, Al Arish, Gaza and Ascalan. I'm hoping we can stay with Jewish families as often as we did on the trip down. Once at Ascalan or Gaza, we'll seek advice on the best route home."

"How long will it take, father?" Jesus asked.

The desert sun gleamed off the sand as if it were a bed of diamonds. Jesus sheltered his eyes with his hands and gazed into seemingly unending space.

"Hard to say, son. Once we get to Memphis, I figure 20 days to Jerusalem and then another six or seven days to Nazareth. That's assuming no dust storms or other reasons for delay. It's a long trip. Your toes will be hardened by the time we get there. And your sandals will probably have holes in them."

The lunch break gave Jesus new energy. I was happy and relieved to see Jesus running ahead, skipping and singing, oblivious to sore feet. He tossed stones across the hard pan desert ground. At one point he chased a lizard until Joseph yelled for him to get back on the path. I smiled at the boy's unbounded vigor and joy.

"Praise the Lord! Praise the Lord, you His servants," Jesus chanted in child-like sing-song as he bounded along the desert road. *"Praise the name of the Lord. Let the name of the Lord be praised, both now and forevermore. From the rising of the sun to the place where it sets, the name of the Lord is to be praised."* Then the singing turned to humming. He had listened to his parents intently and devotedly, soaking up Jewish culture like a sponge.

The refrain and words, from familiar psalms, were those we often intoned, especially at mealtime. Jesus knew most of it by heart. Joseph looked back at me. We grinned, knowing each other's thoughts. Jesus was singing about himself. I muffled my mouth to keep from laughing out loud.

The Nile River valley was filled with mountainous caves, many used for human habitation. There were similar cave homes in Galilee, and while Jesus was born in a cave-like stable at Bethlehem, such accommodations never appealed to Joseph. Too damp, he had complained to me on several occasions. He blamed a persistent cough on cave conditions.

"Aba! Aba! Look," Jesus pointed from his advanced point on a sand dune. He jumped as if that would give him a better view. "It's the river. And buildings. And trees."

"That would be the Nile River, Jesus," Joseph said. "It flows north to the Great Sea, or as the Romans say, the Mare Nostrum. That's Latin for 'our sea.' The Romans think they own everything. Latin, you should know, is the language that Romans speak. We speak Aramaic, but when you go to school you will also study Hebrew. Our Scriptures are written in Hebrew, the language of Jews. You may even study Greek. And Latin."

"That's a lot of studying, Aba. Why do Romans think they own everything?"

"I can't say for sure, Jesus, but I suspect that it can be blamed on Adam and Eve. That's the Bible story your mother has read to you many times. The Romans, like Adam and Eve, seem to be unsatisfied with what they have, always looking for more. As you know, the Romans rule in Israel as well as in Egypt."

"What does rule mean, father? And who is this King Herod?"

"Well, son, it means Romans place themselves in charge of things. They make most of the decisions, and they put heavy taxes on people. The poor have barely anything left to live on. As for King Herod, we'll talk about that another time. Ah, yes," Joseph peered over the dunes. "There is the town of Asyut. By the time we get to the river the temperature will rise another ten degrees. I hope we can find transportation north."

Joseph's plan worked. He found a down-river sailboat operator who needed another hand and we soon departed. Joseph's labor plus some of the money Zechariah had given them three years earlier provided for our passage. In eight days, we were told, we would be in Memphis, with night rests, sufficient wind and assuming stopovers for loading and unloading proceeded in due time. The boat owner, a Capt. Ammon, was a barrel-chested, shirtless man of about 40 or so. He was full of questions for Joseph.

I could tell Joseph's answers were guarded. He was still mindful of the threat made by the deceased Herod and concerned about the successor to the murderous Judean king. He told Ammon that we had been visiting friends and that we were now on our way back home. He provided no details. Jesus was more interested in the scars and pictures Ammon had on his chest and arms, symbols of birds and snakes. He stared at the sailor's left hand, which had only three fingers.

I tried to redirect Jesus' attention and cautioned him not to ask questions about Ammon's disfigured hand. There was no need to provoke the person in charge of our trip north. My concern was quickly nullified by Ammon's spirited laugh. He slapped his knee in mirthful performance.

"Ah, you can't fool old Ammon," he looked at Jesus. "You want to know why I'm down to three fingers on my left hand." His laugh permeated his explanation like an echo fills a canyon. "It was like this. One hot day when one of the sails took ornery and refused to unfold properly, I spent nearly an hour fixing ropes and ties. Well, sonny, sweat leaked from my body like tears from the pharaoh's jilted lover. I was hot and filthy."

Ammon clearly was a storyteller, and embellishment may have been his middle name.

"So, I stretched out on the floor of the boat," he continued, "dangling over the edge, getting things untangled. There I was, flat on my stomach near the bow," he pointed, "with my feet hooked under an anchor to keep me steady. Now, you look like a smart boy and are aware that the Nile River is full of snakes and other nasty creatures." He motioned to the pictures on his chest.

Jesus' eyes bulged as Ammon's tale unfolded.

Ammon continued. "I reached down to scoop some river water to clean my hands and body when smack! A big crocodile – must have been 10 feet long – snapped his jaws on this hand. Lucky for me, he only got two fingers for his supper. Oh, there are big crocodiles in the Nile."

Jesus moved closer to me and hid his face in my blue cloak. I placed one hand behind Jesus' head to minister motherly protection and comfort and ran her other hand through his curly, dark hair. Ammon's chest heaved in laughter, so much as to nearly set the bird drawings in flight. Joseph looked away, hiding a smile from both of us, striving not to be complicit in Ammon's story.

"Boy, what's your donkey's name?" Ammon inquired.

"We call him Dynamo," Jesus replied shyly.

"Dynamo, heh? That's a good name for a reluctant donkey. Now, see here. Be sure to tie up old Dynamo good so he don't wander to the boat's edge and tempt a crocodile." Ammon thundered another laugh, but Jesus saw no humor in it.

No crocodile or other critter interrupted their travel. The southwesterly breeze not only nudged the sailboat northward, but refreshed the passengers, tempering the 85-degree Saharan day. Their hope was to reach Minya the next day. In the meantime, Joseph was assigned to mend a torn sail. It gave him time to give Jesus a geography lesson.

"Son, would you please bring me that large needle and thimble. This old cotton sail is still tough." When unfurled, the square sail more than spanned the width of the boat. This one was an auxiliary sheet ripped in a storm weeks ago. The mast for the 40-foot craft was toward the bow. Side oars were employed on calm days. "Rivers can be riled by storms, just like lakes. Ammon said this sail was torn two months ago, yanked from several grommets. But no need to worry."

"Father?"

"Yes, Jesus."

"What is a jilted lover?"

"What? Where . . . oh, I see. Ammon's colorful words. He was comparing his sweat to tears shed by a person who feels rejected and hurt. Jilted means rejected."

"Oh." There was a brief pause. "Have you ever been attacked by a crocodile, father?"

"I've never seen one, Jesus. But Ammon is probably right. There are some in the swampy sections of the Nile. By the way, Ammon says the Nile is the longest river in the world. According to one of his seamen, the river starts in central Africa and flows more than 4,000 miles north. He said it's 20 miles wide in some places. It must be fed by mountain streams somewhere."

"Father, if crocodiles are so mean, why did God make them?"

"Hmm. Good question. Why does a hammer sometimes slip off a peg and hit one's thumb?"

"Well, that's an easy one," Jesus chuckled. "Poor aim by the person with the hammer."

We entered the large city of Minya as the sun faded in the west. After we docked, Ammon's small crew unloaded stores of flax and wheat. He reminded Joseph that the north-bound skiff would take off approximately one hour after sunrise.

"And be mindful, as I was telling the missus, about buying things at the bazaar," Ammon shook his finger in caution. "Never, never pay the price a merchant is asking. He will start out high. When you begin to walk away the price will come down. If you shake your head as to be disinterested, the cost will drop even further." He laughed. "Tis one of the miracles of Nile River commerce."

That night we stayed at the riverside home of Dana and Yacov, a Jewish couple with two children. Joseph had obtained their names from another couple who had provided us shelter on our trip southward. After a meal of miqpeh, a stew of lentil and greens, Joseph and I were quizzed about our travels. An herbal tea accompanied the conversation. The children were asleep.

"What a frightening time that must have been for you," Yacov said. "This Herod must have been possessed by the devil." Joseph nodded. "I am surprised that you traveled beyond Minya. This is such a nice area. You said you took your family far south of Memphis?"

"It isn't that we wanted to travel so far," Joseph explained, "but we heard from Jewish people in Memphis that Herod may even have spies there. I didn't want to take a chance. Even now, after three years, I watch what I say in public. While we understand Herod died in Jericho, we know little about his successor. We will ask about the current Roman rulers as we proceed home."

"We wish we could help you on that count, but down here we have heard nothing," Yacov said. "I will say that Jewish families have been treated fairly in Egypt. Of course, there is history on that count, going back to another Joseph, son of Rachel and Jacob in Canaan. Ironically, as you know, jealous Jewish brothers sold that Joseph into slavery only for him to become the Egyptian vizier, the top man next to the Pharaoh."

"Yes, the Romans aren't the only ones to displease God," I said. "We had friendly, helpful neighbors in the Asyut area," she said. "There are good people everywhere."

"If you want to talk about the old days, Yacov, don't forget our people were slaves of the Egyptians for a long time," Dana injected. "The 12 tribes of Hebrews, as they called us, escaped and then wandered around the Sanai for 40 years. Rome has ruled this area for a long time," she continued her history lesson.

"When Octavian defeated his rival Mark Antony, he deposed Cleopatra and took over the Ptolemaic Kingdom. Octavian, as Augustus, became the first Roman Emperor after he ended the republic. Augustus introduced land reforms that encouraged wider private ownership. And, for the most part, there has been religious liberty. Augustus likes to talk about what he calls "pax Romana," a peaceful and prosperous time. Sure, prosperous for the Roman privileged and peaceful at the point of a spear."

"Enough politics," Yacov injected. "Joseph, what are your plans after returning to Israel? I know you are handy with a saw and hammer."

"Yes, I plan to return to carpenter work in the Galilee area," Joseph replied. "I started work with Mary's father some years ago. We build and repair houses in the Nazareth and Cana areas, but we have also gone to Sepphoris. It is the fastest growing city in the region. Most houses are built of stone, so we must be skilled in masonry, too. Mary's father is an expert in masonry.

"I'm hoping the young fellow will also take up carpentry," Joseph said, "but that's a ways off yet. He may choose other ambitions. What is your work here in Minya?"

"We have a tentmaker business. There are four employees. We repair boat sails, too. Minya is a good location, a favorite place for traders to resupply, then either continue down the Nile or head into the desert. My father had a similar business in Alexandria. Tell you the truth, Joseph, I wanted to start a cosmetic business, but father and culture overruled."

"What do you mean?" Joseph's interest was nudged. "Don't women here wear perfume?"

"Well, my father convinced me that tent sales and repairing are more lucrative than cosmetics. Cosmetics sales would depend primarily on non-Jewish customers. Our women tend to look at cosmetics with disdain, although some paint the nails of their fingers and toes with henna. And a few use perfumes – aloes, saffron and myrrh, for example."

"Interesting," was Joseph's singular response.

"So, you are destined for Galilee and Nazareth?" Yacov prodded. "Wouldn't there be more opportunity for you, and the boy later on, if you settled in Judea, say Jerusalem? Bigger city, growing area, more building and more money. Galilee is pretty remote."

"I have considered that," Joseph answered, "specifically settling in Bethlehem, which is just to the south of Jerusalem. We would be near the Temple and all of Jewish life. However, on second thought we concluded that Jesus should be raised in a smaller community. We'll be fine in Nazareth. We may or may not go through Jerusalem." He didn't mention anything about an angel's message.

More family talk ensued, but after a while Joseph's internal clock and the pending morning departure time took his notice. We retired and awoke early to a meal of wheat bread, date juice and figs. Jesus' eyes could not believe such choice. He was accustomed to barley bread and goat's milk for breakfast. After we prayed the Shima, Jesus broke some bread from the round loaf and chewed it with delight. Dana appreciated the unspoken thankfulness.

"Sana and Yacov, we are so grateful for your hospitality," I said. "People have been so wonderful. It is amazing how God provides. Should you ever travel to Galilee, I beg you to stop for shelter and meals. I wish we could stay longer, but Joseph is anxious about getting to the boat on time. May God bless you all the days of your life."

"It has been our pleasure to have you," said Dana. "Safe travel home and God be with you."

I looked at Joseph and smiled.

"Ah, welcome aboard again," Ammon bellowed. "And how is the young fellow this morning? Still sleepy, eh? Well, just to put you at ease, I checked with the dock people, and they say we will have good weather as we head toward Memphis. And there are no reports of crocodiles." That ignited his laughter and sent the bird drawings on his chest flying. "But you can never tell. They are sneaky."

"Mr. Ammon? Will you be extra careful when you wash your hands in the river?" Jesus implored. He looked the man squarely in the eyes.

The crusty seaman was taken aback by Jesus' concern. Apprehension about another person's well-being was not a hallmark of river culture.

"Why thank you little boy for your worry. I will take special caution and think of you when I do."

Ammon looked at me. Clearly, he had not bothered to clean his hands and face to start the new day. Yet, his eyes looked kinder, his entire countenance less brusque.

"You have a mighty fine young fella here," Ammon said. "With such benevolence I wouldn't be surprised if he grew up to be a big success." The big man smiled. With that he launched the boat and steered it out to the main channel. As Ammon foretold, the trip north proceeded unhindered. As they approached the capital of Lower Egypt, the captain turned educator.

"Mr. Joseph, they tell me that in ancient times the Great Sea came further south than at present, maybe as much as 80,000 cubits. Over the centuries, the mud carried by the Nile filled in coastline to create a great delta." Ammon enjoyed being a tourist guide. "The pyramids and Sphinx are a short distance northwest of here."

"What is a Sphinx?" Jesus asked. "Is it bigger than a crocodile?"

"Oh, yes, my boy" Ammon laughed. "The Sphinx is huge, carved out of limestone. It has the head of a man and body of an animal. It's a mythical creature of some kind. And don't ask me what mythical means because I don't know, except that it's a strange make-believe creature."

"Is it dangerous?" Jesus asked.

"Naw. It's just a big piece of rock."

"What's a pyramid?" Jesus' curiosity subdued his shyness.

"Ah," Ammon smiled. "Your interest in things is a wonderful thing. The Great Pyramid," he was happy to explain, "is a magnificent expression of man's imagination. Its base covers a wide area, has four triangular sides that reach high in the sky and come to a point. It's an architectural masterpiece, precise in its design. Some believe it was constructed by a lost civilization. Too complicated for me."

"Lost civilization?" Jesus inquired. "Do they mean these people were lost and never found?"

"No, no," Ammon chuckled. "They mean that the Great Pyramid builders were highly intelligent, but history has no record of them."

"Oh," Jesus replied. "No one wrote down their story like they did in the Scriptures?"

"Something like that," Ammon patted Jesus on the head as the boat floated northward.

"Will we see the Great Pyramid?" Jesus asked.

"Look over there," Ammon pointed, "in the distance behind that grove of palm trees. See the Great Pyramid's point stretching into the sky? And there are smaller pyramids in the same area."

"I see it!" Jesus cried. "Wow! It would be fun to climb it all the way to the top."

"I'm not sure if they'll let you do that," said Ammon. He started to shift things on the boat in preparation for landing. The history lesson was over.

Within the hour, the craft was steered to dock at Memphis, the terminal for his river run. Operators of boats of all sizes and for all purposes jockeyed for position in tight spaces. It was a zoo on water. Ammon's voice boomed and invoked the names of Egyptian gods as he irreverently sought a parking place amid the chaos and shouting.

"You son of 60 dogs!!" Ammon directed his vilest judgement at a man blocking the entryway to his mooring. "Are you newly born? Our family has rented this spot since the Sphinx was a baby. Move that floating pile of junk or I swear I'll run through it." The captain of the *pile of junk* hastily made way for Ammon and his threats.

"Never mind Ammon's colorful ways," Joseph said, attempting to mitigate the blue air. "He has an unusual way with words." After we loaded most of our belongings on the trusty back of Dynamo, we began the long trek northeastward to home.

Chapter 5

NEAR MEMPHIS (Cairo) EGYPT – We walked until midday when I proposed lunch in the shade of a waterside grove. As we rested near the town of Heliopolis large and small caravans of travelers – mostly merchants – passed. Dust would barely settle when another group marched by. The hooves of pack animals stirred and kicked the sandy dirt into clouds of grungy powder.

This was clearly a major trade route. It was like a two-way parade, travelers headed to and from the Nile valley. Some people – and animals, too – were ornately costumed, indicating wealth. Others had modest dress. Their animals were draped with faded and torn blankets that had been exposed to elements for many years.

Filtering through the cavalcade was an overture of brays, snorts, moans and whinnies. Shouts of various animal tenders were evidence that not all of beasts of burden were happily plodding along the prescribed path. Some directives clearly were unintended for a little boy's ears, especially those that colorfully condemned a creature to hell.

For a minute I considered urging Joseph to move on to escape the grime and bedlam. But there was shade here and a public well. Mixed thoughts were evident on my face. Joseph understood.

"Remember Genesis, Mary," Joseph beseeched, "for dust thou art and unto dust shalt thou return. I think we're turning to dust."

My look clearly conveyed I was not impressed with his attempt at humor.

"OK," Joseph said, shucking off rejection of his dismissed levity. "We had better be on our way again."

Jesus, Mary and Joseph shook their garments to free collected residue as they watched the almost carnival-like procession. I watched Joseph brush his growing beard to scatter the powdery deposit. I wondered. Was it age or dust he was trying to dislodge. Speckles of gray infiltrated his hair and beard. And he was only in his early 30s.

Even so, he was still strong and able to protect the family from any type of threat. He was thoughtful and kind. How many other men, I thought, would have stood by me when they discovered I was pregnant?

How many other men would have believed the voice of an angel? He is special. Then I looked at Jesus.

He, too, was growing in strength. His mind seemed to be always exploring, full of questions. His limited world was nevertheless unlimited in things to investigate. He hunched over a mound of sand, unmindful of the cacophony around him, and seemed to be meditating. Perhaps, I thought in motherly conjecture, he was praying. That must be it.

"Immah, check out this funny-looking bug," Jesus glanced up.

"It has whiskers just like Abba. And it looks like it has three heads. Wow, look how fast it moves! It appears angry about something. Honest, I didn't poke at it with a stick or do anything to make it mad. Maybe it's just hungry. Should I give him something to eat?"

"How do you know it's a him?" Joseph surveyed the developing drama. He spotted the object of Jesus' study, then offered an opinion. "It may be a she who's upset because there is dust in her hair." Mary cast that look again. "I think your bug buddy is a sand scorpion," Joseph declared, "and I wouldn't provoke her. She has two pincers, and it wouldn't take much to make her bite."

Jesus rose and then backed off. Joseph laughed.

"It appears the crisis is over," he jested. "The standoff ended."

"I don't think it was funny," I said. "He could have been bitten. Bugs are creepy." I quivered at the thought of them. "It looks as if the caravan traffic has eased. I want to bathe Jesus before we go on. Scrub some of that sand from his ears."

"Immah. I don't need a bath," Jesus protested. "Can't we wait until tonight, or tomorrow. What's the hurry?"

He was learning that mothers tend to give little or no attention to such petitions. The bath followed lunch. He also learned that unlike back at their cave residence, where bath water was warmed in the hot desert sun, this well water was cold. He shivered like tree leaves before an advancing storm. I quickly toweled him, partly to warm him and partly to make sure he was dried off before another caravan-induced dust cloud came along.

Cleansing completed, we traveled on. That night we camped on the outskirts of a central Nile delta village northeast of Memphis. From

Memphis north, the Nile fans its way through many channels and flood plains before reaching the Great Sea. With Jesus asleep, his parents pondered the unfolding events.

"God made the night so peaceful," I said, prodding the conversation. "Look at the twinkling stars and tranquil heaven. The vastness of the heavens symbolizes the vastness of the unknowns that lay ahead for us." Joseph said nothing about the future, but to me life had already changed dramatically.

"Sure a lot more peaceful than when we came down," Joseph added quickly. "Back then, we were worried to make it safely through the night – or for that matter, through the next day. How could we be sure to outrun Herod's soldiers? And I was wary of his minions, to be honest, until we were far to the south. Even then, I kept vigil."

"It was more than awful, Joseph. To think of all those baby boys Herod executed in hopes of killing our son in the process. Sometimes, in my worst nightmares, I still hear the screaming children. How could a person be so cruel?" I gave a protective glance at Jesus, confirmation that he was restfully safe.

"I must say that the years in Egypt were peaceful," I whispered after a time of silence. "I think Jesus also enjoyed our time there. We made good friends, Joseph, and we had a nice neighborhood. Many people welcomed us and helped us, and I'm not just talking about Hebrew families."

"I agree, Mary, and I know you left with some reluctance, but we had to return home. We are bound to fulfill all the dimensions of the Scriptures. It isn't anything we decided. It's God's will."

"God's will has been a part of us, Joseph." I looked into his eyes. "We have been blessed beyond comprehension. To think, in all of history, two unknown people from an unknown place could be chosen to be parents of God's human presentation." Mary's eyes glistened with joy. Joseph held her closely.

"And, Joseph, I don't say it enough. Thank you dear husband for standing by me when others were ready to throw stones."

Unable to fall asleep, they wondered about the future.

"Mary," Joseph said with more than a tinge of anxiety. "Are you worried about the years ahead? I mean, knowing what we know, that

Jesus is more than an ordinary child? How do we raise him? Can we just let him grow up like any other youngster, not overly worried about a scrapped knee, dog bites or falls from trees? How do we protect him from all the usual problems of childhood, knowing who he is?"

"We trust in God, Joseph."

"Mary! What do you mean, 'We trust in God'!?" his voice loaded with bafflement. "Aren't you forgetting a slight detail there?"

"We have been over this before. I realize it's complicated. Life is complicated. We'll manage somehow. Oh, there will be scrapped knees and much worse, but we'll manage. Go to sleep Joseph. Tomorrow is a big enough challenge."

Life is complicated? Joseph let that circulate in his brain, his brow raised in uncertainty before fogginess and sleep captured him.

When the sun rose over the scrub vegetation to the east, slowly casting away shadows, the peaceful sounds of chirping birds were overtaken by the hubbub of more passing travelers. Joseph couldn't believe the traffic. I was worried about the dust and how to keep the breakfast bread from turning into dirt cakes. Dry bread and water were breakfast staples.

"Wake up son. It's time to greet another day," Joseph pulled at Jesus' garments. "It's not just another day, Jesus. It's a great day, and mornings are especially wonderful because we have been renewed and are full of energy."

"I'd say one person here is still full of slumber," I said, urging prayer before morning meal. "Come, the two of you. We must pray. Wake up Jesus."

Jesus rubbed the sleep from his eyes.

"Are you awake?" I led the prayer. "*Baruch atah Adonai, Eloheinu melech haolam, hamotzi lechem min ha-aretz*, (Blessed are you, Lord our God, Ruler of the universe, who has given us the bread from the Earth.) Come Jesus. Repeat it. Say your prayers."

He did, and Joseph urged a second prayer. "What do we say now, every morning and evening?" He looked at Jesus' sleepy face.

"The Shema," Jesus yawned.

"Well? How does it go? Just the first part."

"You want me to start?" Jesus asked hesitantly. Joseph nodded. The birds chirped. Dynamo brayed. "I don't know if I remember it exactly." Joseph extended his hands in encouragement. Jesus placed his hand over his eyes.

"She-ma yisrael, eloheinu, adonai echad. Baruch shem kavod malchuto l'olam va-ed. (Hear O' Israel, the Lord is our God, the Lord is One. Blessed is the name of His glorious kingdom for ever and ever.) Jesus stumbled his way through the prayer and Joseph patted him on the head in approval. "Amen. Can we eat now? Where are all these people going?" Jesus said in wonderment.

"Here and there," Joseph responded in fatherly detachment, the same question on his mind. He didn't notice the approaching man.

"Good morning to the three of you," said a traveler leading a horse packed with supplies. Joseph looked up. "I trust you slept well during the night, because you won't get any rest in the daylight," the stranger laughed. "Which way are you headed, up or down? Oh, sorry. My name is Eleazar. From the Maccabean branch, and this is my wife Kalatha." She bowed to Joseph with her introduction. "You can call me Mac," he said with an impish look.

His tan flaxen tunic, peppered with stains and grime, appeared only slightly more soiled than his straggly beard. A blue cord around his midsection was frazzled. A folded tannish scarf, which at one time was presumably white, protected his head from blowing sand and the hot midday sun. None of this nondescript appearance could diminish his broad smile.

"Yes, and good morning to all of you. I am Joseph of Galilee north of Judea. This is my wife Mary and our son Jesus."

"Well, Joseph, it is a pleasure to meet you. You are a long way from home. Hebrew, I presume?"

"House of David," Joseph replied, perhaps too quickly, he thought. *I don't know this fellow from Adam.*

"We are Jewish, also, as you probably know," the 40ish man replied. He was shorter than Joseph, and from the looks of his dress could be classified as neither rich nor poor, but in between. "Just so happens we have a son, too. Marcel. He's a kvell kid, but he tends to putz along, playing with his dog. I don't even see him now, but he's around here somewhere."

"Maccabean?" Joseph repeated.

"Yes. We were those troublemakers who kicked the Greeks out of Jerusalem some 150 years ago. They were actually known as the Seleucids, and when they took over our Temple it was the last straw. It's what led to our alliance with Rome. Big improvement, eh? But you probably know all about that, being Jewish yourself."

Joseph nodded.

"We are on our way home to Jericho," Eleazar continued. "Spent a couple of weeks down here visiting relatives, two weeks too long, if you know what I mean. I managed to sell some grain and fruit dates, so it wasn't a complete loss of time. I'm just kidding, Joseph. We had a good time with relatives."

Joseph nodded.

"Have you ever been to Jericho? It's an old town, domicile to many civilizations. The abundant water, springs, attracted people down through the centuries. Why, I think the town has changed hands more often than some Roman bigshots change wives."

Eleazar chuckled and Joseph nodded.

"We like it there. Mild winters and just enough action to make life interesting. Tourist place. Lots of travelers. Herod, so-called king of the Jews who added Great to his name, had his winter palace there. By birth he was part Jewish, but he never acted much like it. He was more interested in power, maybe being god himself. He died not too long ago and is buried in Jericho. But you probably know that."

Joseph nodded.

"Mr. Eleazar," Joseph addressed his new acquaintance, not comfortable with the "Mac" moniker. "Is Herod's son, Archelaus, in charge now?"

"That's the rumor. My political friends say he may have a rocky term. We'll see. It's politics. Don't you know that everything is politics? Archelaus, good ol' Archy boy, I should clarify, is in charge in Judea. The Romans appointed his brother, Antipas, ruler of Galilee. Anyway, Archy got off to a bad start after his father died. It was just before Passover, and he got all dressed up in white and made a big speech about appeasement and the end of political imprisonment.

"Well, Joseph, that went over like bacon at a rabbi banquet. Some Jews wanted an apology for the deaths of several dozen protestors in Jerusalem who were burned to death by Archy's father. His father was an animal. These Jews had protested the erection of a golden eagle over the Temple entrance as blasphemy. Instead of making an apology on behalf of his father, Archelaus headed off to party with his friends.

"Maybe you know all this. Just say so if you do. I don't want to jaw you to death, Mr. Joseph. By the way, you never did say in which direction you are headed."

"We are going in the same direction as you. Toward Judea," Joseph replied.

"Are you traveling alone?"

"Yes. Just the three of us. We've come down the Nile to Lower Egypt."

"Visiting with relatives? Taking a little flight from the routine?"

"You could say that," Joseph answered.

"Joseph. I don't want to tell you what to do." Eleazar rubbed his chin. "But your family really shouldn't be traveling alone. It's too dangerous. Too many robbers. Tell you what. Why don't you travel with us? We can walk together. Talk together. We can camp at night together. If you want, we can even eat together. What do you say?"

Joseph looked at me. He pondered the "talk together" offer. Then he surveyed Eleazar's caravan of family members, attendants and nearly a dozen camels and donkeys. And the dust. And smell. I could sense the dilemma on Joseph's mind.

"I guess that would be fine. You don't mind?"

"Joseph!" Eleazar said with a mixture of conviction and pique. "Glad to have your company. The days will go faster with someone to talk to."

Joseph read my wrinkled forehead like a Memphis swami. He could tell I was something less than enthused. When we fled Bethlehem nearly four years ago, we barely stopped to rest. Joseph, filled with panic, trusted no one. Now, he accepts this Eleazar's offer, content it was the right decision?

"Jesus. Come. We're going to travel with this caravan. Don't forget your sandals. They are still over there by the tree."

So, we walked with the Jericho contingent, bound for Nazareth. After a while, Jesus took Dynamo's strap, gently tugging the animal that carried most of our belongings. The road weaved in and out of tropical-like vegetation, from green to brown depending on proximity to delta streams. Sometimes it was in shade; then again stark sunlight reflected off baren silt that was ground to powder.

I wondered how many thousands of people, not to mention animals, had trodden these highways. Who knows? This could have been a passage for Pharaohs, hoisted on palanquins, with legions of attendants. Maybe the Great Ramses himself, who scorned Moses and the Israelites, traveled here. No doubt trade companies from Damascus and Media plied these routes. Roman soldiers likely marched along this path to carry out military objectives.

The wind picked up and tiny swirls of sand formed in the distance. These vortexes were a projection in miniature of what often happened in the open desert of the Sanai. These were merely part of the horizon, as commonplace as sand fleas. The convoy proceeded uninhibited.

"My feet hurt, father," Jesus said. "Will you carry me?"

"Well, son, we've only traveled about four miles. There is a long way to go, so your feet better get . . ."

"What's this?" Joseph was interrupted. "Do I hear that the boy has sore feet? I do, too. This hard ground can be pretty tough on such young toes. Maybe," Eleazar suggested cautiously, eyes cast downward, "maybe he could ride one of my tame camels. I assure you, Joseph, he will be safe." He pointed to the animal in question and looked at Jesus. "The camel's name is Grunt, because he seems to do that more that chew his cud."

Joseph again looked at me with that what-do-you-think unspoken question. I shrugged my shoulders, and before we knew it Eleazar had lifted Jesus atop the camel. Instead of indicating fear, Jesus smiled broadly as he took the reins in one hand and patted Grunt on his neck with the other. Joseph inherited Dynamo's tether.

"Grunt and your boy seem to get along fine," Eleazar said. "Maybe he'll grow up to be a camel herdsman. You know, there is good money in breeding and selling animals – especially camels. They take a little managing, camels especially. I swear, they can be more stubborn than a donkey. Joseph, do you have a career in mind for the young fella?"

The caravan seemed to have picked up other groups, Joseph thought. There were more pack-bearing animals and their handlers. More women balancing jars on their heads. More of everything, including thickening dust and magnified noise. Ah, the price of security in numbers, he pondered. He watched Jesus in rhythmic bounce atop an indifferent Grunt, the animal seemingly unaware of a passenger.

"Oh, yes, Mr. Eleazar. Jesus seems to be satisfied with Grunt. Just the other day he was telling us how camels had a bad smell, made terrible moaning sounds and tended to bite. He said he didn't want anything to do with camels. Amazing, how he's had a change of mind now that the critter is doing the walking for him."

Jesus waved, somehow sensing they were talking about him.

"Ah, Joseph," Eleazar laughed. "Youngsters can reverse their minds faster than weather changes in the desert."

"How far do you plan on traveling each day?" Joseph asked.

"Ordinarily we move just during daylight, and we make several stops to eat and rest the animals. And ourselves. Some groups like to travel at night, especially during the extremely hot days, but I like to see where I'm going. That means, Joseph, I like to see if there is any potential trouble ahead. Don't worry. We have scouts and sentries at night."

They had traveled to a crossroads when the expanded group halted. The direct heat of the sun and its reflection off the sand made for a hot afternoon. Sporadic groves of trees were being replaced by more frequent sand dunes. It was an omen of what was ahead. There was the satisfaction that it was late Nisan (or springtime) on the Hebrew calendar, not the blistering months of Tamuz and Av.

Joseph noted a signpost that directed travelers west to Alexandria or continuing north to Belbeis on the Farma road. He helped Jesus dismount from Grunt, and then in choreographic-like routine everyone shook the dust from their clothes and footwear. Waterskins were passed about to wash the grime from mouths and relieve parched throats.

"After a brief rest, we will travel a little longer before making camp for the night," Eleazar explained to Joseph. "We should have no trouble reaching Belbeis and beyond tomorrow." He looked Jesus in the eye. "Did you get all the sand removed from your face? And was it fun riding atop Grunt?"

Jesus nodded, but it was not with enthusiasm. The truth was the sore feet had been replaced by a sore posterior.

"Joseph. I would like you and your boy to make acquaintance with our son Marcel. He was off playing with his dog when we first met. I swear he's a magician. He disappears all the time. A convenient way to avoid chores, don't you know. Come, Marcel. There are people I want you to meet." Marcel and his dog ambled along as if the halt was going to last the rest of the day.

"You putz along as if your feet have anchors on them."

"Father, Mo injured his left hind leg. See, he has been limping, almost dragging himself. I sometimes have to carry him. Poor fellow."

"How long has he been hurting?" Jesus inquired.

"Jesus, don't you think you should first say hello to Marcel," Joseph suggested.

"Sorry, father. Hello, Marcel. Nice to meet you. How did your dog get hurt?"

"Hi, Jesus. Don't know what happened to Shlomo. Father calls him Slow Mo. I just call him Mo. Couple days ago I noticed he was shuffling along. Maybe he got into a fight with another dog. Or was kicked by a camel or ass. The worrisome thing is, he doesn't seem to be getting any better. Father says he'll be OK, but I'm worried."

Jesus looked at Mo's big brown eyes and began to pet the dog. The animal's ears lay back as if he were receiving a massage. His tail wagged. Then, Mo rolled over and Jesus scratched his belly and ears.

"Ol' Mo likes that," Marcel laughed. "You've made a quick friend. Do you have a dog?"

"No, but that would be great," Jesus said quickly. "What do you think, father? Could we get a dog? I would take care of him. He would be no bother."

"Jesus, getting a dog is a long way away. Probably 300 miles away. We'll talk about it later. Much later."

"Take another swig of water," Eleazar shouted so everyone could hear. "Then we'll move along."

The so-called Farma Road swung into more fertile land, changing directions like it didn't know where to go. Joseph was amazed at the diversity of the landscape, from a swath of barren wilderness to rich delta agricultural land – across and along canals flowing to the Great Sea. Late in the day, the procession stopped south of Belbeis.

That night the Holy Family had the unexpected peace of finding a secluded stand of trees. Eleazar's family, the rest of the caravan, and the attendant clamor, set up camp some distance away. Joseph collected rocks to build a make-shift fire pit and Jesus hunted for sticks and burnable brush. I surveyed the food supply in Dynamo's pack. I cooked. We ate.

"I really would take care of a dog, father," Jesus said, still chewing on figs. "What do you think we should name the dog?"

"How about Sleepy," Joseph said, "as in 'you look sleepy'? Bedtime for you."

The stars portrayed an extraordinary sense of serenity. The solitude, and the security of nearby companions, made the journey back home more bearable. Jesus, captivated by thoughts of wagging tails, fell asleep quickly.

"Looks like we'll have only ourselves to chat with tonight," Joseph said as he snuffed out the suppertime fire. I smiled with gratitude.

Chapter 6

NAZARETH, GALILEE (about 4 AD) – "Did you finish building the table for Rabbi Shimon and his wife Gittel?"

Anne, already busy preparing the evening meal, quizzed her husband as he walked through the portal of their Nazareth home. Joachim, his faded blue tunic wet from perspiration, wasn't ready to participate in a "how was your day" discussion. His body ached and his blackened thumbnail throbbed in rhythm with his heartbeat.

He didn't respond. Instead, he grabbed a basin, went back outside to the nearby village well, drew water and poured it over his head. For an encore, he removed his outer garment and pitched another basin across his sweaty chest before proceeding to wash his hands and face. He relished the breeze that wafted from the southwest, across the plains from Mount Carmel.

Joachim sat down on the two-foot-high circular wall that surrounded the well. An empty bucket and a rope-like lift system for procuring water hung from the upper structure. His mind was a jumble of conflicting questions. He ran his calloused hands through his wet hair as if that may bring order to a subliminal collision of thoughts.

Just where was history headed?

The Mount Tabor region in the far distance brought back the story of Israel's victory when its army leader Barak defeated forces of the Canaanite king of Hazor, commanded by Jabin. How many opposing forces have walked the hillsides of Nazareth? And today? How would the town fare under the rule of Herod Antipas, son of the late Herod the Great?

More precisely, how would their grandson, knowing what their daughter Mary said about his conception, fare under the Romans? Jesus' future was a mystery in many ways. The immediate question was the location of Jesus, Mary and Joseph. Joachim had confidence in Joseph providing safety for the family, but that didn't wipe away worry.

Little Nazareth, he pondered. A Jewish village of 450 souls in the middle of nowhere. Of little consequence to the world. Mostly poor people, some with fertile plots for agriculture on the plains to the south.

Any wealth in the region was in Sepphoris, the luxurious Greek-style city where Antipas had his headquarters.

Joachim often worked in Sepphoris, which was several miles northwest of Nazareth, an hour's walk. It was a gleaming place with a colonnaded main street set atop a hill, a fortress city rebuilt by Antipas after a civil war among Roman antagonists. Workmen like Joachim knew little about such conflicts and politics but profited from Antipas' ambitious restoration projects.

However, he and Anne were aware that Antipas' father, Herod the Great, had caused their daughter, Mary, and son-in-law, Joseph, and grandson, Jesus, to flee Israel for Egypt. Word of Herod's killing of innocent boys in hopes of doing away with Jesus had been relayed from family members and other Jewish friends in Jerusalem.

Elizabeth, Mary's distant cousin, gave information through a personal messenger that Herod was on a warpath and seeking the death of the infant Jesus. The informant told of the Holy Family's escape to Egypt. She and her husband, Zechariah, had become close friends of Mary and Joseph, and were present at Jesus' circumcision. In keeping with Jewish law, the Brit Milah ceremony took place eight days after his birth.

All that was more than three years ago.

The relatives in Jerusalem, like immediate family in Nazareth, could only wait and hope for the best. They were aware of the sizeable Jewish population in Egypt, people who would take in the refugees. They had confidence in Joseph's keen protector sense. And Elizabeth often recalled Mary's visit when both were pregnant and the comforting thought that Mary was mother of the Messiah.

God would watch over them.

Elizabeth, a good deal older than Mary, after all was part of God's mystery. She was six months into her pregnancy – a surprise to everyone because of her advanced years -- when Mary came to visit her in the Judean hill country on the western outskirts of Jerusalem.

She rejoiced in the recollection that her baby, John, kicked wildly in her womb when Mary unexpectedly arrived. She knew then that Mary was with child, too. During the visit, Mary told her about Jesus' conception, how the angel explained that she would conceive by the Holy Spirit and her child would be called the son of God.

Talk about the Scripture coming alive!

She and Zechariah were faithful followers of God's law as outlined in the Hebrew bible. That's why they were so disappointed not to have been blessed with a child. What had they done to be rebuked by God? Neighbors had whispered scornfully about their fate. No longer.

They could recite Isaiah's prophecy by heart. Frequently one of them started a passage and, like long-married couples, the other would complete it. The prediction of Jesus' birth and its impact upon the people of Israel was among their favorite passages.

Therefore, Isaiah had written some seven centuries before, *the Lord Himself shall give you a sign: behold, the young woman shall conceive, and bear a son and shall call his name Immanuel.* The couple frequently reassured themselves that Isaiah's words of *God with us* would show favor to the Jewish people. The prophet cast Jesus as wonderful counselor, mighty God, everlasting father, and prince of peace.

Mary and Elizabeth became more than friends. Despite their age difference, they were like sisters. They giggled about changes in their bodies, food cravings and a mutual dislike of goat meat. They shared concerns of their babies' health and if the offspring would have the prescribed ten fingers and ten toes. And they discussed the rigors of childbirth.

Elizabeth could hot forget how much Mary had helped her during those last three months of pregnancy, with cooking, cleaning and tending the small garden. Mary, confronted with morning sickness and other issues of early pregnancy, stayed until John was born. And Elizabeth treasured that day when Mary first came and the exchange that followed.

"Blessed are you among women, and blessed is the fruit of your womb," Elizabeth had said.

And Mary's response was:

"My soul magnifies the Lord,
and my spirit rejoices in God my Savior,

for God has looked with favor on the lowliness of the Almighty's servant.
Surely, from now on all generations will call me blessed;
for the Mighty One has done great things for me,
and holy is God's name.
God's mercy is for those who fear God
from generation to generation.
God has shown strength with God's arm;
God has scattered the proud in the thoughts of their hearts.
God has brought down the powerful from their thrones,
and lifted up the lowly;
God has filled the hungry with good things,
and sent the rich away empty.
God has helped servant Israel,
in remembrance of God's mercy,
according to the promise God made to our ancestors,
to Abraham and to his descendants forever.

Just how long he had been sitting on the well rim, pondering events, Joachim wondered. The more he sized up his grandson's destiny under Antipas the more he convinced himself the Roman ruler was not the threat that his father, Herod the Great, had been. For one thing, Antipas had family politics and his own place in the Roman hierarchy to worry about.

"Just when do you plan to come in for supper," Anne yelled from a nearby walking path. "Whatever you're thinking about, I doubt if wishing at the well will bring answers. Come. We're having baked sacra and bread with dates, one of your favorite combinations."

"Sorry," Joachim shouted back. "I'll be right in."

He walked the short distance eastward to their modest home. Anne was placing the fish on the table as he walked in the door. The fragrance ignited his appetite. The hungry craftsman temporarily set aside the matters of the world. The demands of an empty stomach took precedence.

"That sure smells good!" he said, giving the word *sure* an elongated prominence. "Anne, you must come from a long line of good cooks," he said, hoping to schmooze his way forward to make up for his tardiness. "I knew when I first saw you at Synagogue lo those many years ago that you were the cook for me. Aye. And, I must say, you keep a good house. How blessed I am."

"And, Joachim, I always admired your chutzpah," Anne said. "I hope our meal didn't cool off too much. What took you so long at the well? Did you have a sliver in your hand? Or was there something in your head? But you are right about me coming from a long line of excellent cooks. For sure," she said with a sly look, "my house has been known centuries for its cuisine."

"Ah. I sense your meaning," he said.

They sat down to supper and prayed. Both knew what would be discussed during the meal. Much of what was on their minds had been talked about before, but, like the food on their plates, there was renewed sustenance in exchanging thoughts again. The fate of their family was never a closed subject and reviewing and praying together eased their anxiety.

"You are worried about Mary and her family," Anne said reading her husband's mind.

"Aren't you?" he replied.

"Of course. My guess is that they are on their way home. Herod is dead. Joseph has been informed of this, and he's decided to pull up stakes in Egypt and return to Nazareth. It will be a tedious trip, one full of unknowns. Will they have enough to eat? What about the weather? Which route is the safest, free from robbers and other danger?"

"What makes you so sure they'll return to Galilee?" Joachim injected. "It's possible they have found a village in Egypt that they like. Good neighbors. Plenty of work for Joseph. Mary has settled in, found new friends. And Jesus. He's probably having a good time playing in the sand. How old is he now?"

"You don't know how old your own grandson is? Oy vey!" Anne looked across the table as if the existence of God was questioned. "Feh!" she said with editorial exclamation. After an appropriate interlude, she declared with exactness: "He will be four at the 17th of Tevet."

"Hmm," Joachim muttered between chews. He ignored her dramatics. "Growing up fast. We haven't heard about him since Elizabith's account of the presentation in the Temple. And that was hardly a family reunion. Faster than you can say mazel tov, the three foreigners visited, brought gifts and praise to Jesus, departed, and Herod goes on a rampage to kill all baby boys. Those Eastern visitors informed Joseph of Herod's maniacal plan, and they left for Egypt."

His graying eyebrows raised to exclaim such frenzy. His face appeared tired, yet he looked at her with profound tenderness.

"How did we get through those days?"

"That was an awful and worrisome time," Anne agreed. "It's difficult to understand Herod's cruelty. We are blessed that Elizabeth and Zechariah have good contacts, not just in Israel but Egypt, too. Within weeks we learned that Mary and the family had escaped and were safe out of Herod's reach. They'll be back. Why do you doubt it?"

Joachim had an even stronger notion that his daughter's family would return to Galilee. He knew Joseph and he knew Joseph's devotion to his family. He could not have hand picked a better son-in-law. He was also an excellent and dependable mason and carpenter. And, he couldn't deny that he liked to hear Anne get riled up and spiel away.

"Do you forget what our own daughter said when she became pregnant with Jesus?" Anne continued. "What the angel told her? His destiny? All that is written in Scripture?"

Joachim smiled. He looked at her across the table. They were on the same page.

"My dear wife," he said with solemnity, and then a pause. "Would you please pass me that last piece of fish?"

Anne returned an affectionate look and handed over the plate. And then a slice of bread. They sat there, a couple in love, proud parents and proud grandparents. Suddenly, Joachim began to laugh. It began with a chuckle and grew to a boisterous rumble, one that required him to put down his fork and place hands on his bouncing stomach.

"What?" Anne asked in puzzlement. "Are you meshuga?"

"No, no. I'm not crazy," Joachim replied, still guffawing. "You asked me some time ago if I finished the table for Rabbi Shimon and his spouse. The answer is no. I didn't finish the table."

His belated response, and Anne's awareness of the matter, produced a duet of chortling. Their mirth was abruptly defused by heavy knocks on the door. *Who could that be*? was evident on both of their faces.

"Open up now!!" a deep-voiced man ordered. "Now!" and he rapped as though intending to break the door down. Joachim motioned for Anne to go to a back room. He approached the front door.

"Hurry it up!! We don't have all night."

Joachim lifted the metal latch and slowly opened the door. The gruff-talking man's stature punctuated his presence. He was at least three inches taller than Joachim, dressed in the uniform of a minor Roman official.

"Good evening. How may I help you?" Joachim inquired. He was not surprised to see Roman soldiers in his yard. But what could have provoked such a hostile arrival? Why did a sense of animosity accompany the visitor? Indeed, what had happened to compel a late-day call?

"Are you Joachim, the so-called carpenter?" the man said harshly.

"Yes. I am Joachim. What is it you want?"

"I am a mere courier," the brusque reply came. "What Antipas wants, and more precisely what his chief builder wants, are workers who will work. The ruler of Galilee is building a great city. He has plans for other great cities. The question is whether he can rely on Jewish carpenters like you. You haven't been to Sepphoris this week. Why? You have agreed to work there."

Joachim nodded. He had signed on to work on Antipas' projects in Sepphoris. The truth was he had no choice, no matter what work he had lined up elsewhere.

"I agree. I should have spent more time there," Joachim answered. It would have gained him nothing to explain that his son-in-law had been gone for several years and another worker was sick.

"We investigated your whereabouts," the courier said sternly. "We know you have been working on furniture for a rabbi. I am here to inform you that the tetrarch of Galilee, the great Antipas, and all Romans for that part, come before everyone else. Rome respects Jews and their culture, but not at the expense of our needs. Do you understand?"

The carpenter stroked his beard out of habit and nodded assent.

"Be there tomorrow!" the messenger ordered, his finger pointed at Joachim's nose. Then he and the entourage departed.

"I guess the rabbi's table won't be completed tomorrow either," Joachim told Anne back inside.

"I hope you are right, that Joseph and his family are on their way back. I can use his help. Anne, I must turn all my attention to work in Sepphoris. I don't have a choice. Other projects in Nazareth, the rabbi's table, the farmer's shed and your to-do list here will have to wait. And who knows how long? Antipas and the Romans are not a patient lot."

They finished supper. Physical hunger was satisfied, only to be replaced by an emptiness rooted in uncertainty. What was the future under Roman rule? Would high taxes lead to Jewish revolt? Was Antipas turning into his father? That was really the big elephant in the room. Where was Mary and her family?

"Your mind, Joachim, isn't on carpentry and masonry work in Sepphoris. I can tell." Anne looked at his weary face. "Your worries concern Jesus once Antipas finds out he's back home and recalls his father's rampage after all the excitement about a new king being born and the Magi coming to pay homage. What will Antipas do? Will he react with similar wrath?"

She had read Joachim's thoughts precisely. He had had the same talk with himself out at the well. He eventually convinced himself that Antipas, even if he did find out about Jesus' presence in Nazareth, had too many other problems. That included dealing with family matters and hanging on to his cushy lifestyle.

"I am positive Antipas will know if Jesus is back in Israel. He will probably know before we do. The Roman intelligence system is extensive, and, sad to say, some of it is fed by Jews. If you are correct that our daughter and family are on their way back, and I hope you are, I have confidence that Joseph is aware of the political dangers. He has good sense."

"Don't I know the same? My fear with Jesus, and it will exist until I die, is the nature of his being, the purpose of his mission, the impact he will have on people. Knowing what we know, Joachim, what Mary and Joseph have told us, how that corresponds with the prophesy of the Scriptures, how do we proceed? What will happen?"

Joachim looked at her, his face in amused agreement. He smiled at her litany of concerns. It was territory he had already traversed.

"That, too, I pondered out by the well. Your questions are my questions. How can anyone know the future?" Anne was about to speak. "Wait, please," he extended his hand. "Hear me out. Even though Jesus is no ordinary boy, perhaps the best thing we can do is to treat him like an ordinary boy." He looked at her for concurrence.

"If he walked in the door right now, are we to get down on bended knee and begin praying to God?" Joachim rambled. "Are we to launch into The Aleinu? Is it our duty to start a session of praise and thanksgiving? Do we light candles and have an incense offering? Or, as I suggest, do we run up to him and give him a big hug?"

This was no mundane matter for the two of them. It was not a new subject either. Sometimes the issue of how to handle Jesus as God became more than a little complicated.

"So, we merely say, 'Welcome to Nazareth. We are your grandparents. It's nice to have you home. How was the trip'?" Anne teased.

Joachim's long day and the unexpected and unfriendly visit from Antipas' envoy coalesced into a drained mood.

"Anne. I'm tired and I'm going to bed."

Chapter 7

"Shalom, Joachim," the woman greeted him curtly on the outskirts of Nazareth. "Here you are, up early, tools in hand and off to work already?"

He hadn't seen her step out from an alleyway and was startled by her brusque voice. She seemed almost offended that he was violating her morning space, as if this corner of the world belonged to her. And, in a way, it did. She fancied herself as the town herald.

"Give your breakfast time to dissolve, Mr. Carpenter," she preached. "Slow down. The world will wait for you. Business goes better on a settled stomach. Don't you agree?" She mellowed. "Looks like it's going to be a blessed day."

Her uncovered head revealed uncombed hair. It looked as if her straggly locks had been in a fight all night long. A blue shawl dangled in disarray across her shoulders and a wrinkled nightshirt brushed her unstrapped sandals. Appearances were not a priority for Chloe Adontz, no matter what time of day. However, information about Nazareth and its people were like sustenance to her.

Chloe not only rose early but made it her duty to help launch the day for any other soul up and about. She had a knack of inserting herself in the life of others, giving advice abundantly and joyfully. She believed it was the right thing to do, unquestionably helpful to whomever she may encounter. And she didn't hoard news. She shared it with all who would listen.

"Blessed hot, maybe," Joachim responded. He kept on walking, pulling his cart full of tools with fragile hopes she had run out of commentary. *She's like a town rooster*, he thought, cackling away and meddling in everything. He looked up in prayer. *Thanks be to God for Anne.* He smiled in satisfaction.

"You are headed in the wrong direction," Chloe instructed. "The rabbi's house is the other way. That table won't build itself."

"Ah, as usual. You are right, Chloe. Have a nice day."

Joachim didn't change direction. Sun at his back, he headed northwest to Sepphoris and Antipas' bidding. Last night's messenger made priorities clear. The weather was fair. A limp breeze did little to tame the expected warm Nisan (May/June) day. The sun would be low in the other direction by the time he returned to Nazareth and supper.

Caesar Augustus had appointed Herod Antipas tetrarch of Galilee and Perea following the death of Herod the Great, Antipas' father. Rome divided the kingdom with Antipas ruling in the north. Perea was a region southeast of Galilee, beyond the Jordan River. Herod Archelaus, another son, took over as ruler of Samaria, Judea and Idumea. Other siblings were assigned other areas.

Antipas, 26, was ambitious. While sibling rivalries are not unusual, his contest with brothers not only embraced pleasing Rome in every way but building the best cities in the empire. And, perhaps even more provoking, he had a wandering eye – initially for his brother's wife. It was family intermingling that was destined for disaster.

Joachim was aware of such connubial shenanigans, mostly through the gossip machine fed by Mrs. Adontz. His only concern was to work on the masonry of temples, baths and other edifices that were part of Antipas' dream city of Sepphoris. There was a subliminal motive for Joachim. He and Anne had lived in Sepphoris for a period following Mary's birth in Jerusalem.

The city, perched atop a hill like a dove in a tree, drew its name from a variant of the Hebrew word for bird. Jewish Hasmoneans ruled Sepphoris until it fell under Roman rule some three generations before Antipas came along. His appointment was not without uproar. Rebels protesting Herod rule burned part of the city. Now Antipas was rebuilding what he called "the ornament of Galilee."

Though Sepphoris was the ruling seat for Galilee, Antipas' designs included a new capital city, Tiberias, on the western shore of the Sea of Galilee.

After an hour's walk, Joachim arrived at the foremen checkpoint on the south edge of Sepphoris. There credentials were reviewed and directions given for the workday. The emphasis on construction details came entirely from Antipas. If he wanted to speed up work on a reflecting pool, that's where foremen sent artisans. On this day work bosses assigned Joachim and a crew to put final touches on circular pillars that formed the portal to a large conference building.

"You were scheduled for work here the previous two days, but didn't show, according to overseer's notes." The foreman clearly wanted answers from Joachim. "Have you been ill? Or attending lesser business?"

"I was not sick," Joachim answered honestly. "I am building a table for our rabbi and his wife. It is my fault. I should have been here."

"Your forthrightness and skillfulness with a trowel favor you this time, Joachim. Antipas wants these projects speeded up. We're behind schedule."

"I understand, sir. It won't happen again."

Romans were architectural masters at building many things, roads, aqueducts and buildings among them. Joachim's assistant mixed the prescribed mortar of pumice, lime and volcanic ash into a lathering compound precise for finishing work. He had a reputation for consummate skills, the reason he was hired and that supervisors wanted to retain his employment.

Assigned to polish portico columns in a garden area, Joachim was thankful to be in the open air, not stuck in a steamy inside building. Each column was a cubit in diameter, or about six hand spans. He was also grateful that the columns were comparatively short, no more than 15 cubits high. His two-section ladder would negate the need for scaffolding.

While many Roman citizens worked six-hour days, slaves and artisans who labored for Antipas frequently toiled nearly twice that long, from sunrise to sunset. While common laborers earned less than a denarius per day, Joachim and similar craftsmen received a denarius or more. Wages weren't taxed, but Roman subjects paid heavy tribute on homes, land, livestock, orchards and fish.

Tax collectors, or publicans, were not popular people – among Jews or Gentiles. Usually, they were political appointees and frequently relatives or friends of the local Roman ruler. Rome honed nepotism, sprinkled with patrimony, to a fine art. Residents especially despised those tax collectors who tacked on a bonus for themselves.

Many Jews associated publicans with a general hatred of Rome. They viewed Roman taxes as a tribute to a god they despised (Caesars were all declared gods), and as a symbol of their slavery to Rome.

Jewish society often regarded publicans as first cousins to sinners. Hebrew publicans were outcasts.

Joachim was neither a politician nor a protestor. He made a good living as a craftsman and did as he was told in silent acquiescence. Not only was he mild-mannered, but he sensed the inherent and impending quandaries related to their grandson's nature. Jesus, as told by their daughter Mary, was not only human, but divine.

He and Anne had not shared such revelations about Jesus with anyone, not relatives or friends and neighbors. Even though Jewish Scripture talked about an expected Messiah, many thought of such an event as deliverance from Roman rule. To suggest a radical concept of a God/man, a spiritual savior, was a belief embraced by some, but most envisioned a conquering leader, someone who would expel the Roman occupiers.

How Jesus' unique nature and mission would play out in Nazareth, both among Roman rulers and Jews themselves, was a question constantly before Anne and Joachim. Even though Jesus was a mere child, it was unknown when his uniqueness may become apparent to the public. Neither did they have any idea when or how Jesus would begin his mission.

Like most Jews, Jesus' grandparents knew the prophesies well. Unlike others, they had personal involvement. Grandparents of God? What could they do? What should they do? An astounding dilemma. It was a subject of never-ending discussion. They were on a merry-go-round that never stopped. Excitement mixed with apprehension. Awe countered by uncertainty.

"Are you dreaming again, Joachim?"

Rufus Gaius was an affable overseer, one who recognized the need to complete a job, indeed, to keep higher-ups happy. He also believed that success was achieved by the carrot rather than the stick. Treat workers right and you get more work done. He had become as close to a friend with Joachim as a boss from an occupying force can be.

"You had that up-in-the-clouds gaze about you," Rufus laughed. "Are you pondering a leisurely weekend, one free of the wife's to-do list? Maybe find a fishing stream somewhere nearby? A peaceful day and the lunkers are just waiting to be hooked. Ah. Certainly, it's too far to walk to the Sea of Galilee where the really big ones lurk. Good to dream, Joachim."

"Sorry, Rufus. I wasn't thinking about fishing, although that's not a bad idea. If I get any days off from this job in Sepphoris, I will have to get back to finishing the rabbi's table. I've told you about that project. The rabbi's wife puts as much emphasis on that as Antipas does on building his temples. How are things with you?"

"Can't complain. I have a job. Plenty to eat," and he rubbed his ample belly. "I never married, as you know, and while I have satisfactory accommodations here, my sister wants me to come back to Ardea. That's a village near Rome, on the Tyrrhenian Sea. Plenty of fishing there, Joachim. And no busy schedule. I could relax and read some of Virgil's poems. At least that's what my sister says."

"Who's Virgil? Some relative?"

"No, no, Joachim," he chuckled. "He's a writer. My sister tells me he has become quite famous with his writings about peace. She reads that stuff, but I'm not much for it. I'd rather talk and drink ale with friends down at the local tavern. No wine for me, Joachim. I have a barbaric streak. Moreover, wine is for the wealthy. Laying on pillows around a table with fruit and wine and doing all sorts of things."

Rufus Gaius uttered an uneasy laugh. He was aware of Joachim's beliefs regarding loyalty to one's wife.

"So then," Joachim asked after a pause filled with images. "Are you going back to Rome with your sister? You are allowed to do that? Just pick up and leave?"

"Well, I know some people. And, as you've noticed and commented on before, I am pretty well peppered with gray hair. I could ask for withdrawal due to age even though Antipas is zealous in his building projects. You heard that he wants to build a whole new town over by the Galilee coast? I want to get out of here before that starts."

"I heard. Looks like plenty of work for carpenters and masons for years to come," Joachim said. "Speaking of that, I'd better get back to work here before some grumpy old overseer comes along and chews me out. Wouldn't want that. Look bad on my record."

The two men laughed.

"Get back to work, Joachim, before I get grumpy and chew you out. And put something nasty on your record."

It was after sundown when Joachim walked into the front door of his Nazareth home, the same aches that followed every other workday. Mixing mortar and troweling it from a ladder is no easy task, and his knees told him all about it. And on this night, his shoulders agreed with his knees. Still, he was in good spirits, and he smiled at Anne, who was washing cookware. He had several days free of the gloom of Sepphoris.

Joachim and Anne had waited years to become parents. They had prayed endlessly that God would bless them with a child. Like other devout Jews, such as Elizabeth and Zechariah in Jerusalem, they grieved as they aged and remained childless.

Joachim especially went through a period of depression after he was declared unworthy at Temple. His sacrifices were rejected because he had no offspring. It was an exasperating whirl. One day Anne was walking near a stream outside Jerusalem, where they lived before moving to Galilee. In her grief, she composed a prayer of appeal to God. Once back home, she jotted down her thoughts and lamentations:

"Oh me," she wrote. "*I was born cursed in front of the children of Israel. I am reviled and they treat me with contempt and cast me out of the Temple of the Lord my God. Oh me, what am I like? I am not like the birds of the sky, for the birds of the sky are fruitful before you, Lord. Oh me, what am I like? I am not like domestic animals, for the domestic animals are fruitful before you, Lord. Oh me, what am I like? I am not like the wild animals of the earth, for the wild animals of the earth are fruitful before you, Lord. Oh me, what am I like? I am not like the waters of a stream, for these waters are fruitful before you, Lord. Oh me, what am I like? I am not like this earth, for the earth produces its fruit in season and blesses you, Lord."*

After months of prayer by both, Anne conceived. Mary was born prematurely, a sign to Anne that she was special. The elated parents frequently referred to similar accounts in Scripture of births to elderly couples. Rachel, also childless, went to the Tabernacle at Shiloh where her prayers were blessed. The conception and birth of Samuel followed. Anne rejoiced in noting that her name in Hebrew was Rachel.

"How was work today, Joachim?"

"The same. The ingredients in mortar never change. The columns and fountains and gargoyles are uniform. Antipas' madness for building things to honor himself is unceasing. The sense of authority and power is constant. So, yes, Anne. Today was much the same as every other day." He finished drying his hands after washing. "The only bright spot was Rufus."

"How's Rufus getting along?"

"He's fine, though his sister wants him to come back to Rome. And I wouldn't be surprised if he left Galilee."

"Maybe we should move, Joachim. We could settle near Elizabeth and Zechariah west of Jerusalem. Or, how about Jericho? I hear that's a nice place."

"Exactly what I had in mind, Anne. We could dig up all our thousands of denarii buried in the backyard and head to sunny beaches of Caesarea on the Great Sea. My shoulders are rejoicing already. My knees are jumping for joy. When should we pack?"

Their amusement burst out in hilarious laughter. It was one of those unrestrained moments of mutual silliness when a mere side glance provokes a renewed ripple of boisterous merriment. The joking and Anne's sparkling eyes masked the discomforts of a long day of labor.

"My dear Joachim," Anne, still chortling, addressed her husband. "Our farmer neighbor, Gideon, brought over some gifts from the vine this afternoon. Some is fermented. Some is not. Before we eat, would you care for a cup of something? And which type?" she added, knowing the answer beforehand.

"Well," Joachim replied in feigned deliberation, "Perhaps I should," he continued in drawn-out fashion, "appraise the medicinal influence of each." He placed a calloused finger upon his lip so as to ponder the matter. "Which will make me feel better? Grape juice or wine?" Anne smiled broadly.

"If it will help you decide, Gideon suggested the wine is good for easing pain of the joints and overall countering tension."

"You have convinced me, dear Anne. I shall have a cup of the fermented version, please." Anne, as was Jewish custom, had grape juice. They moved outside to the small garden that adorned the front door of their quarters. The smell of lilies and the spectacular view of the Jezreel Valley expanded their sense of contentment.

The anemones, or lilies of the field, would only be in bloom a week or two more. Their crisp, sweet fragrance competed with the licorice scent of olive tree blooms. The tiny, white olive flowers congregate in clusters. The trees produce fruit every other year. The mournful song of doves in the grove of cedars across the road did not diminish the serenity.

"Remember when we first married Anne, how we talked about life and that we would be equal partners? Our culture is based on the household of the father, or what is called bet'av. But we decided on bet'av and bet'em to reflect the equality of man and woman. I hope I have lived up to that, even though I sometimes take you for granted."

"Joachim, you are a wonderful husband. I couldn't dream of a more loving, loyal and caring man. Many fathers would have gone meshuga when they discovered their unmarried daughter, though betrothed, was pregnant. But you trusted both Joseph and Mary and believed. Believed!" she said with tender emphasis.

"And what a role in history that belief has bestowed upon us," he noted.

"Joachim, my dear, are you disappointed that we have had no sons?"

"Not at all, Anne. We have a great son-in-law, Joseph. It would have been nice to have a son, but we have Jesus. What more could we ask of God?"

They sat and looked at each other and the surrounding Galilean countryside. Orchards, vineyards, wheat fields and rows of olive trees dotted the agrarian landscape. Agriculture was the main occupation in the area. Barley fields occupied the better soil. Pastures yielded a variety of legumes for cattle and sheep.

"Listen," Anne sat up in her chair. "Do you hear that?"

The tinkling of a bell drifted from a nearby hillside. That was followed by the fragmented and alarmist bellowing of sheep. Sheep were noted for their stubborn behavior, slow and resistant to direction, especially guidance by a herding dog. Baffled herdsmen could not understand a flock's reluctance to move to new grass after chewing through a pasture.

Joachim nodded to her question.

"I love this time of year," he said. "Nature in all its forms is reinventing itself, sprouting new wood and producing fruit from last year's growth. Flowers of every variety are competing for attention. As for the sheep, ewes may be particularly defensive now because of their lambs. Moms, no matter what the specie, are fiercely protective."

While springtime launches life, the Israeli agricultural year – and thus its calendar – begins in the autumn with the olive harvest. Seven more periods of grain planting, late planting, barley harvest, harvest and feasting, vine-tending, and summer fruit, follow. Household activities, and thus the economy, are centered around the cycle of the agricultural year.

Everyone in a farming family is involved in harvest. In the fields, men reap the crops using sickles, while women and older children gather sheaves of wheat and tie them into bundles. Women and young girls also carry bundles on their heads as the whole family proceeds toward the village threshing floor.

"Do you wish we were involved in agriculture, lived outside Nazareth?" Joachim inquired. "You could have a pet lamb. Or several."

"No," Anne was quick to reply. "I like it here. With you."

Chapter 8

SINAI *PENINSULA, about 4AD* – I gazed at the vast heavens above, the night uncluttered with clouds. The depth of God's universe is overwhelming. I glimpsed for a second at Joseph and could sense his mind. *What is Mary thinking?* Finally, I gave voice to my thoughts

"Scripture says that God blessed Abraham and would make his descendants as numerous as the stars in the sky. Just look up, Joseph. That's a lot of descendants."

"I can't disagree with that," he replied. "How many stars are there and how many years will God's pronouncement take? And, on top of that, how many of those promised descendants will believe in God?"

"Joseph. It's not like you to question God's plan. What I was getting at, is why, among all those stars, did He choose us."

I swallowed hard, pondering my own question. Time passed. A soft breeze stirred as if to carry an answer.

"He selected us to be parents of Jesus, God's way of coming among us? It's been nearly four years and the angel's words never leave me: '*Do not be afraid, Mary, for you have found favor with God. Listen: You will become pregnant and give birth to a son, and you will name him Jesus.*' Me. A teenage girl from nowhere. Now I'm 20 and it's still all mind boggling."

The road out of Egypt was silent, except for the whispers of nocturnal creatures. We were cloaked in the darkness of night save for the twinkling stars. Yet, we also knew the light was within the little boy sleeping on the ground next to us. We knew Scripture and what we were told at Jesus' conception. We were the ones chosen.

Oh, there will likely be dark days. We had often discussed that. Many of those challenges are still hidden in the shadows of choices made by the human race. How any suffering would play out for our family was not a new subject. But for now, on the way back to Israel, we rejoiced in the light near us.

"Just look at him, Joseph. Isn't he beautiful?" I couldn't help but smile.

"And then the angel says: '*He will be great and will be called the Son of the Most High. And the Lord God will give to Him the throne of his father David, and He will reign over the house of Jacob forever, and of His kingdom there will be no end.'* The angel said not to be afraid, but it's hard.

"Sometimes I'm terrified, Joseph, until I concentrate on God's love. That comforts me. Still, why me? Why us?"

"I can't answer your question, Mary."

Joseph knew that entwined in the mystery of Mary's deliberation, and the genuine excitement at being the mother of Jesus, were all the unknowns that the future held. Her face reflected quizzical joy. He looked at Jesus, then at Mary.

"I know why He picked you, Mary. What I don't understand is why He picked me and not some younger fellow. Someone more energetic. Someone more athletic, who can understand the twists and turns of boys. Someone without flecks of gray hair. And while God was deciding all this, why not an architect rather than a carpenter with callouses and blackened thumbnails. It makes little sense."

"You sell yourself short, Joseph. You are the perfect man to be Jesus' father. From you he learns to be humble, to serve. You are a just man, fair in your dealings. He learns skills. You don't broadcast it, but often you put aside your carpenter tools to help someone else in the field. And not once, even at Passover when there was a lot of boasting going on, do I hear you brag about Jesus or suggest how he's special."

She let her words settle, and then added.

"Joseph, I am blessed to have you as my husband. I love you deeply."

It was not uncommon for Joseph to be lost for words, but here his vocal cords seemed to stiffen into knots. He wiggled on a makeshift seat next to the fading embers of the cooking fire. He looked at Mary, and eventually brought forth a murmured utterance.

"You know that I love you, too. I will do anything to protect you and Jesus. As for nattering about Jesus and who he is, and who we are, I always figured that would be asking for trouble." He thought more on that, and then added.

"Who would believe our story anyway, Mary? And I'm not one to stir any pots of controversy."

"Look, Joseph! A shooting star!"

"Hmm. I didn't see it. What does it mean, Mary? One of Abraham's descendants headed for trouble? I hope it's not us."

"Be serious. It's God working with his art brush. Didn't anyone ever tell you that? That's what some of my friends said when I was little. And you know seers suggest that viewers of shooting stars will have good luck."

"In that case, since you saw the falling star and I didn't, I'm appointing you to be in charge of our safety committee on the way home."

"Only if you become head of the cooking committee!"

"You don't really mean that, Mary."

I laughed and made a sour face.

"I can remember my parents sitting in the garden at night, looking at the heavens," I said. "Often, we prayed. They are such hard workers, Joseph. You know that. And they are holy and generous. Like you. My mom held me on her lap when I was small, taught me prayers and so much of the Scripture. Did you look at the stars?"

"Not so much," Joseph laughed. "My father, Jacob, was not as religious and sentimental as Joachim, your dad. He was on the gruff side. Maybe that was because he had all those stepchildren to raise. My Uncle Heli died, and as you know, my father then married his widow, who became my mom. I'm more complicated than you think. But, no, we didn't look at stars much."

"Joseph? Do you think we'll have any trouble on the way back through the desert and then Judea and Samaria? And once we get back to Nazareth, will we always have to be looking over our shoulders for the Romans and soldiers? Does this Herod Antipas have the same agenda to kill Jesus as his father did?"

Joseph looked at me tenderly. My questions were the same ones that preoccupied his mind, but he wouldn't say that.

"Mary, I feel much better about our trip home now that we joined up with this Jericho assemblage. Mr. Eleazar is right. There is security in numbers. And I have the feeling that if we were accosted by any would-be robbers, he would be able to talk his way out of it. We'll just have to put up with the dust and his penchant for gab. Maybe his wife, Kalatha, has some new recipes she will share with you."

"Oh, you think I need new recipes, do you? Remember, you are inching toward being head of the cooking committee."

"With that dreadful thought, I think we should get some rest. Another long day tomorrow."

"Joseph?"

"Yes, Mary."

"Why do you suppose the angel of your dreams, back after when Jesus was born and Herod threatened to kill him, urged us to flee to Egypt? Why not Thessalonica or Patmos? Why not some place other than where Rome rules?"

"I haven't the foggiest idea. Maybe because of all the Jewish people in Egypt. I never really thought about it. I just knew we had to get far away from Herod, and even then, I was concerned his Roman friends would find out."

He looked up at the twinkling stars and pulled the woolen shawl around his shoulders. The desert can get chilly at night. The caravan animals went through their systematic grunts, groans and shuffling. Otherwise, it was silent.

"Joseph?"

"Yes, Mary."

"Don't you find it curious that ours was a flight to Egypt, and 1,400 years before, Moses led the Jewish people out of Egypt? What do you make of that?"

There was no response from the other side of the blanket.

"Joseph? Are you asleep already? I was wondering if we will we be traveling all the way to Jericho, or be taking a different route?"

"I don't know yet. Goodnight, Mary."

Jesus rose with the dawn, before his parents were awake. Joseph was snoring his way in a deep sleep. I lay content next to him. The boy stood, rubbed his eyes, and routinely brushed the sand from his clothes. He looked around. There was sporadic movement among the caravan some distance away. Herdsmen were tending the animals. Afar, to the northeast, I could see the outline of buildings in the town of Belbeis. Soon we would pass through the heat of the desert.

Jesus' mind wandered. He contemplated walking toward the caravan animals, just to watch the watering and feeding, but that could get him into trouble. He circled a nearby palm tree, glanced up at its fronds, observing how they cut a pattern and interrupted the dark blue of the early morning sky. A slight breeze sent them scurrying to new forms. A pair of doves, suspicious of his movements, flew off with their wings whistling.

In a nearby arroyo, he spotted a lizard sitting on a piece of driftwood. He tip-toed closer, and for a minute the critter wiggled its tail in greeting. Jesus smiled. *What are you trying to tell me.* He moved several steps closer. The lizard was surveying escape routes. *You don't need to be afraid of me.* It had two tongues, and both were wavering in a nervous dance.

It turned its head as if to slither away, but unexpectedly lunged at Jesus. He had seen the species before and was told they were harmless. Yet, instinct caused him to leap away, ever eyeballing the critter. He stumbled backward. His left heel brushed into a pear cactus. A thorn punctured his skin. He forgot about the lizard and ran for help.

"Father! Help!" He yelled, racing back to their little encampment. Quickly his parents were roused.

"What's wrong?" I implored. "Why are you crying and moaning?"

"I have a thorn in my foot. See!"

"And just how did the thorn get in your foot?" Joseph asked, minus a great deal of sympathy.

Jesus explained. I pulled him to my lap, examined the foot and thorn.

"Joseph. Please get my sewing kit."

Needle in hand, I ignored Jesus' yowls and carefully dug the thorn out. Blood seeped from the prick.

"Lucky you didn't fall into the cactus with your head," Joseph said, still nigh of pity. I looked with disapproval of Joseph's comment, bound the wounded heal and slipped on Jesus' sandals.

"There. You should be good to travel."

Eleazar, the caravan leader, rushed up to discover the source of the caterwauling. He saw Jesus walking around, favoring his left foot.

"Ah. Stubbed your toe on a rock, did ya," he exclaimed in clairvoyant style. "I always tell my Marcel to watch where he is walking. But does he listen? No, I tell ya." He looked at Joseph. "I think little boys are deaf."

Joseph clarified that the culprit was a thorn, not a rock, and that the point of distress was the heel, not the toe.

"Actually," Joseph laughed, "a rock would have been kinder. Pear cactus are mean. I hope he doesn't have to contend with thorns again. What time are we departing this morning?"

"The animals are tended to and as soon as we can get the humans in line we will take off," Eleazar said. "Can you be ready in half an hour?"

"See you then," Joseph answered.

The wind picked up as they entered Belbeis. The tributary of the Nile was wider here than Joseph envisioned. However, soon the northeast-bound contingent moved away from the village and river, destined for barren lands. Presently, Eleazar approached Joseph with a worried look on his face. His son Marcel and Marcel's dog tagged along.

"What did you say," Joseph leaned toward Eleazar to hear over the whine of the wind. "I didn't hear you."

"I was saying," he raised his voice, "that we can expect increasing winds today. I visited with a group headed south, and they said there have been gales nearly every day. I suggest that everyone make sure their head covering is secure and a face wrap handy. If we run into a sandstorm, try to keep your eyes looking down as much as possible. And you may want to devise a covering for your donkey's head, too."

"Will we halt if it gets too bad?" Joseph shouted. "And how long will it last?"

"That's difficult to say. Could be short or maybe all day. Once there was a sandstorm in the Sinai that lasted a week. They called it a Khamsin." Joseph frowned. "My sense of the weather is that these are spawned by squalls and won't last long. I'm not good at forecasting the weather, but then who is." He laughed. "Anyways, it's good to be prepared."

He practically yelled in Joseph's ear.

"I doubt the severity will require us to stop. I'll wave a sign or send Marcel to notify you if we halt. Nevertheless, as a precaution, you may want to tie a rope between the three of you, just in case the dust gets so thick that it's difficult to see where you are going. We do that for our animals. These storms blow sporadic, unpredictable. Sort of like when my wife gets angry," he winked.

Joseph nodded. He explained the weather situation to me and Jesus, and then tethered us with Dynamo. Off we proceeded across the desert sands. Before mid-day, as Eleazar warned, the winds intensified. Camels snorted in protest and the column slowed to half the pace. It was as if someone was sweeping the desert floor with a wild, out-of-control broom. Billowing, brown clouds greeted the travelers.

Heads down, they plodded along, the intensity steady. Mary pulled the covering tightly about Jesus' face. Tiny pellets of sand bounced off their bodies and stung exposed skin. A burst of sand and debris swept by, and Dynamo brayed. Jesus rubbed his eyes to get rid of dust particles. Joseph saw his predicament and lifted him to his shoulders.

"Blink your eyes, don't rub them," Joseph advised Jesus. "And keep your head buried in my neck."

Suddenly, the wind abated, and the follow-up breeze circulated rain droplets. Some of the animals, and people, too, stuck out their tongues to catch the globules as if they were liquid gold. Slowly, the desert air was cleansed of its anger and took on a pristine flavor. Skies cleared. A brilliant royal blue dome blanketed the desolate desert.

"I can't believe such a change," I said, holding my arms upward. "And the air! Joseph, the air smells like freshly washed clothes. Look over there, Jesus. A huge boulder. It must be 10 houses high. And there in the blue sky. God has taken his white paint brush and whisked several long irregular lines. Just amazing."

"That bolder you see is more like a small mountain," Joseph said, ever the carpenter with a measuring eye. "It's a long walk from here, maybe a quarter day. Now where is that boy dashing off to? Oh. I see. He's running to greet Eleazar and his son."

"Hello again, Joseph," Eleazar waved. "How do you like the desert weather? Hot. Then breezy. Then a sandstorm followed by rain. And now? Perfect. If you don't like the weather, just wait a little, eh? Truth is it's a place of contrasts. In the summer, this is a hot place. But in the mountains, it gets below freezing."

Joseph nodded. The caravan proceeded, as did Eleazar. The two kibitzed, though Joseph mostly listened and nodded.

"And it snows in the mountains," Eleazar explained. "The mountains are mostly in the south part of Sinai. Yes, quite a place. The Sinai is east of the Red Sea, but desert is desert, whether it's this one or the Sinai. They run together. Mount Sinai is a long way east of here. That's where Moses received the Ten Commandments. But you knew that."

Joseph nodded.

"This is the same desert, where we are now, Joseph, that Moses led the Israelites out of Egypt and across the Red Sea. About a thousand years or so ago. I couldn't say where Moses made that crossing, but we'll be traveling through the same Land of Goshen west of the Red Sea and no doubt will cross the Moses' path. However, I doubt we'll see any markers that say *Moses' Trail,"* and he laughed at his humor.

Joseph smiled and nodded.

"Then your plan is . . ." Joseph started, but Eleazar wasn't finished.

"Incredible. Don't you think, Joseph? Here's Moses leading thousands of people out of Egypt and into the desert. I don't think he has the supplies, animals and guides that we have. Incredible, I say. Of course, after the plagues and no food, choices were limited. And then crossing the Red Sea. Do you believe the sea parted as Moses directed?"

Joseph was formulating his response.

"I'll tell you what I think," said Eleazar. "It was an especially dry season, and the sea level was low. After Moses and the people waded across, there was a downpour and flooding that caught the Egyptian soldiers by surprise. Or," he rubbed his whiskers, "it could be that God caused the waters to recede. Whatever happened, it will keep Jewish scholars debating for centuries.

"I will tell you this, Joseph. I will never understand such an ungrateful group of people. Moses saves their necks from bondage, and they expect a bazaar full of milk and honey when they get to the other side. I'm surprised God didn't hand Moses a thousand commandments instead of ten." He stopped to think about what he'd just said.

"I suppose that churlish bunch could be representing all of us. God gives us so much and still we gripe and want more. I hope it doesn't take us 40 years to get home." He stroked his chin again. "What do you say, Joseph? Maybe time for a short afternoon stop to rest the animals. It'll give us time to visit some more."

"Sounds like a good plan to me," said Joseph.

Joseph conveyed the schedule to me.

"We won't halt for long." Eleazar wants the caravan to get near the banks of the Red Sea by nightfall. We will eat a few figs while we wait," Joseph suggested. "That won't spoil our supper. Jesus, see if you can find some plant leaves for Dynamo to chew on, but watch out for cactus. Mary, I assume everything came through the sandstorm unscathed? Did we lose anything?"

"All our precautions paid off, Joseph. I still can't believe how quickly the weather changed for the better. I pray we don't run into a more serious weather situation. By the way, did you have a nice conversation with Eleazar?" she snickered. Joseph flinched and was forming a retort when their exchange was cut short. Eleazar, Marcel, and his dog Shlomo, approached.

"All ready to go?" the caravan leader asked.

"We're ready," Joseph answered.

"Marcel!" Jesus injected. "Shlomo's leg is better. He is not limping."

"I know," Marcel said. "He seems to be good as new. Ever since you petted him the other day, he is more frisky, and the limp has gone away. You must have a magic touch. Maybe you should be a dog doctor when you grow up."

Eleazar chuckled. Mary and Joseph exchanged curious looks.

Jesus approached Shlomo and rubbed his belly. The dog's tail wagged in gratitude.

Chapter 9

The Jericho caravan and Nazareth tag-alongs plodded toward the northeast. As the sun disappeared behind the endless sand, darkness slowly sucked up the scant shadows. Eleazar ordered a cease to the day's travel. Nighttime camp was formed, cooks began to prepare supper, animals were watered and fed, and guard positions established. Joseph, as usual, sought a place removed from the main group. He wrapped his tent shelter to branches of a Sayal tree to fashion a covering, and Mary began to prepare the meal.

"What's for supper, Immah?" Jesus inquired. "I'm as hungry as a starved camel, and Marcel told me camels have three stomachs, so now you understand how hungry I am."

"You ate two figs when we stopped earlier," I reminded, brushing my fingers through his dark hair, dislodging dust at the same time.

"Ah, Mary. He's a growing boy," Joseph chimed in. "Why, those two figs only satisfied two of his stomachs! Why don't you search for some firewood, Jesus. The sooner you find some, the sooner we'll eat."

Other caravans, headed southeast toward Memphis and Nile River towns, shuffled past. Soon after supper. Eleazar approached Joseph to explain travel plans and routes. He carried drawings that outlined geographical features and the main roads between Jerusalem and Egypt. His flickering oil lamp marked his advance.

"Ah, Joseph. I trust you and the Mrs. and the boy, had a satisfying meal," Eleazar said by way of greeting. "I think our cook has some baked honey cake left over if anyone is interested."

Jesus glanced at his parents with a look of anticipation, but Joseph answered before his son's expectancy could turn into words.

"Thanks, Eleazar, but I think we're good."

Jesus' disappointed face spoke volumes, but he said nothing. Instead, he rubbed his stomach, then went off to prepare his bed. I gave Joseph a look of disapproval, but the matter was settled.

"What are your travel plans for tomorrow?" Joseph asked. "I see you brought some maps. Eleazar, are these your drawings?"

"Yes and no. I purchased the base map from a veteran tradesman, and then scribbled in my own landmarks and lesser roads. Here. Take a look. This is about where we are tonight," he pointed to a spot on his map. "Joseph, beyond a giant bolder to the north, it's impossible to see it in the dark, lies the town of Succoth. Some call it Tharu, but all the caravan people refer to it as Succoth.

"Moses and the Israelites, traveling east, came through there. Next, they passed what we call Etham. A short distance from Etham, south of that mountain range," and Eleazar pointed northward, "you can see the shadowy peaks up there, they reached Yam Suph. That is where Moses crossed the Red Sea with the Egyptians in pursuit. But you probably knew that."

Joseph nodded.

"What isn't clear is if God parted the waters for Moses and the thousands of men, women and children to escape, or if they crossed a dry wadi that separated lakes between the Red Sea and the Great Sea. But see here. What is definite, still today, is that there is a fork in the road at Yam Suph. One road goes northward to the Great Sea and the other leads south along the coastline to Mount Sinai.

"Well, we all know Moses' flock trooped to Mount Sinai, grumbling all the way. Can you imagine? Moses saves them from servitude and who knows what else, and their response is a litany of complaints. We'll be taking the north fork or the Farma road. We should be there in a couple of days. Unless, Joseph, you want to follow Moses' route into the wilderness!"

Eleazar laughed and Joseph smiled and shook his head, "no."

"Scriptures say that our people once settled in Goshen, up near the Great Sea, because of famine," Eleazar felt compelled to launch one of his history lessons. "As years went by many more Jews came there and the new pharaoh, Ramses, became alarmed. He enslaves them, orders them to build new cities – one of them named after himself. Modest fellow, don't you see?

"Then comes the worst. I guess he was worried about the Israelites taking over by sheer numbers because he then orders the slaughter of all newborn Jewish babies. Well, you know the story. Moses' mother puts him in a basket and places it in the Nile River. There he is discovered by the pharaoh's daughter, rescued, and grows to become a great leader – both in and out of Egypt. She actually gave him the name Moses.

"I guess that's not news to you."

"I'm familiar with the readings," Joseph said.

"OK. I have a question for you. As you know, Joseph of the Scriptures, your namesake, also the son of Jacob, was thrown into a well by his jealous brothers and rescued by an Egyptian official. He was taken to Goshen, which is a ways north of here, between the Red Sea and Nile. That's where famine forced his brothers and other Jews to come. It was fertile land.

"OK. The Jewish people multiply over the years, become slaves, and suffer many atrocities. Four centuries after Joseph, Moses comes along and leads the people south out of Goshen to the very land ahead of us. Are you with me, Joseph? See what I'm saying?"

"Not sure. What's your point, Eleazar."

"My point is why did Moses come south right away? Why not flee east to get out of the main part of Egypt quickly?"

"I see," answered Joseph, eyebrows raised. It wasn't a question that he'd ever considered before. "Maybe Moses didn't want to confront any Philistines to the east. Maybe he wanted to stay south along waterways for food and drink. Maybe he knew the country well and where the best crossing was. Maybe he didn't want to face the perils of the desert with that many people."

"You could be right, Joseph. Such a spiel! You are quite the talker. Well then," Eleazar waved in departure, "I'll see you and your family tomorrow. We will continue to face the perils of the desert. I am assuming that the wadi near Yam Suph will be dry, and we won't need our swimming attire. If there is a stream there, I'm not sure I have enough pull with God to get him to part the waters."

Eleazar chuckled at his own remarks and Joseph grinned.

"We should be on the Farma road by early morning. Goodnight, Joseph."

With that the evening returned to its normal stillness. Joseph shook his head and smiled at Eleazar's propensity to prattle. He walked to the family campsite. Jesus was already asleep. Joseph and I looked at him with wonder.

The overwhelming challenge of rearing the human manifestation of God never left their minds. They sensed their role in history and in God's plan, but not in any defined way. In that ambiguous but glorious circumstance, they were a little like parents in all places and all times.

"How is he holding up with the journey?" I asked Joseph.

"He's doing fine, maybe having a better time of it than we are. I think he's made a friend in Marcel, and he sure likes that dog. I'm sure his little legs get tired, but so long as he keeps his sandals on, doesn't chase lizards and backs into cactus, he'll manage the trip. How are you doing, Mary?"

His question brought tears to my eyes. I couldn't help it. They trickled down my cheek and dropped to the ground. I watched as the droplets were immediately absorbed by the grainy sand. I bowed my head.

"Mary. What is it? Are you not feeling well?"

"It's the opposite, Joseph. I am beyond happy. How is it that I should be the most blessed woman in creation? Not only the mother of Jesus, the mother of God, but the wife of a man who couldn't be more considerate, more understanding. Instead of being angry and ashamed, your steady faith caused you to accept me and my pregnancy, and you have guided us ever since."

Joseph embraced her, holding her tightly in his thick arms. His own eyes moistened as they stood as one in the deep darkness of the desert night. At first, they didn't speak, but much was said. The wind's slight murmur blended with the soft, breathing hums of Jesus. They looked at each other, then at the child.

"Do you remember when he took his first steps?" Joseph whispered. "He was like a drunken sailor. He'd walk a little, arms flailing, then fall, walk a little further, then fall again. Finally, he managed to wobble upright from you to me, about 10 cubits. Oh, was he proud of that stroll. I can still see his big smile as he clapped his chubby hands."

"It was just before he turned one year old," I said, picturing the exact time and place, "at our second residence in Egypt. And then, a day later, he proudly walked to a storage room door, pulled it open, and waddled right in. He had been curious of where that door went."

"Now he backs into cactus," Joseph laughed.

"And his first attempt at saying father?" I smiled. "He said 'fada,' and then shortened that to 'da'. And when praying to God, Abba became 'Ba-Ba.' It sounded as if he was mimicking a lamb."

"I recall how you tried to get him to say Immah," Joseph laughed. "He would have this impish smile and after a while say 'fada'. That was cute. His pronouncing of Immah was shortened to mah. Remember? He sometimes still calls you mah."

"I hope he doesn't miss his friends from Asyut too much," I said. "The other day he talked about spinning tops with Horas. You remember him, Joseph? He was taller than Jesus, but a pleasant boy. I think his father was Amsi, the baker."

"You would remember a baker's name," Joseph teased. "Jesus will be fine. Like us, he will miss his acquaintances back there, but he will make new friends. It's easy for him to make friends. He and Marcel connected the first day. Of course, there was the dog."

The following morning there was exhilaration among all in the Jericho camp. They knew that soon they would cross the Red Sea area where Moses and their ancestors walked – and ran – to escape the pharaoh's army. We were excited, too, to behold this significant place in Jewish history, the climax of the first Passover.

Joseph noted that several years before, in our flight to Egypt, we had taken a more northern route, then meandered through the delta maze before reaching Memphis.

There was no lagging this Friday morning. Plans were already made. The day's journey would end in the Sinai with Shabbat. Children ran and skipped along the dusty trail. A joyous air enveloped the entourage. Soon Eleazar's "big rock" was passed. The mountains to the north became closer and bigger. But the land ahead was fairly level, except for scattered knobs and boulders, with signs of marsh and greater vegetation.

As they trekked past mid-day, there was no dimming of enthusiasm. With the sun still bright in the west, the cacophony of songs and regular caravan din were suddenly overpowered by a sudden eruption of echoing sounds to halt. Eleazar had given the signal to the caravan master to stop, and each camel driver repeated the words.

Camps were established, food supplies unloaded, and camels hobbled. With sunset, the Jewish Shabbat meal would begin. Grains would be mixed with goat cheese, cabbage and peppers, items purchased along the way. Leftovers would be served for breakfast. Most of the camel tenders were non-Jewish hired hands and prepared their own meals.

For those observing Shabbat, there would be no work until the day of rest ended – after Saturday sunset. Three meals had already been prepared, the first for Friday evening, the second for lunch on Saturday and the third later that afternoon. All would be eaten in a festive manner. Once gathered at Friday sunset, Eleazar presided. He asked all to cover their eyes with their hands and recite the blessing:

Blessed are You, God, Ruler of the universe, who sanctified us with the commandment of lighting Shabbat candles.

Next came the blessing of the children. Then Eleazar called upon a male singer. "Ariel has the best voice in our caravan. If I sang, it would open all the ancient tombs in Egypt and cause the animals to stampede. We don't want that. So, Ariel will give our song of welcome."

Shalom aleichem mal'achei hashareit mal'achei elyon mimelech malchei ham'lachim, ha-kadosh baruch hu

Bo'achem l'shalom mal'achei hashalom mal'achei elyon mimelech malchei ham'lachim, ha-kadosh baruch hu

Barechuni l'shalom mal'achei hashalom mal'achei elyon mimelech malchei ham'lachim, ha-kadosh baruch hu

Tzeitchem l'shalom mal'achei hashalom mal'achei elyon mimelech malchei ham'lachim, ha-kadosh baruch hu

(Peace be with you, ministering angels, messengers of the Most High, messengers of the King of Kings, the Holy One, Blessed be He.

Come in peace, messengers of peace, messengers of the Most High, messengers of the King of Kings, the Holy One, Blessed be He.

Bless me with peace, messengers of peace, messengers of the Most High, messengers of the King of Kings, the Holy One, Blessed be He. Go in peace, messengers of peace, messengers of the Most High, messengers of the King of Kings, the Holy One, Blessed be He.)

Eleazar recited several other blessings and then asked Ariel to lead them in praying festive hymns. Once completed, Eleazar proceeded to derasha, the Jewish homily usually given by a rabbi.

"I pray that no one will take offense if I say a few words," and he glanced at Joseph. Joseph questioned if *a few words* was a sincere measure of Eleazar's intended discourse.

"Tonight, is a special celebration," he began. "I know you are aware that on Sunday we will walk on holy ground. Our sandals will touch the very path of sandals worn by Moses and our ancestors. It was near here that Israel fled the pursuing Egyptian soldiers and crossed the Red Sea to freedom. It was near here that God once again interceded on our behalf. It was the redemption of our ancestors from slavery that foreshadows the messianic redemption yet to come."

Joseph and Mary instinctively looked at Jesus, then at each other. They smiled knowingly.

"While we will cross this sacred place and turn to the northeast, Moses led the people south to Mount Sinai where our holy laws were given to him by God. It was then that God asked us to keep holy on the sabbath, to rest on the seventh day as he did when he created the universe.

"This should be a place, then, where we recommit ourselves – me included – to all of His Ten Commandments. Don't steal, don't cheat, don't swear, don't lie, don't covet another person's possessions and don't honor false gods. You know them all. We are a blessed people. All God asks is that we show it by following his laws."

Eleazar hesitated in his commentary. He then looked skyward.

"I don't know about you," he said to the assembly, "but I feel a singular presence of God here. While God is always with us, I believe he is close to us today in a special way. Praise be to him, now, in this place and wherever we may be." He clapped his hands as if to say it was time to move on. "Now, I think it is time to eat,"

Mary and Joseph again exchanged perceptive glances. *God is here, close to us!* Indeed.

Joseph was surprised at Eleazar's brevity. He also scolded himself for internal judgements that labeled Eleazar as a windbag.

"Jesus, are you excited to be walking Moses' path?" I inquired.

"Yes, Mah. I remember your Scripture lessons about Moses and our people running to freedom. But I'm glad we won't be going into the wilderness. It's probably filled with cactus."

We laughed.

"And what did you think of Eleazar's comments about the Ten Commandments?" Joseph asked.

"Mr. Eleazar may not be a rabbi," Jesus responded, "but his words make us think." He paused, looked at the ground and picked up a stick. Then he sketched a heart in the sand.

"He left out loving our parents. And we must love God and our neighbor." He looked at me for motherly endorsement.

"Can we eat now?"

While there was a feeling of excitement afloat among the Jericho caravan, it was tempered by the solemnity of religious history. Prompted by the uncommon level of enthusiasm among adults, the children skipped and sang as if it were the harvest festival of Sukkot. For elders, however, traveling the path of Moses was more jubilation, a sense of joy enfolded in the sacred.

Sukkot came at the end of the growing season, when families traveled to Jerusalem to give thanks for God's bounty. It is a time of merriment for children of all ages, with dancing, singing and eating. Sacred rituals are also part of the celebration, readings and chanting that link the cycle of nature with human life. All that was later in the year.

"Did you get enough to eat?" Joseph asked Jesus as preparations were made to re-start the caravan. Jesus nodded and rubbed his stomach.

"I think this will last me 'til mid-day," Jesus answered. Bread, olives and dried fruit made up the first-meal menu and were designed to ward off hunger until supper, usually the main meal. Traditionally, there were only two meals a day. A heavy breakfast was reproached in Scripture.

"Good. We have a long day ahead of us," Joseph said, "and there will only be dried figs to munch on along the way." The caravan master signaled the animal tenders to start, and the procession of camels, donkeys and people was again underway. Nose rings were yanked, and the animals got the message. A symphony of camel whines and donkey brays ensued.

Home, Jericho, was on the minds of dozens in Eleazar's party, including Bedouin animal drivers, even though they were yet to reach the half-way point. Pronounced, too, for the Jewish contingent, was the stirring enkindled by Moses and their ancestors. One could almost sense the joy of freedom from generations past, hear their shouts as they escaped the Egyptian soldiers and once again were headed to the promised land.

Walking was easy. Morning air, fresh in the nose, seemed to make our feet lighter. Even the animals, laden with linen, papyrus, metals and stone objects, moved compliantly in a rhythmic cadence. Eleazar was a trader, bringing cedar, pottery, olives and other products to Egypt and hauling imports back.

Mo, Marcel's dog, barked in nonsensical frenzy, chasing its tail. It bounded in Jesus' direction and as quickly reversed course. Soon Marcel loped in the same direction, waving, yelling and blowing a whistle as if Mo were headed to the unknown. Jesus laughed and clapped his hands. The dog ran to an outcropping of rock elevated above the dry wadi below. He howled as if imparting instructions, then ran ahead of the column.

"Are you sure Mo isn't short for Moses?" Jesus yelled to Marcel. "It looks like he wants to lead us across that marsh."

"Maybe that's what he's trying to tell us, to hurry to the other side," Marcel replied. "I knew he was a smart dog," The chase resumed.

"I hope Ol' Mo doesn't take the right fork toward Mount Sinai," Joseph laughed.

With little fanfare from Eleazar, the caravan crossed the wadi in a zig-zag fashion, avoiding muddy spots, and walked up the bank on the Sinai side. There, Mo waited and barked a welcome greeting. Suddenly, Hebrew voices began humming and then singing, first the children and then the adults. Their song was from the Book of Exodus, a melody engraved in their minds, a story of freedom known as Shirat HaYam, or Song of Moses.

"I will sing to the Lord, for He is highly exalted.
Both horse and driver He has hurled into the sea.
The Lord is my strength and my defense;
He has become my salvation.
He is my God, and I will exalt Him . . .

They skipped up the embankment and never looked back. At the fork in the road, they proceeded left, northeast on toward Farma and the Great Sea.

That night Jesus was restless, could not get to sleep immediately. Darkness consumed the bleak landscape. Not even the peaks of hills and mountain ranges could be seen. The moon was lit elsewhere in the universe, and stars struggled in vague dimness to take its place.

He sat up and stared at the emptiness. Joseph snored softly. I was awake and quietly went over to his corner of the tent.

"Jesus, what's the trouble? Are you ill?"

"No, Mah. I've just been thinking."

"Thinking? About what? Are you worried about something?"

"No, no. It isn't a worry."

"What then?"

"Well, it's about Moses."

"You are worried about Moses?" Mary asked patiently. "You are still thinking of walking in his footsteps today. Is that it?"

"Yes, Mah. But there is this other thing."

"And what would that be my son?"

"Our Scriptures, and you have read it several times, says Moses was the greatest prophet and leader in all times. He actually talked with God. And he wrote down the first laws for us."

"Yes."

"But then Moses tells the people that a greater prophet would come after him. Who is that? Who is he talking about?"

"Your question, Jesus, has kept people awake at night for generations. Kings and emperors have read those words and wondered the same thing. Maybe, just maybe, this new prophet, this greater prophet, will come along in our time. What do you think of that?"

"Maybe. Never thought of that. I guess it would have to be somebody old. Like Moses."

"Well, perhaps. Moses was born a long time ago. Some say 14 centuries ago. And there have been many prophets and people claiming to be prophets ever since. Maybe we can talk about it more tomorrow. OK?"

"OK. I am getting sleepy. Goodnight Mah."

I kissed him and returned to my side of the shelter. Joseph was still making funny sounds.

The next morning I told Joseph of the bedtime talk with Jesus about prophets. We agreed that the questions would only get more difficult in the years ahead.

"Your response to him was perfect, Mary. I couldn't have said it better,"

"Joseph, you couldn't have said it at all because you were sound asleep." I gave him a look that ended that subject. "We better prepare breakfast and then pack things. It looks like Jesus is still dreaming about Moses. Let him be, Joseph. He needs his rest."

"He also needs to be responsible for his duties, like gathering wood for our fire."

"Perhaps you could gather the wood today."

Joseph didn't quibble. The wood was gathered, fire started and cooking under way when a still sleepy Jesus woke up. The smell of breakfast caused his body to stir. He put on his sandals, rose, and stretched.

"I hear Moses and the prophets kept you from falling asleep last night," Joseph probed. Jesus smiled.

"Father?" he began, still stretching and yawning. "Does Grandpa Joachim have a dog?"

Chapter 10

OUT OF EGYPT (about 4 AD) – As Joseph led his family home, the political climate in Jerusalem worsened. There was a time when he intended that they return to Jerusalem, not permanently but at least long enough to visit Elizabeth and Zechariah and thank them for their help prior to the hasty trip to Egypt. Not only would Mary be able to spend time with her cousin, but the stop would give Jesus a chance to meet his relative, John.

However, the Jerusalem route became uncertain once Joseph learned that Herod Archelaus had assumed power in Judea. While he knew little about Archelaus, the news was that he inherited his father's thirst for complete control. He had discussed the matter with Mary, and she left the decision to him. He would inquire further once they reached Gaza. Gaza was not under Archelaus' thumb, and honest information perhaps more readily available.

At Gaza, there would be the choice of continuing with Eleazar and the Jericho party on the road to Jerusalem, or travel alone up the coast toward Ashkelon, Joppa and Caesarea. Also, at Gaza he would hear the status of the Roman occupation and whether Archelaus was a benevolent dictator or despot. Little did Joseph know that Jerusalem was in chaos.

For Archelaus it was a political dilemma. He could show muscle to his Hebrew subjects in an attempt to impress Rome. Or he could be lenient and witness a decrease in tribute to Rome. Too much force may lead to rebellion, another outcome that would sour the emperor. There is no easy answer for an autocrat. He was dancing on a tightrope.

Many of his problems were inherited from his father, Herod the Great. He hadn't forgotten his father's declaration nearly four years ago to kill all Bethlehem Jewish boys under two years of age in a paranoid fit over Jesus' birth and claims by some he was the long-awaited king. But Jesus' whereabouts and what to do about it were not a priority for Archelaus. He had more immediate problems. Like the long memory of Jews.

Herod the Great, half Jew, had blustered into power and declared himself king of the Jews. Rome conquered Judea from the

Hasmoneans, some 20 years before Herod took over. His rule was erratic, touched with spurts of goodwill and spasms of obsessive suspicion. He shifted from benevolence to brutality.

While credited with building the port of Caesarea, completing the second Temple in Jerusalem, and even opening Roman grain bins during a famine, Judeans remembered the bloody encounter that put him firmly in control and his harshness in routine matters. And they were weary of outside rule.

Before the Romans they lived under the control of Hasmoneans, the Greeks, Persians, Assyrians, and Babylonians. They were looking for a leader, as promised by the prophets, to set them free. Herod's death at his palatial winter home in Jericho was not mourned.

The surging unrest with Rome was aggravated by disputes among the Jews themselves. They were far from a monolithic people. There were Sadducees, scribes and Pharisees, zealots and Essenes. Sadducees associated with Temple priests and the Sanhedrin, the Jewish governing body. They adhered strictly to Mosaic law.

Pharisees were the teachers. They believed the writings of prophets were divinely inspired. And they believed in resurrection after death. The Sadducees did not. Zealots looked for a military leader to overthrow Roman occupation by force.

Even before Archelaus' formal appointment as successor, while he was in Rome awaiting Caesar Augustus' decision, the vacuum in leadership back in Judea generated insurrection. Like his father, he forced his rule upon return. As the Holy Family plodded toward home, bands of revolutionaries in Judea fought to overthrow Achelous' new reign. Thousands died in the futile attempt.

"You look deep in thought, my friend."

Joseph did not see Eleazar approach. Pondering which route to take after Gaza had filled his mind to the point of overload. He turned with a jerk.

"Oh, sorry, Eleazar. Yes. I was thinking about which road to take beyond Gaza. Have you heard anything more during the last several days? I mean about the situation in Jerusalem?"

"Not anything firm, Joseph. I was visiting with a southbound caravan out of Jericho yesterday. The head tradesman told me they are still dancing in Jericho over Herod the Great's death. Herod was a major figure there you know. He had three winter palaces near Jericho. Imagine! Three!! Few could afford one. Did I tell you about that?

"I'm told the first palace he leased from Cleopatra, the queen of Egypt. Then he constructed his own, but I guess that wasn't big enough. So, with the help of Roman architects and local artisans, he built another bigger place. There were courtyards decorated with frescos, gardens, and pools. On top of a large mound there was a portico that gave him a stunning overlook of the oasis Jericho."

"But," Joseph pressed, "any more news about Archelaus?"

"Just bits of this and that. Maybe a little more conflict and the usual protests." Eleazar paused as if to rediscover his train of thought. "All that wealth. All that grandeur. What good did it do old Herod, Joseph? He still died. In fact, I'm told he was a miserable man, by that I mean he was tormented. Some say he was crazier than a mad camel.

"Did I mention to you about Jericho? Wonderful place. Mild weather. Better than Jerusalem. Maybe you have heard the expression, 'Up to Jerusalem?' Well let me tell you the road from Jericho to Jerusalem is a climber. Twisty like a snake and steep. From the Mount of Olives on the eastern edge of Jerusalem, it's all downhill to Jericho. Takes a long day to make the trip down to Jericho.

"That's if there are no delays. It's not the safest road. That's why, Joseph, it's best to travel with a group. There are a lot of beatings and robberies on that road, so many that some now call it the Way of Blood. But Jericho is safe. Much activity. Because of the friendly climate, we produce many things – date palms, spices, wine, perfumes. Maybe you and Mary and the boy should settle down in Jericho."

Joseph wasn't sure if Eleazar was finished with his Jericho sales pitch.

"What say you, Joseph? A carpenter like yourself would have no trouble finding lots of work in Jericho. It's like living on the intersection of the world. It's home to the rich and poor and everyone in between. Of course, it once had huge walls around it, like Jerusalem and many other cities. Scripture tells us Joshua and his army blew trumpets and the wall came tumblin' down. But you probably knew that."

"Sounds like a nice place, but we have family in Nazareth. Maybe someday we'll visit."

"Suit yourself, Joseph, but remember your family is always welcome to travel with our caravan."

"Thank you for that. You have been most kind. Jesus has made a new friend, or I should say friends if you count Marcel's dog. You know, Eleazar, you are always welcome at our home in Nazareth, too. It's just a six-day walk. I know you trade people come to Capernaum at least yearly. Like Jericho, it's a major trading hub and Nazareth is just a short distance away."

The two parted company as the caravan proceeded northeast to the Great Sea and Farma. They would arrive there tomorrow, then follow the seacoast out of Egypt into Judea. After the evening meal, Mary and Joseph talked about many things dealing with the future, and especially imagining the arrival home.

Jesus had heard the discussions between his parents about which route to take once they reached Gaza. He did not understand why it was a significant issue. It seemed as if they were talking in a foreign language, using words with a hidden meaning. Parents are funny that way, saying things in a roundabout way. He aimed to find out more.

That night during the evening meal, his pursuit of details about travel plans took shape. He certainly didn't want to worry them with his questions, but he was curious. It's only natural for four-year old boys, well almost four, to wonder about things. How else can one learn?

"Father, why do you and Mah talk so much about which road to take? Is one way shorter than the other?"

"Well, son." Joseph, caught off guard, was formulating his response on the run. "Not really. I suppose each route has its good and bad points."

"What are the bad points?"

"The bad points? Well, the bad points. Yes. The road from Gaza to Jerusalem is mostly through a desert. It can be really hot."

"What your father is trying to say, Jesus, is that the path along the Great Sea has the benefit of breezes from the water." I tried to help explain. "Isn't that right, Joseph?"

"Yes, of course. Breezes."

"But we're traveling through a desert now. And we did before," Jesus responded.

"True," said Joseph, still fumbling for words. "Some say the path is smoother along the sea." He was happy with his response.

"Who makes the roads?" Jesus shifted gears.

"Well, people do," Joseph scratched his head. "People pick out a good place to walk and eventually by walking and riding donkeys there is a path. The path grows as camels come along and there is more traffic. And now the Romans, who are masters at road building, have really improved the paths. They remove the rocks, or rather tell Jewish workers to remove the rocks, and put little drainage ditches along some roads."

"What are drainage ditches, father?"

"You see, that allows water to drain off to the side of the road."

"But it hardly ever rains in the desert."

"Isn't it about time you go to sleep?"

"Father, who is this Archelaus person?"

"Why, he is the ruler of Judea and several other places. Have you taken an interest in politics, Jesus? Maybe you will grow up to be a leader."

"What's politics?"

"I think it's past your bedtime. Don't you, Mary?"

"We have another long day tomorrow. Instead of riding on a camel, Jesus, you may have to take a turn at leading Dynamo. Are your feet OK?"

"They're fine. I don't know why I need to go to bed so soon. Marcel's father lets him stay up later. And I bet his dog never sleeps but is on guard all night. He sure is a nice dog."

"That's enough jabbering tonight. We'll take up your other questions and world problems another time."

Jesus awoke at the sound of his parents preparing the day's first meal and repacking Dynamo's cargo. He propped himself on one arm and saw that Joseph was approaching, intent on stirring the lad and gathering the blankets and tent.

"Ah, ready for another day on the road, Jesus?"

"Why do they call it the Great Sea, father?"

"Why do you suppose?"

"Because it's big?"

"Correct. It's big. Enormous. The biggest sea around. I guess you don't want any bread and olive oil but are going to live on questions. Is that it?"

By mid-day the column faced an uphill trek that produced snorts among the camels and brays among the donkeys. Not only was the grade long, but the sand trail was soft. Hooves and feet sank with every step. It felt as if the ground were giving away, ready to swallow you. Jesus halted to re-tie his head wrap. Then he yanked the bridle leash, trying to convince Dynamo to keep moving.

The wind picked up and flecks of fine sand struck Jesus' cheeks. Joseph, who was trailing, ran ahead, and pulled Jesus' face cover upward. Jesus could barely see. He instructed Mary, who was hanging onto Dynamo's tail, and Jesus to keep their heads lowered. "Look down and follow the tracks," he yelled. "Don't fall or the animals behind may step on you."

Caravan guides read the boulders and distant acacia trees as guideposts. It wasn't their first trip through this Sinai wind tunnel. They knew that in a short time they would crest the mammoth dune, winds would abate, and the sandstorm subside. The Great Sea winds that filled the sails and propelled ships for centuries also whipped across the desert landscape and slowed land travelers.

One by one, animals and humans, strained their bodies up and over this blowing and drifting natural obstacle. Abruptly, it was all downhill to the sea, coasting after climbing the mountain. Jesus didn't notice at first, still keeping his head down, still following the tracks before him as instructed. He noted a lessening of the wind. Then shouts! It spiked his curiosity. He looked up.

"Mah, father!! Look at all that water! It looks like it never ends. Father. Is the rest of the world all water? How can all that water be next to all this sand? God made all the Earth, and he could have put more water in the desert. Look, Dynamo. You can walk right in and take a bath for days. And splash without worrying you will get someone else wet."

His parents, relieved at reaching the sea, marveled at the child's delight in discovering new things. Indeed, the Great Sea was something to behold. It made the Nile River look like a trickle. The wind, which only a brief time before spit sand and menaced travelers, now painted the sea with sparkling white caps. They walked the level plain with ease.

In a short time, the group reached the town of Farma. The gated Egyptian fortress, a brief walk from the sea, sat at the easternmost point of the Nile delta. Instead of rushing directly to the sea, caravan herdsmen directed everyone to a nearby wadi and fresh water. Eleazar had warned Joseph that the Great Sea "is almost as salty as the Dead Sea."

Suddenly, shouts of panic filled the air. Eleazar rushed along the caravan yelling at anyone and everyone.

"Our Marcel is missing! I can't find him anywhere! Has anyone seen our son Marcel?"

Eleazar's wife Kalatha, arms waving hysterically above her head, ran after her husband with loud and reverberant shrieks. The ensuing bedlam of people racing without direction engulfed Joseph's family. His first reaction was defensive, ever thinking about Jesus' safety. Even after Eleazar calmed down enough to explain the situation, Joseph didn't drop his guard.

"He must have become disoriented during the sandstorm," Eliazar suggested. "I should have been watching closer. We must go back, Joseph, and look for Marcel. He can't be too far, maybe a mile or so back over that sand dune. Please join our search party."

Joseph nodded.

"May I go along?" Jesus asked his father. "I think I know how to find Marcel."

Joseph, Eleazar and a half dozen other men, including weather-hardened camel tenders, all ready to double back to the dune area, gaped in astoundment. The high-pitched pronouncement of a four-year-old boy brought an unexpected calm to the search party. Joseph was reluctant to allow Jesus to join the contingent, but curiously did not forbid it.

"Let's unpack our things from Dynamo and you can ride on him," Joseph said. In minutes, the group left the Farma wadi and plodded up the dunes to the south. Once at the apex, the swirling winds spit sand particles in every direction. The heaviest gusts were at their back. Shouts yielded nothing, so the searchers trudged along using recently made but fast-vanishing tracks as a guide.

During a rest stop minutes later, Joseph approached Jesus and asked what ideas he had to find Marcel. He had mixed feelings about bringing him along in the first place and that hadn't changed.

"Father, my guess is that Marcel and his dog Schlomo are together. Mo wouldn't leave Marcel," Jesus said convincingly. "I know these men who direct the camels have whistles. If we can get them to blow their whistles, and if the rest of us whistle, Mo will hear it."

"Well, it's worth a try, Jesus," Joseph said. "I'll suggest that to Eleazar."

Soon the desert wind had competing sounds, shrill wails from the whistles of camel tenders and man-made toots and screeches. The disorganized din was sufficient to wilt cactus flowers. The cacophony went on for more than a minute. Then Eleazar raised his hand to signal a halt and turned his ear to the empty space ahead. There was no reassuring answer from the desolate reaches.

Jesus urged a reprise and the discordant call bounced off every nearby scrub bush and grain of sand. This time there was a response. A caravan guide to the far left of the trail was the first to hear the barking. Then Dynamo brayed. Shouts followed. Men rushed as if gold had been discovered. Marcel and Mo were found hunkering on the downwind side of a boulder. There was excitement and rejoicing. Mo chased his tail.

Jesus walked back to Farma, yielding his seat atop Dynamo to Marcel. That night Eleazar called upon cooks to prepare a festive meal like none other they had had on the journey. Jesus and Marcel were hoisted in celebration, and they gave thanks to God.

They embarked the next day along the coastal plain toward Gaza. Sea breezes continued to make the trip enjoyable. The entire caravan was in a jubilant mood. There was singing and spontaneous dancing. Jesus continued to be in awe at the expanse of water. He and the other children ran to the shoreline, squealing as they splashed through the water.

That night Joseph, hoping to head off a barrage of questions, decided to present a geography and government lesson.

"We have now entered Judea," he addressed Jesus after the evening meal, "but this part has a different ruler than in Jerusalem. When we get to Nazareth, there will be yet another ruler. To the east of Jericho, where Marcel and his family live, is Peraea and north of that is Decapolis. You see . . ."

"Father, why are there so many rulers? The psalms say the Lord is king of all nations, forever."

"Yes, Jesus. You are right. But people have disagreements about many things. Families have disagreements. One brother thinks he is not getting his fair share. Sometimes instead of following God's rule of love to settle things, there is fighting. And this hatred can be passed down for generations until there are new borders, new nations. We are a sinful people."

"That's because Adam and Eve decided to disregard God's instructions."

"Yes. And now the Romans want to rule the entire world. You see, they have their own gods. Julius Caesar even declared himself as a god. The Romans defeated the Greeks, who had their own gods. A long time ago this very land was occupied by the Philistines. They formed an ethnic state and fought with the Israelites until the Babylonian empire took over. It never ends."

Jesus was submerged with enough history to drown all his questions.

"And, Jesus, the Great Sea was the scene for many of these battles. The Romans give the sea a Latin name, Mare Magnum. We don't use Latin but speak in Aramaic, the ancient Semitic language. You will probably study all these things in school. We have the Sea of Galilee up north, you'll see. Much, much smaller than the Great Sea but more peaceable. Fishing and farming are the main occupations in Galilee. Although your grandfather, Joachim, a fine carpenter, may disagree. Isn't it time for bed?"

"Father. How deep is the Great Sea? Are there big rocks in it? And who owns it? Does the wind always blow out of the sea? Does it have lots of fish? Are there any crocodiles in the Great Sea?"

"I don't know the answers to those questions. What I do know is that it is time for you to go to sleep."

"Aw, father. I have more questions. Why did you become a carpenter? Was Grandfather Joachim always a carpenter? Are there any crocodiles in the Sea of Galilee?"

"You are sure worried about crocodiles," Joseph said. "I guess old Ammon, that boat captain on the Nile, is the reason. He liked to spin stories. Anyway, there are no crocodiles in the Sea of Galilee. As for your grandfather, Joachim, he once was a shepherd near Jerusalem. After he and Grandmother Anne were married, they lived in Jerusalem. That's where your mother was born."

"Why did they move to Nazareth?"

"I don't know. You can ask Grandfather Joachim why he moved to Nazareth. Now, it's bedtime and past."

The following morning the Jericho contingent arrived in Gaza city. They were greeted by an air of festivity. They passed through the sea gate and were thrust into Ambarvalia, the Roman festival for purification and agricultural fertility. Chanting citizens led a bull, sow and sheep around the plaza before the animals were sacrificed to ensure a state of blessedness.

Gaza city, like Jericho, is one of the oldest places in the world. At present it is prosperous and comparatively peaceable. After the destruction caused by many wars, Gaza was virtually rebuilt by the Romans. Now the port city was booming, on the crossroads to both Jerusalem and Caesarea. Nearly all the Jewish protests were in cities to the north, primarily in Jerusalem.

Eleazar had an inner distaste for Gaza. No fan of the Romans, he informed Joseph that they would not stay long in the city but would make their encampment outside the north gate. Gaza, he imparted, once was the capital for the Philistines, a long adversary of the Israelites. Joseph thought there was more to Eleazar's objections but had his own decisions to make.

That night he and Mary resolved to leave the Jericho group bound for Jerusalem and instead follow the sea road north. Near Caesarea they would take the path toward Nazareth. Mary had reservations about leaving the security of the caravan. Joseph worried about the uprisings in Jerusalem and the possibility of Herod Archelaus learning about the presence of Jesus.

Jesus, when told of his parents' decision, was sad to part with his new friend, Marcel, and his dog Mo. Joseph suggested that he would meet many new friends in his life and possibly see Marcel again. "There are many children in the Nazareth area, and some will be in your school." Joseph tried to soothe the separation. He allayed Mary's concerns by finding a small group also bound north toward Ashkelon.

"Have you made up your mind on the route to take?" Eleazar asked Joseph after the early meal was taken. "We will be pulling out soon."

Joseph approached Eleazar and wrapped his arms around the smaller man. Eleazar had his answer, but Joseph wanted to put it in words. A tear trickled down his cheek and found refuge in his beard.

"We are so grateful for your hospitality, my dear Eleazar," Joseph grabbed both of his hands. "I guess farewells are among the most difficult part of life. We will miss you, and Jesus will be without his new friend, Marcel." The two men watched the boys, half playing with the dog and half trying to say goodbye.

"We will miss you and your family, Joseph," Eleazar said. "Your boy is perceptive for his age. Maybe he will grow up to be a famous prophet.

"I must say, Joseph, no one has your patience and tolerance in discussions about religion and politics." Joseph laughed. "I know. I know," Eleazar went on. "I do most of the yammering. Kalatha says I talk too much, but out here visiting is about the only entertainment available. Oh, here comes the boss now. Kalatha, my dear, I have some bad news. Joseph and his family are taking the sea road."

Kalatha sought out Mary and the two women embraced, each also wishing for a reunion in the future but inwardly doubting if that would ever happen. "I hope we meet again, just for the children's sake," Kalatha said. "The boys have had such good times together. They will miss each other."

"True enough," said Mary. "We will miss all of you. You were so kind to invite us to join your caravan. We left good friends in Egypt and now we leave good friends again. I must admit it will be good to settle down in Galilee, but I know Jesus will never forget Marcel and his dog. We will remember you and your family in our prayers. Please pray for us. As the boys get older there will be difficult times."

"We will pray for you, Mary. I have a feeling that whatever trials you and Joseph face, God will be near you and watch over you."

"I know you are right, Kalatha. I see Joseph coming, so I suppose the time has come. Please, be safe. God bless." Jesus and Marcel laughed as Mo barked and chased his tail.

"I think he's putting on a goodbye dance," Marcel speculated. "Or, he could be saying that he wants you to stay in our circle. He's a clever dog. He has a great sense of what's going on."

"Marcel, my son," Eleazar injected, "Ole Mo doesn't have a clever bone in his body, but he is a life-saving companion."

"Maybe he has a bee in his tail," Jesus suggested. "He's trying to run away from the bee, but he'll never succeed that way."

"Time to go, Jesus. Time to meet some new friends," Joseph motioned. The Nazareth family waved goodbye to the Jericho family and resumed the walk along the sea. Shortly, they met up with another Jewish family, the Cohens from Caesarea. They were awaiting Joseph's family in the shade of a gnarled palm tree, inland from the sea and just off the walking path.

"Good to see you again," Aharon Cohen extended his hand in greeting to Joseph. "We saw you leave the caravan back at the Jerusalem road. You and your family are most welcome to travel with us. As I mentioned at our first meeting, we are small compared to the Jericho group. I have only a few donkeys and just one camel. But Esther and I are rich in children – five daughters."

"Indeed, you are rich, Aharon, "Joseph replied. "We thank you for allowing us to accompany you. Mary, my wife, was quite concerned, as I mentioned to you earlier, about traveling by ourselves. So, joining your family will be a great consolation to her. We just have the one boy, Jesus. And one donkey." Joseph looked at Mary, "Come," he invited. "Come and meet Esther and Aharon Cohen."

The families walked until the setting sun touched the sea, exchanging family information, then took the evening meal together. Jesus had never witnessed so many girls, all talking at the same time. He finally found the courage to ask Leah, one his size, a question.

"Have you ever seen a crocodile?" Jesus led with one of his favorites topics.

"Oh, no. They are mean," Leah said. "But I have seen a cobra. That's a killer. If they breath on you, you're as good as dead." Jesus was surprised at her knowledge of cobras.

"I saw a lizard once," Jesus said, "and it made me back into a cactus. See, right there," he pointed to his heal.

"I don't see anything," Leah said.

"Well, my mom pulled out all the thorns and put some stuff on my skin for healing." He returned to his reptile account. "While I didn't see a crocodile," Jesus continued, "I did see this man on the Nile River whose fingers were bit off by a crocodile."

The parents exchanged family details, minus any mention of Jesus' special place in the future of the world. Joseph finally proceeded to a question for Aharon that had been pestering in his mind since their meeting.

"Please Mr. Aharon, I'm curious. Do you find daughters more difficult to raise? And does Esther agree with your opinion?"

"Ah, Joseph. How would I know?" He paused. "The secret is that I'm partial to girls," he whispered. "But as Esther says, all are gifts. If we had a boy, she says, we would be blessed. And if Esther says it, that's the way it is."

Joseph nodded. "I hear you."

The two men talked more family, shop and politics. Aharon worked at pipe building factory and was active in the local Synagogue. They were returning from visiting Esther's kinfolk in Alexandria, Egypt. Joseph, without giving any background, said his family had lived in middle Egypt for some years and decided to return home and his carpenter craft in Nazareth.

"Better turn in," Aharon advised. "Another long walk tomorrow. We should be in Ashkelon by midday and Ashdod by evening. Ashkelon was once another Philistine stronghold. It's one of those places that changed hands many times down through history, the site of many battles. My goal is to reach Caesarea in six days. Now there is a city.

"You can't believe the new port the Romans are building there," Aharon spread his hand in demonstration. "I see you have your hand raised, Jesus. Do you have a question about Caesarea?"

"No," Jesus replied meekly. "I just wondered if you had a dog."

Chapter 11

GALILEE, about 29AD – As I was saying, while I've become a good friend and follower of Jesus, I have not found favor with his mother. My brother suggests the next time I visit over at Nazareth that I should scrub up good, be on my best behavior with a more serene demeanor, and perhaps wear a clean tunic that covers my chest and all the bird inkings. Andrew is so caring.

Recently, I suggested to the merchant, Philip, that he should visit Jesus. He has heard him preach about love and charity. His fishing supply business could use a little more charity with its customers. Like many, Philip wonders if Jesus is the real deal. "Could he be the one, Simon?" he asks, without saying the word Messiah.

I said he could find out for himself. It looked like rain. Business at his store will be slow. Why not go visit Jesus? Maybe Philip's happy demeanor can bring Jesus some relief.

On my last visit to Nazareth I could tell something heavy was on his mind. Really, for both Jesus and Mary I sensed a time of reckoning had arrived. They seemed to squirm in uncertainty regarding the months ahead, like a fish hanging on a hook, darting between unknowns, captives of God's plan for salvation.

I have accepted Jesus as the Messiah and he has accepted me as a follower. Eden and I know this man is also the visible presence of God. Jesus and I are more than just good friends. I was present at many of his sermons before the people of Galilee. But his ministry is at a crossroads.

I know a good deal about Jesus' life story, the pain of Joseph's death and his difficulties in the process of realizing he is God as well as man. Recently, he told me how he was absorbed with the future, how he continues to pray to God the Father for guidance regarding his ministry and salvation course.

Jesus greeted the new day at his favorite place, the grove with the big sycamore tree. Nearby, aspens lined the path like sentinels. He prayed, first thanking God for all His graces and then hoping he could syphon some insight on the days ahead, some sort of roadmap to guide him on his mission.

"I think I'll wander down to father's grave," he told Mary after a brief breakfast. She had already drawn water from the village well and was planning the day's meals. It was just the two of them, or so she supposed.

She wanted to know if he'd be home for supper. There wouldn't be too many more of these quiet family meals. She had no idea what the agenda of Jesus' ministry may look like, but she imagined it would be full of people – the hungry, the sick, the poor and many looking for a glimpse of the healer and miracle worker.

It is not the kind of scene she was comfortable with. Mary reflected the village of Nazareth, quiet and unassuming. She loved people, but crowds made her uneasy. The thought of people rushing here and there, shouting and jostling for a position near Jesus, made her anxious about his safety. Such are the dimensions of the accordance she made with the Angel Gabriel three decades ago.

"It looks as if it may storm," Mary cautioned Jesus as he grabbed a head covering and walked out the door.

"I expect there will be many storms ahead," Jesus replied. He wished he hadn't said that, adding to her worries. "I will be back before midday."

Jesus was 19 when Joseph died, still a young man in every sense of the word. He had completed his lesser schooling and continued a rigorous rabbinic-like study of Scripture. Like others that age he explored the challenges of adulthood, including social and employment options. He gained proficiency as a carpenter but had a way to go before he would be the equal of Joseph as a craftsman.

His circle of friends expanded, and like all young men that included several young women he had known for some time. It was not uncommon for young women to be married at 15. Jesus, however, though partial to a farm girl nearby, had not contemplated marriage. For sure, he was fond of Naomi. She and most of his close friends attended the same Synagogue in Nazareth.

Joseph had had several bouts with pulmonary issues, but no one expected death so soon. Jesus and Mary were with him when he died, grateful that he did not suffer. Nevertheless, it was a shock and they were grief-stricken. It was especially hard for his mother.

It was not a large funeral. Aside from Jesus and Mary, and close friends, most of those who attended were Joseph's customers and neighbors who had been benefactors or witnesses of his gentle manner and natural kindness.

At the service, Rabbi Shimon made special mention of Joseph's craftsmanship, both in building things and relationships with people. As to the former, he singled out a certain cherished dining table that belonged to the rabbi's wife. Joseph had managed to follow the pattern outlined by Joachim, his father-in-law, many tears before. When prayers ended, Jesus talked briefly. He noted that his father loved people, "without reservation, an example to all of us."

Then the procession, with Joseph's body carried on a platform, headed down the narrow path leading out of Nazareth. His remains were placed in a tomb hewn out of rock on a hillside that commanded a broad vista that included Mount Tabor to the southeast. That's where Jesus stood again this morning, alone, praying for the man who had faithfully stood by him and his mother.

It was a peaceful place. By now the sun had muscled in daylight. As usual, it forced night's blanket of stars to take cover, go into hiding until the day completed its tour of duty. But dawn's early light was itself dimmed by an approaching storm front. Unperturbed, doves softly practiced their mournful morning song. Sparrows, those pervasive commoners, indifferently blared their noisy cheeps.

In the distance, bleating sheep were ushered to pasture. There was no marketplace bartering noise yet. Commerce was just waking up, too. There was no sawing, no hammering, no splish-splashing of mortar being applied to stone, although all those sounds would have been music to Joseph's ears.

Jesus bowed his head in meditation at the tomb.

My dear earthly father. Thank you. Thank you for accepting God the Father's plan for salvation. I'm sure it was difficult as it was for my mother. But there was no simpler way to reopen the gates of heaven to all mankind. I had to become human, work to establish your kingdom on Earth, teach and heal and show the path to eternal life.

You and mother went through many difficult times to protect me, rushing me as an infant from Herod's grasp, fleeing to a strange land, returning to Galilee and teaching me how to work with my hands, to make things, and more importantly, how to treat people. And if you were here today you would probably try to intercede on my behalf all the way to the end. Thank you.

I tell you this dear Joseph, my earthly father. You will become known forever as the protector of all, a quiet man whose heart shouted with love. Now I must leave, and as I said once before, I need to be about by heavenly father's business."

It was a difficult goodbye for Jesus. There was a chance he would not again venture down that narrow side trail to the grave, now nearly overgrown with wild plants and brush. However, with uncertainty prevalent, Jesus wanted to say a formal goodbye. He was not sure where he'd be in the months ahead.

Mary, he knew, would be with him to the last day. How much should he tell her? Mothers have a way of reading between the lines, but he was hesitant to fill in the blanks, particularly those gruesome and torturing trials. She didn't have to visualize any of that, and in particular, the final days in Jerusalem and the pain through its dusty, twisting streets.

As he headed back, he heard the rumbling of thunder in the distance. The storm was coming. He felt a few drops of rain, that forerunner of gusty winds and torrents. The birds knew it. Their wings flapped in a determined drive to reach a known shelter. He laughed to himself. Should he fly away to some sanctuary, a haven from the pending tempest? No doubt that was the devil rapping at his door. The rain intensified.

Ah. The cavern. He had passed it on the way to Joseph's tomb, but his mind then was dedicated to the visit and what he would say. Now, as if Joseph were coming to the rescue again, the cavern was in plain sight. He picked up his pace to match the mounting downbeat of the rainfall. As he darted beneath the twisted bluff, he was immediately aware that he was not alone.

A man, with his arms wrapped around himself to simulate a warm shawl, stood shivering in a corner. He had no head gear and was woefully underdressed for the rainy, chilly weather. He appeared fearful and insecure. He was younger than Jesus, and shorter. The stubble-faced cavern companion suddenly presented a small, defensive smile, accompanied by a corrugated brow, even as he shrank deeper into the fissure.

Jesus smiled, too, not in a faked manner designed to ward off possible peril, but a warm, welcoming beam that immediately put his new neighbor at ease. His memory told him that he had seen this fellow before. But where? It may have been Nazareth, Capernaum or places in between.

"Here, take my wrap," Jesus offered as he approached the stranger. "You appear frightfully uncomfortable and I am just a short distance from home." There was no response until Jesus spoke again. "There is nothing to fear. Have I seen you in the area before? It seems so. Here, put this around you."

"Thank you," the man sheepishly replied, head downcast. He pulled the cloak about his shoulders. It immediately warmed his body and had what he inwardly sensed as a healing influence. It had an impact on his physical and mental well-being. Who is this person who gives up his coat to a stranger during a cold rain?

"My name is Philip," the man said somewhat guarded. "I live in Bethsaida."

"Philip, you say. Isn't that Greek?"

"Yes," he replied, still not comfortable about revealing too much. "You say we have met before? What is your name?"

"I'm Jesus of Nazareth. I was returning home from a visit to the tomb of my father, Joseph, when the downpour began. I ran into this cavern for protection. I'm sorry if I startled you."

Philip's eyes blossomed like spring flowers. He fixed on Jesus' face and slowly walked toward him. His own countenance changed from doubt to joy. After a pause, he advanced and threw his arms around Jesus.

"I was on my way to see you," he said with excitement. "I've heard you speak, though it was from the outer edges of the crowd. Simon suggested I visit you. There is talk that you are the one mentioned in our Holy Scriptures by Moses, whom prophets named as Jesus of Nazareth, son of Joseph. I can't believe this. I meet you in a cave?"

"You know Simon and Andrew?"

"Yes, yes. I work as an outfitter for fisherman. We sell supplies to fishing crews, mend nets, fix sails, just about anything they need. I've known the two of them and their father for some time. When Simon began telling me about you, with fervor, I listened. He isn't one to be convinced easily about anything, but he was persistent about you and your ministry. His head is thick, but his heart is warm and sincere."

"That would be Simon," Jesus laughed.

"Well, Simon kept pestering me to go find you, to 'see for yourself', as he put it. This went on for some time, so I finally said I would go just to shut him up. I should tell you that I also know the man called the Baptist, and he has also told me about you and your mission."

They stood looking at each other like two old friends who had just met for the first time.

"So, here I am and there you are. Amazing," Philip stuttered.

"Philip," Jesus said, the diminishing rain patter and fading thunder the only other sounds, "Follow me."

"My Lord," Philip said softly. "I will follow you, but right now I must return home and tell others that I have found what I was seeking, especially tell my friend Nathanial about our meeting?"

He returned Jesus's shawl and stepped gleefully out into the drizzle. He was whistling some tune as he ran eastward. Jesus watched as Philip skipped away, then turned toward Nazareth. The brief encounter with Philip lightened his load, pushing images of the future to the background. The sun slithered its way between lingering clouds. Droplets of rain smothered trees and bushes, making the entire countryside appear as a field of diamonds.

"Mother, I think I have another follower, a fellow by the name of Philip," he effused, walking in the door. "He knows Simon and Andrew and others who may be interested in spreading God's word. I must finish building those shelves for Mrs. Esther, and then perhaps tomorrow travel over to Capernaum and Bethsaida to visit Philip's friends."

"Please close the door, Jesus. The outside air is chilly. Does this Philip have birds all over his body?" Mary asked.

"Birds? What are you talking about?" Then Jesus laughed. "Oh, you want to know if he's like Simon. I don't know about bird images. His body was covered. But he is shy compared to Simon."

"All mankind is," Mary countered.

"Mother. Simon is a good man. Rough around the edges, but genuine. I'll give him your friendly regards when I see him tomorrow." He grabbed slices of barley bread, slathered them with honey, ate and left for his carpenter job. The shelves turned out well, he thought. Early the next day, on his way to Capernaum, he smiled as he pondered his craftsmanship: *Joseph, I think, would be proud.*

Capernaum is a long day's walk from Nazareth. Jesus arrived as the sun dove toward the western hills behind him. The town of 1,500, mostly merchants and fishermen, hugs the north shore of the Sea of Galilee. It is strategically located about midway between Damascus and Jerusalem and hence a busy trading point. Caravans pass through almost daily.

It is not only a place where travelers stop to feed themselves and their animals, but where news is exchanged along with goods. Already there was growing talk in the town about a healer, stories of a man who casts out demons and makes the blind see. These reports were carried along the trade routes and found various forms all the way to Jerusalem.

Broad sloping hills drift northward from Capernaum's coast. To someone in a boat on the Sea of Galilee, looking toward the north, the Capernaum landscape is cast as one vast, painted canvass. The hills in the background reduce the town to a squiggly line on the earthen panorama.

Capernaum's streets are laid out in grid fashion. The town has no defensive walls. Most of the houses are one-story, with stone steps leading from a courtyard to a thatched roof. Jesus was familiar with the town and residence of Simon and his wife.

"Hello, Jesus," I said opening the door. "Good to see you again. Come in please." I was scrubbing fish entrails and scales from my hands and arms. "We had a busy day. Good catch last night."

"Oh, Simon," Jesus replied quickly. "I didn't mean to interrupt anything. I'm on my way to Bethsaida to see some of your friends."

"You are on your way," I said briskly, "to having evening meal with us. Don't say otherwise," I argued as Jesus raised his hand and was about to speak. "We have plenty, and you preach that we must always share. And you will stay here. Bethsaida is about a two hour walk from here. It is settled," I pronounced, drying my arms. "Besides, I have some questions, something to get settled. Will you have a glass of wine with me?"

"Must be serious matters," Jesus said. "I'll try to be of help."

I poured wine and after we dispensed with small talk, I decided to raise the things to be "settled."

"Well, here's the deal," I began without hesitation. "Eden and I had a little disagreement the other day. OK. It was more than a little disagreement."

"Well, it's not unheard of that husbands and wives have differing opinions," Jesus said diplomatically.

"True, but this was basic stuff," I persisted, scratching my ear. "I say wives should be submissive to their husbands. Genesis says Eve was made from Adam's rib. That's clear she was second to him. When I said that to Eden, she had a fit. One would think I said it was OK to pray to a foreign god, or to steal.

"What were you initially disagreeing about?" Jesus inquired.

"That's not important."

"Could be," Jesus countered. "No one has the correct answers to all questions, and some of the answers may have varying colors."

"Don't muddy the issue."

"Fair enough. Then I will be plain-spoken. A women's opinion has no less value than a man's. Marriage is a partnership. Neither partner is superior. To think so defies the entire concept of leaving one's parents and two becoming one. This isn't some legalistic complication, a splitting of scriptural hairs. It's a question of dignity for all.

"Think of it this way, Simon," Jesus continued. "Eve was not made from Adam's head so that he was more intelligent and could have power over her. She was not made from his feet so that he could walk on her. Rather, she was made from his rib, near the heart, so that he could love and care for her."

I couldn't argue with any of that, so the matter rested there for some seconds.

"Do you still want me to stay the night?" Jesus asked, pondering this stubborn man he had chosen as a disciple. Jesus vowed one thing: He would not mention this discussion to his mother.

"Aw, don't mind me," I smiled. "I've been called pig-headed by my own father. Who are you seeing in Bethsaida?"

"I'm going to visit your friend, Philip, and his acquaintance, I think he said his name is Nathaniel."

"Philip? Whose family runs the fish outfitter business?"

"Yes. Seems like a nice fellow, a person who believes in the Lord and the kingdom to come. Loves the Scriptures."

"They charge plenty for their supplies and services," I injected. "Where did you meet him? Was he trying to sell you a piece of second-hand junk for your carpenter business?"

"He didn't try to sell me anything. I had seen him Bethsaida before and met him again outside Nazareth. The truth is he was looking for me. You and Andrew, he said, spoke highly of my planned ministry and suggested a visit with me. You talk as if Philip is some sort of bad guy. He had nice things to say about you."

"He's OK, just a little different."

"He's just a little different?" Jesus looked directly into my eyes.

"Well, yes. He always wears fancier clothes and is well groomed. You never see him without footwear. I would bet a day's catch that he has never had fish guts on his hands. You don't see any dirt under his fingernails. But I have to say, he does know his business. Prices, though, are a little on the expensive side."

"He's never cheated you, has he?"

"No. No. I can't say that."

"Good," Jesus replied. "I asked him to be one of my followers."

Eden walked in before I could protest Philip as a follower. She said the evening meal was ready and proudly announced she had prepared tilapia that was caught by the family crew the night before. She sprinkled the fish with caraway seeds and black cumin and then fried them over hot coals. She also served fresh bread.

Eden is an attractive woman. She is diminutive but strong. She is generous, both with her attending to others and with her opinion. She is a hard worker. If necessary, Jesus thought, she could do most of the chores associated with running a fishing business. However, Simon would protest having a woman on the boat and handling the nets.

"How's your mother?" Jesus inquired, knowing that Eden had long cared for her.

"She's about the same," Eden replied. "We're so glad you can have meals with us and stay the night. Simon tells me you are going on to Bethsaida tomorrow."

"True. I hope to see Simon's business friend, Philip," Jesus said, glancing at his host across the table, "and perhaps some other people. Thank you, Eden, for a fine meal and your great hospitality."

As Jesus departed the next morning, heading down Capernaum's main street, he spotted a young man sitting in one of the merchant cubicles. He looked at Jesus, his face a composite of distress and doubt. He slouched like a person without a spine, appearing as if he wanted to be somewhere else. There were boxes and stacks of papers on the ledge before him.

The sun was shining, but the man behind the wooden stall was as gloomy as yesterday's stormy weather.

He glanced at Jesus cautiously and sporadically, hesitant about risking any steadfast connection. Adjoining booths were abuzz with shoppers, avoiding, it appeared, the young fellow as if he were afflicted with leprosy. Why was he the target of such revulsion? It was a pitiful sight to Jesus' mind, one that stirred him to investigate.

"Good day to you," Jesus smiled at the man. He was short in stature and apparently short in confidence. There was no immediate reply. "You don't seem too busy. Perhaps customers will come later. What is your name?"

"They call me Levi," he said timidly, as though he was ashamed of his identity. It was a strain for him to say that much. He feigned busyness, reaching for papers behind him, nervous about this visitor, his hands shaking. Then he forced a look at Jesus again, reading kind eyes with perhaps less to fear.

"Are you ill, Levi?" Jesus asked.

"No, sir."

"Is there something I can do for you, Levi? You appear distraught."

"No, sir. Thank you."

"I am Jesus of Nazareth, passing in the direction of Bethsaida. Where do you live?" Jesus inquired. "What are you selling?"

"I live with my mother in Capernaum. I am employed here," he said, without explanation. "My father died several years ago. I really had to take this job." He looked away.

"I'm sorry to hear about your father. Having no father makes it difficult for the entire family. It's good that you have a job."

"I suspect so," Levi said indifferently, "but I am hated for it."

"That seems curious," Jesus said, "being disliked because of your work. May I ask why?"

The question seemed to nullify any confidence he had gained. Levi began to shake again, but he found the courage to look at Jesus again. That visual exchange quickly steadied his wobbly demeanor.

"I am a publican," he said, almost breathing the words. "It was the only job I could find. It was the alternative to starvation. Because of it, I am universally hated. I am a Jew who a took a job from the Romans and work for the Romans. Hence, my own people consider me unclean. And I am a sinner."

"You are a sinner?" Jesus asked.

"Well, in my job I collect taxes and then add a little for myself. It's a common thing."

"A little?"

"Well, well sometimes it's more than a little."

"Sometimes?"

"I charge more to rich merchants who I think can afford it."

"So, honest, rich merchants are acceptable targets?"

"Yes. I mean not really, but it's the way the system works." He paused. "Not only am I hated by my own people, but I also don't think my Roman boss trusts me. Even though I keep precise books. I collect all sorts of taxes, but mostly duties on imports from merchants and caravans. Others collect taxes on local farmers. The system says I must pay the Romans in advance, then collect taxes owed. I charge some a little more than what's due, and people say that makes me wealthy."

Levi began shaking again. He was talking too much, he feared. He didn't know this man, so why should he rattle on about the Roman tax system and collectors. If the Roman tax official heard talk like this, he would probably kill him. And if a strict Jewish person, say a Zealot, heard him, he would possibly do the same thing.

"Are you happy, Levi?"

"Sir, who are you?" Levi asked in a nearly inaudible voice.

Jesus smiled.

"Fear not," he said, reading Levi's mind. "I am neither a Roman official nor a member of the Zealot party. I am Jesus, the Lord God who was often mentioned by prophets in our Scripture. What is wealth, you ask. I say wealth is love and peace and serving one another. I invite you to this wealth, Levi, seeking the kingdom of God, eternal life."

The sun suddenly appeared even brighter, as if a new day had been born.

"Follow me," Jesus beckoned.

Levi stood tall, shuffled some papers, and abandoned his stall.

"Henceforth," Jesus said, "you will be known as Matthew."

Chapter 12

THE LAST STRETCH TO HOME, about 4 AD – The weather along the Great Sea was invigorating. The two families walked briskly, making better time than Aharon had imagined. Jesus' feet had become accustomed to the mostly sandy paths and developed callouses as tough as the bottoms of his sandals. His dark skin, bathed by the subtropical sun, took on a bronze-like appearance.

As they trekked northward, the coastline began to change. Occasionally, where the path neared the shoreline, Jesus dashed toward the water to taste the salty spray. His arms outstretched, he sang as he splashed through the surf.

"Not too close!" his mother yelled after him, when he splatted through a receding wave. At one point, he stopped and stared at the immensity of the water. Mary watched him, wondering what was going through his mind.

"Where does it end, Mah?" he turned toward her.

"Are you talking about the sea, Jesus?"

"Yes, Mah. The sea. Does it end somewhere, or does it just go on forever, like the heavens?"

"Those are big questions for such a little boy," she smiled. "I don't know for sure, but my guess is that there are many shores like this one. The world is a huge place, and we are just like a grain of sand."

"Mah, we are much more than a grain of sand. You have told me how special we all are in the eyes of God, that we were made in His image. And the psalms say, *I praise you, for I am fearfully and wonderfully made.*"

"That is true, Jesus. I was just trying to compare our size to the hugeness of the world, not how important we are to God and his mercy."

After midday, the shoreline became rockier. Boulders twice as tall as Joseph jutted above the sand, forcing the walking path ever further inland. Jesus darted in and around the maze of stones until a creeping creature caused him to skid to a stop. He hadn't forgotten his encounter with a lizard, so he gave the strange waddler plenty of space.

"What do we have here?" Joseph approached.

"I don't know father, but I'm not getting any closer to it."

"Good choice. I think this is a turtle, Jesus. It's not likely to harm you. There are turtles in the Sea of Galilee, but not this big. Let it be and come up to the road."

That night, during the meal, Jesus' head kept bobbing as he alternately dozed off and jerked awake. The rigors of the long day had consumed his energy. Sleep gradually overtook any remnants of motion. Mary and Joseph couldn't help quietly laughing at this involuntary entertainment -- Jesus nodding like palm fronds in the wind. Finally, Joseph removed a half-eaten fig from Jesus' hand, gathered him in his arms and gently placed him on a blanket in their lean-to shelter.

Mary and Joseph gazed at the sleeping child, as they often did. The mystery and amazement of their circumstance never ceased to be overwhelming. She had agreed to be the vessel that brought humanity to the face of God. Where would all this lead? How many times would they have to flee for his safety? Joseph, as bewildered as she in these events, always presented a calming demeanor. That and faith in God were her primary comforts.

"Joseph, I know we've been over this a hundred times, but I'm still mystified, and I don't mind telling you, more than a little frightened at the coming years. What should we do? How should we act? Sometimes my head spins in absolute confusion. I am aware of the Scriptures foretelling the coming of a Messiah, but me, a simple Jewish girl, his mother!?"

She pulled her faded red shawl tighter around her head and neck. The breeze off the sea was surprisingly cool. She sat in Joseph's arms, tears slowly trickling to her weather-beaten cheeks. He dabbed them away with the sleeve of his tunic.

"You must read my mind, Mary. I, too, am flabbergasted about my role in all this. Why you? Why me? His coming, as you say, is well foretold in the Scriptures. But I am a simple carpenter, twice your age. So, I ask myself every day, why didn't God pick a younger fellow. Please don't misunderstand. I am most happy to be your husband and blessed to be his father, but shouldn't I have a few more denarii in my pocket and less gray in my beard for this undertaking?"

He paused, then placed a straggle of hair behind her ear. He tenderly raised her chin and looked deep into her eyes as to inject a full portion of serenity while not ignoring reality.

"No doubt he will need the best education. He will not only have to be fluent in Aramaic and Hebrew but understand Greek and Latin. And he will need clothes and books. It's not like Nazareth is chockfull of rabbi teachers. I think of these things always. But then I say to myself, *why not us?* Mary, we just move forward the best we can and trust in God." Her loving smile was all the answer he needed.

"Mary, we are good people, good parents. I am not saying great. I still think God should have solicited a younger father, but, I suppose, He could have done worse. You and God have a special understanding. You perhaps see further ahead than I. We can talk all night, but I doubt if I will find any more answers. It will be just be as big a mystery tomorrow morning."

Mary's eyes closed; her breathing relaxed. Joseph looked to the stars.

"And, you know what else I think, Mary?" Joseph said softly, probing the heavens for insight. "I think they will still be talking about a lot of these things two thousand years from now. You will still be the mother of God, and I will still be the carpenter from Nazareth. And there will still be debate about who Jesus is. But we know."

Joseph looked downward to Mary, but she was fast asleep.

The next morning, as they approached Caesarea, the travelers stopped at a Bedouin camp. The nomadic group had items for sale or trade and directed Mary to a well where she could get water for doing laundry. She hadn't had an opportunity to wash the family clothes since they were adjacent to one of the streams in the Nile River delta. She was scrubbing garments on a nearby rock when another woman approached.

"Marhaba," the woman said. Mary wasn't sure what that meant, but guessed it was a word of greeting.

"Shalom," Mary replied.

"You speak Aramaic," the woman said. "I know some Aramaic. Marhaba is Arabic and means hello. We are Nomads, mostly from the Arabian Peninsula. When one travels to many regions like we do, one learns a little about many languages. I know some Greek, also. Are you going to Jerusalem?"

"No," Mary replied without elaboration.

"Good," the woman said. "There is much unrest there. Young Herod Archelaus is not making many friends. We met a group of Jewish families recently, working class people, who decided to abandon Jerusalem and take up residence elsewhere. The irony is that Roman Emperor Augustus proudly speaks of Pax Romana, a time of peace, but Archelaus must not have received the word."

"And what is your destination?" Mary asked.

"We have no destination except to find new grass for our goats. Our clan shuns violence and conflict. When we heard of the turmoil in Jerusalem, our leaders chose to avoid it. So far, with some exceptions, the Romans have not bothered us. We seek no land, want no power. We simply desire the freedom to move about independently."

"I'm nearly finished with washing our clothes," Mary said. "May I help you clean your items?"

"Oh, no," the Bedouin woman replied. "I finished just as you arrived. Now I must hang them out to dry. Peace be to you and safe travels."

"It was nice to meet you, too," Mary replied. "And peace to you and your family. Peace, I agree, is a precious gift."

Mary rejoined her family and draped the wet clothes over nearby bushes. Joseph had gathered an armful of dry branches for cooking fires and was stacking them in the pack saddle atop Dynamo. Jesus was sitting on a small rock, drawing figures in the sand with a stick. He looked up as his mother addressed his father.

"You were wise to avoid Jerusalem," she told Joseph, and then related what the Bedouin woman had said. "When will we arrive in Caesarea?"

"Mr. Aharon says we should arrive as the sun sets. He recommended we set up night camp outside the city. They will go on to their home on the far side of Caesarea, beyond the road that heads northeast to Nazareth. Did you finish the washing?"

"Yes. Were you able to purchase any food for us?

"I traded some denarii for goat cheese, bread, and figs. And I even acquired some dried grass for our donkey. It's good that we will be in Nazareth in a few days because most of the coins that Elizabeth and Zechariah gave us are gone."

"Why are people fighting in Jerusalem?" Jesus asked, "and why didn't we go there? Is there fighting in Nazareth, also? Why so much fighting?"

"Questions. Always with the questions," Joseph said.

"I know, father. But how else do you learn things?"

"You are correct, Jesus," Joseph scratched his head in reply. "It is good to ask questions. There are strong feelings by workers in Jerusalem, Jesus, that they are not being treated fairly by the Romans. Injustice often ignites turmoil. I decided it was best for us to avoid any troubles. Remember, Jesus, it's always best to avoid trouble if you can."

"What if you can't avoid trouble, father? What if the injustice requires action?

"You ask questions like an adult, Jesus, and I must answer like a child. I don't know. There are always disagreements. Always will be. The real diplomats are the peacemakers. It seems to me there is less trouble in small places. Jerusalem, you see, is a big city, the holiest of all places for we Jews. And not everyone agrees with us. We sometimes don't agree with ourselves."

"I would like to visit Jerusalem some time," Jesus looked at his father.

"You will, Jesus. You will."

"Ah. I see you are back from your shopping, Joseph," Mr. Cohen said. "Did you find what you needed for the rest of the trip?"

"We should be able to finish our travels without going hungry," Joseph answered. "I even purchased some forage for our donkey. These Bedouin have everything. It's like walking into a large city market."

"Good. You are right. The Bedouin are merchant masters. In a short time, we will arrive at the Nazareth junction. Our home is further north. We would like to give you bread and figs for the rest of your journey. Dana makes the best matzah in all Israel. Just the right dash of herbs with the usual whole wheat flour, water, olive oil and salt. Just talking about it makes my taste buds jump for joy."

"That's really not necessary . . ."

Aharon raised his hand to interrupt Joseph.

"It has already been settled, my traveling friend. But I can't give you the complete recipe," he laughed. "Here," he handed two loaves to Joseph.

"That is generous of you and Dana," Joseph said.

"Now," Aharon continued, "I have brought a jar of wine to share, some fresh goats milk for the children. You see, I, too, shopped at the Bedouin store." He smiled from ear to ear and handed out cups. "I want to tell you and Mary and your son a little about my hometown. Please. Let us sit here in the palm tree shade." He sat and the others followed his lead.

"The first thing to know is that there are several places called Caesarea. I guess there was a compulsion to please Caesar. My town is really Caesarea Maritima. It is virtually a new town, launched by the late Herod the Great about two decades ago. His architects oversaw the building of two large jetties that became the bulwark for developing a deep-water seaport, known as Sebastos Harbor. Sebastos is Greek for Augustus.

"Herod wasn't the most popular fellow in the region, as you may know, but he directed a number of big construction projects."

"Yes. We have heard about his brutality," Joseph said pointedly..

"Herod," Aharon continued, "though he had palaces everywhere, made Caesarea the principal city of Judea. His Caesarea palace was built on a promontory jutting out into the sea, with a decorative pool surrounded by porticos. The harbor rivals the one in Alexandria built by Queen Cleopatra. It is an architectural and construction marvel.

"He constructed storerooms, markets, wide roads, baths, temples to Emperor Augustus, and imposing public buildings. Every five years the city hosts major sports competitions, gladiator games, and theatrical productions in the theatre overlooking the Great Sea. Equally amazing to the harbor project was the aqueduct built by Herod."

"What's an akiduck?" Jesus inquired.

"Aqueduct is a long word meaning a water canal, except this canal is elevated, built like a high-level bridge."

"Will we see it?" Jesus asked,

"I'm afraid you won't be able to see it, Jesus," Aharon replied. "The road to Nazareth angles inland to the northeast. The aqueduct is north of here."

"Is it designed to bring fresh water to the city?" Joseph asked."

"Exactly," said Aharon. "Caesarea had no reliable source of fresh water. So, Herod ordered that the aqueduct be built, extending it many cubits to the northeast to where he tapped into hillside springs. The water flows southward to the city where a pipe system distributes it to homes and businesses. That's where we get our water for drinking and bathing."

"That's amazing," said Joseph. "The people of Nazareth still walk to nearby wells for their water. So, we can say Herod did some good for this area."

"Yes, you can. Remember he was part Jewish, but I'm not sure that factored into any of his construction decisions," Aharon said. "He was the Jewish client king for the Romans, and it was Caesar that he tried to impress. Actually, Caesarea has replaced Jerusalem as Judea's civilian and military capital for the Romans. It is the official residence of the Roman procurator, Antonius Felix, and the prefect, Pontius Pilate. They say Pilate has been groomed to eventually move up to procurator."

"Yet," Joseph said, "Caesarea doesn't seem to have the importance as Jerusalem,"

"You are right, Joseph. No place compares to Jerusalem. It is our holy city, where the Ark of the Covenant and our God reside in the Temple."

Joseph looked at Jesus but said nothing.

"I do have one other question for you, Aharon, if I may," Joseph said.

"Yes, by all means."

"Do you know anything about the trail to Nazareth? I know it is not well-traveled like roads going to Jerusalem. I'm familiar with the Jerusalem to Nazareth road, but not this one."

"Ah, Joseph. I can tell you are concerned about safety and that is wise. About possible robbers or worse. I, too, know little about the road to Nazareth from here, but I can tell you that we have not heard it to be populated with thieves. But rural Samaritans are not fond of Jews. There is historical resentment.

"Your trip to Nazareth will be short. You have adequate supplies. I would just avoid stopping at any rural household. I think you will be without troubles."

"I appreciate your words. Mary is one to worry, you see. But, as you say, our time on the road will be brief."

"Well, here is to safe travels and a good life in Nazareth," and Aharon hoisted his wine cup in salute. Joseph did the same.

"Again, Aharon, thank you and Dana for your hospitality and allowing us to travel with you. It meant a great deal to have your company. With an early start in the morning, we should be in Nazareth by sunset. The rocky path and hills won't be as easy as walking along the Great Sea, but the anticipation of getting home will offset all that.

"And, Aharon. Mary, Jesus and I wish all of God's blessings for your family."

After goodbyes, the Cohen family proceeded the short distance to their residence. Mary, Jesus and Joseph took the diagonal road through the outskirts of Caesarea. After walking until the sun set, Joseph set up camp for the night. They could still see the flickering lights of Caesarea, candles on the ground that dimed in contrast to God's heavenly canopy.

"We are fortunate, Mary," Joseph said after the evening meal, "that we'll be home tomorrow night. Our food supply is getting low, but enough for another day. We have the bread Aharon gave us and the little I purchased back in town. I refilled the water skins so we're good if it gets hot tomorrow. I guess I should have bought more food for us and less hay for Dynamo."

"Listen," Jesus said, almost whispering. "I think I hear an owl."

"I think," Joseph said, "you are hearing the coo of a mourning dove. It does sound a little like an owl, only softer. The dove has many chirps. Soon you will hear a whistling sound. That's not part of a dove's song list, but rather is from the vibrations of its wings."

"Wow, father. You know a lot about birds," Jesus said. "They never seem to run out of songs or things to eat. While we worry about having food, the birds seem to get along just fine. They always find enough."

"True, Jesus," Joseph switched on his fatherly voice. "Would you rather peck away at seeds on the ground, or have warm bread? How about digging for ugly insects in the tree bark rather than eating a juicy fig? Or you could nibble on a worm. Or, maybe . . . "

"I think he gets the picture, Joseph," Mary interrupted. "How about we all listen as the dove sings us to sleep?"

"Tell me again about Grandpa and Grandma Joachim and Anne," Jesus begged.

I've told you everything," Mary said, running thin of patience.

"But you never did say if they have a dog."

"All I can tell you is that we didn't have a dog when I was growing up. My guess is they don't have one now, but I couldn't say for sure. Now, close those eyes."

While Jesus slept, Mary remained awake. Her stirring kept Joseph from falling asleep.

"Are you so excited about getting home that your eyes won't close?" Joseph asked. "It will be good to be back among our people," answering his own question.

"Not only that, Joseph. It will be such a relief not to travel. We've been walking every day for several weeks. Maybe our legs won't stop when we get to Nazareth. Or perhaps we will sleep two days."

"I know the trip has been wearing for you and Jesus. But home is not far away. Try to sleep now."

"I am so looking forward to being with my mother and father. It's been nearly four years, Joseph. Your family will be so happy to see you, too."

"I agree, Mary. Let's never take a trip that long again."

The next morning was sunny and mild, a day perfect for walking home. They left the Caesarean region early. The trail was rough with stones, up and down, winding around the hills of Samaria. While tired of the routine, their bodies had become accustomed to walking. The desert sun had given their skin a leathery shield. Their legs muscles were strong.

The nearly constant sun painted Jesus' already dark skin a coppery look. The little boy who frequently wanted to be carried early in the journey now skipped along with more vigor than his parents.

They were unaware of boundaries. There were no signposts, but by mid-morning Joseph believed they were nearing Galilee. Coming over a steep hill, he noticed two approaching men. As they neared, he motioned Mary and Jesus to halt off the trail as he went ahead. The bearded duo looked menacing. Their soiled tunics were torn in places, and each carried knives.

Joseph was not one to pre-judge, yet Jesus' presence and the duo's unkempt appearance altered circumstances. He was forever mindful of Jesus' nature. A large, shaggy dog that was baring its teeth made the situation more threatening. The animal stepped into the path as though directed. There was no alternate way around them.

"Shalom," Joseph greeted the pair. They said nothing at first, sized up Joseph's stature and then glanced down the trail at Mary and Jesus. Joseph, likewise, tried to assess their next move. He gripped his ever-ready staff in case the dog would lunge.

"Where are you going?" one of them asked.

"Home, to Nazareth," Joseph replied.

"Don't recall seeing you in these parts before."

"We've been away nearly four years," Joseph said, not wanting to explain further lest the pair had contact with the Herod family.

He had scarcely replied when the unexpected happened. Jesus, spotting the dog, ran toward Joseph and the two men. Before Joseph could intercede, Jesus approached the animal with a big smile.

"Mister, what's the dog's name?"

"Be careful, boy," one of them warned. "Titus don't take kindly to strangers."

"Titus looks like a nice dog to me," Jesus said, approaching the animal. "But he could use a bath."

The men laughed, and Joseph wasn't sure what to do.

"Titus hasn't had a bath ever," one snickered, "except when he's caught in the rain. And he wasn't too happy about that."

As Mary joined the gathering, Titus decided there was no threat from anyone. His bared teeth were replaced with the usual pant. He nuzzled up to Jesus, his slobbery nose pressed under Jesus' hand. Jesus responded by rubbing the dog's chin, then its belly. In less than a minute, perceived trouble was changed to new-found friendship.

"See," Jesus looked up at the two men and then at Joseph and Mary," Titus likes strangers."

Chapter 13

NAZARETH – Anne, Mary's mother, was outside her Nazareth home shaking the dust from a rug when Chloe Adontz ambled down the street. Anne spotted her out of the corner of her eye, but it was too late to avoid the busybody – although Anne pondered some sort of evasive move. Alas, she was captured by the yenta's soprano singsong "shalom" that was familiar to most of the town. In this case the greeting was an elongated, "Shalommm my dear Anne!!"

"Shalom, Chloe," Anne said as she grabbed a stick and beat the rug with unusual force. "And how are you this fine day?"

"Never better," Chloe chortled with her response of choice. Her eyes sparkled with anticipation of discovering the latest news or spreading her already mined hearsay. "Dispensing some of Joachim's sawdust?" she laughed. "I understand he has yet to finish the table for the rabbi's wife. One would think that would be a priority, but then what do I know about business."

"You know, Chloe, there is a lot of truth in what you say," Anne answered, without being specific about which part of the gossiper's statement she was referring to. "I just know Joachim has been busy and tries hard to please all his customers. He seldom gets home before dark and usually is exhausted. And how is your Noam?"

"He's fine. Goes about his work but doesn't say much. He still tends the olive trees for the orchard owner. The workers there are underpaid, but he doesn't complain. Noam is a patient man."

"He has that reputation," Anne said, about to excuse herself from Chloe's clutches and attend to other matters.

"I assume your sister Mary of Clopas is doing well, busy with her two babies," Chloe pressed on. "Does she plan to have more children?"

"Now, Chole, that is entirely the business of Mary and Clopas. They and their family are doing well, thank you. Clopas loves farming. The boys are starting to help with chores. Anything else today?"

"Have you heard anything from Mary and Joseph?" Chloe asked directly, sensing Anne was making a get-away. Always tuned in to Nazareth's news channels, she already knew the answer. Joachim and Anne had little but rumors and faith to lean on, but there had been no direct word from Mary and Joseph. Relatives in Jerusalem had informed them about the flight to Egypt after Jesus' presentation in the Temple. That was nearly four years ago, but there had been no word since.

Being of the House of Levi, Joachim and Anne were called to a different city to register according to Caesar Augustus' census call. Joseph, being from the Davidic line, took Mary to Bethlehem. Hence, the grandparents were not present for Jesus' birth. Nor were they at his presentation at the Temple in Jerusalem, a ritual in accordance with Torah law.

"We have heard nothing, Chloe. But both Joachim and I have great faith in Joseph's wisdom and of course great faith in God." Neither of them had revealed any of Mary's secrets about the conception of Jesus. Nor had they mentioned anything to town folks of Herod the Great's threats and the forced trip to Egypt. "I have a grandmother's intuition that they will be home soon."

"And, dear Anne, is that womanly intuition shared by Joachim, and what is it based on?"

"Ah, my dear, Chloe," Anne swallowed deeply, after tinting her response with more sarcasm than intended. "Intuition, as you know, is a personal feeling. There is no defined basis for it. One just seems to know things before they happen. You seem to be extraordinary at that." That comment needed no translation.

"Well, I hate to just run off, Anne, but I must get going."

"May your day be a happy one," Anne waved a goodbye, "and may it be filled with intuition."

Later, after Joachim had returned from work in Sepphoris, Anne's conscience kicked in. She asked him if her remarks to Chloe were unkind, too biting. She included Chloe's repeated "dear Anne" greeting, "as if she was my closest sister." He was drained from a long day's work, but the question seemed to revive him. He began to laugh.

"Ah, dear, dear Anne," he looked at her with tired but impish eyes. "That is a question, I would say, for the rabbi. Personally, I think you were overly charitable. I'm afraid I would have gone off the path with her."

"I see," Anne replied. "You are most helpful. And, by the way, when are you going to get around to work on that table for the rabbi's wife?"

"Here is what I think about Chloe's inquiry regarding Jesus, Mary and Joseph and their whereabouts." He ignored her dig about the table. "We know they fled to Egypt because of Herod, and we know Joseph wouldn't risk a return while Herod was still alive. Herod had a paranoid streak and a long memory. But now that Herod is dead, Joseph will come home. I know it."

"Oh, I agree. I certainly hope so, Joachim."

They mulled those optimistic thoughts as Joachim washed for the evening meal.

"I've prepared fish for supper. I hope that's OK with you. Won't it be exciting to see Jesus, and, of course, Mary and Joseph, too?"

"Yes, and yes, Anne"

"Yes, and yes?"

"Yes, fish sounds good and I, too, will be excited to see all of them."

"Jesus is almost four, you know," she reminded, dishing up the cooked tilapia. "Amazing how times flies, but these have been long years. What will he be like, Joachim? What will our little God-grandson be like?"

"I haven't the slightest idea. Maybe we should consult Chloe," he chided.

"Be serious. She would be the last person I would ask. I treasure my time, too."

"Now, Anne. Chloe is Chloe. She is one of God's children, too."

"Right. Go religious on me. You, the in-house rabbi!"

"Let's eat."

Of the 400 some residents of Nazareth, Anne and Joachim lived in average accommodations. They weren't poor. They weren't wealthy. Because of his steady construction work in Sepphoris, they could afford a two-room house. Most townspeople lived in single-room accommodations. Some dwellings were remodeled caves. The men worked for others or had small farms. Families lived a marginal existence, with nothing for savings after payment of heavy taxes.

Like most hillside communities, Nazareth was not planned on a fancy grid system designed by an architectural engineer from Athens. The streets and houses evolved haphazardly, pretty much as the bluffs and boulders dictated. Builders prefer the softer limestone, and that's where the chiseling and pounding took precedence. Natural fissures also figured in the process.

There were no plots, an orderly row of structures. It was a spattered array in which soft rock dominated hard rock, unless if course you wanted to pay more. A street, or more accurately a path, showed up as a barely included afterthought. Except near the well area, which had some semblance of planning.

Nazareth was off the beaten path. It was not listed among Galilee towns by historians of the time, nor mentioned in the Talmud, the Jewish summary of religious teachings. The poor attracted even less attention. Aramaic was the primary spoken language in the region, although Roman colonization led to a greater mix of populations and language. A growing number roughly spoke or understood Greek and Latin.

Hebrew was the mother tongue, the language of the sacred books of Judaism. It was spoken by the high priests in Jerusalem, rabbis in Synagogues and in most households. Even though Rome conquered the Greeks, the Semitic environment of Israel sustained Jewish cultural identity through customs and lifestyle.

"Do you really think they are on their way back to Nazareth?" Anne asked as she picked at her food. The question and subject didn't impede Joachim's appetite.

"Like I said, Anne, Joseph is aware of Herod's death and he would want to come home directly. My question is whether Joseph will want to live in the house of his father, Jacob. He died over a year ago, and I don't think anyone has lived in his place. Or will Joseph and Mary choose to live in the residence they had when they were first married. Would you please pass the fish?" He paused as he refilled his plate.

"I remember well talking to Jacob before Mary and Joseph were betrothed. He was a good and honorable man. We dispensed with dowry obligations, but Jacob a traditionalist, proposed that Joseph work in my building business for a couple of years as a sign of earnest intent to care for Mary. Joseph is a good carpenter, and I expect he will again take up that work. "

"How soon do you think they will get here?"

"Anne, if I were smart enough to know that I wouldn't have to measure twice. I have a hard time remembering Mary's birthday. 18 Kislev, right?"

"No, Joachim. It's 8 Kislev. I can't believe you'd forget the date your own daughter was born!"

"I do remember the initial turmoil surrounding her pregnancy. Here she was, 15 years old, betrothed to marry Joseph, and she tells us she is with child. Joseph was so patient. The angel explained it all to him, and Joseph had faith. Would we all have that kind of faith. You could say that Mary and Joseph's faith saved us all."

"True enough, but where will it all lead, Joachim? We are the grandparents of Jesus, the Messiah. While that is an incredible honor for us, it is also scarry."

"You worry about everything, Anne. Put your trust in God."

"God should be in charge of your memory."

"Is there any bread left?"

"Yes, I baked several loaves today, but I'm saving some of them. Saving them for Mary and her family when they come," Anne stated evenly.

"You're expecting them tonight?"

"Women have intuition. Men, not so much."

After the meal, Anne mended several garments and Joachim went to his adjoining tool shop where he sharpened saws. He scrapped dried mortar from trowels, polished them and cleaned out his tool vest. Later they talked about his work and the fact he was spending a lot of the time in Sepphoris. Neither liked it, but Joachim pointed out that the money was good and he felt constrained by Roman demands.

Anne suggested that Joachim was overstating the mandates of Tetrarch Antipas and his construction superintendents. The spousal squabble was interrupted by a feeble rap on the door. It was nearing bedtime. They looked at each other, part in puzzlement and part in relief that the knock halted their verbal engagement. There was no reason for

Antipas' cronies to show up. Joachim had been working steadily in Sepphoris.

"Well, are you going to open the door?" Anne asked with residual pique. It was unusual to have late visitors in Nazareth. Ordinarily it signaled an emergency or that someone had a special need.

"Maybe it's Chloe with some late-breaking news," Joachim said, aiming for his wife's sensitive spot.

"Just answer the door already."

Joachim, the clever carpenter, had fashioned a small peek hole just above the door handle. It had become his signature creation and the whole town knew about it. He bent down, pushed a small, sliding flap to one side, and peered outside.

A small boy's nose appeared in the dim light. In the background were shadows of two adults. He looked at Anne and raised his shoulders in blankness.

Suddenly, like the lifting of fog, reality came into focus. His face transformed from quizzical to wonderment and lit up like a menorah. He looked at Anne with all the boundless rapture of a new father.

The return of Mary and her family had absorbed their minds. It was part of their daily prayers. It was the focus of their attention at Shabbat, Friday night services usually held privately in Jewish homes.

Anne read the look on his face with seasoned marital precision. She leaped up and ran toward the door, a tentative smile spreading on her face. Joy captured her entire being. Her clasped hands reached for her chin in guarded expectancy. Joachim looked at her with a confident grin. He slowly opened the door.

There he was. The Lord in little boy form.

Anne and Joachim knew Mary's story. They knew the Scriptures, notably the words of the prophets. They trusted their daughter. They believed.

"Shalom, Savta (grandma) and Saba (grandpa)!" a soprano-like voice said with excitement. He stretched out his arms to Anne, inviting a hug. "Father feared you may already be asleep, but I knew you'd still be up," Jesus chirped.

For a moment Anne was so stunned at seeing her grandchild for the first time, simultaneously meeting the Son of God, that she was frozen in nervous bewilderment. It took abrupt prodding from Joachim to release her daze.

"Are you going to dither all night, Anne? Give the child a squeeze!"

"Ohhh, my," she said softly. "Ohhh my."

"His name is Jesus," Joachim coached her. "Mary and Joseph, please come in. It's so wonderful to see you. To know you are safe. What a great surprise, although Anne knew you were coming. She has intuition," he winked.

Mary and Joseph were unable to translate Joachim's sly words. Mary embraced her father. Joseph, too, gave him a bear hug. Anne clung to Jesus as if he were going to suddenly evaporate. Jesus, in turn, wrapped both of his tiny arms around his grandmother's tunic-covered leg. He stayed there as Mary and Joseph exchanged kisses with Anne.

"This takes my breath away," Anne finally managed to say. "Yes, I did expect you, but when it was real, I had to blink my eyes to be sure. Oh, Mary. How did you manage all your trials? We heard from relatives in Jerusalem about Jesus' birth in a stable and how Herod went crazy after learning about a new king. You fled to Egypt in the middle of the night."

"Joseph was by my side," Mary smiled. "We managed."

"I am so relieved you are home," Anne said. "Let me take your outer garments and headwear."

"Well, come. Sit down," Joachim urged. "We have much to catch up on. Are any of you hungry? We have some fish left over from the evening meal. The fire is still going. We can reheat the fish and warm the barley bread. Jesus, would you like some goat's milk? I bet you have some good stories about life in Egypt and from the trip home."

Jesus looked at his father for approval of the goat's milk. Getting a nod, he walked to Joachim.

"Please. Could I have some milk?" Then a serious look came over his face. "Saba, are there any crocodiles around here?" He jumped up on a bench, his short legs dangling beneath the table. "Crocodiles are dangerous."

"Crocodiles?" Joachim laughed. "Whatever caused that question? Did you see some on your trip?"

"No," Jesus said after a sip of milk, "but I saw a man on the Nile River who said a crocodile bit off some of his fingers. I saw that! Thank you Savta for the milk," he looked at Anne. "This big man had only three fingers on one hand. He said there are a lot of crocodiles in the Nile River, some really large ones. I'm glad we didn't run into any."

"Well, Jesus, I doubt if you will see any crocodiles in Galilee, but anything is possible. Perhaps some fishermen on a slow day on the Sea of Galilee, their minds fogged by over-tipping the wineskin, may see leviathans, but doubtful even then. There are feral dogs. Bears have been . . ."

"Really, Joachim," Anne cast him a lethal look, "must you scare the boy?"

Joachim raised his hands in surrender. Mary and Joseph exchanged mirthful glances.

"Saba, do you have a dog?" Jesus said hopefully.

"No, Jesus. That decision was made for me years ago. Tell me, Joseph. Was the travel to and from Egypt difficult? How did you manage to subsist?"

"Elizabeth and Zechariah graciously gave us some money as we left Jerusalem after Jesus' presentation in the Temple. We were able to stay with many Jewish families along the route to and from Egypt. People are generous. We joined caravans along the way for safer travel, and those folks often shared meals with us. The biggest problem was finding forage for the donkey."

"I'm glad to hear about the goodness of people."

Tell us about the rituals in the Temple," Anne requested as she heated the leftover fish and bread. "Who was present? I know Mosaic law requires purification ceremonies."

"As prescribed by Mosaic law," Mary explained, "we arranged the offering of two pigeons. We couldn't afford a lamb," she hesitated. "You see, we brought the true lamb." Anne and Joachim understood what Mary was saying. They were aware of Jesus' role as Savior. "We walked into the Temple and met a man named Simeon."

"Simeon?" Anne said with a puzzled look. "Who is he?"

"We were not sure, but we learned that he is a holy man," Mary said. "He took Jesus in his arms, looked at him with love, said blessings and then he said, 'Lord, now let your servant depart in peace, according to your word.' He spoke with great joy, adding that he long awaited the Messiah. He felt his yearnings finally had been met. He said Jesus would bring salvation to all people."

"Oh, Mary," Anne said, and tears formed in her eyes. They all gazed at one another in awe, understanding fully the dimensions of what Mary had said. Then they all looked at Jesus.

"Mah," Jesus interrupted their meditation. "What are pigeons, and what happened to them at this blessing?"

"Pigeons are large birds, Jesus," Joachim explained amidst a mixture of laughter and sniffles. "They are used as a means of sacrifice."

"What's sacrifice, Saba?"

Once again, the room became somber.

"It's a word you'll understand when you get older," Joseph said. Anne informed them that the reheated food was ready. She set plates on the table. Joachim offered milk, water or wine.

"Old man Horovitz still makes the best wine in the area, better than any you'll find in Sepphoris," Joachim said. "You remember him, Joseph. He has a sizeable vineyard on the west hillside. Good man." He looked at Anne. "And I'm not just saying that because of his wine. He's a charitable fellow. He sees a need and acts on it. And he makes no big deal of his good works."

"Mary," Anne asked. "Was Jesus wiggly during the ritual?"

"Not at all," Mary replied. "He was still a suckling infant, but he took to Simeon like kinfolk. He didn't cry once. I was surprised. But with all the celebration when he was born, animals galore and singing shepherds, people coming and going, he wasn't fussy then. He likes people, don't you Jesus?"

"People are nice, but sometimes I don't understand their words," he said, chewing on a piece of warmed bread. "I like dogs, too."

With that clarification, Jesus jumped off his chair and explored the rest of the house. He was unfamiliar with such a domicile, having lived in caves in Egypt for several years, and then in a tent on the way home.

"We are so happy you are back home," Anne said, "and relieved to know that you are all safe. Mary, through this man Simeon, don't you see, the Savior is revealed to the entire world. This holy man refers to the prophet Isaiah who wrote, *I will make you a light to the nations, that my salvation may reach to the ends of the earth.* It is all so breathtaking and humbling," she whispered. "God working through our family. I pray that He will give you the courage to sustain you in all that is ahead."

"Mother, I know there will be trying times, but there will be many joyful years, too. True, it is unbelievably amazing that we are so blessed to host our God, to nurture and cherish the Son. We will raise Jesus, fully knowing he is the God-boy, but treating him like any other Jewish youngster. He, then, will ultimately decide when to reveal his real identity. Does that sound appropriate to you."

They both paused their discussion as Jesus walked back to the eating area.

"To be honest," Mary said leaning toward her mother and again lowering her voice, "the greatest challenge right now is to assimilate Jesus among neighbors here. Joseph and I have talked about that and decided, at least for the time being, to keep all these matters in our hearts."

"I'll have another piece of fish please, if there is any left," Jesus said. "Mah, what are all these things in your heart?" He looked into her eyes, confused by their talk.

"You are the hungry one," Mary said. "Yes, there is more fish. What's in my heart, and Joseph's and your grandparents, too, is that we love you more than you can imagine. There is one slice of bread. Would you like it?"

"Yes, please."

For the next hour they talked about a myriad of things, from life in Egypt to travels down the Nile River and caravan companions. The only intermission in the warm, homecoming chatter was when Joseph noticed Jesus' half-asleep, bobbing head. They smiled as Joseph lifted the boy in his arms and placed him on a mat in a corner of the room. He returned with an obvious question on his wrinkled brow.

"Joseph, what's on your mind?" Joachim inquired. "The look on your face suggests something is troubling you. Are you worried about a residence for your family? I can assure . . ."

"What I was wondering, Joachim, you know that my mother died some time ago, but my father, Jacob. Have you seen him lately? You and he visited before Mary and I were betrothed. He pretty much keeps to himself in his wood shop, so you may not . . ."

"Joseph, I'm sorry," Joachim interrupted, "but your father died last year. We didn't know about it for a week, and only learned of it from a neighbor, Chloe Adontz."

"Father, do you know where Jacob is entombed?" Mary asked.

"I inquired after we heard of his death. His remains are in the family tomb in the cemetery at the east edge of Nazareth. We can visit there whenever you like. He was a good man, Joseph."

"I intend to uphold the agreement and work for you," Joseph said.

"Joseph, Joseph," Joachim intoned. "These are things to talk about in the 'morrow."

Chapter 14

NAZARETH – "Shush! Get out of my house!" Anne yelled. She swung a broom at three chickens that were pecking their way through the rear entry to her kitchen. "Who left the door open anyway?" she inquired.

"I'm sorry, Grandma," Jesus confessed, running back inside. "I forgot to close it when I went out to Grandpa's shop. I'll help chase them away."

She laughed and in grandmotherly fashion converted a would-be scolding into a gracious "thanks" for his help.

"Are these chickens yours?" Jesus asked. "They are funny looking. They are smaller and a different color than chickens in Egypt," he said, directing the cackling critters back outside.

"Do little boys in Egypt let chickens roam inside the house?" Anne asked playfully. Jesus got the message.

"No," he replied. "That part is the same."

"Did you bathe and put on a clean tunic this morning?" his mother asked. "Yesterday was a long and dusty trip."

"Yes, Mah. I washed and put on clean clothes."

"Did you wash in and behind your ears?"

Jesus nodded.

"Good. What was Grandpa doing?"

"Oh, he and father were talking about stuff, carpenter work and houses and things I didn't understand."

When Mary and Joseph were betrothed, an arrangement overseen by their fathers, it set off a two-stage process under Jewish custom. Mary was 15, Joseph nearly 30. The age difference was not uncommon. The betrothal meant the two promised their love to each other according to Jewish law.

Joseph, in the months prior to the planned marriage ceremony, established a residence for his future bride and himself as there was no room for them at his family's house. His father and brothers and their families shared a residence. Joseph was born in Bethlehem, but the family later moved to Galilee. He was already a skilled carpenter at the time of his betrothal.

Then God intervened. Hebrew prophesy became realty.

Mary, while engaged to marry Joseph, accepted the pronouncement of the Angel Gabriel to become the mother of God. She was fully aware of Isaiah and the others in Scripture who foretold the coming of Jesus. But her assent to a role in history and divine design did not answer the questions that were sure to come from Joseph and her own family, not to mention neighbors.

She was overwhelmed by a mixture of awe and fear, gratification and puzzlement. What an unbelievable, blessed summons, to be the mother of Jesus, the mother of God. What a frightening, awkward dilemma, to be with child and not only unmarried but engaged to a man who knew nothing about it. Besides being "highly favored" she had a thousand questions she wished she had asked Gabriel.

Who should she tell? Her mother? Father? Joseph? Best friends?

She had to share with someone this incredible honor, this worrisome predicament. When she told her mother, it was with a combination of sureness in her mother's love, faith and judgement. Mary was validated on all points. She related the entire Gabriel message.

"You are indeed blessed," Anne had told her daughter. "You, my cherished one, are part of the fulfillment of Scripture, a figure that will be known in all of history, a woman who elevates the dignity of all women." The two embraced for an extended period. Then Anne looked into Mary's eyes.

"Oh, Mary. What a blessed honor! You, the mother of God! Me, the grandmother of God! I can hardly breathe."

They savored each other's presence for some time before Anne continued.

"My suggestion is that, for now, you attend Elizabeth's needs. Let's not tell your father and Joseph just yet. We will sort this all out when you return."

"But Joseph will want to accompany me to Judea," Mary said,

"I will arrange for a guardian with an animal to transport you to Judea. Joachim and I will convince Joseph of your safety. You will leave tomorrow."

It had been a mild springtime. The flowers that signaled new life began to emerge, spreading the Galilee countryside with glorious beauty, bouquet and promise. It was the perfectly designed time for Jesus' conception. For now, Mary was called to another mission. Elizabeth lived on the outskirts of Jerusalem.

Elizabeth, six months pregnant, knew immediately upon seeing Mary that she, too, was with child. Her unborn baby (the future John the Baptist) leapt in her womb. Since both Elizabeth and Zechariah were elderly, Mary's help with household chores and preparation for the baby were crucial. Mary returned home after Elizabeth gave birth and was faced with the multiple aspects of her own pregnancy.

At three months pregnancy, her thickening waistline would soon require explanation. How could she assure Joseph that she had not been disloyal? How could she convince him of the mystery and miracle of Jesus' incarnation? Who would believe such a story? Like herself, Joseph had a deep faith in God, but her story pressed the limits of credence. Human words fell short.

Joseph's love for her defused any consideration to humiliate her. She was subject to stoning under Jewish law, a consequence he rejected. After solemn deliberation, he decided that breaking the bonds of betrothal was the proper solution. It was his meager resolution to an impossible dilemma.

Again, God intervened.

As in Mary's case, an angel brought Joseph into the divine plan, and he married her. Yes, the neighbors chattered about the bulging bride. But Joseph knew the truth. As important, the immediate family believed them. He and Mary treasured their role in God's salvation strategy. They knew the small town of Nazareth would become known forever.

"The house down the street where you and Mary lived after the wedding is in good repair," Joachim assured Joseph. "I did some minor repairs to the north side of the roof, and secured a side door, but it has otherwise held up well the last four years. But you are welcome to stay with us as long as you'd like. The neighborhood has changed some. Your father died as did old Ephraim, the storyteller. Roman taxes and poor weather combined to bankrupt a couple of farmers in the area.

"Joseph. You remember Ephraim." A smile spread on Joachim's face. "He was as old as Methuselah, people would say, and had enough children to start his own town. But his ability to tell stories beat all. He could bend your ear for as long as the wine held out. He and his family seemed to survive on the good graces of everyone else. I remember you once expanded his table."

"I recall," Joseph said, his thoughts meandering like a nomadic stream. "Thanks for your hospitality, but I would like for us to move into our own place as soon as practical. And, Joachim, I want to fulfill my father's promise to work for you. I must do that. My father didn't have much so he pledged my labor as a wedding gift to your house.

"Joseph, you know that is not necessary. So much has happened."

"But Joachim, it is necessary for me."

"Well, OK. In that case, as soon as you get settled, I have a job for you. I've been working almost all the time in Sepphoris. Herod Antipas has spectacular plans to rebuild the city. It's good money, but my work in Nazareth has been put off. For instance, I promised the rabbi's wife months ago that I would build a new dining table for her. Perhaps that's a job you can do. I have the wood and all the materials."

"I would be honored to take on such an assignment," Joseph replied with a satisfied look. "Just tell me what you have in mind, or rather what she has in mind. That's the important part."

The weekend was filled with more stories of the last four years. Mary acknowledged that they had made many friends along the way and that "people were so nice and generous." She admitted it was especially difficult to leave the Asyut region, their last Egypt home. "But Joseph was determined," she said, "and I knew, too, that we must come back to Galilee."

"I still remember the fear we all had when you and Joseph left for Bethlehem to register for the census," Anne said. "Here you were, nearly nine months pregnant, and you have to walk or ride that donkey for a week's trip? I don't know how you did it. It had to be terribly uncomfortable. And then there was always the danger of bandits or bad weather.."

"We were fine, mother. Joseph took care of everything. As you know, the only problem was finding a place to stay when we got there."

"Emperor Augustus had to have his special census," Joachim injected, "so that he could double check property and income of citizens to make sure no taxes were missed. And he didn't trust free-agent tax collectors. Rome doesn't have its own tax collection agency."

"I didn't realize that," Joseph said.

"Herod the Great always sent his tribute to Rome in a timely fashion," Joachim continued, "but now that he is gone the system isn't working as smoothly. Taxation is a slippery process."

"Have the two of you considered how you will explain your absence to friends and neighbors, and how it all began?" Anne asked after the small talk had subsided. "I confess I'm thinking of Chloe Adontz, the local chinwag, and how she will spin the story of your return. Going to Bethlehem is easy to explain because of the call to register for the census. And, while there, Jesus was born."

Anne's question created a ringing silence. How could they tell the story of the shepherds coming in from the fields at the behest of angels, the unusual star guiding distant visitors and, because of Herod the Great's paranoia, the need to flee to Egypt in the middle of the night? What sort of narrative could they create to justify an absence of four years? Joseph eventually spoke up.

"I'm opposed to constructing some big story, a falsehood, to explain what happened, why we did what we did and Jesus' presence," he said stoutly. "That doesn't seem an appropriate way to accommodate the Christ child, one sent by the God to redeem the world."

That muted conversation. They sat, a jumble of thoughts, and listened to a little boy who was outside feeding and talking to Anne's chickens.

"Why not the truth?" Mary suddenly broke the stillness. "Why not say that conditions in Jerusalem, political unrest, was such that we were advised to leave town. And others did the same. It so happened that we ended up in Egypt, enjoyed it and stayed awhile. If there are persistent questions, we can say we'd rather not go into detail."

Mary's proposed strategy produced gradual nods of approval. Joseph smiled broadly, as if he had just come out of a dark tunnel and into the sunlight.

"Mary, you are amazing," Joseph shook his head in awe. "When we open our own carpentry business, would you please handle all complaints from the public?"

Having solved a major question, Joseph turned to another issue that had occupied his mind since they left Egypt. More than Jesus' heralded divinity, his God-man nature, Herod the Great feared a rival in the making, a baby who some proclaimed as a king. For Joseph, it was almost as if Herod's despotism had been passed wholly to his sons, Archelaus in Jerusalem and Antipas in Galilee.

"Joachim, you have been to Sepphoris often with your work. What is your calculation of Antipas? Aside from his desire to outbuild his brothers, has he inherited his father's ruthlessness? If he found out about Jesus, really found out the full story, and aware of his father's reaction to the perceived threat from Jesus, would he react violently?

"We avoided Jerusalem on the way back from Egypt because I don't trust Archelaus. We were told he is quick-tempered like his father, easily provoked, constantly on the lookout for any imaginary threat to his position. Would you say Antipas is equal to that?"

"Always remember Joseph," Joachim responded, "power first seeks to protect itself, to perpetuate itself. Does that mean it's impossible for power to accommodate benevolence and freedom? There may have been exceptions, but history favors autocratic rule. As for Antipas, his attention right now is on women and building temples. Unlike his brother, who I wouldn't trust any further than I could throw a crate of plaster, I wouldn't worry a lot about Antipas."

"What do you think we should do?" Joseph asked. "How can we better protect Jesus?"

"I don't know, Joseph. Maybe you are overly concerned. Things tend to fade with time. Not always. I heard a story about this old merry maker who went to a party without his wife. He was most fond of wine. Over the course of the evening, he found himself in the grip of the grape. Arriving home, he knew the missus would be angry, so he took off his sandals and tip-toed into his house. His stealthy return was successful so it seemed."

"What happened?" Joseph asked. "The wife said nothing the next morning?"

"That's right. The next morning, she said nothing." Joachim began to snicker. "But two years later, when she wanted a bigger house, she remembered."

Joseph laughed and Mary did, too. Anne was less accommodating.

"Joachim," she said, "your story doesn't address Joseph's concern. He, and Mary, too, are worried about Jesus growing up under a system where the ruler is always looking for a potential enemy, whether it be from the outside or in his own region. You are in a position at your work to hear such threats."

"You are right, Anne. I didn't mean to make light of Joseph's apprehension. It is valid to be vigilant. I will listen for any unusual talk. At the same time, we all must live our lives. We cannot be constantly encumbered by the possibility that something will go wrong."

In the new week, Joseph started work on the table for the rabbi's wife. Joachim resumed his masonry work in Sepphoris. Anne, Mary and Jesus went to the little house that Joseph found upon their engagement. Like many residences in Nazareth, it was cut into the chalky limestone hillside in the southeast part of town overlooking a nearby valley. Stones had been mudded along smoothed limestone to create interior walls.

"I like the arched door leading to the back area," Anne assessed. "Joseph did well. The main room is big enough and it appears venting is provided in the ceiling." The house Joseph remodeled also had a small room used for storage. An outer courtyard surrounded the entrance with a garden area to the side. They spent the next weeks preparing furniture plans for Joseph, deciding on window and door covers and other decorations. Soon plans were sufficiently complete for the young family to move in.

The cooking area was directly below the vented area in a corner of the main room. Pots, cooking utensils and a loom were housed in a covered part of the courtyard where a ladder gave access to the roof.

Life moved on in Nazareth, the remote hillside village some disparaged as "a one-camel town". The environs were tucked in a hillside and basin that had been occupied for centuries, lately by Greeks and more recently by Hasmonean Jews. Herod's takeover ended

Hasmonean rule. Jews from other parts of Judea, including ancestors of Joachim and Anne, then moved in.

In the months after Joseph's family returned, Mary became acquainted with neighbors, including Chloe Adontz. Mary quickly became one of the "women at the well." It was a daily trip, some days twice, and the center for dispensing of news. Mrs. Adontz was the chief reporter, both informant and interviewer. Mary, forewarned by Anne of Chloe's busy agenda, was prepared for her questions.

Two women, Adah and Eunice, soon became Mary's close friends. She met both at the well. Adah was unmarried and cared for her widower father and two brothers. Eunice and her husband Jeremiah had two children. She shared a lamb stew recipe while Adah's most famous dish was fish with wine and tahini. Mary exchanged humas and bread recipes.

Joseph's skill as a carpenter had already been known. He had no problem in getting customers and easing Joachim's workload. Nearly all the local carpentry jobs, new and repair, fell to Joseph. Gradually, Joachim even cut back on his work in Sepphoris. It troubled Joseph when he noticed Joachim's shortness of breath. He mentioned it to Mary, and Mary talked to her mother about it.

Anne was aware of Joachim's "wheeze," and attributed it to breathing construction dust, especially the powdery lime used in masonry.

Jesus, too, made many new friends. He was especially popular among boys looking for help with problems in language skills and Scripture studies. The well and town center were no longer the outer limits of his discovery. He wandered outside the town and took great joy in observing shepherds and their dogs move sheep between pastures. It was on one such excursion that he noticed a lamb with a bleeding leg. It could barely walk. He struggled to pick up the squirmy animal and carried it to the farmhand.

"This little critter was limping along," Jesus informed the shepherd. "It appears he became entangled in a bramble."

"I expect your diagnosis is correct young fella. I noticed its limp, also. Let's see," he said, examining the lamb. "Well, it appears the bleeding has stopped. Did you rub some balm on the wound?" he said, teasing.

"No, sir," Jesus replied. "I don't have salve of any kind. Maybe the injury was not as bad as we thought."

"Maybe," said the shepherd, "or perhaps you have a special touch with sheep in trouble. What's your name, little guy? I haven't seen you in these parts."

"Oh, I've been here for some time now. My name is Jesus and I live in Nazareth. My father is a carpenter, a real good carpenter."

"Well, I see you are also a good salesman. Jesus. Let's see if the lamb still has a severe limp. It's all but trying to jump out of my arms." He placed the sheep on the ground and it sped off as if being chased by a wolf. "I guess that answers that. The lamb is fine," he said scratching his head. "I'm not sure how that happened."

"I admire your dogs," Jesus said. "They are smart. I love dogs. I'm hoping to get my own dog. I'd better return home."

"I hope you get a dog," the man said, still baffled by the lamb's quick recovery. "God be with you," he waved.

The routine of life unfolded in Nazareth in the months to come, except that all were shocked by Joachim's worsening health. It all happened so quickly. Anne believed the heavy demands of masonry, especially as directed by the Romans in Sepphoris, hastened his quick demise. Jesus, now 5, had his first experience of death. He had scarcely got to know his grandfather.

"Why are they washing Saba's body and rubbing it with oil?" Jesus asked his mother during preparation ceremonies.

"It is part of the Jewish ritual," she explained. "We give great respect to the dead, even an enemy. The body is washed, anointed with nard and sometimes myrrh," That done and final prayers said, the next of kin, including Anne and families of Joseph and Clopas, and friends, said their goodbyes." By custom burial occurred the same day as death.

"Why did Saba have to die?" Jesus persisted.

"We don't know what God has planned for us," Mary struggled for an adequate response, "but we do accept that if we believe in God sincerely, we will live forever with him." She felt odd telling him about faith in God, but it wasn't the first time or last that Mary had peculiar emotions when discussing God with Jesus.

Less than a year after her father's death, Mary's mother died. She mourned Anne's death with greater loss than she had her father's. She had had a close relationship with her mother, in large part because Anne appreciated the complexity of Jesus' divine as well as human nature and its consequences for her daughter.

In their short time together following the return from Egypt, they had talked often about Jesus and his fulfilling of the Scriptures. Anne and Joachim had not seen their grandson until he was nearly four years old, and then both died within two years. They packed in a lot of grandparenting in that brief time, and Anne developed a special relationship with her daughter.

Now the salvation story was focused on three – Jesus, Mary and Joseph. Perhaps it always was.

Jesus made Anne's death easier as he remembered her for the little things, which were big things to him. He told how she scratched his back, rubbed his feet and gently patted him on the head. He said she "didn't rub as hard" when she cleaned his ears. "And it didn't hurt when she took that wood splinter out of my finger."

Grandma, he said, had taken walks with him, down by the stream, and let him wade in the water and pick up frogs. He recalled how she let him help pull weeds in her garden, "and she didn't even yell at me when I stepped on her beans."

"She's in heaven now, with Grandpa," he declared the day following burial. He did have one concern.

"Who will take care of Grandma's chickens?" he asked.

Chapter 15

NAZARETH, about 6AD – "Please close the door, Jesus," Mary said with some annoyance. "I don't expect there is any guidance in Hebrew Scripture that suggests you should automatically close a door after entering a house. But do it anyway. Okay? It's become a habit with you to walk in, look for something to eat, and leave the door open."

"I'm sorry, Mah. I will try to do better," Jesus replied with a distinct lack of enthusiasm. He grabbed the honey jar, a piece of barley bread, slathered the bread with honey, sat down and ate.

"What?" he responded innocently as he gazed upward at his mother's stern look. Even at age 6, Jesus was already aware of "the look", but this time it was underlined and in bold face.

"The door!!" she said, with emphasis.

"Oh, yeah." He rose, chewing as honey ran down his chin, and closed the door.

Jesus was on a growing spurt, as were his friends. Playing games ranked second only to eating. Except for Jesus Mary saw to it that Scripture lessons came first. His friends frequently came to him with questions. For example, Caleb, age seven, could never remember the name Mordecai, the Book of Esther figure.

"That's a tough one," Jesus admitted one day when they were reviewing lessons, "but this is the third time you've asked about Mordecai. Think of him as, let's say, *more* of something. Think of *more* and maybe the rest will come," Jesus advised. A week later Caleb inquired again: "Who was this Most-guy?"

Like waifs, they ran the narrow streets of Nazareth, often racing. The town's central well typically was the turn-around point. They played games by drawing in the dirt. Wealthier boys had archery equipment. Most of the games Nazareth boys played were imported by the Romans. There was tug-of-war, jacks and a form of kickball, with the balls made of linen, hair and string.

Caleb wasn't the best student when it came to Scripture, but he certainly didn't lack inquisitiveness. Names intrigued him, except the hard-to-spell names like Mordecai. One day after school he quizzed Jesus about Moses and how Moses received his name.

"I know how the Pharaoh's daughter rescued him from the river, named him Moses and raised him. But what happened to his parents, why did he end up in the river and why was he named Moses?"

"You must have missed school the day Rabbi ben Shimon talked about Moses," Jesus said. "It seems there is disagreement about Moses' name, according to the Rabbi. You are right about Pharoah's daughter finding a baby in a basket in the river. It seems the Hebrew population at that time was growing too fast for the comfort of Egyptian leaders. One story says the Pharoah ordered the death of Hebrew newborn males to subdue that increase. Some say it was because of famine.

"Now the Moses' parents, Amram and Jochebed, hid him for about three months, and then – the Rabbi didn't say why – decided to place him in a basket and launched him in the river. My guess, Caleb, is that the Egyptian soldiers were about to move in. Anyway, the Pharoah's daughter was swimming and discovered the baby."

"Moses, or Moshe in Hebrew, comes from the Egyptian word *mose,* which means 'is born,' according to the Rabbi. There is also the opinion that the word Moses comes from the Hebrew word 'to pull out of the water.' Some claim he grew up with a different name, but the Rabbi says we should say Moses."

"Wow, you sure do know a lot of history," Caleb said.

"No, I'm merely telling you what the Rabbi said."

"OK. Now, I've also been wondering about your name. Why did they name you Jesus? I don't know another Jesus in all the Nazareth region. I know two other Calebs, but no one else named Jesus."

"Hmm. You got me stumped there," Jesus replied. "My mother says that it's really Yeshua in Hebrew. She says an angel suggested the name. I guess she had a dream. My father said he would go into more detail when I'm older. He says that about a lot of my questions."

Caleb and Jesus, though special pals, were playing near a small stream one day when the subject of farming came up. Caleb's father was a respected date grower, and head of the local dendrology alliance. The group promoted sales and quality improvement of various trees associated with wood and fruit products. It was a chance for Caleb, out of the blue, to do some bragging.

"I would say my father is smarter than your father," Caleb said, as he skipped a flat stone across the water. "He knows everything about trees, the ones that grow fruit and the ones used to build stuff. Your father is a good carpenter, but that's just sawing wood."

Jesus picked up a rock, tossed it in the water where it landed with a plunk.

"My father is not only a good carpenter, a craftsman," Jesus said, "but he is thankful to all the good things trees do, and thankful to God for producing trees in the first place. And I'm sure he is grateful to your father, especially for his palm trees and those juicy dates."

"I knew you would find something about God or Scripture in regard to trees," Caleb said.

"Here's something to ask your father about trees," Jesus suggested. "After God himself and people, what is the most mentioned thing in Scripture? Maybe he knows the answer."

"Are you saying trees? How do you know that? Did you count line by line?"

"No," Jesus replied. "The Rabbi said it one day."

Jesus was nearly three cubits (50 inches) tall, average, but despite the honey consumption weighed less than most of his friends. Mary also required Jesus to spend time in Joseph's carpenter shop. He quickly picked up the names for tools and sawing cuts. He learned many things, save for remembering to close the front door.

He was studying both Hebrew and Aramaic. While his parents, mainly Mary, taught him about the Jewish prophets, psalms, proverbs and other writings, all in Hebrew, they also coached him in Aramaic. Aramaic, a Semitic language that originated in the Euphrates Valley some seven centuries before, was the spoken language of Galilean Jews.

"Jesus, what is the most important part of Scripture?" Mary asked one day prior to his Synagogue lessons.

"I'm quite sure that would be the books written by Moses," he replied quickly as if it were a no-brainer. "Mah, did you know that Josiah Stern has a dog? His name is Rex, and he is funny. He likes to greet you by racing around you, but Josiah taught him never to jump on people. He is black with a white stripe on his nose and he has white feet. He sure is a nice dog."

Josiah was the same age as Jesus. The two met at Synagogue school and became good friends.

"What does that have to do with Scripture and studies at Synagogue?"

"Nothing. Josiah was just telling the class about Rex's latest trick."

"Does Rex read from the Scripture scrolls?"

"No, Mah. You're being silly. But it wouldn't hurt if we had a dog. I'd take care of him." Mary ignored his comment.

Jewish boys entered school at age six. The Synagogue School was in a room adjacent to the main worship area, which was near the marketplace in central Nazareth. It was a five-minute walk from Jesus' home. Jesus and the other pupils sat on the floor in a semicircle facing the teacher. Until the age of 10, Hebrew Scripture was the only text used.

At 10 emphasis switched to the oral Torah and interpretations, and at age 13 rabbis stressed the importance of following the commandments of Moses. By 18 a young man was considering the laws of marriage and soon after focused on a vocation. For exceptional students, those keen on Scripture, the prescribed teaching or rabbinical age was 30.

Girls were given instruction in domestic duties, such as spinning, weaving, the preparation of food, and caring for children. Women were also formally trained in such things as midwifery and medicine.

"Tonight, we will review some spelling words," Mary declared. "You need to expand your vocabulary beyond kalba (the Aramaic word for dog). And you should start learning some Greek words. The people near the Jordan River and some in Sepphoris speak Greek." Greek was spoken throughout Palestine for many years.

"Mah, if I grow up to be a carpenter like father and work in the Nazareth area, why do I have to learn Greek? Now, if I become a wealthy trader-merchant or well-known rabbi it might be different. Besides, Greek must be hard to learn. My friend, Josiah, when he doesn't understand something, says, 'It's Greek to me!' He's funny, like his dog. Mah, What's the Greek word for dog?"

"Feh!," Mary said with vexation, throwing her hands in the air. "Your father will conduct tonight's spelling lesson."

In the Mediterranean world in which Jesus lived, half the children born did not reach the age of puberty. Disease and malnutrition were prevalent. It was not uncommon for extended families to live in a clan-like cluster. That was the case with Jesus' friend, Josiah, for example. He and other related children had the run of several houses or rooms.

Often married brothers lived in the front section of a house while their wives and children slept in the rear room. The oldest brother, or their father, served as the patriarch.

"Now, Jesus, be attentive. We must review these spelling words," Joseph said after the evening meal. "Orders from your mother."

Joseph was more at ease talking carpentry and construction than conducting spelling practice, but he followed his wife's directions.

"We have 20 words to review. First, how do you spell 'ժողովուրդ' (people)? That's an important word."

Jesus rattled off the 20 Aramaic words without a miss.

"Are we done?" he said hopefully. "Father, I know quite a few Greek words, too. For example, kalba (dog) is σκύλος in Greek. Did you know that?"

"Yes, Jesus. I know that. You sure are persistent. We'll think about getting a dog. Your mother still isn't convinced. I'll say this, Jesus. If you study your spelling words and your Scripture lessons and prayers, without fail, she might be easier to persuade." Joseph made Jesus promise not to raise the subject of getting a dog until a decision had been made. The decision, he stressed, could go either way.

Jesus' eyes lit up. He read it as a done deal. He learned new Aramaic words by the dozens. He memorized Hebrew Scripture figures and their roles in Jewish history. He even studied Greek. To say he grew in wisdom would be like saying he hoped for a dog. From then on, he developed an image for "his" dog, things they could do together, tricks he would impart, and, of course, a name.

At the time, few regarded a dog as a pet. Except for those used in herding and hunting, dogs were seen in a negative light. Often, they ran in packs. Like swine, they were considered unclean. To call a person a dog implied they were of low status. But Jesus envisioned his dog as a companion, a dog that would befriend everyone.

I know, he said one day, talking to himself. *I think I'll name him Slama. That means peace*.

That was in summer. By late in the year, Joseph had swayed Mary into getting a dog, but not without several conditions. She insisted that Jesus, and only Jesus, be responsible for feeding and caring for the animal. That included picking up messes of all kinds, walking the animal, always securing it and maintaining an outside shelter. Joseph said he would enforce her rules. The dog could sleep in a lean-to next to his shop.

"This is my best birthday ever!" Jesus shouted when Joseph brought the Canaan pup home. Jesus hugged it and let the dog lick him on the nose, all the time while Mary frowned and Joseph laughed. Joseph said he purchased the animal from a sheep farmer who assured him it would be docile and friendly. "Mah, would it be OK if I showed him to Josiah?"

"Hold on there, young man," Joseph interceded. "You haven't even picked out a name for the dog. Besides, it may not be a good idea to introduce the puppy to an older dog like Josiah's Rex just yet. Give it some time. You must teach it manners, how to get along with others. Herding sheep is in its blood. The pup needs to expand its horizons."

"Father, his name will be Slama. Maybe we'll shorten it to Slam."

Jesus groomed Slam's pale gold and white fur nearly every day. The dog had black spots on its front legs. The time came, in the months ahead, when some of Mary's rules were bent. Slam was allowed in the house for short periods. He became known in the neighborhood, all the way to the well. Rex and Slam became buddies, and Jesus once took Slam to Synagogue School. But just once. Chewing marks were discovered on an entryway bench and Slam was blamed.

Like all dogs, Slam made other blunders, the most serious when he dug up some of Mary's hyssop plants. Fortunately, Jesus was able to successfully replant most of them. Then there was the time when the pup chewed on a piece of finished chair leg in Joseph's shop. Those sins of Slam were transferred to Jesus. He was not allowed to let Slim have the run of the property until he had trained the dog not to dig or gnaw on things. At Joseph's recommendation, Jesus soaked some plants and wood in vinegar and let Slam chew on them. Slam got the message.

There was one other incident that put Slam in the doghouse. Jesus and Josiah had taken their dogs for a run outside the village. On the way back home, Slam discovered a fresh pile of donkey dung and rolled in it. Mary turned several colors of fury as soon as they entered the house. Not even the Archangel Gabriel could have rescued Slam from eviction.

"Get that animal out of my kitchen immediately," she bellowed in an unmotherly mandate. "Scrub that animal front to back, rinse him off, then scrub him again. Check his ears, paws and between every hair." She barely paused to breathe as she appended her decree. "I don't want any donkey smell when that dog is present."

Slam had even lost his name in the process, being reduced to *that animal* and *that dog.*

One day Joseph returned from a carpenter job with what he thought was good news. "I have some interesting information, Mary," he said. "A customer was told by the rabbi that Herod Archelaus has been removed as ethnarch of Judea and Samaria. Seems Emperor Augustus heard enough about Archelaus' mistakes and banned him to Gaul. To Gaul! That's the end of the world. Judea will now be ruled directly by a Roman governor."

"Have they named this governor?" Mary asked.

"There is a rumor that Quirinius, who governs Syria, will also rule Samaria and Judea. He was a personal friend of Julius Ceasar, I'm told, and later served in the legion under Augustus. If that's all true, Herod Antipas, Archelaus' brother, won't be happy. He was building new cities to honor Augustus and hoping to succeed his father as king of the entire region."

"Well," Mary said with little emotion, "that's politics. I know you have always feared Archelaus, felt he carried his father's paranoia about Jesus. But, Joseph, what's to say the Roman governor will be much different?"

After the death of Mary's parents, disposal of their estate was by custom relegated to Joseph. The status of women in Jesus' time was substantially changed from that of their ancient sisters. While women were held in high regard by Jewish society, their role was confined in large part to the private family domain. Hence, Joseph handled court matters involving the sale of the property.

In ancient Israel, by contrast, women participated in most of community life except in the Temple priesthood. They were involved in business and real estate. Some held leadership roles, including that of judge. Some were engaged in political issues. They took an active part in public events.

On the contrary, first-century Jewish women were separated from men in private, public, and religious life. They could go to the Temple but could not venture beyond the confines of the Women's Court. They were also encouraged to have private prayer lives at home.

Mary ended up with Anne's chickens. She also kept one of her mother's woolen bedspreads. Anne had made it herself, and it became Mary's favorite keepsake. Feeding the chickens and gathering the eggs were added to Jesus' chores. Joseph constructed a small coop in the courtyard for Anne's chickens. Jesus was also required to put away various shop tools Joseph used every day and sweep the floor. The sawdust was spread inside the chicken enclosure.

Jesus seldom wore his sandals. His long tan tunics, held in place by sashes of various colors, gave way to shorter garments as he grew by inches. The brown curls on the back of his of his head seemed to multiply with his height. He was seldom late for a meal. Unlike most students, he relished studying Scripture, which the local rabbi presented as "exploring our family tree."

As a result, he was always excited for the springtime Passover trip to Jerusalem, an event steeped in ancestral history. He was eight years old when he made his first Passover pilgrimage. It was special. For him there was not only the novelty of the week-long journey, but the adventure of meeting new people, a caravan of Nazareth relatives and friends.

(It is approximately 280,000 cubits from Nazareth to Jerusalem, or 80 miles.)

Passover was the beginning of the seven-day Festival of the Unleavened Bread. Normally, the trip and festival take nearly three weeks. It was on this initial pilgrimage that Jesus met Eli Abrams from Nain, a town a short distance southeast of Nazareth. The boy was better known as Eli of Nain since it was custom for most Jews in that time to disregard last names. Hence, Jesus of Nazareth, or Jesus, son of Joseph.

Nain, like Nazareth, was a nondescript town, a farming village that clung to Mount Moreh on the eastern side of the Jezreel Valley. Eli's father tended a hillside olive grove that basked in the afternoon sun. Since Josiah did not make the trip (he looked after Slam), Jesus spent much of the journey running around with Eli. They were the same age, but Jesus knew more Scripture. Eli knew more about olives.

The Hebrew Bible asks that all able male Jews make a pilgrimage to Jerusalem three times a year – in the spring for Passover, in the summer for Shavuot and in the fall for Sukkot. Passover is the most important for it commemorates the Biblical story of Exodus, where God freed the Israelites from slavery in Egypt. Jesus knew the story and many of the customs associated with Passover.

The meal was preceded by several days of purification rituals, including washing of feet by servants. There were prescribed procedures for seating (based on hierarchy), placement of tableware. and for nearly every step and prayer associated with the ceremony. The Seder meal consisted of roasted meat of a one-year-old, unblemished male lamb, unleavened bread, and wine. The lamb was brought to the Temple court for slaughter amid the sound of trumpets.

Passover drew thousands of Jews from throughout the world to Jerusalem. The city of 20,000 swelled by six times. Jerusalem and the Temple Mount were considered as their home away from home. Every room in the city was occupied. Most of Jesus' caravan became part of a hillside campsite above the Kidron Valley. For a first-time visitor like Jesus, it was an awesome adventure.

Jesus accompanied Joseph's group to the Temple where the courtyard was filled with the sounds of bleating lambs and goats. Money changers were yelling prices to those lined up to purchase an animal. The lamb or goat was slaughtered, skinned and eventually hung by hooks to bleed out. The entire procedure was supervised by Temple priests according to specified rituals.

The noise was deafening and the reek from burning entrails stung the nose. Jesus pinched his nostrils shut to minimize the stench. Inwardly, he was more disturbed by the notion of using the holy Temple area for bustling business. But he said nothing.

Pilgrims would regularly congregate in the Temple area for prayer during the festival time, but only high priests were allowed in the Temple's innermost sanctuary, the Holy of Holies, and then only on the Day of Atonement. It enclosed the Ark of the Covenant, God's residence, the junction between Heaven and Earth. The high priest was an appointee of the Romans, making him and his edicts suspicious in the minds of many Jews.

Passover had a powerful impact on Jesus. Mary and Joseph noticed that he was quieter than usual after they returned from Jerusalem. His mind seemed adrift. Not once during the following week did he take Slam on a long walk or play with friends. Joseph became concerned when Jesus asked if the rabbi would be present for Shabbat services on the weekend. He seldom missed Synagogue, but never before inquired about particulars of worship.

"I know our rabbi has congregations in several other towns and I hoped he would be in Nazareth this time," Jesus explained. "We are a small place, but God doesn't care about size. Does he father? I think he wants us to be like Moses, full of faith. When God promises something, like freedom from slavery or everlasting life, we can count on it."

"You are so right, Jesus. And, yes, God doesn't care that we're small. And as far as I know, the rabbi will be here for our Shabbat. Why are you so concerned about the rabbi's presence, my son?"

"Not concerned, father. I just like to hear him talk about God. I hoped he would be here."

The Synagogue in Nazareth was indeed small, a public building that was also used for town meetings and other functions. It was located near the center of town and at one of the area's highest points. Most residents were Jews, and the Synagogue also drew families from nearly agriculture valleys. It was not uncommon, especially when the rabbi was in town, for people to be standing – even out the front door.

Unlike in many larger places, the Nazareth Synagogue did not have three doors but one. The entry faced south toward Jerusalem. Like most, there was a mikveh (ritual bath) where worshippers symbolically cleansed their hearts before entering. Inside there were stepped benches on two sides, chief seats for important members. The common people sat on the floor.

Speakers and readers stood on the bema, a small platform in front and next to a menorah. Those who read from the Torah sat in a special chair called the Moses' seat. Jesus pictured the day when he might sit in Moses' seat and read from the Torah, but he kept the thought to himself. The weekend came.

"Shalom!" Rabbi Shimon addressed people as they entered the Synagogue. "And shalom to you Mary and Joseph, and the young fellow, too. How are you Jesus?"

"I'm doing well, Rabbi, and I'm happy that you are here."

"Well," he patted Jesus on the head, "I'm happy that I'm here, too. Is there something on that young mind of yours?"

"Yes, Thanks for asking. I was hoping," Jesus explained, "that you might talk about the coming of the Messiah."

"Jesus!" Joseph interrupted. "Don't be so impolite as to suggest what the Rabbi should speak about. That's . . ."

"No, no, Joseph," the Rabbi injected with a laugh. "That's perfectly OK, although unusual coming from a little fellow. You must have read my mind, Jesus, for my discourse today does mention the Messiah's coming, as does the Amidah prayer. But please excuse me. I must get ready for services." The Rabbi gave a small wave and Jesus waved back. A smile angled across Jesus' face. They walked inside.

Jesus saw Josiah across the room. They motioned something to one another with their hands until Mary poked Jesus to end the unspoken conversation. Rabbi Shimon entered the bema and the service began with readings, stories going back to creation. "Please stand" the Rabbi then requested. Following prayers of blessing, petition and thanksgiving, they recited the Amidah prayer.

O Lord, open my lips, and my mouth shall tell your praise.

Blessed are you, O Lord our God and God of our ancestors, God of Abraham, God of Isaac, and God of Jacob, the great, mighty and revered God, the most high God, who graciously gives loving kindness. You create all things. You remember the pious actions of the patriarchs, and in love will bring a redeemer for their children's children for Your Name's sake. O King, Helper, Savior and Shield. Blessed are You, O Lord, the protector of Abraham.

You are Lord, are all-powerful forever. You resurrect the dead, You are mighty to save . . . You favor people with knowledge and teach human beings with understanding. O favor us with knowledge, understanding and applied wisdom from You. Make us return, O our Father, unto your Torah . . . Forgive us, O our Father, for we have sinned . . ."

The prayer ended with a plea for peace. It was then time for Rabbi Shimon's sermon. He began in his normal fashion by asking God to bestow good health and good life "on all of Galilee and Nazareth in particular." He looked at Jesus and smiled.

"Today, while I intended to speak on that part of the Amidah prayer that speaks of God's love and his bringing of a redeemer, I want to give some random thoughts about when that will happen. And I want to thank a young member of the congregation for steering my mind, no, I will say inspired me in this direction." He took a deep breath and continued.

"When I was a little boy, I often wondered when the savior would come to Israel. When will a redeemer, as the prayer says, come? We know God's love never fails. We know that our Temple, Solomon's Temple, was destroyed nearly six centuries ago by the Babylonians and our people taken captive. We know that 60 years later King Cyrus freed our ancestors who then came back to Jerusalem.

"We know a Jewish man named Zerubbabel led the rebuilding of the city's wall and the Second Temple. There are many things we know about our faith and our people, but we still don't know when the Messiah will come. Now here is what crossed my mind today. Maybe, who knows, the Messiah is in Israel now. What do you think of that?"

A murmuring rippled through the congregation. People looked at one another.

"I know. I know," the Rabbi continued. "That's an extraordinary thought. In truth, it is mind-boggling. Then again, how else would a Messiah come except in a mind-boggling way? He wouldn't just ride in on a camel from Damascus." That produced chuckles from the kids. "He wouldn't merely show up on a boat from Ionia. He certainly won't come from the Romans. He will come from among us. And maybe, just maybe, he is here.

"Now, having said that, I want to tell you a story. There was a shul, a prayer place, in the hills. It was run by Zealots and many people came there to pray. But jealousy and bickering among the Zealots led to its decline. The leader was dismayed that animosity had replaced the peaceful spirit of the shul. He took his plight to a good friend, Rabbi Miska.

"Some days later Miska told the leader he had received a vision that the Messiah was among the ranks of the Zealots. The leader was stunned. Who could it be? This was unbelievable. He shared Miska's words with the other Zealots. Silence filled the shul. They looked at one another. A new respect was born. Anger was replaced with forgiveness. It became a peaceful and joyous place again. News spread. The people returned. They were renewed. Everyone was happy."

Rabbi Shimon looked out at the congregation. Then he concluded.

"This all happened because the Zealots believed the Messiah was among them."

Again, he looked up. This time his eyes met Jesus' eyes and the two smiled.

The following week playtime between Jesus and Josiah had a common theme. Instead of tag or spinning tops, Jesus, every day, insisted on playing Synagogue. He played the role of the rabbi and Josiah was the helper, or shamash. On the fourth day, Josiah claimed the part of the rabbi.

Attending the Passover festival also meant carpentry work piled up for Joseph back in Nazareth. It usually took him weeks to catch up on orders. As Jesus grew, so did the need for his assistance in the business. He slowly moved from helper to apprentice. Joseph was a gracious manager. Jesus wrangled time off to go fishing with Josiah, first in a stream that flowed eastward into the Sea of Galilee and later in the sea itself.

Most commercial fishermen used nets to catch fish, but Jesus, with help from Joseph, fashioned metal hooks that were decorated with bright red threads of wool for additional enticement. Sometimes the musht and biny would bite; ofttimes not. Once, Josiah came home with seven keepers and Jesus caught none. "He didn't even get a bite," Josiah chided in days to come. Jesus laughed.

Shortly before he turned nine, Jesus received his first assignment as a carpenter. A friend of Joseph had mentioned that an uneven rock floor in the family eating area caused the table to wobble. Jesus overheard the problem and later suggested that a shim may be the answer. Joseph chuckled in satisfaction: *He's thinking like a repairman. At least he didn't recommend shaving off the other three table legs.*

"Great idea, Jesus. Why don't you arrange to inspect the table and measure what size shim is needed. Then we can fabricate the piece and you can attach it."

Jesus beamed with dignity. He had picked up nails, swept sawdust, fetched tools and held long boards while Joseph sawed. He even learned the critical matter of measuring. But dealing with a customer was new territory for him. He was determined to please.

The customer was happy. He smiled and paid Jesus for the work. But customer satisfaction, Jesus learned, was the biggest reward.

Chapter 16

NAZARETH, about 8AD – "Father. What is a tekton? I heard a boy at Synagogue class the other day say that you are a tekton, not a carpenter."

"Well, Jesus. I suppose the boy is technically correct. Tekton is a fancy Greek word for someone who is a carpenter, mason and a general all-around handyman. But carpenter suits me just fine. Masons make more money, and often work on big projects, but carpenters and handymen deal more with regular people.

"The truth is in these parts a carpenter must also know how to hew rock because most houses, like ours, are carved out of the bluff hillsides of Nazareth. And wood for building is scarce and precious."

The two were in Joseph's carpenter shed, a small building he had erected next to the family living quarters. Two sides were solid limestone. It was bounded by an enclosure where Mary's chickens pecked at grit and a lean-to that contained laying nests. The hens had scratched several holes in the yard and frequently took turns fluffing themselves with dust.

A work bench was the shop's main fixture. There were all kinds of tools and papyrus ropes hanging on the back wall. A comforting smell of nature, a mixture of soil, damp stone and wood and granite shavings, permeated the workshop. Jesus frequently spent time in the shed, when he wasn't at Synagogue school, playing with friends and after he had convinced his mother that he had completed Scripture study.

"What are you working on, father? Jesus asked.

"I'm trying to form a new door handle for Maurice the tanner and his wife. They live just beyond the village well. Right now the door won't stay shut, not a good thing on a street where there are a lot of people coming and going. They couldn't agree on a design but finally asked me to build anything that seals the door. I found a piece of scrap lumber that will serve the purpose."

"Do you and mother ever have disagreements?"

"Oh, sure," Joseph said without hesitation. "Every couple has disagreements. It's only natural. Two independent minds sometimes arrive at different conclusions. Life would be dull if everyone agreed on everything all the time. Maurice and his wife eventually agreed that the important thing is that the door closes properly, not how it looks."

"What have you and mother disagreed about?"

"Let's see, Jesus. How shall I put it. Your mother convinced me we should have chickens. She inherited them from her mother. That pretty much nullified my opposition. You remember another disagreement. We had lively discussions about your getting a dog. We won that one.

"When we returned from Egypt several years ago, I wanted to keep ole Dynamo in our back yard. Mary said the donkey would irritate everyone with its braying and stink up the neighborhood. She vetoed the idea, so Dynamo is now housed on a farm outside the village. I do repair work for the farmer. He takes care of Dynamo.

"About the only time we need him is for our trips to Passover in Jerusalem." Joseph looked down at his inquisitive son. "If you are keeping score, that puts your mother ahead 2 to 1. Don't tell her I said that."

"Father. What is a chisel?"

"This is a chisel," Joseph held up a tool that he had retrieved from his work bench. "They come in various sizes depending on what kind of work you are doing. That big one over there is for cutting stone."

"What would you use the one in your hand for?"

"This particular chisel has a narrow blade for finishing work. You strike the top gently with a mallet, carefully guiding the chisel along a prescribed path. With a chisel one can shape wood to achieve whatever structure you want, for example, an arm on a chair. I'm using this one to round off the door handle for Maurice the tanner and his wife."

"What happens if you make a mistake, if you accidentally hit the chisel too hard or if it cuts a place where you didn't want to go?"

"That happens," Joseph said, "even with skilled carpenters. All people make mistakes. Show me a carpenter with a black fingernail and I'll show you a carpenter who has made a mistake. Wood is precious in Galilee. That's why a carpenter has to be extra careful. If he makes a mistake, sometimes it can be rubbed out. If it's a bad mistake, he may have to start over."

"Father, what's the worst mistake you ever made?"

"You sure are full of questions this morning, Jesus. And that's good. Asking questions is how one learns. If you don't ask a question, then there will be an empty spot in your head where the answer was supposed to go. But not all answers to questions may line up with what's already in your brain. Some answers require evaluation, contemplation and even meditation.

"Now to answer your question," Joseph continued, "I think the worse mistake I ever made was to doubt God. Some questions came up before you were born, and I was not comfortable with the answers. Eventually, faith in God prevailed and calmed my mind. But your question probably had to do with a carpentry mistake, right?"

"Well, it did," Jesus replied, "but now I am interested in why you doubted God. What was that all about? Did you doubt that God would stand at your side?"

"Well, Jesus. It's a complicated matter, and when you get a little older, I will explain all the details. For now, let's just say I learned my lesson that one should always trust in God."

Jesus would soon be eight. He was growing physically and mentally. His curiosity was in high gear. His hair had been longer, but Mary trimmed it against his wishes. She also ordered him to change his under garment and short tunic twice a week. His dark arms and legs were even browner due to frequent exposure to the sun.

He liked Synagogue school, had several good friends and, of course, doted on Slam, his beloved Caanan sheep dog. Slam was fully grown, his gold and white fur shining from Jesus' frequent bathing and grooming. Mary said she would be happy if Jesus paid as much attention to his own personal care. Slam was asleep in a basket of pine straw in a corner of the shop.

"Have you fed Slam and taken him for a walk?" Joseph asked.

"Yes, father. Right after I had my breakfast I gave him some scraps from last night's supper. I swept the floor of barley breadcrumbs and other things. Slam likes the breadcrumbs and goat cheese curds he may find, but I don't think he has a taste for cummin and spices. And we went for a good walk. Only Slam ran off."

"What happened?"

"Well, we were at the western edge of town and Slam spotted a fox in a nearby woods. I guess he thought it was a wayward lamb because he chased after it down through a gully and up a ridge. I called for him to come back, but he ignored me. I ran after him and finally found him sitting and staring in the distance, whining. He was surprised, I suppose, to learn that a 'lamb' could run that fast."

Joseph laughed at the story.

Jesus stepped around the dozing Slam and picked up a large spike. The dog half-peeked with one eye and gave a flick of an ear, as if dispensing a flea. The spike was five inches long. He turned it over in his small hands and touched its sharp tip. Joseph glanced at Jesus and wondered what was going through the boy's mind.

"I would sure hate to have one of these stick me in the hand," Jesus said. "What are they used for?"

"Spikes are just big nails," Joseph explained. "They are used to attach heavy boards. I seldom use them. They tend to split the wood. But you are correct in saying they can be dangerous, say if you accidentally step on one. Here, let me put it in the spike can."

The sun crept its way high enough in the late morning sky to cast a steep ray into the woodshop's lone and tiny window. The beam revealed dancing dust mites and wood flakes that were otherwise hidden in the shadows. The large door to the shop, usually kept open, admitted abundant light.

"Father, how much money do you and mother make?"

"Enough. That's all we have to make. We don't worry about it. God will provide what's enough. We pay the taxes, although Ceasar seems to want more every year. We trade with people. I do work for the flour maker so your mother can bake bread. I repair plows and machinery in exchange for farmers' wine and lamb, though we rarely have lamb to eat. Mary trades eggs for cloth. We get by."

"Why did you become a carpenter, or should I say tekton?"

"My father, Jacob, was a man of many talents," Joseph explained. "He could fix anything. I was his youngest, and he showed me how to use certain tools. As I grew older, I taught myself some skills. Sometimes, Jesus, you have to figure things out for yourself."

Joseph made a few more chisel strikes on the door handle, rubbed out the rough spots, then brushed the dust from his apron. "There. I think that will do. I will stain it to match the door, let it dry, and take it over to Maurice this afternoon. Do you want to come along?"

"Father, there is dust in your beard. I've heard you say that Grandfather Jacob and his past generations were Canaanites. And Slam is called a Caanan dog. What does Caanan mean?"

"That's an interesting question," Joseph said. "I've always been told that Caanan was a wide area along the Great Sea, most of it west of the Jordan River. Some 10 or so generations ago our people, the Israelites, moved here and declared it the Promised Land. I suppose after roaming the deserts for years, it did appear promising.

"I suspect the Canaanites were a rather disorganized people, somewhat nomadic. The Scripture identifies them as the descendants of Caanan, a son of Ham and grandson of Noah. As for Slam, I would guess his breed was so named because some Canaanites used dogs for tending sheep. Now, are you drained of questions for today?"

"No. I still have lots of questions."

"Like what?"

"Why was I born in Bethlehem and not in Nazareth? Do they have better birth assistants there?"

"I think I have explained this before," Joseph said. "Ceasar Augustas ordered a census be taken, that is a counting of all the people. It was mostly so the Romans could keep track of taxpayers. Since we are of the House of David, we are required to register in our hometown, Bethlehem. While we were there, you were born. It was a hard trip for your mother, sometimes walking, sometimes riding on Dynamo, for seven days."

"And then you couldn't find a place to stay."

"That's right. For a while I thought we'd have to pitch a tent in the open field, but a kind lady let us stay in her barn and even helped with your birth. It was a cave-like structure and cows and sheep shared a place with you. It was a hectic time. Then you had lots of visitors. And right after your presentation in the Temple in Jerusalem, we went to Egypt."

"That was because of mean Herod."

"Right. Jesus, let's have something to eat, then deliver this door handle."

"OK. C'mon Slam."

Chapter 17

NAZARETH, about 12 AD – It was unusual for Jesus to toss and turn in his sleep. Ordinarily, he slept like a bushed Bedouin. Finally, he rose from his mat, quietly put on his outer garments and slipped out of the house. Joseph saw him leave but said nothing.

Jesus walked a short distance from home, then stopped and stared as the sun inched over the hills east of Nazareth. The more he gazed in the distance the less things came into focus. Questions drifted through his mind. While the red morning sky was cloudless, his head was laden with a muddle of competing and intertwining issues. Serenity was overcome by mystification.

It was not the first time he pondered life's meaning and his role in it, but never before had he lost any sleep over it. This episode came on like a swarm of chaotic bees, a buzz of unorganized thoughts. It shook his developing body and disturbed his expanding mind. Jesus was facing maturity from a whole different perspective.

He was 11, educated in the Scriptures and aware of prophesy. His parents had told him about his conception and birth, their flight to Egypt. Slowly, like spring rains seep into the soil, his destiny was coming to light in the back recesses of his mind. But the ultimate proclamation of his mission and his real identity was still being forged.

Instead of the flat-out declaration that God said to Moses, *I am who am,* Jesus was asking, *Who am I.*

As he continued a slow walk down the hill the rising sun, unable to keep up, fell behind the hills. The shadows reflected his mental state. Near the bottom of the incline he sat beneath a stately sycamore tree, standing tall and unconventional amid a grove of competing undergrowth. He'd been down the path many times before but now the sycamore took on a new distinctiveness. He looked up at its proud canopy.

The sun gradually escaped the blocking hills, converted shadows to elongated contortions and made the sycamore even more unique. A smile of nascent understanding spread on Jesus' face. All the talk about what his parents said about his birth, why Herod the Great was so concerned about him as a baby and the prophesy down through the centuries. How did this all add up?

Was he more than just human? He didn't feel he was any different than his friends. When he fell down last year on some rocks, his knee bled just as Josiah's finger oozed blood when he caught it in a door. He became hungry, tired, sick and restless like any other child. Yet, he seemed to fit what was outlined in the Scriptures.

Could he be the fulfillment of Isaiah?

According to his parents, his conception and birth accounts say so. The visiting magi said so. Simeon said so clearly at Jesus' circumcision at the Temple in Jerusalem. According to Jewish law, Mary and Joseph took their son to the Temple eight days after his birth. The Holy Spirit had revealed to Simeon, a devout, elderly Jew, that he would not die until his eyes had seen the Savior. That day he saw Jesus and took him in his arms.

"'Sovereign Lord, as you have promised, you may now dismiss your servant in peace," Simeon had declared. "For my eyes have seen your salvation, which you have prepared in the sight of all people, a light for revelation to the Gentiles and for glory to your people Israel." Looking at Mary, he continued, "'This child is destined to cause the falling and rising of many in Israel, and to be a sign that will be spoken against, so that the thoughts of many hearts will be revealed. And a sword will pierce your own soul too."

The words, as recalled by his mother, were burned into Jesus' memory. What does it all mean?

And then there was the idea expressed by the prophets that the Messiah would not only come from God but be God. God would take on human form. As Jesus contemplated the complex concept of the Messiah having two natures, divine as well as human, he vowed to explore that and other matters with rabbis and elders at some future Passover visit to Jerusalem.

"You seem to be a captive of your thoughts," a voice accompanied a tap on Jesus' shoulder. Joseph sat down next to Jesus. "Anything I can do to help? Your mother and I saw you leave. She said you looked troubled. Mothers always have unique ability to diagnose." Jesus smiled, relieved to have the disruption.

"Father, thanks for being here. Have things ever popped into your mind while sleeping, and rattle around keeping you awake?"

"Yes. I think that happens to everyone. What stirred you awake?"

"Things."

"What things?"

"Well, what will I do when I grow up.?"

"I had questions, too, when I was your age," he said softly, "but I suspect your questions are different than mine were. You are a unique person, Jesus, a young man with a divine nature. That's difficult to comprehend, to grow into. But that's what God has told us, that you are the fulfillment of the scriptural prophesy.

"How this will evolve in the years ahead I cannot say. My meager suggestion is that you just let it happen. You will know the way. Now, let's go to breakfast."

Josiah came over at midday, the issues of adulthood set aside. They had been goofing off in general, then racing and playing kickball. Strong appetites developed and led to hunger declarations as to who was the most famished and a dare about who could eat the most.

"I could devour a whole lamb," Josiah crowed.

"O, yeah!" Jesus countered. "I could gobble down a lamb, eat some bread and fruit, finish off leftover fish and still be hungry."

Mary had placed bread, honey and milk on the table and reminded the boys that there was fruit in the storage cellar. She had gone outside to work in the garden, and then returned. By then, the boasting boys had stuffed themselves until they were green in the gills.

"Mah, I don't feel so good. My stomach hurts." Jesus groaned and rubbed his belly to accentuate the location of his discomfort. On the other side of the table his friend, Josiah, was having similar distress. He said nothing, only swallowed deeply to counter any propensity his gurgling stomach may have to release.

"It must have been something I ate," Jesus said with a hangdog look.

"What did you eat?" Mary asked, caressing his head in a loving, maternal manner. She entwined her fingers in the curly locks of his nape.

"Mah, please! It doesn't hurt up there. It's my stomach."

"I know. I know. How many honey sandwiches did you have? Two?"

"It was more than that."

"How many more?"

"It was more like four."

"Four? No wonder . . ."

"And I had some grapes and palm dates. And a few figs."

"My oh my," Mary gasped. "Your stomach is not that big. What about you, Josiah? Do you feel sick, too?"

Josiah nodded and hoped the mixture of consumed bread, honey, fruit and figs would stay down.

"I'm going to give both of you some herbal medicine," Mary said. "Then lie down on the mats over in the corner. Perhaps rest will calm your upset stomachs. What were you boys thinking?"

It wasn't the only time the two courted trouble. Josiah accompanied Jesus one day to gather eggs from Mary's hens. In the process, an egg toss game materialized. Each successful catch meant participants took a step backward. Gravity and errancy took their course. The cost was a broken egg and Jesus had none for two weeks.

On another occasion, Jesus and Josiah returned from a fishing trip with no fish but with tunics caked in mud. Both were ordered to scrub their dirty britches on a stone and hang them on a clothesline next to Joseph's shop.

While spending time with buddies had a high priority for Jesus, it didn't trump Synagogue school. Mary saw to that. When Jesus turned 10, his religious education focused on the Oral Torah, statutes and legal interpretations that were not part of the Five Books of Moses – the written law. It encompassed a general array of worship practices, guides to relationships with God and other people, festival observances and rules of civil procedure.

Jesus loved Passover. As a little boy he accompanied his parents to Jerusalem though was not old enough to be considered part of the official Jewish community. Last year his friend Josiah took care of Slam while Jesus went to Passover festivities. But now Josiah and his family went on the pilgrimage, too. They were excited to make the trip together, but first they had to find a caretaker for Slam and Rex for three weeks.

The good news was that an acquaintance of Mary's agreed to watch the dogs. The bad news was that this neighbor lived next door to Chloe Adontz, a situation that made Joseph uncomfortable. He envisioned some sort of problem that would be magnified and "who knows, end up in the emperor's court in Rome." Mary said he was overreacting.

She was right. The dogs would be the least of their problems during Passover journey.

Getting ready for the trip to Jerusalem was a sizeable task. Mary packed various colored tunics, mostly pastels, and mantles for herself, and tan shades of garments for Joseph and Jesus. Since it was the unpredictable time of Nisan (spring), she had to plan for both cool and warm weather. They took dried fruits and herbs, foods that would not spoil along the way, and cooking utensils. Joseph boxed up tent materials.

All would be piled on a rented ass, not unlike the arrangements for their trip to and from Egypt when Jesus was an infant. Dynamo, the trustworthy donkey that hauled all the family's belongings then, died nearly a year ago. Because of pasture and barn rental fees, Joseph decided not to purchase a replacement animal.

The unusually large caravan from the Nazareth, led by a hired guide, included many relatives and friends of Mary and Joseph. Soon a group from Nain, including the family of Jesus' friend, Eli, joined them. Farmers and their families, pulling supply-laden animals, merged into the parade. The three boys, now more mature, helped with the daily chores associated with being part of a large troupe. They had assigned jobs and a new sense of independence.

Josiah and Eli, still not ready to totally abandon the carefree ways of youth, noticed a change in Jesus, now 12. It was hard to explain. He certainly hadn't surrendered his penchant for conversation, but he tended to talk more about faith, emphasizing the importance of the Passover festival and how it honored Jewish life and tradition. They tried to loosen his serious side.

"Jesus," Eli probed on the third day of travel. "Did you happen to notice that yafa (good-looking) almah (young woman) in the family up ahead?"

Jesus smiled.

"Well. Did you?" Eli persisted.

"What? Do you think I am blind," Jesus responded, getting a poke in the ribs for his honesty. Josiah picked up on the levity stream.

"Here's a Passover joke," he looked at the other two with a wide grin of anticipated acceptance. "Why did the matzah quit his baking job?" He waited for a response, but none came. He was disappointed.

"C'mon guys. Think." Still, no answer. Finally, the punch line begged for release. "Because he didn't get a raise!"

Eli and Jesus joined in the guffawing, affirming Josiah's joke telling. True to nature that beget another story.

"OK, OK. Here's a good one. An Egyptian task master fell down a wishing well. The Hebrew slave was amazed. He said: 'I never knew they worked'."

"Enough already," Eli cried.

The pilgrimage was a joyous one, a celebration of song, prayer and food. The air was infused with the strains of many harps. Trumpets blared their praise. When the delegation reached the outskirts of Jerusalem, Roman officials noted that one of the few campsites remaining was in the hills north of the Mount of Olives. That's where the Nazareth group pitched tents.

Mary had suggested that they stay with her cousin Elizabeth at the west edge of Jerusalem, but Joseph said there was not enough room there for the entire Nazareth group. He believed they should remain with their own caravan.

The city and region were jammed with 120,000 visitors. The environs were filled with caravan animals and their tenders. It required massive preparations to accommodate that many people and livestock. It was an amazing spectacle. Smells and sounds added to a setting that was unforgettable. The streets were crowded; vendors overwhelmed.

On the second day, as some were still arriving and others getting settled, claps of thunder echoed in the deep valleys surrounding the city. Then the rain came, not in torrents, but a gentle and warm drizzle that felt like the touch of God. It didn't send anyone scurrying. Rather, many looked heavenly, arms stretched upward. Children, and older people, too, danced. It was especially delightful for the desert visitors. Jerusalem is mostly an arid climate, with the so-called rainy season occurring earlier.

It was not an easy journey from the Mount of Olives campsite to the Sheep Gate, the closest entrance to the holy city. The narrow, hilly paths were congested. Assigned times of visitation and numerous Roman soldiers eased the procedure. Once purification rituals were completed, families were permitted to begin the Seder meal.

At a specific time, Joseph and male relatives purchased a one-year-old male lamb and took it to the Temple courtyard for slaughter and skinning. Chanting of psalms accompanied by brass transpired during the butchering process. Then the gutted lamb was taken to the campsite and roasted, later to be served with matzah (unleavened bread) and wine. Prayers attended the feasting.

Blessed are you, O Lord our God, king of the universe, who has created the fruit of the vine. . . And you, O Lord our God, have given us festival days for joy, this feast of the unleavened bread, the time of our deliverance in remembrance of the departure from Egypt. Blessed are you, O Lord our God, who has kept us alive, sustained us and enabled us to enjoy this season.

Jesus inhaled the full parameters of the festival, reveling in his Jewish culture. He already attached meaning to Passover beyond the freeing of his ancestors. His thoughts burned to the point where they yearned for expression. By now familiar with the layout of the city, especially the Temple area, he decided to test his ideas with elders.

On the night before the Nazareth caravan was to return home, Jesus and his two buddies helped pack up. The Mount of Olives campsite, as upon arrival, was a cacophonous mass of disorganization. Like on any trip, the thought of going home to familiar settings and life was comforting. But Jerusalem pulled at Jesus. It was almost a feeling that he was already home. He aided Joseph in bundling and securing all the components of temporary living, but his mind was elsewhere.

Jesus rose with the others before daybreak. Early meal was taken, and then they loaded supplies atop the donkey and strapped them down.

He moved down the road, assisting others along the way with departure chores. Once the caravan guide checked with all the family heads, the trumpet sounded to signal the start home. The group slowly proceeded northward.

The sun lazily announced the new day as it stretched over the eastern hills. The air was clear, a fine time for travel. There were similar scenes in all directions as Jerusalem exhaled the horde of visitors. Another Passover Festival was completed and ordinary time ticked into place.

As on the way south, the home trek for the Nazareth families would take most of the week. Joseph and Mary believed that Jesus was with his friends.

Rather, Jesus lingered behind.

He had hardly slept, thinking most of the night about who he was and where he was going. Once again he was lost in the perplexity of a dual nature. For some time, he suspected he was different, but was it all because of his love of Scripture? Was it because he, like his parents, had a profound love of Mosaic law? There seemed to be an accumulation of signs that it was more than that.

When he was six, he had asked his mother about an unusual vision. Mary knew that day would come. She struggled with it. What to say? How to explain? He told her that sometime the previous year, when he was in the carpenter shop with Joseph, he had bent over to pick up some heavy nails. Sunlight beamed through a window. As he stooped, he told her he noticed the shadow of a cross behind him.

Mary, fearing an incoherent, stammering response, had asked a frivolous question: *You said that happened last year?* When Jesus replied that that was the case, she was pressed to come up with a real answer. At first, she thought the best course was to talk over the matter with Joseph. After a brief debate with herself, she had said: *I believe what you saw, Jesus, was a sign that there are crosses in life, things we all must endure.*

She was surprised at his easy acceptance of her words. He said 'OK,' and ran off and played. But the incident prompted her to talk with Joseph about the right time and place to fully explain to Jesus about his special nature, that he was both human and the son of God – a divine person. They waited. At eight, they overheard him in prayerful discussion with "God the Father," talking as in a normal way. They waited.

At age 10, before Passover, they had decided to tell Jesus the story, the details of his conception, his birth in Bethlehem, the flight to Egypt, how God had planned to take human form to reconcile the sin passed down as described in Genesis. Mary suggested they withhold talking about the final chapter.

When they finished, Mary added: "That's why, my child, you are and will always be known as the son of man and son of God."

She and Joseph were surprised to learn that Jesus knew it all. He cited the Scriptures that foretold it and the prophetic references about God's plan for salvation. He, too, omitted any reference to the final days, saving that discussion for another time. Now, in the wake of another Passover, he contemplated all these things as he looked back toward Jerusalem, the focus of this mission.

He started walking toward the city, down through the Kidron Valley, nodding to those streaming in the other direction. After a time, he sat on a stone in the shade of an oak tree, head down, thinking, apprehensive but determined.

"Are you lost, young fellow?" a man tapped Jesus on the shoulder, startling him from mediation. Like nearly every other visitor, the man was leaving Jerusalem.

"No, not exactly," Jesus replied awkwardly. "Just thinking. I'll be OK."

"Thinking, eh? That's a mighty big assignment for a boy. Sure you're OK? What's running through that young mind of yours? Family issues?"

"You might put it that way, although not what you think," Jesus replied, putting a puzzled look on the stranger's face. "I'm going one way," he said. "People are going another way. I hope that's not a bad sign."

"Sounds to me as if you are lost."

"I guess I'm still caught up in all the meanings of the Passover festival," Jesus said. "God led Moses and our ancestors out of slavery.

Our people wandered around for another 40 years and have always been on the move. Are we still lost in some ways?"

"Son, the day is getting along and my feet are already tired. These questions are beyond my thinking right now. Maybe tonight, in the glow of some wine, I would be better able to respond." He reached in a sack that was slung over his left shoulder. "Here are a few figs and some bread. That'll fill up some of the hollow spots in your stomach. Is there something else I can do for you?"

"No. Really, I'll be fine. But thanks for your concern, and thanks for the figs. The Lord be with you always."

With that the man departed, a strange look on his face. Jesus was once again alone with his thoughts. He proceeded up the rock-strew path toward the old city. Just outside the Sheep Gate at the northeast corner of the walled city, near the Bethesda pool, he found a tent and blanket, remnants of a discarded shelter. He decided to camp there for the night, feasting on his figs and pondering his future.

His mind drifted. *Jerusalem.* The word reverberated in his mind. This was his fourth visit and he was still in awe of the city, particularly the Temple Mount. He knew it was the center of Jewish faith. For centuries the Temple housed the Holy of Holies, the Ark of the Covenant. The golden-plated cedar chest contained the two tablets of law given by God to Moses. The Ark was placed there after King Solomon constructed the First Temple.

Jesus also knew that the Temple was destroyed by invading Babylonians nearly six centuries ago and the Ark of the Covenant removed. Even now, as he looked toward the walled city, it saddened him to realize that the Ark was still missing. After the Jewish people returned from exile, construction of a second Temple was begun. It was completed by Herod the Great.

Jerusalem. Jesus' mind was captivated by one of the oldest cities in the world. But for him it was more than a place. It was the holy presence of God. It was the real home for Jewish people. It was his home. Yet, his human nature resisted the idea of waltzing into the Temple precinct and discussing Scripture and the intentions of God with appointed leaders and elders.

But his divine nature persisted and prevailed.

The next morning, he rose with new fervor. He was bursting with questions that were imbedded with his own observations. He walked through the northern gate, ambled past the Antonia Fortress, the citadel constructed by Herod the Great to protect the Temple, then continued southerly through the western portico (later the western wall area). As he strode around the south side of the Temple, he was awed by the facades and pinnacles.

Once on the east side, he faced the massive 15-story Temple. Jesus, the son of man, was still nervous and second-guessed his presence. But Jesus, the son of God, advanced to the men's court. Only selected priests were allowed in the Temple sanctuary.

He paused at one of the steps. As the day progressed and with Passover visitors gone, the usual Temple teachers and elders, some dressed in vivid robes, congregated in the outside court. As Jesus approached, he could hear a general buzzing, mostly a Passover review. God would be pleased, one said, at the record crowds. Another expressed pleasure that so many had paid tribute to God's mercy in leading Moses and the Hebrew nation out of slavery.

Suddenly, these grizzled veterans of Jewish Scripture and culture, men learned in the law, were confronted by a smooth-faced juvenile whose drab tunic barely covered his knees. Who was this upstart who invaded their space? Relieved that the tumult of Passover was over, and the routine of everyday life restored, now comes this interloper to muddy up the day.

Similarly, Jesus didn't know any of them. Ananus, father-in-law of Caiaphas, was the high priest, but neither he nor his court was among the gathering. Jesus approached them as if he were in Synagogue school back home.

"God be with you," Jesus addressed the group with accuracy. "Please, may I join you in your discussions and deliberations?"

Six men unaccustomed to interruptions from strangers, least of all from a child, were aghast at Jesus' spirit. Most 12-year-olds would rather be fishing or playing kickball than discussing Scripture.

"Who are you and where are you from? Are you lost?" one of teachers asked.

"I am Jesus of Nazareth, and I'm not lost. I just want to ask some questions."

"How old are you? Is your father a rabbi?"

"I am 12, and my father is a carpenter. Of the house of David."

"Twelve, you say. Well, you are still a year away from being a full member of the Jewish community. What's on your mind?"

"May I sit down? At home everyone sits on the ground around the rabbi for our lessons."

Some in the group were members of the Temple Sanhedrin, the high tribunal of the Jews who oversaw religious, civil and criminal matters. When not in court, they were accustomed to visiting and teaching in the court area. They looked at one another with bewildered faces. Eventually, one of the elders with eyebrows raised, decided to reply.

"Sure. Sure," he said, baffled as to what else to say. "Please. Sit down."

"May I ask some questions."

"Oh," the designated responder hastened to answer. "By all means. Ask whatever you'd like."

There was a low gurgling of laughter as the elders anticipated a form of entertainment, some easy queries that a rookie rabbi could answer in his sleep, certainly no issues of significance. The lad, one whispered, may end up embarrassed for his chutzpah.

"Thank you," Jesus said, his confidence growing. "I heard some of you talking about the Passover festival. It was wonderful. But I wondered. What do you see as a possible extended meaning of the annual celebration? The Pharaoh released our people from slavery. They were freed from physical bondage. Are we still, today, in spiritual bondage? Are we so bound by all the laws as to be blinded to our real goal – everlasting life with God?"

Some of the raised eyebrows pressed upward on foreheads. Clearly, that was no ordinary question and this was no ordinary young person. But these men were not novices, untrained teachers devoid of the elements of debate and discussion. A good device is to sometimes answer a question with another question. A man cleared his throat.

"Are you suggesting that the laws we administer somehow diminish our genuine purpose in celebrating Passover? What, pray tell, would you change?" he asked.

"I'm not sure about Festival events," Jesus replied, "What would you say if more emphasis was given to changing ourselves, changing how we treat one another?"

"Well," the elder said, "we can always be more generous in how we get along. Have you witnessed discord among our people, a lack of respect?"

"People are basically good," Jesus said, "but I would ask – in your deliberations of disputes – do you sense real forgiveness? Is mercy, even common courtesy, in evidence? After loving God with our whole heart and soul, shouldn't we love our neighbors as ourselves?"

"You show unusual insight for a youngster," the elder said. Others in the group, which had grown two-fold, nodded their agreement. "Your teacher is exceptional or you have innate abilities of your own, or maybe both. What other matters interest you?"

"When do you think the Messiah will come? Jesus asked.

"Aha. "That's a good question," a teacher replied, "to which there are many answers. Just as there are many answers to other questions. For example, as a Sadducees, which by the way is the party of the high priest, I have no idea when or if a Messiah will come. We don't believe in the resurrection of the body. My Zealot friend sees the Messiah as a sort of military leader who will chase out the Romans.

"And my Pharisee brothers believe in an afterlife. While they reject the influences of the Greeks, they sincerely believe that the Pharisee authority is most accepted by the common people. And they claim we Sadducees mostly represent the elite and wealthy. So, you can see, young fellow, that while we believe in the same God, the God of Abraham, there are differences."

"He exaggerates," an elder stood up in the rear. "We agree on far more things than we disagree, though I will say the Sadducees speaker enjoys being contrary. We all wish the Romans would leave. Some of us just say it a little louder. But I am intrigued by your inquisitiveness. I have more questions for you. Are you surprised by all our differences?

Are you in agreement with some of us about resurrection and an afterlife? And are you a believer in the God of Abraham?"

Before Jesus could answer, the elder popped a final question. "About the coming of the Messiah, your original question. What do you say?"

"I think he could be among us," Jesus replied directly.

The teachers looked at each other, puzzled by the reply. *Ask him,* one whispered to a colleague, *why he thinks such a thing.* The suggestion eventually found its way to the front and gained form.

"Those in the back wonder: What causes you to think the Messiah may be among us?" the Sadducees elder rounded out the probe. "Why do you say that?"

"I am confident in myself," Jesus answered.

So concluded the mysterious exchange between the boy and the elders. There was a general mumbling as they departed, some shaking their heads in wonder. It was not a confrontation, but a spiritual dialogue that at least in the moment had the teachers questioning themselves.

Jesus returned to his patched-together shelter outside the city for the night, his entire being lifted by the Temple experience. His head swirled with more questions. He was bent on a second day of discussions with Temple teachers. The notion of going home to his life in Nazareth was suffocated by the excitement of being in Jerusalem and talking Scripture with the Jewish teachers.

He ate the two remaining figs before he went to bed. His make-shift tent featured gaping spaces, overhead openings for a generous display of the heavens. He reclined on his back, hands folded beneath his head for a pillow. He gazed upward, his mind a kaleidoscope of thoughts that spun him into a deep sleep. He envisioned lines of people, marching toward the Temple, laughing, talking, helping one another when needed. Children played. There were no arguments or shoving. Rather, people shared bread, sang songs and prayed.

The sun was already shining brightly when he was startled awake by something licking on his right toe. He abruptly sat up, rubbed his eyes and watched a lamb nibble the scant grass around his feet. Jesus smiled broadly and reached out to pet the wooly creature, but it suddenly darted away and rejoined the flock. He stretched and quickly reinserted himself into the wonders of a new day in Jerusalem.

He prayed.

Mary was half out of her mind. Joseph tried to calm her, assuring her that Jesus, though apparently missing from the caravan, was safe. She was worried the night before when he didn't appear for supper. Now, the next morning, he wasn't present for the first meal of the day. Skipping a meal, she noted to Joseph, is not a common thing for Jesus.

"Mary, he is 12, and at the stage where he is capable to care for himself," Joseph said. Silently, he was troubled, too. And more than a little irritated. Why would Jesus wander off without saying anything? "I'll check with everyone in our group, and perhaps those ahead of us. I have already asked Josiah and Eli, and they say they haven't seen him either. Josiah also said that Jesus can fend for himself, get along on little. I asked the two if he seemed upset or in any other way not himself."

"Not himself!" Mary broke in. "That's a loaded question, Joseph. Which himself? Don't complicate the matter, Joseph. Did they answer your question? I realize he has special gifts but he could be hurt."

"Eli said Jesus seemed distant the last couple of days, that his mind was far off sometimes. He said Jesus wanted to talk about the deeper meaning of Scripture. Eli suggested that Jesus may never have left the Jerusalem area. I am going to make another round to check with people, and if there is nothing new, I say we turn around and return to Jerusalem."

Finding no new information, Joseph informed the caravan leader that he and Mary were headed back to Jerusalem. It would be a long day. The season of spring was moving to hotter days. It was a solemn trip. Nary a word was spoken. That evening, exhausted, Joseph pitched camp on the Mount of Olives, near the place they had lived during the festival. They ate little, retired early, and rose at daybreak.

Even three days after the festival had ended there were pilgrims leaving the city. Joseph scanned each group, asking guides if they had seen a 12-year-old lad dressed in a light brown tunic. No one had. They walked through the Sheep Gate on the northern side, eyes probing every place and every group. It was approaching midday when they rounded a corner near the outer court of the Temple. Joseph tethered his donkey and they entered the court area.

There he was!

Mary began to run, so excited she nearly tripped on her blue-green tunic. Her cream-colored mantle was flying in all directions. A smile filled her face. Her outstretched arms preceded her body, anticipating holding him tightly. She suppressed a scream. Joseph saw him, too, but strolled along at his usual pace, staff in hand. He was excited and perturbed at the same time.

At first Jesus did not seen them. Once again, his questions and comments astounded the teachers. He was standing on some steps, surrounded by rabbis and elders, a crowd three times the size of the previous day. Others approached, leaned in to get a drift of the discussion, which presently centered on Scripture figures and prophets who wrote about a future Messiah or redeemer for the Jewish nation.

"The visionary, Isaiah, made several mentions of a Messiah when he wrote some seven centuries ago," one of the elders noted. Others cited the words of Jeremiah and Ezekiel. Some argued that whenever a Messiah-like king would come it would likely mark the end of the world.

Several stood and argued that this notion of an apocalyptic concurrence with a redeemer king was so much meshuggeneh. Jesus, without revealing his own heritage, asked a question to which he already had the answer: "Didn't Isaiah specify that the redeemer would come from the house of David?" he piped up, hoping to break through the verbal fog of a half dozen speakers.

Then he saw his mother. He ran down the steps and past the crowd. The two embraced. He was nearly as tall as Mary. Her eyes flooded with tears. Her body shook with joy. He held her briefly, somewhat surprised by her emotions. Joseph smiled and watched. Finally, she gathered her feelings and looked him in the face.

"Son, why have you done this to us? Your father and I have been looking for you with great anxiety."

Joseph said nothing but was thinking plenty.

"Why were you looking for me? Did you not know that I must be in my Father's house?"

Neither Mary nor Joseph understood his words. Mary was too overwhelmed at finding Jesus to prolong her inquiry. As on other occasions, she wrote the matter on the journal of her heart. Joseph had plenty to say but decided it would be best to postpone any rebuke. Mary knew he was fuming. She took him aside and gently soothed his anger.

"All I can say is that you can't enjoy the glory of sunshine," Mary counseled, "until you pass through the storm."

The family returned to Nazareth.

Chapter 18

CAPERNAUM, GALILEE, about 30 AD – I have to be honest. I was shocked when Jesus told me he had selected Levi the tax collector as one of his followers. I suggested to him that Levi is about as popular as a leper at a festival, one of the most hated guys in all Capernaum. Levi is more likely to spread conflict than the kingdom of God. To think that I, Simon, and my brother, Andrew, are on the same team is embarrassing.

Jesus said it is wrong to hate anyone, and that Levi is a new person who is sorry for his wrongful actions. Jesus even gave him a new name, Matthew, like that will erase his history of gouging people and working for the Romans. Jesus has this warped sense of forgiveness. I say maybe forgive once, but not for years of transgressions. Jesus said I should pray about my attitude toward Levi, as if I am the one who needs help.

He spent the night with Enid and me, and after first meal left for Bethsaida to the east. It's usually an easy two-hour walk, but Jesus has a habit of talking with nearly everyone along the way. He intends on seeing Philip and his friend, Nathaniel. He also plans to visit Andrew and our father Jonah.

The path to Bethsaida is a meandering one. In places it follows grassy plains, and in other areas it shifts near the shores of the Sea of Galilee. Beads of sweat formed on Jesus' forehead. He looked northeastward and saw barren hillsides. It reminded him of the scant faith some have in God. His mind then focused on his second cousin, John the Baptist, and Herod Antipas. Rumors were flying that John's criticism of Antipas' extra-marital lifestyle was making the tetrarch's household tense.

Somewhere far off on the sloping meadows he heard the faint tinkling of a bell and assumed it came from a herd of sheep. However, the tall grasses concealed any animals and herdsman. His nostrils were awash in the competing fragrances of legumes and sea water.

Suddenly, he came to the ford where travelers cross the narrow Jordan River. He waded across and was soon at the outskirts of Bethsaida. A short distance away the Jordan, fed by several tiny streams to the north, enters the Sea of Galilee. Eventually, the Jordan exits the south end of the Sea of Galilee and flows into the Dead Sea.

Some fishermen, who had gone out early in the day, were already returning with their catches. As he walked into town, Jesus noticed a group of rough-looking men talking outside a building festooned in nets and ropes. He quickly surmised it was the outfitter run by Philip's family. The smell of fish and what was left after cleaning them saturated the air and punished the nose.

As he neared the business, a bearded fellow glanced toward him and immediately the greeter's facial hair parted into a wide smile. It was Andrew.

"Jesus of Nazareth!" he yelled. He walked quickly toward Jesus and hugged him. "What?" he grinned, "have you decided to give up the preaching profession to become a fisherman?"

Jesus grabbed the shorter man by both shoulders. "Andrew. It's good to see you. Praise the Lord. I'm afraid I would make a poor fisherman. Too many things to remember – currents, depths, water temperature, weather. No. I'm still fishing for men to join my ministry, and I thank you for saying *yes.* I've come to visit Philip, who has joined the band, and he wants to introduce me to Nathaniel."

"Good luck on that," Andrew said. "You heard what Nathaniel said after Philip told him about you?" Jesus shrugged. "Well, Nathaniel, some call him Bartholomew, comes from your neck of the woods – over at Cana. He and Philip are good friends. One day not long ago, Philip saw him sitting beneath a fig tree and told him: *'We have found the one Moses wrote about in the Law, and about whom the prophets also wrote – Jesus of Nazareth, the son of Joseph.'* And do you know what Nathaniel said?" Jesus didn't reply.

Andrew continued. "Nathaniel scoffed, *'A Messiah from Nazareth!! Can anything good come from there?'* But Philip encouraged him '*to come see for yourself*'. Now I don't know the background of all this, if Cana residents just have a superior attitude or if Nazareth has a bad standing. I can tell you this. Nathaniel is one skeptical man."

"Skepticism is not all bad," Jesus said. "It keeps people from stepping into quicksand. Or being taken in by a false prophet. I'll talk to him. Like always, it will be his choice. I just came from Simon and Eden's place, and they are fine. They say 'hello'. Her mother is sickly. Now, how have you been and the health of your father Jonah?"

"My father is doing OK, but the rigor of running a boat is taking its toll. He says his knees and back are paying the price. I would expect Simon to be hale. He's too ornery to get sick. I swear the man has an unending supply of energy. Let's go up to the store. Father has gone home, but Philip should be there. And he'll know where to find Nathaniel."

Before they reached the front door, Philip exited. "I saw you approach," he said, arms extended. "It's wonderful to see you again, Jesus. I see Andrew almost every day, and I was hoping you would visit before too long. I trust your mother is fine and the carpenter business is going well."

"All is well with mother and the business," Jesus replied. "As for Nazareth, there are those who doubt my mission. Like Nathaniel they question if anything good can come from Nazareth."

"Ah, I see that Andrew has been telling you about Nathaniel. He can be a stiff-necked sort, but then we all have our cantankerous days. Just for your information, he doesn't think highly of Bethsaida either. Unless you want a tour of the family business, perhaps you would like to meet him now? Andrew, would you mind if we went off to talk to Nathaniel?"

"Not at all. I wish you good fortune, Jesus," Andrew said. "And you must promise to come back and have supper with us. And, we have an extra mat for sleeping." Jesus agreed.

Nathaniel was only a year younger than Jesus. While a native of Cana, he had worked odd jobs in the Jordan River area for some time. Like most Galilean men his dress was simple. His beard was long. His father, Tolmai, and brothers operated a fig tree farm outside Cana. In the off-season, Nathaniel often sought work elsewhere.

"I think we'll find him down by the water," Philip said. He often finds work in helping fishermen unload." They walked the short distance through a glade of willows and soon heard the gentle lap of waves. There were a half dozen fishing boats in the small harbor and others approaching in the distance. Nathaniel was with a crew working with nets on the far end.

"Nathaniel!" Philip shouted. "Nathaniel! I have someone here you should meet." The Canaanite dropped some ropes and walked toward Philip. He rubbed his hands together, brushing off sand. He was bare-chested and sweaty.

"I'm not too presentable for a social meeting," Nathaniel said as he thrust a greeting hand forward to Philip. He suspected the man with Philip was Jesus. He nodded in Jesus' direction.

"Nathaniel. This is Jesus of Nazareth, the man I recently told you about. Remember? You were sitting beneath that old fig tree east of here. You said you were trying to figure out the world and your place in it. You were not in a good mood that day."

"Yes. I recall, Philip," Nathaniel replied with a look of discomfort. "How do you do, Mr. Jesus," he extended his hand.

"Greetings, Nathaniel" Jesus replied, shaking Nathaniel's grimy paw. "You have been laboring."

"Yes, but it is fun work."

"Behold, here is a true Galilean," Jesus continued. "There is no duplicity in him."

"How do you know me?" Nathaniel asked.

"Before Philip called you, I saw you under the fig tree."

"Rabbi," Nathaniel said in astounding conversion, "you are the son of God; you are the king of Israel."

"Do you believe because I told you that I saw you under a fig tree? You will see greater things than this."

Nathaniel was aghast. *He sees what I was thinking under the fig tree and what is in my heart.*

"Amen, amen, I say to you," Jesus referred to Jacob in Genesis, "you will see the sky opened and the angels of God ascending and descending on the son of man."

Later, Jesus, troubled about the safety of his cousin, talked with Philip about it. Philip, who knew John the Baptist long before he met Jesus, had little new information except that the unconventional man was still baptizing people in the Jordan River and preaching the nearness of salvation.

Philip surmised that Herod Antipas loathed John because of his preaching about Jewish law regarding marriage and divorce. It all began when the Herod brothers, Antipas and Philip the tetrarch of Decapolis, both sons of Herod the Great, became involved in a marital muddle. Antipas with a wandering eye, formally left his own wife and married his brother's wife though the latter had not yet been divorced.

That night Jesus stayed at Andrew's house. The following day he returned to Nazareth. When Mary greeted him, she also handed him two more orders for work. It was clear the carpentry business and his ministry on behalf of the kingdom of God were competing for time.

"Are you hungry?" Mary asked, "or did your friend, Simon the birdman, pack you something for the road?"

"Mother, I'm more convinced than ever that Simon is one of my strongest followers. And I have also convinced a fellow from Cana to be a herald of the good news. And, no, Simon didn't provide a knapsack. I'm famished. How about some of your famous bread and honey?"

"There's plenty," Mary answered. "I'm just surprised that coming back from the region's fishing capital that they didn't provide you with at least dried fish for the return." She then gave him a motherly squeeze and pat on the head. "It's good to have you back home." She knew these days were getting short. The future and his destiny never left her mind.

Jesus licked the honey partially off the bread, then bit into the fresh barley loaf. "When and how should we end the carpentry business?" he asked. He still spoke of it as a family enterprise. For Mary, the question had a final ring. He may as well have said, she thought, *When do I proceed to Jerusalem for the last days.* The clock had been ticking ever since his birth.

"I don't know, Jesus. You have developed a reputation in carpentry almost the equal of Joseph. You heard that I emphasized *almost.*" She tried to divert reality by shifting the discussion to the elements of woodworking. "Even Chloe, though she has become quite crippled, came by yesterday and said she had heard many excellent comments from your customers."

"Speaking of Chloe, is there any other news from the area?" Jesus inquired. "There is talk, and a fellow over in Bethsaida says it's true, that Herod Antipas is angry with my cousin, John. John, as you know, pulls no punches. He baptizes and preaches according to Scripture, and God is surely grateful to him. He does not follow a book on etiquette, just God's book."

"Chloe didn't mention anything, but then her sources may be drying up. How could baptizing people and preaching upset Antipas?"

"It has to do with marriage and divorce," Jesus replied.

"Well, I don't know if I ever told you, but when I became pregnant with you, before marriage to Joseph, divorce was something he considered. This is while we were betrothed. Neighbors were talking and upset. My parents were distressed. I could have been stoned. But the angel informed Joseph of the Holy Spirit's plan, and we were married. Now, trusting Joseph, holy Joseph, that's a loyal man."

"This is a different situation, mother. I was told that Antipas divorced his wife, married his brother's wife, even though she was not divorced. John called him out on the arrangement, making Antipas furious. Apparently the Herods have no room for decency and the law."

"John, for his own well-being, needs to remember that Antipas and the Romans are still in charge," Mary said, "and that means in charge of everything."

"He won't capitulate," Jesus replied. His mind returned to his own future. "Maybe Simon has some ideas on how to wind down the carpenter business. He knows a lot of people, and so does his father. Perhaps there is someone in Capernaum who would take over our shop."

"Maybe," Mary said. "Maybe Simon's bird artisan consultant would want to start a new profession."

"Really, mother. I tell you that you don't know this man, Simon."

Chapter 19

NAZARETH, 13AD – Joseph sat at the kitchen table and looked over the work requests. He shook his head. When would he ever catch up? He, Mary and Jesus had just returned from Passover in Jerusalem, and being gone had a price. It would be mid-summer before he would complete the job orders, not to mention newly gained projects. It was fortunate that he wasn't required to work in Sepphoris like his late father-law once had.

"That's what you get for being a good carpenter who charges a fair price," Mary said to cheer him up. It didn't work. She was beginning her daily baking chores after the early meal.

"I don't want to turn people away," Joseph continued, "nor do I want to disappoint them by pushing off their needs for weeks. I just wish there were more carpenters in the area. Fortunately, many farmers are also good fixers. They have a natural knack for doing things themselves rather than calling a repairman. Otherwise, I'd be smothered in work. Don't you agree, Mary?"

"What? You think I should have married a farmer, Joseph?"

"No. No. I didn't say *that*," he said, mildly agitated. "You took my comments out of context or something." He ran his fingers through his graying hair in contemplation. "Maybe, just maybe, "he half muttered to himself, "Jesus can be assigned some of the less complicated work. He must be trusted at some point."

"Joseph," Mary flitted about wielding pots and pans, "I have laundry to get caught up with, baking to do, a garden that needs hoeing, and chickens to feed. Do you know a house collects dust even when you are gone? And I want to thank neighbors who helped with chores while we were at Passover." She paused in matrimonial deference to let her words sink in.

"Would you rather be a beggar making his pleas at the edge of town? Or, a busy carpenter?"

That was sharp enough to raise Joseph out of his chair. He walked out the back door to his shop without another word. It was one of those times when a couple's conversation reaches a plateau of no return.

Later, as he was sanding a customer's cabinet, he glanced at an order for building a latticed fence to pen in a family's chickens. He had built such an enclosure for Mary's chickens. Why couldn't Jesus use that as a pattern for a similar fence. Joseph smiled, satisfied with his idea.

That night at table, earlier discussions forgotten, Joseph launched his strategy, fully expecting Mary to object at trusting Jesus with hammers, nails, saws and wire. He carefully plotted a proposal to circumvent a protective mother's shield. He was secretly congratulating himself on the plan's dimensions, smiling inwardly at his creative approach.

"Jesus, did you have a busy day?" Joseph inquired.

"Not really," Jesus replied. "After Scripture study, I delivered mother's thank you notes to neighbors, fed the chickens and hoed the garden. That didn't take long. My friends were busy, so the rest of the day was kinda boring. I wish I had some more challenging chores to do."

Joseph looked at Mary, a tiny, judicious grin seeping out the corners of his mouth. He couldn't have written a better script. It was almost too good to be true. Not only did Jesus complete Mary's chore list, but he also sought more confronting work, 'challenging', he had said. Joseph wasn't going to push that button too hard.

"I see," Joseph smiled. "What do you think of doing additional projects in the shop, beyond picking up nails, sweeping and organizing of scattered boards? Maybe a thinking project?"

"Really? What do you have in mind?" Jesus responded, his eyes sparkling with anticipation. Do you mean real jobs with hammering, and nails? Sawing?"

Joseph again sought out negative signs from Mary, expecting a decisive objection from her maternal bench.

"Well, yes. But I would be there to assist. You already know how to measure, saw and use other tools. I think you understand the importance of safety." He was going to add that a wood sliver, commonplace in working with lumber, was part of the maturing process, but he didn't want to push his luck.

"I have this request to construct a chicken fence for this woman, not far from here, just a short walk," Joseph explained. "I figure it could be just like the one we put up for your mother. You can dig holes for the posts, cut the proper length and number of slats here at the shop, carry them over to their back yard, and go at it."

Jesus, imagining the scope of responsibility, was all smiles.

"When you are finished, I will come over and inspect the work. If the customer and I are satisfied, I will send them a bill for the materials involved. Whatever they give you in talents for labor will be yours to keep. What do you think, Jesus?"

They both looked toward Mary for any motherly protests. Joseph's sales strategy was immune to any strong rebuttal points. He couldn't revisit his argument about the load of back orders. He had covered the safety element. Jesus knew the elements of carpentry and seemed delighted with the prospect of independent contracting. What, beyond their appealing faces, could be said for additional support?

"I think it is a splendid idea," Mary said in a nonchalant manner. "If no one wants any additional bread and honey, I will put them away."

Settled. Just like that. Not a single note of demurral. No questions. No warnings that 'he's just a boy'. No side reminders that 'you are dealing with the Son of God here so be careful'. Amazing! It was almost, Joseph regurgitated, as if it were her own idea.

"When do I start?" Jesus asked, shaking Joseph from a mixed state of achievement and surprise. He searched Mary's face again for belated disquiet and found none. He smiled.

"How about right now? We can walk over to the customer's yard, measure the area to be enclosed and present a plan to them. What do you say?"

"Let's go!" Jesus said.

The unnamed Nazareth enterprise of J&J Carpentry won the contract. Jesus completed the project, and not surprisingly took twice as long as Joseph would have. Joseph reviewed the work, made some trifling adjustments and sought the customer's approval. That received, all were happy. Jesus was ecstatic. For him responsibility, acceptance and accomplishment added up to success.

In ensuing weeks, Jesus was entrusted with other jobs. He grew in proficiency, speed and customer relations. Joseph whittled his back orders and by the following year Jesus had gained unofficial recognition as a junior partner in the operation. He simultaneously grew in stature, in favor with God and men, though he would never match Joseph's physical height. His voice became deeper and fuzz appeared on his chin.

That fall, after postponing it several times, 'for no good reason', as Mary put it, she and Joseph decided to have 'the talk' with Jesus. Joseph argued that it was her place to tell him, she being the principle party in Jesus' birth. Mary objected, saying that they should share the responsibility of telling Jesus about his complex identity. Joseph played the "I'm just a poor carpenter" card, which merited a raised eyebrow from Mary.

"Jesus," Mary said one night after supper. "Your father and I have something to discuss with you. Don't we Joseph."

Joseph nodded.

"We probably should have mentioned this some time ago, but we didn't. It's sort of a complicated and difficult subject to discuss."

"Mother," Jesus laughed. "I know all about girls and how babies are conceived. It's not all that complicated."

Joseph and Mary looked at one another, smiles slowly grew on their faces. Perhaps that was another talk too long postponed.

"Where did you learn all that stuff?" Joseph proceeded down the new path.

"We were messing around down near the stream a couple years ago," Jesus explained. "Eli of Nain brought up the subject. He's one of my best friends. Eli knows about a lot of things."

"And?" Joseph prodded. Mary thought enough was said.

"Well," Jesus continued, "Eli says you can't live in a farming region and not have an idea about reproduction. Eli says sheep don't multiply by magic. We all knew what he was talking about. Then Eli says that the same thing happens between a wife and her husband. All of us had pretty well figured that out, too. Eli say it's how life goes on. I agreed but said it was the consequence of love, committed love.

"And then Eli says the same thing happens with fish and plants. Now that was news to most of us." There was a moment of silence and absorption.

"You're right. Eli sure knows about a lot of things," Joseph observed.

Mary made a throat-clearing sound that signaled the subject was closed.

"Actually," she said, "we wanted to talk about something even more complicated. It's about your birth and your identity." She looked at Joseph, waiting for him to pick up the explanation, but he was content to leave it to her. "Jesus, you have a divine nature as well as a human nature," she said, glancing at Jesus for any facial reaction.

"You know Scripture well. You know all the references to a Messiah, to a savior for Israel and all people. Jesus," she hesitated, and looked deeply into his eyes. "You are that Messiah. You are the fulfillment of prophecy. You are the hope of centuries past and centuries to come. You are the key to salvation." She took a deep breath.

"Jesus, you are my son, the son of a woman. But you are also the son of God. You are the divine son of God, the son of the Most High."

For the next half hour, she related the story of her pregnancy, those difficult days when she and Joseph were betrothed but not married. How the angel Gabriel explained Jesus' incarnation and her acceptance to be the mother of Jesus and how Joseph stood by her and was likewise informed by an angel of all that had happened and his role in protecting the infant savior.

Joseph finally spoke up, explaining the need to travel to Bethlehem because of the census, even though Mary was about to give birth. "I was afraid your mother may deliver on the way down, but she insisted everything was fine. Sometimes she rode Dynamo and sometimes she walked. Of course, by the time we got there every room was taken. And then Mary tells me you are about to come. We knew no one in Bethlehem. Eventually, a kind woman, seeing your mother's condition, allowed us to stay in their barn. That's where you were born. She helped with the birth and told all the neighbors. Your birth raised quite a fuss. Even shepherds were informed from on high and came."

Jesus was enthralled at his story. His mind was full of questions, and finally he found an opening.

"First, I have figured out most of that, too. Mother, you have taught me a lot of Scripture. Second, do you have any more bread and honey?"

Joseph laughed at a growing boy's priorities and brought the bread and honey. "Here," he said. "I guess a hard-working carpenter needs extra nourishment. Where was I? Oh, shepherds came and eventually esteemed visitors from Persia and regions to the east brought gifts."

"Joseph, you forgot to tell about the circumcision and presentation in the Temple, all according to Jewish rituals."

"Oh, that, too. By now, word of your birth had spread to Jerusalem, just north of Bethlehem. Not everyone was excited at your birth. There were some high Jewish officials, though aware of Scripture prophesy, who refused to recognize your salvation role. And Herod and the Romans saw you as a threat to their power. Herod was so paranoid he put out a death order on you."

"Well, I'm still here," Jesus said. "Is that when we fled to Egypt?"

"That's right," said Joseph. "The same day we heard of Herod's plot, we left the area. We packed supplies on ole Dynamo and headed south. We came back several years later when we learned of Herod's death."

"I don't understand," Jesus said, "why Herod was so worried about an infant. What threat was I to his earthly rule?"

"I never met the man, and for that I'm thankful," Joseph said unequivocally. "My guess is that when some people talked of a 'new king' being born, Herod went off the deep end. He saw you as grown up and somehow wresting power from the Herod family."

"What you have told me fulfills much of what I have been thinking," Jesus said. He was more solemn than they had seen him before. "All of this became more clear to me in my discussions with the elders at Passover in Jerusalem, although I am sorry for causing both of you such worry. I have been meditating on this divinity thing nearly every day, and I must say while I understand the prophets' words it is difficult to grasp its essence.

"I don't begin to understand what this means for my future, but I pray that our God will slowly reveal it to me. I have some sense of its importance, just from hearing the rabbis deliberate. I appreciate the difficulties both of you have encountered on my behalf. Fleeing to

Egypt and living in a foreign land must have been a trying time for you."

There were other questions as Mary and Joseph cleared the table and put the bread and honey back on the shelf. "I assume you are finished eating," Joseph laughed. Jesus nodded, but there were still many things to digest.

"My parents knew the full story of who you are," Mary said. "I'm so grateful they were able to meet you before they died. We have never told anyone else. The truth is we aren't sure how to go about it. As you grow older and God reveals more to you and the path to your mission, I'm sure matters will unfold. All will be disclosed in good time."

When he turned 13, Jesus became a bar mitzvah, which literally means 'son of the commandment'. He transitioned from child to adult, and formally took on the yoke of the Torah and responsibility to follow all the commandments of the Sinai covenant. There was no formal ceremony, except at Synagogue he was recognized as being among those who could read from the Torah.

Jesus and two other young men who turned 13 were accorded wearing of phylacteries, small, black Scripture boxes that were strapped to the forehead and right arm in obedience to the words of Deuteronomy: *Fix these words of mine in your hearts and minds; tie them as symbols on your hands and bind them on your foreheads.*

Occasionally, Jesus and other young adults, including women, would review Scripture readings following formal Synagogue prayer and services. At one such session, a young male probed the incident in which Jesus stayed behind at Passover in Jerusalem when he was 12. By now it had become a well-known story, sometimes told with embellishment.

"I hear you got quite a scolding from your mother," Caleb teased, "and that your father was so angry he couldn't talk or spit. What were you thinking, Jesus?"

"I'll admit mother was more than a little upset," Jesus answered. "And you are right. My father tends to hide his anger. The veins in his neck stood out and spoke plenty. Honestly, I felt I had to explore the Scriptures with the best teachers, and I became lost in the wonders of

God's mercy and love demonstrated over the centuries. It is an awesome thing to ponder, Caleb." There was a pause.

"Do you like dates, Caleb?" Jesus asked. "Or honey?" Caleb nodded. "So do I. Sometimes one can't get enough of sweet food. That's how it was talking with these learned men. I was immersed in a Synagogue of the open air, a dialogue on the wonders of God. How could I not be there? How could I not participate? God's house is anywhere where two or more people gather in his name. I just lost track of time."

"For three days!?" Caleb continued his query.

"Yes, for three days," Jesus laughed. "Now, do you want me to summarize our discussions from the Temple court?"

"No thanks," Caleb said. "I think I'll go home and eat some dates."

Caleb, who came from one of the wealthier Jewish families in the region, was a good friend of Jesus. In truth, everyone who met Jesus became a friend, some closer than others. He made people feel important. He was always concerned about the welfare of others. He focused on their lives, their families, and always turned a conversation toward them.

By contrast, Caleb liked to talk about himself and his family's good fortunes. Most citizens of the Nazareth area were poor to moderate income farmers or craftsmen, people struggling to make ends meet. Caleb's father was a trader and dealt with vast numbers of caravan merchants in nearby Capernaum. Caleb lacked for nothing, except perhaps – and Jesus sensed it – a sense of self-worth.

There came a day when the two of them, both 15 now, were meandering the narrow streets of Nazareth, kicking around stones and various teenage topics such as fishing and girls, when Caleb brought up what he called the "mysterious nature of females." Jesus said nothing at first, waiting for his friend to elaborate. Silence finally provoked Jesus to seek explanation.

"What's mysterious about them?" he asked. "You realize you are casting your mother among the mysterious."

"No. No. My mom is not mysterious. When she speaks it's clear to the whole family what we need to do. It's a waste of time to object or ask questions. There is no appeal from her orders. I'm talking about women in general and girls in particular."

"OK, Caleb. What happened?"

"What are you talking about?"

"Something happened to set you on this mystery prattle. What was it?"

"You know, Jesus. You have unusual deduction abilities, or maybe you've been spying on me."

"Spying? You're the mysterious one," Jesus said, shaking his head. "It's like a math equation, Caleb. Out of the blue you say girls are mysterious. One plus one means something happened. Spying? What did she do? Give you the cold shoulder?"

"You have been spying!" Caleb claimed. "OK. Here's the deal. I sort of like this Margola, daughter of Baruch. She goes to Synagogue. I'm sure you know her. I thought she liked me. The other day I walked her home after Scripture study, and we strolled hand-in-hand into this olive tree alcove north of the central well. We talked about this and that, and when I tried to kiss her, she acted like I was a Samaritan."

"Well, first of all, there is nothing wrong with a Samaritan," Jesus began. "My guess, Caleb, is that you like her a whole lot more than she likes you. Or, just maybe, you misinterpreted her feelings and that she likes some other boy more than you. Or, maybe she's not ready to be kissed by anyone. Or, maybe you had sticky honey cake residue on your face."

"Some help you are," Caleb protested. "I think you proved that girls are mysterious. I don't get it. I'm not exactly the son of a beggar. And by the way, Jesus, my advice to you is stay out of the counseling business. If, for example, newlyweds seek a favor from you, make yourself scarce. Your explanations don't lift my spirits."

"Now, Caleb. Calm down. There is nothing wrong with you. Margola has every right to be herself, do things when it feels right to her. My guess is that she is more interested in *what* you are than *who* you are. Perhaps she gives no regard to your father's bank account. She wants to first find out who Caleb really is. And eventually she'll learn that you are an OK guy."

"Do you think?"

"Well, I said OK guy. I didn't say spectacular," Jesus joked and punched Caleb in the arm. "Next time pick some roadside flowers and give them to her. Or if she's thirsty, get her a cup of water. Little things may lead to bigger things. Don't force things, Caleb."

"Who told you all this stuff?"

"Nobody. I watch my parents. My father has calloused hands but a tender heart."

"You mean he really brings your mother flowers?"

"No, but he carves little lilies out of scrap material, paints them white, and places them in a wooden vase that he made. He gives her a new wooden flower every year."

The following year the two Nazoreans were again walking the streets, exchanging teenage appraisals of life in Galilee. Jesus, by now, assumed more of the family's carpentry business. He was a good wood craftsman, but Joseph still did most of the masonry work. Working with mortar is taxing, and it was reflected in Joseph's overall health. Their business extended south to Nain and east to Capernaum and Bethsaida.

Caleb, too, became more involved in his father's trading operation, a business that took him to Sepphoris and Tiberias, both cities being developed by Herod Antipas. The two young men seldom talked politics, but it seemed Tetrarch Antipas, who became ruler of Galilee after his father's death, was on their minds. It appeared that for now Rome and Antipas were content to leave Galileans to their own lives so long as heavy taxes were paid.

"What do you hear about Antipas?" Jesus asked his friend. "You get over to Tiberias frequently. What's the talk? Is there a change in his mood?" It was an unusual inquiry on Jesus' part. He had never discussed the matter with his parents.

"Well, as you know, Jesus, Antipas was appointed tetrarch by Caesar Augustus about a dozen years ago. From what I hear he is an odd duck. Little is known about him as an administrator and politician, but rumor has it that he has a wondering eye when it comes to women. Why do you ask?"

"Just curious," Jesus said. "I know his father was extremely distrustful of any perceived threat to his authority. You may have heard about Herod the Great's order to kill male infants in the Jerusalem region when people talked about a savior being born, a new king for Israel. I just wondered if Antipas inherited such a cynical mind."

"I can't answer your concerns, but I'll ask around in Sepphoris and Tiberias. My question has to do with his tax policies. He's a spender, Jesus, and I fear that means he will be asking for more money from citizens. Our company can afford it, but there are many marginal farm and business operations in Galilee."

Jesus discerned a change in Caleb's demeaner in the past year. He was less egocentric. They stopped at the central well for a drink of water, then happened by that same olive park where Caleb's kiss was turned away. Jesus couldn't help himself but raise the question of Margola and the 'kiss' that never happened.

"She's a wonderful girl, Jesus. She's not only beautiful on the outside but even more beautiful as a person. You were right. I was hiking in the Jezreel Valley and spotted some calanit (poppies). I picked her a bouquet. Red is her favorite color. She was delighted. I still can't believe how excited she was. You would have thought I brought her a gold crown."

"Caleb, it was your thoughtfulness that excited her. The flowers were just an instrument."

"Whatever. It sent her humming."

"Well?" Jesus smiled.

"Well, what?"

"What happened next, goofus? Did you get that kiss?"

"That's none of your business," Caleb grinned.

Their banter was interrupted by loud groans and a cry for help a short distance away. The two ran toward the voice in distress. They soon found Chloe Adontz, crumpled on the ground, her right hand shaking in apparent pain. Next to her on the stoney path were the scattered contents of her basket, including smashed fruit and broken eggs.

"Mrs. Adontz. Please lie still," Caleb requested. He removed his shirt, folded it and placed it beneath her head. "Jesus, see if you can find some sort of platform to carry her." There was no doctor in Nazareth, but there was a woman known as a healer. Jesus ran the short distance home, grabbed two poles and cross ties and quickly assembled a carrying device. Within 10 minutes he was back at Mrs. Adontz side.

"How is she?" Jesus inquired.

"I believe she has a broken wrist," Caleb responded. "She has a lot of discomfort. We need to get her to that healer. Stay with her. I'm going to run down to the well and get her some water."

"Mrs. Adontz," Jesus said. "Caleb is getting some water and then we will carry you to the healer woman." He picked up her arm tenderly and stroked her wrist. "I think you will be fine. I am Jesus, son of Mary and Joseph. We live in your neighborhood."

"I know who you are. I remember when you and your parents came back to Nazareth," she said. "I'm feeling better. Would you please retrieve my basket and the unbroken eggs?" She tried to sit up. "I'm embarrassed. I don't know what made me fall. I guess just old age and clumsiness. I am so grateful for your help. Believe me I will tell all just what fine young fellas you two are."

"I believe you," Jesus said. Caleb returned with water. They helped her onto the platform and carried her to the town healer. There the woman examined her wrist, cleaned a cut on the woman's knee, then rubbed a homemade salve on the wound.

"You will be OK, Mrs. Adontz," the healer said. "My opinion is that you didn't break any bones. Keep a bandage on those cuts. See me in a couple days and I'll clean it and put a new bandage on. You took a nasty tumble. Caleb thought you may have broken your wrist, but it seems to be OK. You are lucky."

The next day Chloe Adontz spread the news of her "terrible" fall. No one in Nazareth was left out. "I really thought my wrist was broken" she told Jesus' mother, "I had so much pain. But Caleb and Jesus were wonderful. Jesus fashioned a carrier and they took me to Mrs. Stein, the healer. You won't find two nicer boys in all of Galilee. Mary you should be proud."

Chapter 20

NAZARETH (16AD) – "Have you ever been to Bethany?" Jesus asked Eli of Nain as the two hiked through a forested area on their way to Mount Tabor.

"I'm not sure," Eli replied. "Didn't we camp there one time for the Passover Festival?" He thought. "Yes. It was several years ago, that time when you decided to hang back and visit with the Temple rabbis. Your parents circled back and returned to Jerusalem. Why would you bring that up again?"

"I didn't intend to stir up that incident," Jesus said. "I'm surprised you didn't remember that as the time we saw that girl that set you off in a tizzy. I'm sure you recall that."

"Oh, yes. How could I forget it, my friend? What's on your mind with Bethany?"

"A fellow named Lazarus and his two sisters live there. We met on one of my first trips to Passover. Like the two of us, Lazarus and I hit it off and we've been friends since."

"Are you sure your mind is not on his two sisters?"

"They are friends, too, but it's Lazarus I'm worried about."

"What's the problem? Is he some kind of trouble with the Romans? That's what you get from living within an hour's walk to Jerusalem. Too many Romans there, especially big shots and soldiers. He and his sisters should move to Galilee."

"It has nothing to do with the Romans," Jesus answered. "Lazarus is about my age. He and his siblings were left to operate the olive tree farm after their parents, Cyrus and Eucharis, died. When I last saw Lazarus, he seemed sickly. He claims he feels fine, but when I asked his sister, Martha, about it, she said he was often tired. But she attributed that to the hard work in maintaining the orchard.

"I suspect his sister is right," said Eli. "I know something about the work involved in maintaining olive trees. While they are drought resistant, they don't like competition from weeds. So, pulling weeds is important. Weeds draw moisture from trees. Pruning and removal of dead branches is necessary. And you must root new cuttings every year to replace dying trees and those damaged by storms."

"Perhaps it is the stress and work in olive farming," Jesus said, "but he seems to have lost some weight, too. A young man his age should be building muscle and weight."

"Maybe Lazarus is eating too many olives. There is not a lot of muscle-building nutrients in olives. He needs to eat more lamb and drink more wine. That's my suggestion. I'll tell you a secret. I don't care for olives. I know. Don't tell my father. Lot of people love the taste of olives. Not me."

"OK, Dr. Eli. I'll pass that along the next time I see him. I've been told that Bethany was – maybe still is – a place for the treatment of lepers. But I saw no indications – skin rash and lesions – of leprosy in Lazarus. It may be, too, that I worry for nothing.

"Here we are," Jesus said, hands uplifted, as they entered a clearing at the base of Mount Tabor. "This is one of my favorite places. It is peaceful and sometimes I will walk all the way to the top. It takes about twice as long to walk up than come down. When I walk to the top, I leave home right after sunrise."

"What's so special about this place," Eli inquired, "that you would spend an entire day there?"

"Want to find out? There's a walking trail to the top."

"What will we do when we get there?" Eli said, with more than a hint of disinterest.

"Just breathe in God's fresh air. Feel the gentle breezes flowing up from the Jezreel Valley. Smell the flowers and pine from the mountainside. Listen to all the birds. See your village and Nazareth as they snuggle on the hillsides. And usually, you can view the Sea of Galilee. Up there it seems as if you can almost touch God's feet. It is the perfect place to pray."

"It's certainly a big bump on God's Earth," Eli said, still not convinced of the need to walk to the top. "Why do you pray so much? Do your parents make you recite all that stuff? Why not spend more time looking at girls?"

"No one compels me to pray," Jesus answered. "And while I do say prayers from the Torah, mostly I just have a conversation with God."

"Really? And what do you talk about?"

"Well, I ask God to bless you and all my friends, keep my parents in good health, to give me the strength to follow His will, and that we can live in peace with the Romans and ourselves. But often I just ask God to open the minds of all people to His beautiful kingdom."

"You pray for me? You think I need it?"

"We all need to pray and be the recipient of prayer. We need God's grace. I ask God to send just the right girl to you for a wife. I know that is one of your wishes, and I hope that happens. I want to be at your wedding."

"Amen to that, Jesus. That's the greatest thing I've heard today. I'll race you to the top!"

They ran for a short time before the uphill strain taxed their lungs and leg muscles into a forced rest. Huffing and puffing, both sat on a shale ledge and munched on dried figs. They were already elevated enough to view the folds of Galilee hills and valleys and the patchwork of color marking fields and forests.

"You are right, Jesus. It's beautiful."

"You haven't seen anything yet, Eli. Wait until we get to the top. It will send shivers down your spine."

They resumed climbing the north side of the mountain, the zig-zag path gradually taking them upward. After several more rest stops, including one at a former Bedouin campsite, they reached the crest. Mount Tabor is shaped like an inverted funnel, minus a pointed spigot. Puffs of white clouds were gradually being ushered in by a gentle west wind born in the Great Sea.

"Wow!" Eli shouted, as his head made a 360-degree panoramic examination of the region. "Double wow! You couldn't have been more descriptive. I do get the feeling that we are at the gates of heaven. No wonder you like to come up here. A talk with God from here has a much shorter distance to travel."

"Yes," Jesus replied. "One gets that feeling atop the mountain, although God hears our prayers no matter where we are at, particularly when we feel lowest."

The comment set Eli to thinking, shifted his attention from the abundant scenery to the young man standing next to him. He had known Jesus for a number of years. Even though they were close friends, there was something that set Jesus apart, and it was more than his vast knowledge of Scripture.

Both were 16 years old. Many their age, including Eli, were giving second looks at young women, and young women were looking back. In one case, a Nazarian couple known to both, had sought permission of their parents and would soon be betrothed. Yet, it seemed to Eli, that marriage was as distant to Jesus as God was near.

Ever since that experience four years ago, when he stayed behind after Passover in Jerusalem and had that question-and-answer exchange with Jewish teachers, Jesus seemed different. There was, Eli thought, a gradual shift in his friend's nature. Jesus still had blackened thumbnails, a carpenter's trademark, but inside something was happening, a transformation.

"I sometimes get a notion that you are closer to God than the rest of us are," Eli said bluntly but reverently. "I mean it. You speak of God as if he were a close relative."

"Here's the straight dope, Eli, and you know it as well as I. We are all daughters and sons of God. We know it from Scripture. Everyone is bestowed with the same graces, and everyone has the freedom to embrace those graces or turn away. But no one is denied the opportunity to follow our Lord and embrace his kingdom. I am not privileged in that regard. You are close to God right now, but it may be difficult to understand."

Eli scratched his head in apparent befuddlement. He once again focused on what he could see, the amazing quilt called Galilee.

"God is before your eyes," Jesus said. "Look, Eli, down in the valleys and along the far hillsides." He stretched his arms in demonstration. "There, among the grandeur of the trees and wheat fields, all the little animal creatures running around, and there in the midst of the valleys and streams is the most beautiful thing of all – human beings. Human life." He waited.

"Made in the image and likeness of God. It's all in the Scriptures.

"You can't see them from up here, these people, just as we think we can't see our God, but we both know that he and they are there."

"Oh! Oh!" Eli blurted and pointed toward Nain. "I think I spot this girl, Joana. Yes, yes. I see her walking in a garden covered with the blooms of white myrtle. Oh, my! The way she walks, Jesus. Wait. She is looking my way and pointing. She sees me. I think she is in love with me," he laughed. "I know it."

"Maybe she is, Eli," Jesus said. "Maybe she is. She is certainly down there in your imagination."

They looked at one another and smiled.

"Jesus. Do you even look at girls?"

"All the time. What? You think there is something wrong with my eyes? I tell you my eyes are fine. God knows what he is doing. Girls are beautiful. There is good reason they are attractive to us. How else would life continue? The only problem I see is that some men treat women as second-class citizens. Some look at them and see only outer beauty. They see them as objects for their own pleasure. In God's eyes we are all equal, men and women, Jews and Samaritans, rich and poor."

"I know. I know. You've said that before. But, Jesus, do you really look at girls? Have you ever kissed a girl, other than your mother, I mean?"

"Yes."

"Who?"

"What? Are you writing a book?" Jesus shook his head in the affirmative. "OK. Her name is Naomi."

"I don't know her."

"Well, you would if you went to Synagogue in Nazareth every week. She lives north of Nazareth, toward Sepphoris."

"What happened?"

"Eli, nothing else happened. It was nice. I gave her peck on the cheek. A couple months ago after Synagogue, down near the well. We had drifted off from the others and were talking about the rabbi's sermon. We had seen each other often at school and at services. It just sort of happened." There. It was said. A pause followed.

"Have you ever kissed this Joana, or is she just someone you made up?"

That caused a shift in topics. Now, Eli wanted to change subjects.

"What do you suppose," he said abruptly, "caused this mountain to be so perfectly shaped?"

"I'm no student of Earth science," Jesus said, perplexed by the abrupt change in subjects, "but my guess is time, a long time for wind and rain and nature's other forces, combining like a group of carpenters and masons erecting a building."

"The work of Mother Nature and God our Father?"

"One could say that," Jesus agreed. "I should be getting back. I must feed mother's chickens. And I have to go over job requests and check on scheduling."

"How high is this big bump? A thousand cubits"

"Eli, my guess is that it is more than that. I'll race you to the bottom."

Once they reached the old Bedouin camp, Eli, the leader, held up to rest. Jesus arrived in less than a minute.

"Did you get lost?" Eli teased, still puffing.

"Not at all," Jesus replied. "I was just coasting along and didn't want to pass you."

"Sure," Eli said with elongated sarcasm. "Say, have you ever thought of entering the Galilee relays? For years, boys and men have represented various towns and competed. You should see if Nazareth has such a team and join in the running. You would do well and have fun. Of course, there is no chance you could beat the Nain team. It has won the race for many years."

"Really?" Jesus responded challengingly. "Perhaps that's because you have had no competition. You wouldn't expect fishermen from around the Sea to be up to it. They have stiff knees from sitting in a boat. Grape growers? Well, they are so busy testing their juice they don't have time to run in races. But craftsmen from Nazareth. Now they have honed muscles. I'll check on it."

"You do that. I can't wait for Nain to run circles around Nazareth."

"Circles?" Jesus laughed. "I thought you were talking about racing from one point to another, not running in circles. Just like someone from Nain."

"You know what I meant."

"Yes. Yes. And these races. They are legal? You don't run on Shabbat, do you?"

"We do not," Eli replied. "And while Jews generally do not like Roman games that are conducted to honor their deities, there is no ban on racing. It's like the Greek Olympiads. You realize that Israelites have long been masters of archery. And our people play other games, too, including tag, as I'm sure you have played. Racing is merely organized tag."

"You sound like the commissioner of the Galilee racing association, a real promoter."

"I like to run and I like to compete," Eli said. "So, are you in?"

"I will check it out, see if Nazareth has a team. Where are the races held and what is the distance we have to run?"

"We have marked out a race place in a shepherd's pasture just outside Nain. You may have to dodge a few stupid sheep, but that's a small price to pay for some fun. The owner does not charge us for use of his land. We have a 200-cubit (100 yards) dash. That's fun. A 3,500-cubit (about one mile) relay is the big race of the day. And there is a relay."

"Sounds good. Last one down is a loser."

When Jesus returned home, he was shocked to find his father in bed. It was not like Joseph to rest at the end of a workday. He always found something to fix around their house, those honey-do projects, or tools to be repaired. But not this day. He told Mary he was tired and planned to take a nap. He was lying on his blanket, his comfort transmitted by a slight snore.

Jesus approached Mary with his palms held out and upward in questioning form. She responded with a shrug and motioned for them to go outside.

"I think he is just tired," Mary whispered. "With your help, he has taken on more projects and I think the strain is catching up to him. Remember Jesus, he is not a young man anymore."

"I know. It's just a surprise to see him in bed at this time of day. Perhaps he should see the healer."

Mary said she doubted Joseph would seek medical attention even if she suggested it. They talked for several more minutes before being interrupted by some groaning and audible yawning.

"I don't know why I'm so tired today," Joseph said, stretching his arms upward. "What's for supper, Mary?"

Chapter 21

NAZARETH, 17 AD – Joseph was in a talkative mood, a rare thing for him. Mary saw no particular impetus for this phenomenon, but she did speculate that it may correspond to times when he had more than a single cup of wine.

It wasn't as if he were a recluse. He loved to talk shop, how he approached a carpentry challenge with a new idea, or his concept of a reshaped tool that he believed would improve his work. He could talk hammer and trowel issues all day. Mary listened, like he listened to her exploits about embroidery.

When he turned loquacious, Mary was happy not to interrupt. They were approaching their 18th anniversary, and it had been that way the entire time. She chuckled inwardly. It wasn't as if Joseph was impassive, she mulled. He was reserved. Oh, on several occasions he had displayed extraordinary emotions. The first was when she accepted betrothal. And, of course, when she told him she was pregnant. Who could blame him for that? She, too, had a difficult time understanding all that had happened.

Joseph went a little off track when Jesus was born. They had no more than arrived in Bethlehem when her water broke. She knew birth was near. The couple had no quarters and couldn't find any. In desperation, Joseph took the advice of a farm woman who not only had a stable for them to stay in but knew something about the process of childbirth.

Five years ago, she had to subdue him as he steamed into the Temple Court in Jerusalem where they found Jesus leisurely and blissfully talking Scripture with elders and teachers. But he kept his mouth shut then, even though smoke was coming out of his ears. Mary smiled as she recalled the scene.

"What are you grinning about?" Joseph asked as he took another sip of Nazareth vintage. It was just the two of them. Jesus was off with a friend.

"Nothing in particular," Mary said, "just that it has been a tumultuous but wonderful life with you, Joseph. I just love to hear you talk. You have been such a great husband, father and craftsman."

"What?" his eyebrows raised. "Did I goof up somewhere? Fail to get something fixed? Track sawdust in the house? Tell me."

"None of the above," Mary replied. "I just love you, especially when you get to chattering about something."

"Well, OK then. I have a question for you. Jesus will turn 17 in a couple of weeks. I was talking to this Greek fellow the other day, and we discussed business and how Jesus was doing much of the work at our shop. He asked about Jesus' age. When I told him the lad was about to be 17, he wondered if we were holding a birthday party for him. I said I didn't think so, and he says, 'Why not?' I said I didn't know why not.

"He tells me that Greeks party for any occasion, including birthday anniversaries. They roll out the honey cakes, hazelnuts and there is plenty of wine. Remember, Mary, they have many gods and goddesses to celebrate, too. He said the Greeks are big on hospitality, what he called xenia, and that they frequently exchange gifts. We don't celebrate the day of someone's birth. How's come?"

"Well, Joseph. I can only tell you what my parents and others at Synagogue have said. Celebrating birthdays and gift giving is a pagan tradition. There have been a lot of mystic notions associated with birth down through the years. As you know, we believe in a single God, the creator from whom all life is generated."

"I know all that, but what is wrong with noting a birthday with cake. I like cake."

"I know you do, And so do I. Actually, I'm told Jewish law does not permit us to make a festival at the birth of our children. We don't even celebrate the birthdays of Moses and Abraham. In fact, there is no mention in the Scriptures when either of them was born. We hold more solemnly the day that our people die."

"Well, don't tell the rabbi, but I would rather remember birth than death."

Joseph poured himself another cup of wine as Mary declined.

"Think about it, Joseph," Mary said. "Even if our people celebrated birthdays, the situation with Jesus is dramatically different. He is the human manifestation of God. The Messiah," she whispered in reverence. "As God, he has no beginning and end. His humanity had a beginning point, but he is divine, has always been and always will be." She looked away in thought.

"Tell me. When would we celebrate his birthday?" She looked at him, both eyebrows and hands uplifted.

"Every day, Joseph, the immensity of our role in rearing the Son of God, our God, takes my breath away. And when I think what this means for all ages, I can barely take it in. How can someone who has always existed have a birthday or a birthday party?"

"Well, I wasn't thinking that complicated, Mary. I was thinking about celebrating his human birthday. But I know what you are saying. When I look at him and he is assembling something, I wonder: Why doesn't he save time and just will it finished. Who am I to question how he does a job? And then I ponder for the thousandth time, why did God choose us?"

"I ask myself the same questions," Mary said. "When I wake up shortly before dawn, these things go around and around in my mind like the Jewish hora. Me, a peasant girl, barely five feet tall, of no status, chosen to be the mother of Jesus!"

"Yes, but you had that beautiful, glossy black hair – and you still do," he hastened to add, "parted down the middle, a robust complexion, pretty smile, and with those gold earrings dangling from your lobes, how could God resist? And most important you had a deep faith in God and were fully aware of His promises."

"Joseph, I don't think God cares two hoots about glossy black hair or dangling earrings. That's the wine talking. But I think, logically, why not a girl from Jerusalem, daughter of a well-known Hebrew teacher, someone who goes to the Temple area every day and not just at Passover? Nazareth is almost as far from Jerusalem as Egypt."

"I protest," Joseph said, hoisting his wine cup in the air. "How dare you, a faithful servant of our God, doubt His choice? He selected Mary of Nazareth to be the mother of His human manifestation. Jesus had to come sometime. Scriptures talk about a savior, Yeshua or mamshiah, 39 times at least. My wife is the perfect person to be mother of God. Don't you forget it!"

Mary laughed. She looked at Joseph, his face slightly redder than before. The wine had definitely loosened his lips. And the words Yeshua and mamshiah had a noticeable slur to them.

"I won't forget it, my dear husband."

"Remember how the neighbors talked when you came back from visiting Elizabeth, and you were," and Joseph gave a hand demonstration of pregnancy. "Those were difficult times for both of us. But we trusted God, had faith in God, and each other. Instead of divorcing you, God instructed that I take you as my wife. So, I did. The rabbi came, the wedding rituals were observed and we were married under the law."

The hour was getting late. Mary was sleepy, but Joseph was still wound up. He tipped his wine cup up and swallowed the last of the fermented grapes. He finished with a distinct "ahhhh."

"Two thousand years from now," Joseph continued his oration, "people will still be talking and arguing about us. Did we get married? Did our parents approve? That's an easy one. Like all marriages, our fathers arranged it. If Joachim asked your opinion, it was a mere formality. What about our age spread? Well, I would say it was about usual for our time.

"And there will still be wagging tongues and doubters, people who deny Jesus' divine nature and unique role in human history. I suppose some will rebuff God altogether. Why, Mary, would anyone find it so difficult to see that Jesus' birth and life are not ordinary and hence could not have happened in an ordinary way?"

"Joseph. I'm tired and going to bed."

"When we were younger," Joseph continued, not hearing her, "I was almost afraid to bring up the subject of Jesus. Other families talked of how their children are honor students in school, how they won a sporting event, or how this one or that one is all-Galilee in something." He paused.

"I hesitated to say our son created the universe." He looked at Mary. "Did your folks ever get into that?"

"No, Joseph. They knew he is special but didn't talk about it much. Maybe that's our fault. How aware is he of his divinity? Does he ever talk to you about it?"

"Not directly. A couple of months ago I asked him if he planned to continue as a carpenter in future years, or if he was considering some other profession. I thought it was a fair question. I don't know how this is all going to play out and I was hoping he would share a little insight."

"What did he say?"

"He said it was a question he was working on, that it would all unfold in good time."

"Maybe he doesn't know."

"Oh, I think he knows. My guess is that he knows where he is headed but the details are unclear."

"I'm scared, Joseph, scared for what it may mean for him."

"Me too, Mary. But it's sort of like a knot in a piece of wood. You see it. You know as you saw the board with that knot that things can go several different ways. We don't know the outcome of Jesus' future. I have learned this. There is not much I can do to change it. We just do the best we can and let the rest up to God."

Mary sat fidgeting. Her fingers pulled at the woven belt around her waistband. Her light blue/grey skirt, which she made herself, was still slightly pulled up and tucked in her belt, the working and cooking position. She had kicked off her sandals and removed her head scarf. She was 33. A few gray strands of hair, noticeable at the center part, had infiltrated her ebony head.

"Joseph, you've talked about so many things that now I'm not sleepy." She had a busy tomorrow. After breakfast and baking, it was her turn to help clean the Synagogue. Garden weeds needed pulling. She had to house. She wanted to visit some sick friends. And she had yet to prepare for tomorrow night's Scripture discussion.

As Joseph concluded his dissertation, Jesus quietly came in the rear door and immediately went to bed. Mary reflexively examined her left hand, still showing the burn marks when she accidentally touched the hot stove. Where would their lives go? How would God's plan for salvation, Jesus' plan, unfold? When would it all happen? Joseph is right, she thought. Do your best. The rest is up to God.

She looked over at Joseph. His eyes were closed. His chin rested upon his chest. Snoring would soon follow.

"Joseph! Joseph! Come to bed."

Chapter 22

Joseph arose later than usual the next morning. Mary had been up for nearly an hour when he finally stirred. It was her movement in the kitchen and the sound of a spoon in a mixing bowl that finally roused him from his mat. He sat up with a jerk, simultaneously realizing he had overslept and had a busy day ahead.

"Why didn't you wake me?" he asked Mary.

"Because you looked so peaceful," she replied.

"Peaceful, eh? Peaceful doesn't get my work done." He dressed quickly and gulped his early meal.

"I forgot to mention last night that Jesus wants to run with a Nazareth team that will compete in some kind of regional racing competition," Joseph said. "I said it was fine with me, but that he should check with you first."

"We already talked about it this morning," Mary said. "I told him that I have no objections so long as they don't compete on Shabbot. He's already out practicing for the race. He said he has to expand his lung capacity. Took Slam with him. I think he said he was going to run on that path along the stream."

"If he wants to develop his lungs, he should run to the top of Mount Tabor, but I guess that's too far away. He has some jobs to complete today. As for me, I'm off to replace a broken table leg for Mrs. Berenise and fix a leaky roof for Mr. Kadesh. Neither will expand my lungs, although Mrs. Berenise may accomplish that. She is hard of hearing."

"Just be careful getting up on that roof," Mary cautioned as he headed out the door. "And wear that heavier coat. It's much colder than yesterday."

Jesus was glad he had worn a light jacket over his tunic. It was cooler than when he had left home. The rainy season had descended on Galilee, and the temperature was less than the 46-degree average day for this time of year. He could see his breath as he slowed down near a sharp bluff in the hills outside Nazareth. He sat down on a level rock and examined the laden skies. Snow? he thought. Could it possibly snow?

Slam snuggled up to his leg, his pink tongue a wave of pants in spite of the cold. Jesus scratched under Slam's chin, and the dog's tail responded in kind.

"Slam," Jesus said, and the dog tilted its head waiting for a question, "do you think I should run in these races? I've never done this before, and I need lots of practice. It's 3,500-cubits, and that takes lung power. Good thing it's a relay."

Slam barked as if he understood every word. Jesus laughed and rubbed the dog's neck again. He was in the midst of looking skyward for another weather check when he spotted a figure far up the trail. It looked like a girl, he thought. She ran like a girl. It's definitely a girl, he decided, and she's jogging toward me. He stood. Waited. Slam also eyed the approaching person and gave a low growl until Jesus patted him, assuring there was no danger.

That's a girl, Jesus repeated to himself, and I know her. He watched in a transfixed state, standing in place until she arrived.

"Naomi!" he said. "What are you doing out here alone?"

"Well, hello Jesus, it's nice to see you again, too," she said, with a tinge of tartness.

"Oh, I'm sorry," Jesus fumbled for words. "I should have said hello. I mean, it's nice to see you."

Jesus' surprise was rooted in a cultural notion that women should never roam outside their routine domain unless accompanied by a male. Such boundaries, far more restrictive than earlier in Jewish ancestry, were said to be imported from the Greeks. Naomi's household was seemingly more open. While women were segregated at Synagogue services, Naomi on occasion gave her opinion and asked questions at school.

Naomi spoke after an awkward silence.

"I frequently use this path to run. You are sweating. Have you been working hard in the carpenter shop or is it from running?"

"I have been practicing for the relays coming up in Nain. I hope to be on the Nazareth team, but my legs and lungs need to be in better shape. My friend, Eli, talked me into running the race. Several towns in Galilee will have teams." He paused. "Oh, this is my dog Slam. Say hello to Naomi, Slam."

Slam barked a double woof, his standard for greeting.

"Slam is friendly," Naomi said. "Woof, woof back to you," she added, patting the dog's head. He wagged his tail in thanks.

"What I meant earlier is," Jesus hesitated, "well, should a girl be out here alone? Isn't this about 4,000 cubits from your home?"

"It is, but I've been down this path many times. One of my friends lives in Nazareth. I was down to see her. I'll be fine, but it's sweet of you to worry about me."

His dark cheeks warmed and took on a reddish look. Naomi stooped to pat Slam again, mostly to hide a growing smile and suppress an emerging giggle. Jesus looked off in the distance as if he were searching for words. None came and Naomi again picked up the conversation.

"Is Slam your running coach?"

"I suppose you could say that," Jesus laughed. "I could never outrun Slam. But I've learned something. Running isn't all speed. It's also about pacing oneself. It's about stamina and reading how much energy you have in reserve. You have to watch the competition, stay close in the pack and know when to kick it up a notch or two. Eli has taught me that running is a mental as well as physical game."

"You do know a lot about running," Naomi said. "I never thought that much about it. Do you enjoy racing?"

"Well, I'd say yes and no. It's something new to me. I enjoy running more than racing, exercise more than competition. Don't get me wrong. I'd love to have Nazareth finish ahead of Nain, but that's only because Eli brags so much about his team. Or, as he puts it, 'Your guys will be eating our dust.' Now, he's not only a fast runner, but he is competitive. I hope I get to run against him, and if I can figure out a strategy to keep ahead of him I'll be satisfied."

The two looked around, not knowing what to say next.

"It almost looks as if it could snow," Jesus said, unknotting his tongue. He looked at Naomi's eyes. They are such a dark brown, he thought to himself, like her hair. And her olive skin looks so soft and beautiful. No. I would amend that to gorgeous.

"Oh, I'm sorry. What is it that you said?" Naomi asked, her mind adrift, also. "Oh, yes. Snow. That would be a wonderful surprise. My father is a weather watcher, and he says snow in lower Galilee is worth a dance, and I've only seen him do a snow-jig once. He says he would dance all night if the Romans left. Weather and politics are his favorite topics."

"I saw some flurries today," Jesus said, "but not enough to cause your father to dance. However, Slam danced around trying to catch the flakes."

"I'd like to see him do that," Naomi said.

Again, uncomfortable, nervous silence.

"Do you enjoy Synagogue," Jesus eventually broke the stillness. Naomi pondered the peculiar question.

"Enjoy?" she said, thinking it was an odd if not forced way to continue their chat. "I think that's an unusual word, if I may be honest. Like my parents, I appreciate the Scriptures and the history of our ancestors. I cherish what our God has done for us and what He continues to do. My father has a firm belief, too, that when the Messiah comes it will be the end of the Romans. My mother would say she enjoys it all. What about you? I think I know your answer."

"Do you?" Jesus said, a little surprised. "I would say I am a combination of your parents, except I don't think the Messiah's job is to run off the Romans. I believe the Messiah wants to extend the kingdom of God here on Earth, convincing people that love and kindness, rather than the sword, is the answer to life and eternal salvation. I must agree with your mom. I enjoy Synagogue and the community aspect, praying together." He waited, then added: "Is that what you thought I would say?"

"Pretty much," Naomi smiled, wondering if there was about to be a quiz on the Torah. "I'm sure you heard yourself referred to as 'little rabbi' by some of the boys. Not so much now, but when you were younger. I think it's a charming term. Don't you?"

"Charming? That's a little unusual, I think, to use your word." That left him again at the end of his thought process. When he is with Eli or Josiah, talk comes so easy, he mused, but here with Naomi it's confusion, like trying to steer chickens. Why are girls so difficult to talk to?

"I think 'little rabbi' is appropriate," Naomi went on, "because you have always known more than anyone else in class about Scripture and our history," Naomi restarted the chat. "And you like to talk about it with other people. You speak about God's kingdom with ease, like parents chatter about all the activities and good things their children are doing."

"That's a pretty combination you have on today," Jesus blurted. "I like the bright blue simlah (tunic) and deep red mitpahath (shawl). Are you warm enough?"

"Why, thank you, Jesus. Red and blue are mother's favorite, too. I didn't know you were a fashion observer as well as an expert on Scripture. And I am sufficiently warm, but thanks for asking."

"I'm not a fashion observer," Jesus said mildly. "Ordinarily I pay little attention to what people wear. It's just that red and blue becomes you, that's all."

"I'm sorry," she said. "I do appreciate your comments and I didn't intend to be sarcastic. And I want you to know that I admire your knowledge about Scripture. We should all know more about God's love and hope for people, His recommendations for how we should live. You know what Jesus? I predict you will grow up to be a major rabbi."

As the two looked into each other's eyes, snowflakes again began to tumble down haphazardly. Their attention was diverted to the zig-zagging flakes, fighting against gravity to stay aloft. Snow, though not rare, was still a novelty in Nazareth. They looked up, palms spread outward, fascinated like people everywhere at nature's artful display.

"I want to squeal," Naomi giggled.

"Go ahead," Jesus said.

A darker cloud drifted in from the western sky and the snowflakes picked up in size and intensity. On cue, both stuck out their tongues to catch the fluffy droplets of water. Slam did his dance. Naomi squealed.

"Are you sure you are warm enough," Jesus asked again. "The temperature is continuing to fall. Maybe I should walk you home."

"Don't be silly. I'll be fine. I could walk home with my eyes closed," she said. "Maybe I will."

Jesus didn't pick up on the subtlety.

"I could walk with you part way," he repeated, "to outside Nazareth, and then run back. I can use the extra exercise."

"Sure," she said. "That would be nice."

Jesus usually ran barefooted. He pulled out his heavy sandals, tucked in the back side of his ezor (belt), and slipped them on. Naomi was already wearing sandals. The snow melted as it touched the ground, but Jesus envisioned that would change. They ran northwest, past Nazareth, saying little. At Cedar Point, where a large tree rose in the middle of the path, Jesus decided to turn back toward home.

"Is it OK if I head back now?" he asked.

"Oh sure," Naomi replied. "I have only a short distance from here. Thanks for the escort. It was nice to have you as company."

Jesus, again looking for the right words, reached out and shook her hand. "Well, goodbye then. I'll see you in Synagogue."

It wasn't his first encounter alone with a girl, but it was the first time it had an impact on his senses. His mind was sort of foggy. His speech had faltered as if an array of cords lay tangled in his throat. He struggled to strain a mixture of thoughts and to find the right words. Amazing, he pondered. So that is the magic of girls. It was an episode, he decided, that he was not about to share soon with his parents and friends.

"Slam," he confided as the pair started back to Nazareth, "that was an unusual, no, an astonishing experience."

At first he trotted along, images of Naomi floating along beside him. He removed his sandals. His pace picked up, a gallop transitioning to a dash. He imagined that she was watching him race as he pulled ahead of Eli, giving his friend dust to eat.

Snow was still falling when Jesus arrived home. He was surprised that he was barely puffing. His lingering bemusement was abruptly checked when he opened the door.

"Father! Why are you lying on your cot when it's not close to bedtime?"

"Jesus," his mother answered calmly. "Please close the door. In case you haven't noticed, it's snowing outside. As for your father, he insisted on climbing atop a slippery roof. He fell and now his back is paying the price."

"I'll be perfectly fine," Joseph protested. "Your mother always makes a mountain out of a mole hill. I was coming down the ladder when my foot slipped off the rung. It isn't as if I fell off the roof." His explanation was quickly followed by a moan. "I think you will have to pick up my work projects for a couple of days."

"No problem" Jesus brightly responded. "I can handle it, father. You deserve a few days off."

"You seem in an exceptionally good mood, Jesus," Mary remarked, a mother's radar always on alert. "Was your run that successful or did you hear some uplifting news?"

"It was a good run. I think my legs and lungs are rising to the challenge of the races." He did not mention meeting Naomi.

"When and where is the race?" Joseph inquired. He was coughing more now, a condition aggravated by his fall and the damp weather.

"The races are in a couple of weeks outside Nain," Jesus said. "But don't worry. I can practice with the Nazareth race team and still tend to our carpenter work. Did you get your tools put away?" When Joseph said he had dropped them on the shop floor, a sure sign he wasn't feeling well, Jesus went out and put things in their proper place. One of Joseph's shop rules was to always hang tools in the place "where they belong."

"Here," Mary said to Joseph, handing him a cup of hot goat's milk. "This will help your cough. I mixed some herbs in it."

Joseph obligingly sipped some of it. His face grimaced in response.

"Please drink it all," she advised. "It'll do you good." She shifted gears. "What's up with this bouncy, over-the-moon manner of Jesus?" Mary asked before Jesus returned. "I could see in his eyes that something happened while he was out running. Did you notice, Joseph?"

"No. He looks the same to me. I think it's your imagination, Mary." The warm goat's milk was not going down well.

Except for time at Synagogue school and Shabbat, Jesus worked Joseph's carpenter and masonry schedule without a hitch. By now he was nearly as proficient as Joseph, especially as a carpenter. In less than a week, Joseph was up and about, checking Jesus' work and visiting with customers. He noticed what Mary was talking about in regard to

Jesus' buoyant disposition. Jesus whistled more while he worked, a cheery overlay a constant. Maybe something was going on. Running in a race isn't that inspiring.

Jesus saw Naomi again at Synagogue, but there was little opportunity to talk, not that he had bushel of things to say. He was disappointed when she didn't come to Nain for the races. Mary came but Joseph rested at home. Slam stayed with him. It was a beautiful day. The smattering of snow had long melted. The air was fresh and the temperature perfect for runners. There were teams from Nain, Nazareth, Cana, Magdala, Hamam and Shikhin. A Capernaum group failed to show up.

"Are you ready to eat our dust?" a voice accompanied a slap on Jesus' back. It was Eli with a cubit-long smile. The two embraced as friends and competitors. "Don't blink," Jesus acknowledged his friend, "or you may not see the Nazareth runners pass you. Thanks for inviting us. It's a wonderful setting."

"It is nice out here and we are grateful to the sheep farmer for letting us mark out a race path." With the runners, families and friends, Eli predicted a large turnout. While the host Nain team brought water, any lunch was brought individually. Mary had packed some bread, cheese and figs.

After runners stretched and ran part of the path in warm-ups, the call was made for entrants in the 200-cubit dash. Sixteen runners were divided into four heats with the winners facing off in the finals. Jesus finished third in his heat with the winner, a young man from Nain, winning the finals, too. Eli glanced at Jesus and nodded a winning grin.

Following a rest period, designated officials arranged for the 3,500-cubit relay race, the feature event. The race would last six laps. A runner from each team would run a lap, then hand off a flag to a teammate. Jesus was matched with Eli and four other runners in the third segment. At this point the Nain team was leading, Shikhin second and Nazareth third. Hamam was a close fourth.

Jesus waited for a loping teammate to pass off the flag, then sped down the path. He spotted Eli in the lead. He knew he could dash off and catch Eli in the first turn, but that would be a bad strategy. Instead, he measured his pace so as to gradually move up on Eli. He soon passed the Shikhin runner. It was now he and Eli in this segment. Eli looked over his shoulder and saw Jesus closing the gap. He ran faster, but soon his lungs were gasping for air.

Jesus matched Eli's stride. In the final stretch, Eli's legs joined his lungs in fatigue. With 400 cubits to go, Jesus kicked into a higher gear. Eli looked back in shock. Jesus was right behind him. Eli was running on fumes. His legs felt like they were turning into chunks of stone. He reached out to hand off his flag to another Nain runner for the final lap when he stumbled.

At the same time, Jesus passed his flag to a Nazareth teammate with his right hand and caught Eli with his left. Both sailed into a group of observers who caught them and steadied them from falling. Eli and Jesus enfolded in laughter and coughs. Neither noticed when a Hamam runner spurted into the lead in the final lap.

"Where did you get all that energy?" Eli said in between long gulps of air. "You must thrive on dust," he added, hands on knees and still searching for oxygen. "You seem to run with a different spirit than the day at Mount Tabor. What's the secret?" he panted. "A new breakfast formula?"

"No secret, Eli. I just shook off your dust message and trained hard, especially in the last week". They again congratulated each other and promised to repeat the competition next year. "That's when I won't be at the finish line to hold you up," Jesus said, getting in his own jab. "I'll already be resting, watching the Nazareth team win."

The crowd yelled and Eli and Jesus looked up to determine the source of the commotion. It was quickly evident. Hamam, the team pegged for last, finished first. Its members jumped up and down as if they had just defeated Athens in the Olympiad. Eli and Jesus shook hands with the winners and met their coach. He was Greek.

Mary approached and gave both boys a kiss on the cheek. "That was exciting," she said. "A healthy sport and fun for all. Jesus, if you don't mind, I think I will walk home with some friends from Nazareth."

"I'll be along soon, mother," Jesus responded. "I want to help Eli get the sheep pasture back looking mostly like it was before. Maybe I'll carve a wooden plaque for the farmer to commemorate the race." Eli said he would bring a bag of olives to the farmer in appreciation. With Mary gone, Jesus felt comfortable to ask Eli a personal question.

"You know a lot about girls, Eli. Why do they act so mysterious?"

"Well, Jesus," Eli began as if he indeed was Galilee's foremost expert on women, "girls and boys are different."

"Really?!" Jesus said with more than a little sarcasm. "You should be a physician."

"No. Seriously. They see things differently than we do. They react to things differently. They are more observant, attentive to detail. I think women in general are more caring, more sensitive to the needs of others. Males can be indifferent, perhaps harder to convince. My mom has eyes in the back of her head. My father often looks right past what's in front of him."

"By golly, Eli, I think you're headed for a career as a doctor. I agree with most of what you say, but my father is a stickler for detail and precision. And I believe men are just as caring, but there is much to be learned from women. Our culture should make them equal in all things."

"Jesus," Eli looked directly into his eyes. "What's going on? What makes you think girls are a mystery? I sense a girl issue here. Tell Dr. Eli about it."

"OK," he said tentatively. "I met Naomi from Synagogue school the other day while I was out running. She's really cute, Eli, but I felt uneasy around her. It's like she cast some magic. I think I made a fool of myself the way I acted and in what I said, or in what I didn't say. It's hard to explain."

"Ah, my friend. I've been there," Eli smiled triumphantly. "I think, to use a term the elders use, you experienced a slight case of being smitten. My guess is you were flustered, maybe even flummoxed, nervous for sure. You are right. It is mysterious."

"What happens now?"

"I would say the feeling will either pass or get worse."

"Some help you are."

Jesus arrived home, tired but happy that he had entered the races. It will be the talk of the town for several days, he pondered, how the Nazareth team fared better than expected. However, thoughts of Naomi sped past any reminiscence of the competition at Nain. With some trepidation, he decided to seek his father's assessment. Joseph was honing a finishing blade.

"Are you feeling better?" Jesus asked as he entered the shop.

"Jesus my son. How did the races go, and yes, I'm feeling better. This place, in the midst of all these tools," and he waved his arms wide, "is the best medicine for me, not some terrible potion your mother created. Oh, she has good intentions and perhaps it has a healing element, but it tasted worse than week-old ale left standing in the sun behind the chicken pen. Now, don't you be repeating what I just said about that life-saving medicine of your mother's."

Jesus laughed. "The races were fun and it was good to see Eli. Actually, that's what I wanted to talk to you about, mothers and women and girls. Are they really that different from men?" Joseph looked at him, a chuckle building in his chest.

"Ah, son. It's a subject that philosophers have been addressing for centuries. Your mother and I have been married nearly two decades, and just when I think I have things figured out, I don't figure that I do. It's wonderful! She's wonderful. Life is wonderful. But what brings up this question about women, which we don't have enough time this week to discuss?"

"You and mother are able to talk about things in a normal fashion. Why is it so difficult to talk to some girls?"

"True enough. Your mother and I can discuss things sensibly and with mutual consideration. Most of our conversations involve you. And who is this young lady that has tied your tongue?"

"Her name is Naomi, but don't say a word to mother."

"Jesus. I would bet my best saw that she already knows."

Chapter 23

CAPERNAUM, 30AD – I told him he worries too much. If it's not about building the kingdom, as he puts it, then some other fret is scratching his neck. Now it's John, his second cousin, or whatever, who's preaching about marital infidelity. And John is naming names, specifically Herod Antipas. Jesus thinks that will get John in a heap of trouble.

"Simon," Jesus says to me, what do you think I should do? John doesn't take suggestions to heart. He won't back off his proclaiming the law and quoting Scripture. He gives the same strong message to Antipas as he does to some poor shepherd. He doesn't know the meaning of tact."

Well, if it's tact Jesus is recommending, he's come to the wrong dispenser. I believe in saying what needs to be said. "And why, Jesus," I said, "would John send a different memo to Antipas than 'some poor shepherd', to use your words. I'm surprised you'd say that."

He says, "Simon, I don't mean to imply that the law doesn't relate to everyone. The thing is Antipas can throw John in jail for any perceived offense. There is no reasoning with Romans. Moreover, diplomacy works better than John's in-your-face style."

"How, Jesus, can you diplomatically condemn sleeping with your brother's wife, as Antipas is doing? Should John say, 'Now Antipas, when you snuggle up to this woman, contemplate Moses' commandment against coveting your neighbor's wife.' That would be diplomatic but lost in the ruffle of the sheets. Do you get my meaning?"

"You make yourself clear, Simon," Jesus replied.

The two of us were sitting in the shade of a gnarly, old oak along the sea, talking and watching the waves make their eternal journey. It's not far from where Eden and I live, where Eden has a list of chores for me. I would rather gab with Jesus. It's good to see him again.

We've been many places together. It's really amazing. I grew up a fisherman because my father was a fisherman. Jesus grew up as God because his heavenly father is God. I tossed a stone into the water and wondered how far the ripples would drift.

Jesus told me he was so worried about John that he actually walked all the way along the Jordan to where John was preaching and baptizing to inform him of the danger he was in. "There were dozens there listening and waiting for baptism," Jesus said. "At first John didn't see me, but then he came out of the water and was all in a fluster.

"I wanted to convince him to tone down his attacks on Herod Antipas. Before I had a chance to talk to him, he jumped out of the river and wanted to know my reason for being there. His arms were flailing as he spoke. I tried to settle him down by first saying that I wanted to be baptized by him as others did."

"I presume he ignored your request." I said.

"He did, and forcefully. 'You are coming to me?' he said, shaking his head as if to say no. 'You should be baptizing me,' he went on. It was funny in a way. We were nose-to-nose, eye-to-eye. Finally, he gave in and allowed it. The people around us were amused and clapped as I was baptized."

"That was it then?"

"Not exactly," Jesus explained. "John and the people were then shocked to hear the voice of the Heavenly Father. I was astonished as well. This was the first time that I heard the Father's voice, audibly. I guess God the Father also wanted to let everyone know of the importance of baptism. As a way of showing that, right then, the Holy Spirit descended over me and a voice from above declared: '*This is my beloved Son, with whom I am well pleased.*' That changed the picture. John followed me out of the water and hugged me."

I have to say that that disclosure was also astounding for me. I knew Jesus was no ordinary man. I had more than an inkling he may be the Messiah. Andrew did, too. That's why we agreed to be his followers. But the voice of God, '*This is my beloved son?*' That is the word. What more proof is needed? It's like when one is a child, and your father says: Do as your mother asks. That's it. Over.

For once, after Jesus said that, I was tongue-tied. What should I say? Lamely, I returned to John.

"So John took your advice?" I asked.

"Not really," Jesus said. "It was then that I asked him to go easy on his Antipas lecturing, for his own good health. He said his plans were to eventually proceed north along the river, 'closer to Antipas', he said, 'so he can hear better'. And then he went back to baptizing the people."

"And the people there," I hesitated, "they heard the voice of our God?"

"They did."

"And what did they do?"

"Some who were already baptized rushed off to tell what they had heard and seen, I suppose. Many there began to sing as John baptized."

Jesus then tells me that he has always felt close to John. Except for Jesus' time in Egypt when he was under four years of age, he explained, he visited his distant cousin nearly every year at Passover. John then lived in Ein Kerem at the western edge of Jerusalem. After his parents, Elizabeth and Zecheriah died, he gave the money gained from the sale of their house to the poor and thus enlisted himself in the legions of Judea's indigent.

John lives off the land, literally, mostly in the desert. He is an ascetic Jew and off and on has been part of the strict monastic Essenes. He worked brief periods as a shepherd, fruit picker and wood collector in regions along the Jordan River.

"John preaches that he is a mere messenger," Jesus continued, "that someone greater is coming, someone 'whose sandals I'm unfit to carry.' John looked at me for some time. Then he went back to preaching and the need to repent. When some Pharisees and Sadducees were baptized, he flat out labeled them as vipers, and required them to show proof of their repentance. He cuts no slack for any soul."

"Wow, I like John's style," I told Jesus. "Either fish or cut bait."

Jesus says that from Jerusalem to Jericho and the entire lower Jordan valley, John has become known as the Baptizer. Many see him as a prophet. His growing prominence is also being watched by Roman officials, particularly Pontius Pilate, and some rulers in the Sanhedrin, the Jewish high court.

Pilate, I should point out, assumed the office of prefect (governor) of Judea four years ago. I never met the man, but the word is that Pilate is greedy and ruthless and has little regard for the Jewish population and our religion. He enraged Jews when he sent troops into Jerusalem and the Temple area bearing standards with the image of ruler Tiberius. He was eventually forced to remove them.

I have seen the works of this Jesus. I have witnessed his miracles. I know his love and mercy. I sense his intense desire to build the kingdom on Earth as it is in heaven. He embraces his Hebrew heritage but wants to give it new direction.

When he touches a leper, he does not become unclean but the leper is cured. The sinner who washed his feet was the one who was cleansed. He has taught me that while faith in God is necessary to gain the kingdom of heaven, it must be accompanied by mercy.

What I don't understand is why he picked me as one of his followers. I am just an ordinary person.

With the baptism of Jesus, the message of John the Baptist spread like sand before a driving wind. Jesus had also sought advice from his follower, Philip of Bethsaida, in regard to John, but Philip, too, shrugged for lack of an answer. Philip, who knew John before he met Jesus, explained that "John was merely being John." Moderation was not part of his being.

With the sun rising high, Jesus decided to return to Nazareth. He found no answer regarding John's spirited preaching. "He won't change and I won't stop worrying about him," Jesus said. Then he left.

Back home in Nazareth, more and more an infrequent occasion as his ministry expanded, Jesus told his mother of his visit with Simon. "I'll bet he was a big help," Mary said, her icy regard of the fisherman still unthawed. "Are you hungry?" she asked automatically.

Mary, a widow now, went with him and his growing number of disciples on some of the trips to the Galilee region, but she often declined more distant excursions. Mary's health was good but she never liked crowds. She was 45 and long treks were a challenge. Most of Jesus' disciples were younger than he was.

"No thanks, but your fresh bread is always tempting."

"Where have you been recently and have you gained any disciples?"

"We've traveled a lot," Jesus explained, "from Bethany in the south to Caesarea in the north."

She brought him a plate with several slices of bread and a jar of honey.

"Mother. I'm really not hungry."

"Fine. Maybe I am."

"The time is short," Jesus said contemplatively, "for selecting other followers. I must do a better job of explaining what I mean by building the kingdom of God. I have heard some of them questioning their decision to drop what they were doing and follow me. 'Where exactly are we going?' one said. 'I don't know what I am supposed to be doing,' another said. They call me rabbi, yet apparently don't get the full message."

"My son, the yeast does not always rise when expected."

"I hope I'm not being impatient," Jesus continued, "but there is much to be done."

"Jesus, time will speed by soon enough. I understand the reason your Father in heaven sent you. As you were conceived in my womb, I knew these days would arrive. Taking on a human condition, living the life of a human, beginning your teaching, revealing your divinity, all culminates in the final act of salvation. God, our Lord, our redeemer."

She hesitated in thought.

"The truth is that your followers don't know you like I know you. And, keep in mind they are 100 percent human nature. Be patient."

Again, Mary waited. She looked at Jesus, pondering what she didn't know, how the end would transpire. Hundreds of times, in the darkness of the night when sleep was elusive, her mind searched for relief, begged for endurance. She was torn between motherhood and God's plan. Did he have to die so others could live?

"I don't suppose you have ever contemplated God's formula for salvation," she said tenderly. "I don't even know if God has revealed to you the full dimensions of how the sins of many will be offset by the sacrifice of one. I'm sorry. I shouldn't add to your own worries."

As she savored the richness of bread capped with sweet honey, she tried to force aside images of the harsh days ahead.

"Please, have a piece of bread and tell me about your disciples."

He needed no additional convincing. He smothered the bread with honey and took a big bite as if the answer lay tucked in its delicious fold. Mary pointed to her chin, with satisfaction and a chuckle, to indicate where honey had trickled down Jesus' face into his growing beard. He wiped his chin.

For a few moments it was as if he were 10 again, far from the rigors of a ministry that would end in his death. They talked about his boyhood friends, school, cuts and bruises, and what Joseph called sawdust stories.

The latter included a narrative about a couple who couldn't agree on the configuration of a new front door. Joseph usually related the episode, how he outlined his normal plan for a front door. The husband was all for a simple replacement unit, "something to keep the cold and animals out," was how he put it. Ordinarily, the man's preference presided. Not this time.

"My, my how your memory has failed you," Joseph would quote the wife in the story, and it was then that Joseph would start his belly laugh, Jesus recalled. The woman told the carpenter crew that her husband came home one evening, "smelling like a wine vat." He couldn't get the heavy, one-piece door open. After wrestling with it for a while, she said, he took a run at it.

Now Joseph was beginning to shake with mirth, Jesus said, at the image of the big fellow crashing through the portal. As he lay sprawled on the floor inside he uttered a promise, "sprinkled with violations of the Third Commandment," to never have such a heavy door, the wife related. She proposed a plan she claimed would satisfy both of them. Here, Jesus recollected, Joseph would pause to wipe his snickering face.

Her idea was to have two doors, a top and bottom arrangement that would not only be much easier to open but add a little "glory" to the entrance, "somewhat like Mrs. Weiss has. It will be easy to open and attractive."

"Guess what," Joseph would ask with the answer evident. "Yep. We built a double door."

"Joseph also got a kick out of the time when Grandma Anne's rooster chased you across the yard," Mary remembered. "I suppose you were about seven years old. After she died, we inherited the hens and one mean rooster. As you fled the rooster's talons one day, you stepped in some hot embers from wood scraps that Joseph was burning. That part wasn't so funny, and Joseph felt bad for laughing."

"Wasn't that the same chicken we had for dinner a week later?" Jesus asked.

"It was. Joseph said the rooster was out of second chances. It seems it flew at him some time earlier. It was one of the few times that Joseph's stoic nature was set aside. Now, you still haven't updated me about new disciples."

"First, I need to tell you news you may not like." Jesus said. Mary frowned in expectation.

"I have chosen Simon to head my church. Haven't told him yet, but he is the one constant among the group, the rock."

Mary dipped her spoon in the honey jar, removed it and placed the contents on her tongue. Jesus looked at her in amazement. She was doing the very thing that on many occasions he was told not to do. Was she trying to sweeten the news about Simon?

"OK, then," Mary simply replied. Did that mean she accepted Simon with all his bird drawings and rough edges, Jesus wondered, or that she acquiesced to his decision? He decided to let his question go unanswered.

"I plan to call him Cephas (Peter in English)," Jesus said, still looking for signs of protest. "Cephas is another word for stone or rock," he elaborated.

"I know that," Mary said curtly, which by translation meant she was not 100 percent sold on Simon, or Cephas, or the rock.

"It still amuses me," Jesus said, "to think of that first day I met him. "I was speaking to a group along the Galilee shore. It was close quarters with the trees and embankment, and as the crowd grew I decided to step in Simon's boat to continue my talk. The impression on his face was priceless. It was almost as if I was in the process of stealing his rig. I explained I was just using it as a podium.

"Before the day was over I asked him and his brother, Andrew, to follow me. A little down the shoreline I met the Zebedee brothers, James and John, and I asked them to join and they did. It was the following weekend, you will remember, that I was teaching in the Capernaum Synagogue when a man possessed by demons cried out for help. I helped him, though some said later I shouldn't have because it was on the sabbath."

"I recall all that," Mary said, "and wasn't it that same evening that you went across the street from the Synagogue to Simon's house and cured his mother-in-law of fever?"

"It was."

"I can slice some more bread if you'd like and there is plenty of honey."

"No, thanks."

"Jesus, I've always wondered why you asked a bunch of fishermen to be your followers, and why they said 'yes'."

"I wondered when you would ask that question. Well, they seem like regular people. Fishing for a living is hard work with lots of disappointment. Fishing for men is hard work and often disappointing. Fishing demands faith, patience, working together and attention to conditions. So does fishing for men. At the same time, I want all of them to understand that the kingdom of God includes everyone. All are invited, but their actions will determine their destination. And God's mercy has no bounds."

"And Simon will be their leader?"

"Yes. And you know about Levi, or Mathew as I have called him, the tax collector. He will be a good manager of day-to-day operations and a historian. Nathaniel, or Bartholomew as some refer to him, and Thomas worked in the fishing business, Thomas in his father's repair shop, and Nathaniel as a handyman. I am still praying about the others. Of course, there are others, men and women, who are part of our group, but my plan is to select 12 as my apostles."

"And you have decided on 12 in deference to the 12 tribes of Israel?"

"Yes. I don't need an army. My battle is to win the hearts of people, to explain to them the path to eternal life. That is why I was born a human and that is also the task of my apostles."

"I'm still puzzled by all the emphasis on fishermen," Mary said. "Why not shepherds, for example. Moses was a shepherd. So were David and Jacob. David sang 'the Lord is my shepherd.' Shepherds were among the first to witness your birth. Or why not include a winemaker? People are attracted to them. Or a craftsman like Joseph?"

"I believe I will have another slice of bread," Jesus said, "but I will get it. And a cup of wine. May I get some wine for you?"

"Sure," Mary replied without a second thought. "I'm not going anywhere." He gathered the bread and wine, at the same time thinking of his answer.

"Look at this way. A shepherd's job is to maintain the flock. Sure, he will go after the lost sheep. But a fisherman seeks all kinds of fish, new fish every day. While the kingdom of God is interested in the lost sheep, maybe even more so than those already in the fold, it is attentive to all, people from every nation and culture. I suppose I could select a farmer, for the kingdom of God is like the man who sows good seed in his . . . Mother?"

"Oh, I'm sorry Jesus," Mary said drowsily. "I believe I will retire."

Chapter 24

NAZARETH, 17AD – Jesus briskly stepped up to the bimah before his Synagogue class and opened the Scripture to Deuteronomy, one of his favorite books and the last of Pentateuch or Torah. He unfolded the holy words until he reached the place where he intended to read. He looked up and spotted Naomi in the women's section.

For a moment, he was disoriented by her broad smile, bordered by lips colored only by natural beauty, and olive skin as soft as morning dew and slightly bronzed by the Galilean sun. She confounded his bearings, similar to what happened when he met her on that path outside Nazareth when he was training for the Nain race. He forced his eyes downward at the scroll only to find them glancing sideways in defiance, like a child playing hide-and-seek who takes a sneak peek at scattering participants.

Reading from the Torah was something he had done for several years. Students were asked by Rabbi Shimon to select a passage and then lead a discussion about it. Jesus had memorized much of Deuteronomy, especially sections in which Moses talked of God's special covenant with the Jewish people. While many recited Scripture, Jesus preferred holding the scroll and simulate reading.

On this occasion he planned to mix the words of Moses about the uniqueness and singleness of God, and those of Isaiah regarding the coming of a Messiah. He anticipated a lively discussion.

Now he had to shift his gaze from this farmer's daughter to the task at hand. It was in the nick of time, too, that he redirected his vision. Others in the class began turning their heads to see what demanded his stare. When they looked at him again, his attention was back on track.

"Fellow students," he said. "It always amazes me, as I know it does you, to hear God speaking. We are so blessed as a people to be favored by our God, and to learn of his prescription for living, how to treat all people, how to conduct our behavior. Today, that message comes once again from God, through Moses. Permit me to read His holy words."

Jesus looked at the students again, but this time he intentionally avoided Naomi. He lifted the scroll and read. "It is written,

Hear, O Israel! The Lord is our God, the Lord alone. Therefore, you shall love the Lord, your God, with all your heart, and with all your soul, and with all your strength. Take to heart these words which I enjoin on you today. Drill them into your children. Speak of them at home and abroad, whether you are busy or at rest. Bind them at your wrist as a sign and let them be as a pendant on your forehead. Write them on the doorposts of your houses and on your gates.

"Now, these words were spoken," Jesus said, "after Moses reminded our people of their freedom from Egyptian slavery, and their wandering in the wilderness until God gave Moses the tablets. And what does he find when he comes down from the mountain? They were paying homage to a golden calf and celebrating in licentiousness.

"In spite of all the transgressions, Moses reminded the people of God's forgiveness, *Yet in his love for your fathers,* Moses goes on, *the Lord was so attached to them as to choose you, their descendants, in preference to all other peoples.* Then he adds: *Circumcise your hearts, therefore, and be no longer stiff-necked.* He implores us to open our hearts.

"There are many more words by Moses, as you know, and I encourage you to read them often. But today I would ask you to consider Moses' instruction about loving God only and words of the prophets about the coming of a Messiah. Does one exclude the other? Some say the Messiah will be an anointed king, a mere human figure.

"Yet, Isaiah tells us that a virgin will bear a son and call him Immanuel, which means 'God is with us.' Micah even prophesizes that this ruler for Israel will be born in Bethlehem. Is it possible that this God-man could come in our time?" Jesus asked. "And if he did extraordinary feats – raised the dead, healed the sick, cast out demons – would he be accepted?"

"All interesting questions, Jesus," Amal said, "but isn't it true that most men believe the Messiah will be a strong military leader who will expunge the Romans? And aren't there many references in Scripture, some precise predictions, concerning the coming of a Messiah? And if, as you suggest, he came in our time, what does that mean for us in Nazareth? We are barely on the map!"

"I can tell you this much," Darius piped up from the rear. "If this Messiah, whenever he comes, is a God-man, that is divine as well as human, he won't be enlisting an army to chase out the Romans. As they say in Capernaum, he will have other fish to fry. He will focus on the kingdom of God, not the politics of Israel. And this kingdom will be world-wide."

"Wow!" Hiram said with a tinge of mockery. "Sounds like you have some inside information. Do you have a relative who is or was a high priest, someone with ties to the inner operations of the Temple? Or, maybe, you are the Messiah and are waiting for the right time to disclose your plans."

There were some who applauded Hiram's chutzpa and others who responded with a hissing sound. Jesus extended his hands in a gesture intended to quiet the commotion. "I agree with Darius," Jesus said. "I don't believe the Messiah will organize an army to combat the Romans. Any other comments?"

"Let me see if I understand the essence of your question," Kenan said. "If Moses said there is a single God to be praised and revered, and Scripture also talks about God coming in the form of a human person, are the two passages compatible. Is that it? To me the question is whether God would lower himself to become one of us." He looked around the room and spread his hands. "I rest my case."

That produced uniform laughter.

"I think you have hit on the question of the day," Jesus smiled. "Just a reminder Benji," Jesus added, pointing to a tall boy in the back. "You have the topic next time. Yes, Piram. You have a comment? Piram was on the shy side so Jesus wanted to recognize him.

"Yes, please." He waited to gather his courage. "Jesus, am I imagining it or did I hear someone say that you were born in Bethlehem? And, and I don't know of anyone else named Jesus, which my father says means *God saves* in Hebrew. Perhaps the Messiah lives in Nazareth."

That sent a momentary hush across the room, a rare quiet that Hiram believed he had the responsibility to change.

"Yes, yes, Piram. I see it now. Our town will go down in history. Little ole Nazareth, which by the way, in Hebrew means lost in the hills."

That led to more laughter and gave Jesus an opening to conclude the session without commenting on Piram's comments. But Benji wasn't ready to dismiss.

"Before we end, I would like to suggest another point of confusion," Piram said after the sniggering halted. "The kingdom of God, I believe, involves more than a heavenly realm. It comprises both a worldly and heavenly kingdom, and that, of course, means life after death. But some of our people don't believe in an afterlife. How does that add up?"

"That's an easy one," claimed Thaddeus. "People who don't believe in heaven won't go there. When their body dies, gamar! The end! To me it makes no sense to say there is no afterlife, no heaven. There are several places where Scripture says that we are made in the image of God. To say it all ends at death of the body is not logical."

"I see the rabbi approaching, so we'll have to wrap this up," Jesus said. "I would end our discussion by asking Thaddeus, what if people repent and believe in everlasting life just before they die? Will God's mercy extend to them?"

"Ah, Jesus," Rabbi Shimon said. "I see you are winding things up. Did you have a good session today?"

"I would say so," Jesus replied, "but we could have benefited from your thoughts."

With that the gathering dispersed. Jesus grinned in satisfaction at the conversation that he had stimulated. He was comfortable in leading the exchange and pictured larger crowds and future talks about the kingdom of God. As he walked out of the Synagogue, he pondered his question to Thaddeus. God's mercy never ends, he mused. That makes it possible for the last to be first.

"That was fun and stimulating," she approached Jesus as students went their separate ways. "You have such a kind way of involving people, even when you may disagree." It was the farmer's daughter and her wonderful smile. "I have to wonder if you are destined for greater things than a carpenter, that maybe you'll study to be a rabbi."

"Hello, Naomi. Those are kind words. I just wish it were more acceptable in our culture for girls and women to participate in Synagogue school. Or, for that matter, in everything. Genesis says *God created man in His own image, in the image of God He created him: male and female He created them.* I would place the emphasis on the last phrase. All are equal."

"Well, Jesus. I think most of the women in Nazareth would agree with you," Naomi responded. "But there are still many men who think women should walk a step behind. What are your plans for the rest of the day?"

"I wish I could say that I'm free like a bird, but my father has a list of projects that must be done, or, as he says, 'Projects we should have completed yesterday.' Will you be here next week?"

"I don't know. Benji has the subject next week, and his readings and topics are not as interesting as yours. I only came today because you were in charge."

"That's nice of you to say, Naomi. As for Benji, I seem to recall a session he conducted that ran twice as long as normal. He read from Genesis and ascribed most of the blame for mankind's sin against God to Eve, to women. I was surprised at the number of male students who were in an uproar. If the young women had joined in, poor Benji would still be running for the hills."

"Well, then. I guess we'll see each other when we see each other," Naomi said. They said goodbyes, but again Jesus wished he had said more. Yet, he was in an awkward position. He liked Naomi, but his destiny prohibited any comments or actions that would prompt matters in a misleading way. It was a dilemma that he had measured before he met Naomi.

Of all the ramifications inherent in the intertwining of divine and human natures, this was among the most complex. Making friends with others – especially young women – is a delicate business, he thought, when one has a divine mission. He had discussed the matter with his parents, but he was unsure who else he might consult.

He knew no one could take his place, but the process of revealing who he was and what he was sent by God to do was daunting. Surely, he had assured himself, it would be a gradual process with his followers, his closest friends, a revelation over time, perhaps not unlike the discovery of himself.

When he arrived home, the first thing he noticed was Joseph lying on his mat in the corner of the house, covered with a blanket. This was the second such occasion for Joseph. It was especially worrisome knowing that he had a full schedule of jobs. It had to be serious for his father to miss work, not only because he felt an obligation to customers but because he enjoyed it.

"Please close the door, Jesus. Your father is not feeling well," Mary said. "I feel it's some sort of issue with his breathing, but he refuses to see the healer." The nearest physician was in Sapphoris, and most of them were assigned to the house of Herod Antipas. "I think his condition is getting worse," she said in a whisper.

"What are the two of you murmuring about?" Joseph suddenly rose to a sitting position. "Don't be planning my funeral just yet. I've got too much work to do. Jesus, now that you have completed leading Synagogue school for a while, you can concentrate on carpenter jobs. We have that one large sheep shed to build for Mr. Kilmer on Cana road."

"Yes, father. I know," Jesus replied. "I've already discussed the project with him. He has the poles for the frame and I plan on starting there next week. But first we have a roof to repair, a door to replace and Mrs. Sara of Olive alley needs her chimney fixed. I can handle all of those projects. You need to rest so that you will be able to supervise the sheep shed construction next week."

"You can do the masonry work on the chimney?"

"Yes, I can. I have watched you and learned the right mixture and how to apply it. Besides, I'm more agile on a roof, and you are better at managing a large project from the ground. I will need your guidance on that sheep shed, but I plan to work on the other projects yet this afternoon."

Jesus was coming into the prime of his life. He was strong and like most young men confident beyond experience. He had become more than a carpenter's apprentice. Joseph had trusted him with jobs of any size, complimented him for his skills and emphasized his pleasure at how he treated the customers. He saw himself in Jesus, the highest praise a father can give.

Before the fat sun hauled its glowing belly over the western horizon, Jesus had repaired the chimney and roof. The following day he rose early for the door replacement project and started preliminary work on the herdsman's sheep shed. Joseph wasn't surprised at his accomplishments and told him so when Jesus returned home. After supper, Jesus was restless and it showed.

"OK," Joseph said, reading his son's quizzical demeanor. "Get whatever is sitting in your craw out in the open lest it festers until it becomes a real problem. Something with the business?"

"Yes and no, father. Actually, there's two matters. For some time, I've wondered why one of Herod Antipas' minions hasn't ordered you to work in Sepphoris like he did with Grandfather Joachim. They are always scouring the region for quality craftsmen and you certainly fill that bill. I'm happy that you didn't have to go and could concentrate on your own business."

Joseph laughed, the kind of snigger that is born in the depths of one's soul and nourished by profound satisfaction. Mary knew the story, so she concentrated on cleaning supper utensils, leaving Jesus the sole audience for Joseph. The subject was like a tonic for Joseph. He sat taller and inched his chair toward Jesus. Then he inclined his head in a fashion suggesting that he held a secret that would make Rome shudder.

"I heard they were coming," he began, whispering as if a legion of Roman soldier spies were outside the door. "It was after your grandfather died. I'm sure Joachim had mentioned my name, thinking that I needed a high-paying job in Sepphoris. I didn't. I love my work and customers here. So, what to do? These are people who don't ask; they order.

"Two days later an Antipas foreman and a couple of soldiers showed up. You were off in school. Knowing they are always in need of masons, I honestly told them my specialty was carpentry work. I am no masonry artisan like your grandfather was. Moreover, I stretched the truth by saying I was afraid of heights and that much of my approach to carpentry was by guess and by golly, not a lot of this measuring stuff." Joseph smiled as the story dribbled from his memory bank.

"I could see the sour looks on this one fellow's face," Joseph relished in the telling, picturing the event as if it happened yesterday. He leaned in closer, the clinching words gathering in his mouth. "Like frosting on a cake, I slathered on a yarn about falling from a scaffold, the reason for my fear of heights, don't you see, and that my one leg now tends to give out. There is some truth to that. I told them I didn't feel comfortable on a ladder anymore. They mulled all that and a short time later took off and never came back."

Joseph leaned back in his chair, grabbed some pistachio nuts for chewing as he gathered his thoughts for the rest of the story.

"Now, the real truth is I never wanted to give them the opportunity to meet you, to possibly learn what Herod Antipas I'm sure knows well. His chief scribe, who happens to be Jewish, knows all about what happened shortly after your birth, how Antipas' father, in a paranoid fit, ordered the death of all male infants because he heard of this newborn king.

"Antipas, like his father, has spies everywhere, and knows we fled to Egypt and probably knows when we returned. He has ambitions and, like his father, doesn't want anyone or anything interfering. Understand, Jesus, he was disappointed when his father's territory was divided by Emperor Augustus among siblings, crushed when given the title tetrarch. He wanted to be king and still does. From the time we left Egypt, we have kept a wary eye on Antipas because of who you are."

Joseph rose, secured the goatskin of water, and poured a cup for himself. He drank, then refilled his cup.

"I must say," he said, "that Nazareth has the best-tasting well water of any town I know. Would either of you like a cup of water while I'm up? Or, maybe Jesus, you'd like some grape juice?" Joseph winked and Mary displayed a frown that definitely disapproved.

"OK, then," Joseph continued. No takers. Where was I? Oh, yes. As you know, Jesus, Augustus died several years ago and young Tiberius became emperor. Now Tiberius, from what I hear, is an odd duck. He is a strongman for sure, using the Roman army to put down anyone he dislikes. But, at least he isn't so vain, so far, as to have months named after himself, as Julius Ceasar and Augustus did."

"Joseph," Mary said. "Get on with your story. It's too late for a history lesson. And, I must trim the lamp wicks before going to bed."

"Right. I should amend my statement to say that Emperor Tiberius is not without arrogance. Antipas knows that, and that is why he is building a new city on the west bank of the Sea of Galilee and calling it Tiberias. They are spelled slightly different, and I do not know why." Joseph proceeded to spell out both the names of the city and emperor.

"What?" Mary said with exasperation. "First a history session and now a spelling lesson? What's next? Geography? What's your point?"

"I'm getting there," Joseph said. "The point is Antipas desperately wants to be named a king, and he'll do anything – including building a city – to get it. And that, my dear wife, spells danger."

"Thank you, father, and mother, too, for all your worries and protection. Worry of Rome is among many things that make broadening God's kingdom so difficult, and there will be many more challenges until the end."

That drew Mary's attention. She looked up as she dried the last of the supper dishes. What does he mean *there will be more challenges until the end?* Is he talking about his end, or the end of the world? Joseph's mind wandered down similar roads, but both kept such questions buried in their hearts.

"I am not saying Antipas' representatives won't come to Nazareth next week so seek more workers to rebuild Sepphoris or work at Tiberias," Joseph continued. "If that happens, I suspect they will want to talk to you, and it will be more than just a quiz about skills. They would probe every move you have made since being born in Bethlehem." That cast another shadow over the small house.

"So, Jesus, you may not want to flood the region with advertising, or send out any of these satisfaction surveys," Joseph added.

It gave Mary, a natural worrier, another thing to ponder. She sometimes would ask herself, as a means to redirect her disquiet, if all these points of apprehension were listed in the fine print of the Angel Gabriel's announcement two decades ago. *You have found favor with God,* he had said. She was troubled then and she was troubled now.

"What's the second issue?" Joseph interrupted her thoughts. "You said there were two matters on your mind."

"Yes, father, perhaps not as serious as Antipas, but, yes, of concern."

"Well, spit it out, son."

"Alright. Her name is Naomi," Jesus began. Joseph began nodding as if he knew the second question all along. "Mother and I have talked about it a little, but I believe the issue has become more intense."

"More intense for you or for Naomi?" Joseph blurted. "I know who she is. I've seen her with her family at Synagogue." He paused.

"I think more intense for both of us."

Mary absorbed the full dimensions of Jesus' "issue" and at the same time sensed Joseph was still on the outskirts of understanding. She had met Naomi several times at Synagogue school and during Shabbot. In the past year, she had also seen her at mikveh, the Jewish purification pool. She was impressed by the young woman's maturity, intelligence and warm personality.

Mary had concluded that Naomi, pushed by hormones, was at the age when girls regard boys differently. One day boys are dorks, the next day they are princes.

"I think what Jesus means, Joseph, is that Naomi has an eye for him, and he is attracted to her," Mary said. "It's what happens when human nature takes its course. Except Jesus has two natures, human, which is pulled toward Naomi, and divine, which is pulled toward God. That all adds up to create a difficult issue."

"Hummpff," Joseph responded.

"Thanks, Mother," Jesus said.

"It isn't fair to keep Naomi in the dark about your plans," Mary said. "She is looking to her future and so must you."

"Yes. I know," Jesus replied. "She is such a wonderful young woman. I don't want to do anything to hurt her."

"Can't you just tell her you have a business to run and eventually have plans that will take you out of Galilee?" Joseph proposed.

"Joseph," Mary said with a disgusting glare. "I don't think that's adequate. You don't cut off matters of the heart with a business plan."

"There is another matter," Jesus said, "but I'm not worried about that."

"Yet a third issue?" Joseph spread his arms upward and shook his head. "We haven't solved the first two. Let's have it."

"Rabbinic Jewish law requires men to marry by their early 20s and be fruitful," Jesus said. "Curiously, as I understand it, a woman may remain unmarried. I desire to continue my rabbinical studies apart from the responsibilities of marriage and family. Is that possible and would it bring more wagging tongues to our household?"

Joseph looked at Mary and laughed.

"Wagging tongues don't bother us one bit," Joseph smiled. He looked at Mary and she smiled back. "We are veterans of wagging tongues. Jesus, you were creating wagging tongues before you were born. Not all people but many were ready to stone your pregnant mother before I was privileged to learn who you are. Then we were married.

"In visiting with Rabbi Shimon and others, too, I have learned that this marriage edict for men is more of a recommendation," Joseph continued. "I would worry more about Antipas."

"However you explain your plans to Naomi," Mary said softly, "be tender and prayerful. She will be hurt no matter what your best efforts are to avoid it. She will somehow think she is unworthy, especially if you are the first special person in her life. So, by all means tell her directly that she would be a pleasing, suitable wife, that it is not her but your plans for further studies and ministry that prohibit marriage."

"Your mother always has the right answer," Joseph injected. "She can melt a knot in a piece of lumber and not split the wood." Mary's brow curled. You may have another problem, Jesus. Have you seen Slam today?" Joseph had already told Mary that the aged dog was ailing.

"No. I haven't seen him," Jesus replied. "Is he OK?"

"I think ole Slam is dying," Joseph said bluntly.

"But, father. He seemed fine when I saw him yesterday."

"Maybe so, son. Remember, Slam is old, and it doesn't take much to tip the scales in a bad way."

Slam died two days later.

Chapter 25

There was no birthday party when Jesus turned 18. His life began to settle into a routine devoted to Scripture study and Synagogue, early morning prayer at his favorite spot beneath the sycamore tree, and of course, work.

More and more, as Joseph's health kept him at home, Jesus assumed operation of the carpentry business. However, he made it a point to keep Joseph involved by consulting him on designs and building procedures. It was also good public relations to inform customers that the master builder was still involved.

Months passed.

Jesus' relationship with God the Father became more personal, a oneness that grew as his physical body grew. The Kingdom, and his part in it, began to take shape in his mind. At some point, he decided, it would become necessary to solicit followers to help spread God's word. Likewise, he meditated on Scripture's salvation commentary. His role gradually took form in an obscure way.

Increasingly, he embraced the concept of being both the Son of God and the Son of Man, the divine co-existing with the human. It meshed with Scripture and what Mary and Joseph had told him. His sense of God's plan slowly emerged. How that would play out with the public, particularly Roman and Sanhedrin officials, was still unknown.

Another subject remained unsettled: Naomi.

Mary, in particular, kept urging Jesus to speak to Naomi in kind but plain words about his intentions, but his inability to form the right explanation delayed the matter. He was disgusted with himself, with his procrastination. His default solution was to consult his friends, Caleb, Josiah and others. He would see them at the upcoming Jewish New Year harvest celebration.

While the Torah marks the beginning of Hebrew months in the springtime, in context with the Passover Festival, agricultural regions also celebrated God's great gifts at harvest time as a 'new year'. Leviticus calls it the Festival of Trumpets, a time when the shofar is sounded 100 times to ring in the new harvest year. Eventually, it became known as Rosh Hashana.

The New Year festival begins on the first day of Tishrei (September-October), the seventh month in the Hebrew calendar. The two-day observance is celebrated by some as the birthdate of the world. In Nazareth, the festival began with services in the town well area. While the ceremony was ordinarily held in a Synagogue, the Nazareth Synagogue was too small to accommodate the expected crowd. Moreover, many believed it was appropriate to hold a harvest celebration outdoors, next to the fields.

Rabbi Shimon carried the shofar, the horn of a ram, accompanied by the baal toke'ah, the so-called master of blowing. People streamed in from all directions. They were engulfed in an air of gaiety and perfect weather. The sky's blue mass was like a canvass, with splotches of white clouds painted at random. They were ushered across the dome by a gentle westerly breeze born out of the Great Sea.

"Caleb," Jesus yelled and waved. "Over here by the tall pine."

Caleb spotted him and worked his way through the emerging crowd. Enos, a younger brother, was with him. It was evident the young people of the village were gathering on the perimeter of the cluster while older residents, including Mary and a reenergized Joseph, were in the center. Joseph insisted on attending.

"Shalom," Jesus greeted Caleb. "I see you brought Enos with you, the bright sibling in the family." Caleb looked at Enos and laughed.

"He knows a lot about Scripture but not a lot about business. Father says Enos is a candidate for rabbi school, and once he becomes a rabbi he can pray for the success of our business."

"Well, let us hope that rabbi Enos here prays not only for success of business, but fairness for everyone," Jesus said. "I like the sound of that. Rabbi Enos. Oh, there comes Josiah. And look who is with him. It's Eli from Nain."

"Hey," Caleb addressed the two as they twisted their way through the assembly. Caleb knew Eli from the Nain races. "Did you run up here, Eli, to get muscled up for the next race? Or is the harvest so poor over there that you must come here to celebrate?"

"And peace be with you, too" Eli shot back. "For your information, Caleb, the olive harvest was better than ever this year. Both the quantity and quality are improved. As for racing, we in Nain do not have to practice to outrun the turtles of Nazareth."

"OK, boys. Enough of the flowery greetings," Jesus said. "I am so glad all of you showed up today. After the service and sounding of the shofar, I would ask you to join me for some apples and honey. To be honest," he added with some timidity, "I need your advice on an important matter."

"Well, Jesus," Josiah teased, "let me analyze. I don't suppose you are stumped by a Scripture question. I suspect it has nothing to do with sawing lumber or repairing a roof. And I know you get along fine with your parents. Hmmm," he stretched his narration. "My diagnosis, and certainly I make no claim in psychotherapy or relational counseling," he cleared his throat, "my guess is that you have a girl issue."

They all laughed in agreement but before Jesus could explain his predicament, the rabbi called for quiet and began the prerequisite reading of psalms. There was chanting and blessings and intermittent blowing of the shofar. The rituals lasted for nearly an hour. Soon after the conclusion of the ceremony, the hubbub of visiting resumed. Families drifted back to their homes to enjoy a festive meal.

"There is something mystical about the piercing wails of the shofar," Caleb pronounced. "I know this a harvest celebration, but for me it's a reminder of our heritage. It's a reminder of God coming down Mount Sinai with Moses. It resonates the cries of the prophets urging Israel to return to God and his commandments."

"Well said, my friend," Jesus concurred. "I agree that it is intended to awaken slumbering souls. The kingdom of God, I believe, has nothing to do with political borders and everything to do with the boundaries of our souls, willing to serve others and accepting even those we don't like. That is the real test."

"Does that include the Romans?" Josiah asked. "It's difficult to accept or like them. To criticize them or in any way demean their ruling conduct could get you into a lot of trouble."

"I suspect, Josiah, that before things are over I will be in a lot of trouble." That produced puzzled looks and quiet questions. "But you are right," he finally forced himself to say, "in stating that my troubles right now involve a girl. She is a wonderful young lady, intelligent, kind, generous and attractive."

"That's a nice problem to have," Eli said. "Does this problem have a name? Are you still pining over this Naomi person?"

"Yes. She's the one," said Jesus. "And there is still some pining, I admit. But I need to tell her in a nice way that I'm not interested in marriage, that I have other plans. But how do I do that without hurting her feelings?"

"I think you are asking the impossible," Josiah offered. "I know this girl, and everything you say about her is true. I think the real problem is you. Why are you fighting this? If I had a girl that attractive and interested in me, I would run to my father and ask him to run to her father and beg for betrothal. Is there something wrong with your eyes?"

"No, Josiah. There is nothing wrong with my eyes. My senses are fully awake, but my heart and soul are aimed in a different direction. I know that's difficult for you fellows to understand, but I must continue my Scripture and rabbinic studies. My life is on a different path than others. You will come to know more about that as the years progress."

"Can't you be a rabbi and be married, too?" Enos asked.

"Yes you can. And that's a fair question, Enos. But my future and my work must be totally dedicated to our Father in heaven. In a few years, I plan to leave the carpenter business and take up the task of expanding the kingdom of God on Earth like it is in heaven."

"Wow," said Josiah. "That sounds pretty wild and ambiguous. Do you have a blueprint for this project, as you say you usually do in carpentry work? Are your parents aware of these sprouting ideas? Will others be involved? I guess what I'm asking is: Have you really thought this through?"

"All good questions. Yes, my mother and father are aware of my mission, and we've had many talks about the challenges involved. There is no blueprint, as you say, yet. I pray every day for guidance. I trust God will lead me to make the right decisions. After all, He is the father of us all, and always has our best interests in mind. That doesn't eliminate our responsibilities.

"But my plans are not as undefined as you suggest. I know I will need help in doing my work. At some point I will seek followers. I know now that my preaching will take place all over Galilee, along the Jordan River, and into Judea and Jerusalem itself. I will even go to Samaria. Eventually, I hope the message of God's love and mercy will be extended all over the world."

Jesus' words ushered the conversation far beyond seeking answers about a girl. What is he talking about in extending God's message everywhere? Who will finance this operation was the primary question in Eli's mind. Caleb focused on the idea of preaching to Samaritans, whom Jews held in contempt and regarded as enemies. They were dazed by his comments.

"Those are some hefty plans," Caleb ultimately broke the silence. He rubbed his baby beard as if it were a meditation aid. "A girl would think twice about getting involved in all that. If you tell Naomi what you told us, I think she will not only understand but run back home. When are you going to talk to her?"

"If I see her at the festival today," Jesus said, "I intend to tell her of my plans. Thank you friends for hearing me out. I know it sounds puzzling, but that's where I'm headed. I suggest we now gather at my house for apples and honey and other good things to eat." The offer of food was something they all understood.

Later in the day at the well area Jesus found children playing and running. A few adolescents were hanging out at the big pine, but Naomi was nowhere in sight. He looked in the Synagogue district, but only a few elders were there. He returned home, relieved that he could postpone the encounter once again. However, the following day, as he walked back from his early morning prayers at the sycamore tree, opportunity came jogging down the path.

From 200 cubits he recognized her gait. Clenched hands propelled her rhythmic stride. She wore a light blue tunic that was pulled up above her ankles and cinched beneath a tan belt. A white head shawl, tied loosely around her neck, bounced along like an afterthought. Her dark, braided hair was free to roam about her slender neck. She approached with a broad and captivating smile.

This Naomi from the road to Sepphoris was the complete package. Explaining his plans would be even more difficult than he'd imagined.

"Hello there," she addressed Jesus, coming to a halt. "What are you doing out here alone," she teased. Those were Jesus' words of greeting the first time they had met on the path. He got the message and they both laughed.

"What a pleasant surprise," Jesus said, his mindset laboring toward a candid gear. "I've been wanting to talk to you. I was looking for you at the festival, but I didn't see you."

"I was there," she said. "I saw you. You were busy talking to a bunch of young men. It must have been an interesting chat. One minute everyone was laughing and then later on the looks on your faces were so serious, as if some prophesy was about to be fulfilled."

"Before I forget," Jesus said, "about that first meeting on the path. I wanted to say that I was glad to see you out running, that you felt confident enough to go out on your own. I was surprised because that is unusual in our culture and, I have to admit, a little risky on this remote trail. Robbers have been known to travel these parts."

"I know," she said. "You were concerned for my safety, not that I was breaking some sort of taboo about women appearing alone in public."

"That's it. You are a mind reader. Somehow our culture, I've been told, assimilated customs from the Greeks. Making women subordinate is now more pronounced than it was in our ancestors' time. The family is what's important, and that obviously includes women as well as men. Women should be able to pursue any interests."

"Jesus, would you come and talk with my mother about that? Curiously, my father is OK with my going out on my own, but my mother worries about it, perhaps more about what other people might think than any concern about robbers."

"That is an issue for your family," Jesus replied. "And don't be judgmental about your mother. She loves you and has your best interests at heart. She's right to be concerned about your welfare, and your father trusts your judgement. How's that for a Solomon response? Besides, after you hear what I have to say you may not want to run on the path toward Nazareth again. But I hope that's not the case."

"Goodness. That sounds so serious," Naomi said with outstretched hands and an upturned wrinkle on her brow. "What is it that you want to tell me?"

"Naomi, I think you are a wonderful girl, everything a young man could dream of. You are devout, intelligent, energetic, affable, confident and, yes, attractive. However, my plans for the future are focused solely on spreading the kingdom of God. I will be studying more, praying more as I seek to fulfill my mission. I intend to preach God's word not just in Galilee but throughout Israel.

"I guess what I'm trying to say is that I want to be forthright with you, Naomi. I don't want to mislead you into thinking our friendship could lead to betrothal and marriage. There," he exhaled, "I've said it. At the same time I certainly don't want to disappoint you. My even greater fear is to sadden you."

"Oh, my Jesus." Naomi smiled. She walked to him, threw her arms around his shoulders and kissed him tenderly on the cheek. She looked deeply into his eyes.

"I understand," she said softly. "I cannot deny that you made my heart flutter and that I had imagined us as a couple. And those were joyous and satisfying visions. But then I sensed that your thoughts were in a different direction." She took a step back but continued to gaze into his eyes.

"I, too, hope you are not disappointed by what I say. I have known this young man for longer than I've known you. He works with his father on a farm that grows grain and raises sheep. He is kind, thoughtful, handsome and is a devout Jew. But he doesn't know Scripture like you do." She laughed. Jesus shrugged.

"We have asked our fathers to arrange for our betrothal."

Chapter 26

"What's up, Jesus?" Josiah asked, as he strode into the carpenter shop, his bearing as free flowing as his long hair. "I mean besides your breaking up with Naomi."

Jesus cleaned the sawdust from a rocker leg he was shaping, looked up, then wiped his sweating forehead. "Hello, Josiah. News sure travels fast around here. Where did you hear that?"

"Down at the well. The guys questioned your mind – ditching Naomi – but I defended you. I said your mind is excellent but your eyesight is really foggy."

"Thanks for your concern." Jesus placed the rasp on a table, pulled a rag from a tunic pocket and blew his nose. He was glad Josiah had stopped by. He needed the company. "Did you also know that Slam died?"

"Holy Moses. No! When did that happen? That's awful. I'm sorry."

"Last week. He was pretty old and had been lethargic for some time."

"That's terrible." Josiah continued. "First you lose your girl and then your dog dies. You must be devastated. I recall when Rex died. That was a tough week. Dogs don't get much respect in our culture, but Rex was a better companion than some guys I know."

"I didn't lose my girl and I didn't ditch her, Josiah. I told her I have a different mission in life than marriage, and I didn't want to lead her down a disappointing path."

"What did she say? Was she crushed?"

"She said she had met another young man and planned to get married."

"Well, doesn't that beat all," Josiah said, his face a contortion of puzzlement. "Go figure women."

The two traded other young-people news, fishing reports, the prospects for Nazareth's racing team and politics. Then, out of the blue, Josiah posed a couple of curious questions.

"Jesus, knowing the Scriptures as you do, is there any chance that a publican can go to heaven? And, I've heard you talk about the kingdom of God. What does that mean?"

Jesus picked up the smoothened rocker base and placed it aside. He brushed the shavings from his carpenter apron, removed it and tossed it on the tool table.

"I don't know," Jesus said off hand, pulling at his short beard. "I don't know if there is an answer anywhere in Scripture. I could see that if a tax collector was simply doing the job ordered by Romans that he could merit God's grace. On the other hand, if he was adding more onto what was owed, in other words cheating, he would have to repent and ask for God's mercy. God's mercy is available to the just and the unjust. Why do you ask?"

"My father had already paid a heavy tax on our wheat crop from last year, and the other day this publican comes by for more. Says it's a shipping duty, that he's sorry, but it has to be paid. We will have to mortgage some of this year's crop to come up with the money. It makes me want to join the Zealots."

"That certainly does sound unusual, Josiah. Do you know this man, this tax collector?"

"Yes. You may know him, too. He sometimes attends our Synagogue. His name is Herman Hakotz. I don't know where he lives."

"I see," Jesus said. "I may know him. While many Romans regard us as dogs, I have heard that some Jews are given jobs like tax collectors with the idea that Jews collecting from Jews will create less ill will. Here's an idea. Ask Rabbi ben Shimon about the additional tax. He knows people and my guess is he will visit with this Hakotz fellow in a general way. See what happens."

"That's a good idea. Do I mention the man's name?"

"No. The rabbi knows everybody and what they do."

"OK. I'll do it."

"Good," Jesus said. "Now, as for your question about this kingdom business, as you put it. God's kingdom, as I see it, is not a place with boundaries but includes heaven and earth. Love is the common denominator. God created us and the world out of love, and we must pay back in love. First, we must love God and then we must love our neighbors as ourselves."

"Wait a minute," Josiah protested. "It would be unlikely, but if a Roman lived next door to me, are you saying I have to love him? Or this tax collector? That's pushing things."

"Is it? Suppose you are walking on a remote path and are bitten by a serpent. You realize the consequences of its venom. This tax collector comes by and offers help. Would you accept his help? And if he saved your life, would that change your mind about him? If the scene were reversed, would you help him? Life is complex. Your neighbor might be anyone."

"If this kingdom has no boundaries, where is it?" Josiah asked. "Like I said, it sounds mysterious to me."

"Think of it this way. If you do everything out of love, for example treat your neighbor as you would want to be treated, you are in the midst of the kingdom. I hope to instill that idea in everyone with treatment of the marginal and most vulnerable at the heart of the matter. We are all part of God's creation. That makes everyone our siblings. We have obligations beyond ourselves and our immediate family."

"Well, good luck with all that. You may want to think twice about giving up your day job."

"Let's get something to eat," Jesus proposed. "We can talk more in the house. Mother baked some fresh barley bread this morning and it's waiting to be smothered with honey."

Over the months, Jesus continued to operate the carpentry business with Joseph less and less involved. Coming home from a roof repair job one evening, Jesus found Joseph lying on his mat, breathing heavily. He knelt down beside him and then placed another pillow beneath his head. Mary was preparing the evening meal, a one-pot stew of lentils and chickpeas spiced with herbs.

"Did you finish that roof repair work for the widow Horwitz?" Joseph wanted to know. His voice was raspy and beads of sweat covered his forehead. His eyes, Jesus noticed, had a socket-like look in his face. His skin had tightened to reveal an outline of his bones.

"Yes," Jesus said. "The job is done, and she thanks you and mother for the years of friendship."

"How is her health, Jesus? She has been a widow several years now and not getting any younger."

"She is fine, father. She inquired about you and mother and I said both of you are doing well, but I didn't know that you were having a breathing problem. Is there something I can get for you, perhaps some bread and a cup of mother's stew?"

"That would be fine. Please help me sit up. I'll be OK right here. It's just a little Great Sea flu. Please bring me a cup of stew and then take supper yourself. I'll be fine. When you are finished, I wish to have a talk with you. Not about business. I know you are doing an excellent job. I want to talk about your future."

Jesus could read between the lines. Joseph's words had all the marks of a dying man, yet Jesus had seen his earthly father weather pulmonary storms before. Joseph was not yet 50. The average age of death for Galilean males, discounting infant mortality, was in the 50s. After supper, Jesus sat cross-legged on the earthen floor next to Joseph, unsure what would develop.

"Jesus, we talked about some of this before, so forgive me if I repeat myself," Joseph began, his voice a little croaky. "I don't want you to fret about the future of the business. You are the son of God, born into a human family, to lead all of us to the heavenly kingdom. How that will unfold I do not know. But as the Messiah, you are far more than a carpenter. You are the ultimate fixer of things.

"Mary and I suspect you know this, but I want to say it anyway: The name of Jesus of Nazareth will be revered down through the ages. We have come to understand, as we were told at your conception, that you, my son, are also the God of Isaiah. You are the savior, the one who will reopen the gates of heaven and reconcile our relationship with the Lord."

Joseph started to cough and Jesus held a cup of water to his mouth.

"I'm fine. Just some phlegm." He looked into Jesus' eyes.

"In a few years, you will begin your ministry. I've heard you speak in the Synagogues and elsewhere, but more importantly I have seen your love for people, particularly the needy. Even so, and I'm sure you realize it, there will always be those who reject what you say, discount what you do and refuse your invitation to embrace God and eternal life.

"Mary and I are astounded to be your earthly parents. Were from the beginning. We've told you that before, but I can say that while

Isaiah may have predicted your coming, he didn't offer procedures for parenting the son of God. By that I don't mean you have caused any unusual worries, except, of course, when you were 12 and decided to stay in Jerusalem and chat with the elders.

"You know that your mother was nearly stoned when neighbors discovered she was pregnant. While I was informed by God of circumstances surrounding your conception, try explaining that to an angry mob. We married, survived that, but you were still regarded as a mamzer, claimed to be illegitimate. That ridicule, because they questioned your paternity, subsided when we returned from Egypt. But some hardliners maintained their attitudes until Rabbi Shimon interceded.

"Your grandparents heard the same gossip and lost friends because of it." He paused and wiped his mouth with a cloth. "Gosh, that stew is good. Would you please bring me another serving? And perhaps a small glass of wine. It will help me sleep." Jesus brought the stew, a piece of bread and wine.

"Thanks," Joseph said. "Where was I? Oh yes, even now some of these rigid thinkers talk in the shadows about why you have not married. You hear a lot as a businessman, not all of it business. And there are those who call you a false prophet, one determined to upset the laws and customs of our people. It will only get worse."

Joseph sat up and smiled. "I believe that wine has cured whatever ails me." Then he laughed, a chuckle born out of memory. "Before and after you were born your mother and I discussed how we should raise you. We worried, I'm serious, whether we should let the human Jesus play rough-house games like ordinary boys or watch your every move lest something bad happen to the son of God.

"God forbid – that's an expression here, Jesus – that something terrible would happen on our watch. Imagine getting to the Pearly Gates and God says: *Were the instructions unclear? Did my angel not explain Mary's pregnancy and that she would bear a son, Jesus, who will save people from their sins? And you let him play with your big saw?* Heaven would be in an uproar.

"Truth is when you were little, after we returned from Egypt, I recall a day when your mother nearly had a heart attack. You were in the carpenter shop playing with long nails. You were using a nail to draw in the dust and Mary yanked it away and tossed it into a corner like it was evil. I guess she thought there was a danger you would poke it into your hands.

"She may not have told you about the day coming out of Egypt when you backed into a cactus thorn. You would have thought we were being attacked by the Amalekites. You were yowling. Your mother was sniffling. She retrieved her needle . . ."

"I was not sniffling," Mary protested, finishing kitchen chores except for Joseph's stew cup and wine glass. "I did what any mother would do while you watched and laughed. I dug out the thorn, wiped off the blood, dabbed some balm on the wound and tied a cloth around his leg. I didn't sniffle."

"Note to self: She didn't sniffle," Joseph conceded. "Our biggest concern was when to talk to you about being the son of God in addition to being our son. At what age would you sense that you were more than human, and how should we handle that. Mary said it would happen gradually, just as every other child grows and learns who they are. She was right.

"Your divine nature trumped your human nature that time someone called you a mamzer and said you should be shunned at school because of the circumstances of your birth. How little they knew. Or that time when a boy called your mother a whore and that you had no father. Good thing I wasn't there. I may have pulled his ear halfway to Sepphoris. You showed maturity beyond human expectations."

"There were times," Jesus confessed, "when the human side was quite active. That boy who insulted my mother has had a troubled life. His vile comment was something he repeated from his father. I perhaps stepped out of bounds one time when I suggested to an adult member of the Synagogue that it was no sin to be poor. He had decried the old man who sometimes begs down at the well.

"As you know in our culture children are to be seen and not heard," Jesus said. " He didn't take kindly to my comment and said he would report my conduct, as he put it, to both you and the rabbi. It didn't help when I added that if members of our congregation assisted with the beggar's needs he wouldn't have to solicit. I'm sure you heard about it. I was probably about 15."

"It's news to me," Joseph said. "Mary. Have you heard anything about what Jesus just said?" She shook her head "no."

"My guess, Jesus, is that if this fellow talked to the rabbi at all, he thought better of complaining more about it. Going back to that episode in Jerusalem when you were 12, I admit I was upset. Your mother and I were distressed that something bad had happened to you. It's a terrible feeling for a parent to not know where a child is.

"After your explanation, which calmed my dander a little – and Mary's understanding aided the process – I came to realize that this was your coming-of-age moment. In the days that followed, I recognized that this time with Jewish scholars, asking and answering questions, was a sort of crossover point for you. Your messianic role took form with the understanding that while you were 100 percent human you were also 100 percent divine."

"That's pretty close to hitting the peg with the hammer," Jesus answered, "but I later grasped your angst at my staying behind. I could have handled the matter better."

"Well, now that we have that settled, isn't it time for sleep?" Mary injected. No one disputed the suggestion, and Joseph was soon snoring.

The next morning Joseph ate breakfast and was sharpening tools in the shop as Jesus returned from his prayers at the Sycamore grove. His cough was still present, but the color in his face and general appearance seemed much better. He greeted Jesus with a smile.

"Good morning, son. Always remember that a carpenter's day starts much better when tools are sharp. Or, you might say a good carpenter is only as sharp as his tools."

"Hello, father. I'm surprised to find you out here this early."

"Just checking on things," Joseph said. "I must say everything looks good. Oh, I did a little cleaning here and there. Put tools in their proper place. And I wanted to talk to you privately about the matter of girls. We can talk more freely out here."

"Sure. What is it you want to talk about girls?"

"Well," Joseph wiped his hands with a rag as if he'd just finished a long day's labor, "girls are different. One of the things your mother and

I talked about, given your divine nature and all, was how to prepare you for this time." He continued to twist and thumb the rag as if he planned to knit something.

"What time are we talking about?" Jesus asked.

"That time when you might get serious about a certain girl. I'm not talking about the birds and the bees and all that stuff. We went over that several years ago, but I suppose it touches on the same subject, that time when the birds and the bees get serious, when a male species concentrates on a certain female species. Like that."

"Father, have you forgotten Naomi? If I were to marry someone, that is if my human self solely directed my decisions, Naomi would have been the one. But we had a long visit about it, and it's settled. She knows my plans and my mission. And mother knows all about it, too."

"She does?" Joseph said quizzically.

"Yes, I mentioned it to both of you one night. Perhaps you were snoozing already."

"Perhaps. Well, good. Then our talk is over unless you have any questions." Joseph tossed the knotted rag on the work bench. "Out of curiosity, what did Naomi say? After you told her."

"She said she was going to marry a farm boy."

Chapter 27

It was an unusually warm springtime morning in Nazareth. Even at sunrise, as Jesus sat beneath the Sycamore tree outside of town, it felt like a sauna. A slight westerly wind was saturated with moisture plucked from the Great Sea. Lower Galilee was draped with a wet blanket of heavy dew that only a strong sun and shifting weather front could offset.

He removed his mantle as droplets of perspiration seeped from his olive-toned forehead and trickled down his nose. He smiled and ran his hands through damp black hair. It was the rainy season, and farmers depended on the dew "to kiss the crop." However, the humidity tended to smother things.

Jesus folded his undyed shawl carefully like the treasure it was and laid it on a large rock. It was made by his mother of fine wool, with small tassels dangling from its edges. His one-piece beige tunic fell just below his knees. He kicked off his sandals, now satisfied that he could pray and meditate comfortably with the Father.

As he approached age 20, Jesus gained insight on the process of expanding God's kingdom on Earth. In the coming years, he would continue to examine the Scriptures, seek signs and prophesies that may shed light on his role and life. Some time ago he had concluded that while he was selected to lead God's mission, he couldn't do it alone. He would need disciples in the near term and for that matter for centuries to come.

He envisioned a kingdom that would live far beyond his tenure on Earth, but thoughts of those times gave way to concentration on the immediate future. He knew he would preach and attend to those in need. He was convinced that the core of his mission should be directed at the marginal and the need for the kingdom to rally around the poor.

There were still many questions. Among the things pondered by his parents as Jesus grew to an adult was whether he had any perception of his final days. In the back of Mary's mind were the words spoken by the angel Gabriel at the time of Jesus' conception: *He will be great and will be called the Son of the Most High . . . and of his kingdom there will be no end.*

And they knew of his salvation role. Joseph was told by the angel that Mary was pregnant through the Holy Spirit and that Jesus *will save his people from their sins.* Mary especially contemplated with anguish words spoken by Simeon at the presentation of Jesus at the Temple a few weeks after his birth. Simeon, a devout Jew who proclaimed Jesus as the long-awaited savior, told Mary that Jesus was destined *for the fall and rise of many in Israel* and that *a sword* would pierce her own soul.

Jesus, as was often the case, sat down on a stool he had made from scrap cedar, quietly thinking of his destiny. Pacing was not part of his meditation formula. Even though he often looked heavenward, he frequently conversed as if God were sitting on a chair next to him. Thanksgiving and petition comprised most of his prayer.

How many times we have had these talks, Jesus said to himself.

He wiped the sweat from his face and reveled in the Galilean surroundings. Doves, sparrows, vultures and a myriad of other birds sang in competition to announce the new day, ignoring the sticky heat. A bell tied to the neck of a sheep or cow tinkled in a nearby meadow. A rooster crowed. A dog barked. The sultry wind added its heavy strains to the symphony.

To the southeast the entire landscape was interrupted by the steep gradient of Mount Tabor, rising like a massive dome from the Jezreel Valley. On this morning, a fog-like halo clung to the base of the mountain. In the distance, Jesus could see vast hillsides of olive trees and manicured rows of vineyards. New wheat poked out of the flatlands. Nearest to him was an expanse of grassland dotted with poppies.

Jesus looked in the opposite direction, back at tiny Nazareth, part of it nestled cozily in a basin, part dangling on a steep hillside. Smoke rose as households started fires for breakfast and daily baking as the process of living started anew. Nearly an hour later his stomach and taste buds sent hunger signals. He walked in deep thought, oblivious to the steep bluffs bordering the north side of the path.

"Shalom aleichem, my son," Joseph said as Jesus entered the tiny house. Jesus responded in kind and kissed Joseph on the cheek. He hugged Mary and she presented her cheek to also be kissed.

"Thank you," Mary said. "Now please go back and shut the door tightly as I don't want our home smelling like a bathhouse. The humidity this morning is as oppressive as Roman taxes." The rock walls in back already glistened with dampness.

"I know mother. My tunic is already soaked. I'm going to wash up before having breakfast." When he returned, he found Joseph back on his pallet, a wheezing sound drifting from his chest. He walked directly to him and propped up his head with additional pillows.

"It's the awful weather," Joseph contended, anticipating a comment by Jesus concerning the rattling sound coming from his chest.. "What projects are you working on today?"

"I need to purchase some cedar to build a new water trough for a farmer near Magdala. It's an easy job, but I'll be gone for a couple of days."

"How did you get a job over there?" Mary asked. "That's near the Sea of Galilee."

"It is," Jesus replied. "I have some friends in that area who said this fellow needed a new trough for his sheep pen. He can't pay much so I suspect we will be having lamb for supper in the coming days. A rock structure set as a masonry fixture would last longer, but he can't afford that."

Jesus followed Joseph's example and charged customers on their ability to pay. Good carpenters and masons made 50 denarii a month, twice the earnings of a laborer or shepherd. (A denarius was a Roman silver coin valued in modern times at 75 cents. It bore a likeness of the head of Caesar and was "the head tax coin" exacted by the Romans from the Jews.)

When Jesus returned from the job, he not only had cuts of lamb but a dozen eggs and two loaves of barley bread. He also discovered that a healer was attending Joseph. After a night of nearly constant coughing and wheezing, Mary decided to seek medical help.

"Shalom," Jesus greeting the healer, who then whispered to Mary and Jesus that the end was near for Joseph. While neither was surprised, the imminence of death is always shocking.

"Healer, what are you muttering about?" Joseph said. "Don't be too hasty in your pronouncements. I will see the sun rise again." And he did.

The next day, though his eyes still visited upon his loved ones, his exhausted lungs gave up. Shortly after Mary lovingly spooned some chicken broth in his mouth, Joseph, begotten by Jacob of the House of David, died.

He was 49.

"Truly, he was a holy and caring man," Mary said, as she laid her hand on his now quiet chest. She closed his eyes. Next, she wiped traces of broth from his graying beard. Then she looked at Jesus. "I could not have had a more loving and understanding husband, and you could not have had a more dedicated and protective father. His gentle nature will be exemplary for all time."

Mary asked Jesus to notify the rabbi and two of her closest friends, Adah and Eunice. After the latter arrived, they assisted Mary in washing Joseph's body. They then anointed him with nard and aloe, perfumes Mary had acquired in anticipation of his death. Mary poured several drops of aloe on her husband's forehead and with a mixture of tears gently rubbed his face.

Once finished, they covered his head with a light blue cloth, tied the hands and feet with strips of fabric and then wrapped his entire body in a shroud. While it was Jewish practice to bury the dead the same day, the unusual warm weather made it even more imperative.

News of Joseph's death spread quickly. Within the hour a few close friends came to comfort Mary and Jesus and bid their farewells to Joseph. Other mourners, mostly customers whom Joseph had assisted, came for one last visit to a carpenter who had become a friend. Several, with Jesus' aid, fashioned a litter to transport Joseph's body to his burial site in a cave just outside town.

After Rabbi Shimon arrived, and said his words of sympathy to the family, the mourners processed northeastward out of Nazareth along the narrow path to the tomb site. Jesus and several other male friends carried the litter. While Mary remained silent and somber, some of the women wailed and tossed dust in their hair.

Joeseph's body was carried through the cavern's narrow passageway and placed on a large stone. Most mourners remained outside. The rabbi again pronounced comforting words to the family and read appropriate psalms. His brief remarks reiterated what everyone knew. Joseph, he said, was not only a craftsman but incorporated in his work the love he had for people.

Jesus, too, offered a short eulogy to his earthly father, noting how he cared for "everyone, without reservation, an example to all of us." Jesus then greeted the mourners and thanked them for coming. He then walked to his mother, embraced her and whispered something in her ear. The two then departed and others followed.

Once back in Nazareth, mourners were invited to a meal of condolence hosted by friends. Mary and Jesus remained at home for the next week to receive others wishing to offer support and sympathy. It was also a solemn time when they could have personal talks and reflections about the man who protected the Son of God.

After several years, following usual Jewish tradition, family members would return to the tomb, collect the bones in an ossuary, then place the box in the back of the tomb to make room for future generations in the same space. Mary and Jesus deemed that that was unnecessary.

Some years after Joseph's death and burial, while Jesus was away at work, Mary had a couple of unexpected visitors. She was pulling weeds in her small garden when a pair of Roman soldiers on horses pulled up just outside the courtyard. She was startled. Soldiers were a rare sight in Nazareth. Everyone knew the tax collector by name, but the soldier was a stranger.

One of them dismounted, his vest armor rattling and squeaking as if it needed lubrication. He removed his silver helmet with the thin red plume atop, tucked it under his arm, and walked directly to Mary with no introduction. He represented Roman power and that was prologue enough.

"You are Mary, the mother of Jesus of Nazareth, are you not?" the man asked evenly.

"I am. How may I help you?"

"We are inquiring about your son," the soldier said. "It has come to the attention of builders who work for Herod Antipas that your Jesus is an accomplished mason. His excellency has begun work on a new city called Tiberias near the Sea of Galilee. Perhaps you are aware of this great undertaking in honor of our new Roman emperor."

Emperor Tiberius had succeeded Ceasar Augustus several years before and was Antipas' patron. Building the new Galilee capital in his name was Antipas' approach to job security.

"There is a great need for artisans of all sorts," the soldier envoy said. "We would like to visit with him. Is he here?"

"He is not," Mary said. "I believe he is helping a farmer repair a gate." Her mind slipped quickly into a defensive mode, searching for words that would keep her son out of the crosshairs of Antipas. As Jesus grew, so had her fears. Would Antipas, son of Herod the Great, somehow associate Jesus with the killing of newborn males in Judea some two decades ago? Did they know Jesus and his parents escaped to Egypt?

Joseph had always tried to calm her worries, but he was gone. Certainly, the Herod family spy network was capable of learning details of every perceived threat. Its tentacles followed Roman rule from the Nile northward to the entire Great Sea region. The one hope, she said to herself, lay in the deliberate lack of communications and overt animosity among the Herod siblings.

"As for his abilities as a mason," she said, "you may have Jesus confused with my late husband. He truly was an artisan, a man with imagination and skills. Jesus is not in his league. He is more of a handyman. Not only that, but Jesus plans to become a rabbi and continues to study our Scripture intently."

Suddenly, her apprehension took a new direction. Had she said too much, mentioning Jesus' rabbi and Scripture interests. Would Antipas' minions connect the dots, research Jesus' birth and all the events surrounding it? Roman rulers are good at taking all information, adding it up and reaching conclusions. Mary stood in limpness, frozen by the unforeseen.

"In that case," the soldier said calmly, "we will come back at another time to talk with him. When do you expect him home?"

"I'm not sure. Possibly later today. Maybe tomorrow."

Mary hoped the uncertainty of her response would pose sufficient diversion to the interlopers. The spokesman soldier nodded and turned toward his mount, his hand firmly on his sword not in a threatening way but to keep it from bouncing. Once on his horse, he and his accomplice rode off toward Sapphoris without a gesture.

Jesus, when informed of the encounter, downplayed any ulterior ramifications and, like Joseph would have, assured his mother that the visit was solely to recruit workers. Moreover, it turned out that the attention of Antipas was being redirected to more personal matters, matters of libido that were associated with his marriage to his brother's wife.

Early in his reign Antipas married Phasa'el, the daughter of King Aretas of Nabataea, a nomadic group of Bedouin Arabs who roamed a large area east of the Jordan River. Several years later, on a family visit to Rome, Antipas' roving eye locked on Herodias, wife of Antipas' half-brother. They were eventually married before Herodias was divorced.

Phasa'el returned home to her father, who carried his daughter's humiliation to war. Antipas' forces were defeated in a battle in western Peraea, but it didn't change the marriage situation. Nor did it stop Antipas from building his new city, Tiberias. Jesus was never contacted again to work on the project.

In the years to come, Jesus continued his carpenter and handyman work. While he was respected for his skills, he was always known as the carpenter's son. More and more his preaching was taking him away from Nazareth to the busy crossroads of Capernaum and even north to Sidon, Tyre and deep into Gentile country. But his mission's focus remained on the Jewish people.

He participated with his Nazareth pals in one more race at Nain, but his life turned slowly to his divine side. For Jesus carpentry became a tool for interaction and service with people. Working in a business, even a small one, also gave him exposure to a host of human imperfections – impatience, dissatisfaction and even anger.

A vintner who asked Jesus to build new tables for the process of plucking grapes from stems complained that the benches were too short, "unlike the ones your father constructed." Without instruction, Jesus had sized up other family members and adjusted the height to accommodate everyone. The owner was unusually tall and insisted the table conform to his size. Jesus rebuilt the tables with adjustable legs.

A woman ordered an ornate chair for her greeting room. She specified costly walnut. When Jesus delivered the chair, the woman was elated at its craftsmanship. "I'm surprised," she said. "It's much like what your father would have done." Upon closer inspection, she discovered a knot that was not sanded to her liking. Jesus smoothed it.

When an olive orchard owner belatedly ordered several new ladders, with the harvest season fast approaching, he complained directly to Mary when Jesus put the request after two other jobs. Mary's explanation of following an orderly process only heightened the owner's anger. Jesus fixed it, getting others to reschedule their projects.

"Some of these complaints are unjust and others trifling," Jesus said to his mother one night after supper. His human nature was reacting.

"We are a flawed people, Jesus," Mary responded. "Sometimes, when we confront such individuals, it's helpful to think about what's really behind their annoyance or anger. Perhaps they had an encounter with a tax collector or had a disagreement with a family member. We just don't know what may be bothering them."

Chapter 28

NAZARETH, about 27AD – It wasn't the first time that he wished Joseph were there to help solve a carpenter puzzle. Mrs. Koppel specifically ordered a new oaken table, gave the specifications and was insistent that it have "those fancy corner grooves." She hadn't decided on the stain.

The one thing he knew for sure: It would be expensive. Wood was costly in Galilee, especially oak. He hadn't figured out the total price yet, including his labor, but he had informed her that the project would take a while. She said neither the cost nor time to build it was a problem. However, her daughter was just betrothed, and she would like to have the table for the wedding.

Those "corner grooves", Jesus understood, is what Joseph described as interlocking edges. They were a challenge even for Joseph, and he had made few of them. Jesus told her that he was inexperienced at such woodworking, but she assured him, "You will do a fine job."

If he worked steady on the table, he guessed it would take most of a month. But he had other obligations, like repairing a shed for a farmer and patching Mrs. Adontz' roof that had been damaged in a storm. It had been this way ever since Joseph died. Like his father, Jesus had business all over the region. He knew the geography well, which also served his ministry campaign.

After Mrs. Koppel left, he washed up and joined his mother for supper. His mind was consumed by the new table order and the list of work. He wondered out loud to Mary whether he could complete it in the time she specified, and to her satisfaction. Mary was busy preparing a meal and half-heard his laments. She set the lentil-bean soup and bread on the table.

"Jesus, please close the door. I declare! Is there something about a closed door that poses a problem for you? It's quite possible to talk, spell out your problems, and close the door at the same time."

"I'm sorry mother. Mrs. Koppel makes me nervous." He explained the table order and details. "I don't know if I can meet her expectations. Sometimes I feel like I'm running on father's reputation. He taught me a great deal but I am not the craftsman he was nor can I work as fast. Besides, I have speaking obligations at various Synagogues."

"One of these days you need to take time for me to trim your hair," Mary said, unimpressed by his litany of carpenter jobs. "It's getting to look a little shaggy, not unlike that of your Capernaum friend. Your Synagogue messages may have a longer impact if your hair were shorter."

Just when Jesus thought his mother was deaf to his busy schedule, she came up with a possible solution.

"My son, you might contact Malach of Chorazin, one of Joseph's nephews," Mary suggested as she placed dinnerware on the table. "He's about your age and the last I heard was looking for work. Too bad none of your friends in Nazareth are seeking jobs.

As it turned out, Malach had found employment, and Jesus was again facing his work alone. But he was fortunate. Buried in a box of records he found an old pattern Joseph had drawn to making interlocking corners. With those instructions Jesus was able to complete the table, minus the finishing stain, in less than a month. Moreover, it didn't interfere with his other projects, including preaching.

"Thank you, Joseph!" he shouted when he had fully assembled the table. "Couldn't have done it without you."

"Who are you talking to?" Caleb said as he entered the carpenter shop.

"Hey there, Caleb. You startled me," Jesus replied. "Actually, I was just admiring the table I built for a customer and was thanking my father Joseph for helping."

"Wait a minute," Caleb said, a perplexed look on his face. "You were talking to your father? I think you've gone around the bend, working too hard."

Jesus laughed and told him of Mrs. Koppel's specifications and finding Joseph's old drawings, which bailed him out in building the table and saved him time in the process. "I was moved to give him thanks, and not say it quietly," Jesus explained.

"That is good news. Now you have the time to help me make some wine," Caleb smiled broadly. "I, too, have found an old blueprint, recipe if you will, for making some really good stuff. We can purchase extra fine grapes from the Horovitz vineyard. I found a used press to squeeze out the juices and we will be on our way to creating a fine product, just like your table."

Caleb circled Mrs. Koppel's table, feeling the fine corners and smooth top. "She will be pleased with this. And think, Jesus, you could hand her a glass of really good wine as you present the table to her." His smile widened, like that of a used camel salesman.

"Where do you come up with this 'we' stuff?" Jesus asked. "I don't recall ever talking with you about making wine. Besides, your family is in the date business. Why don't YOU consider making date wine? You heard me expressly use the word 'you'? Your father would probably give you all the dates you want."

"Really, Jesus. That shows how little you know about making wine," Caleb said with a sour look. "That would be like making a fine table out of seaweed. You must have the finest grapes to make really good wine. Fine wine, Jesus, is the blood of the grape. You mix various juices from various grapes to get the exact taste you want, sweet or dry."

"I can see you've studied up on wine making," Jesus said. "Do you plan to make a sweet non-alcoholic grape juice, or the kind with a little kick to it?"

"Probably both," Caleb continued. "I'm told that our yeast only yields about six percent alcohol content in the wine. That's pretty mild. So, what do you say? Are you in? You have all this extra time now. Besides, the fermentation process nullifies all of the bad stuff in our water. Wine is a health drink."

"In moderation, Caleb. In moderation. I don't know if I have the time. I'll have to think about it. I am traveling more, preaching on the Scriptures. I wish people would get as intoxicated with God's word as some get on wine. I'll let you know in a couple of weeks, but if you can get another partner, go for it."

Mary joined Jesus on the day Mrs. Koppel came over to inspect her table. She still had to pick out the kind of stain, if any, that she wanted. The final step would be hardening the surface with a rubbing material he purchased from an oil mill. When she entered the shop, Mrs. Koppel was overjoyed. She clasped her hands to her face in a gesture of marvel.

Jesus had used pegs to secure the grooved corners, then placed wooden caps on the awl-carved holes. She was fascinated by the workmanship. Her hands caressed the table's legs and surface with the gentleness given to a new-born baby. She was so ecstatic that she rushed to Jesus and embraced him.

Jesus wondered if anyone would ever gather for a meal at the table or if was primarily a showpiece.

"You have done a masterful job, Jesus, son of Joseph," she said. She continued to adore the table as if it were heaven's gates. "I want to pay you a bonus. You have exceeded my expectations. I don't think I want it stained. The natural wood is so beautiful. It would be a shame to alter that."

"I'm happy that you are pleased with the table," Jesus said, "but there is no need for a bonus. If you feel you want to give something extra to our Synagogue's poor fund, that would be okay. However, my charge will only include labor and materials. I know you understand that the oak is expensive. I will have it delivered after I apply the clear finishing oils."

With that, Mary invited Mrs. Koppel in the house for fruit juice and figs. However, she declined and apologized, saying she had another appointment that demanded her presence. She gushed more accolades in Jesus' direction and abruptly departed. Jesus was noticeably relieved, so much so that he told Mary he planned to help Caleb make wine.

"I can't imagine that Joseph would have been as nervous as me in building that table," Jesus said, exhaling as if a weight had been lifted from his shoulders. Mary laughed. "Imagine Joseph when he first learned I was pregnant with you – before we were married. Now that's nervous. Panicky nervous. Mrs. Koppel had faith in you just as Joseph had faith in God and in me."

Jesus hired a man with a large cart to deliver the table and in two days was in Caleb's storage barn assisting with the wine-making process. "I've decided to make mostly a blend of grape juices," Caleb explained, "but some fermented wine, too. There is more demand for the juice than alcoholic wine. Although it is the wine that relaxes uptight table makers like you."

"Okay, okay," Jesus joined in Caleb's amusement. "Maybe that was Joseph's secret in dealing with busy times and impatient customers. Finish the day and have a sip or two of wine tonic. What is it you want me to do? Take the grapes off of the stems? Turn the press? Strain the juice? Or, maybe you want me to taste the various juices and recommend the perfect blend."

"Well," Caleb became serious, "perhaps you could peal the grapes."

He looked at Jesus and couldn't withhold his laughter. "I had you there for a second. Admit it."

Caleb already had half the grapes pressed with juices placed in containers and properly labeled. "The important thing," Caleb said like a veteran wine maker, "is to keep the various grape juices separated and itemized. Then we experiment with blends to see which combination makes the palate joyful. For some we will add a little yeast, the same kind your mother uses for baking, to activate fermentation."

The process began. With their chins red from juice dribble, they agreed on blends. "First, we must boil the juices, then place them in clay jars and seal it with bees wax," Caleb explained. "That prevents fermentation and protects the purity. When you are ready to use it, just add a little water."

Then they started on the alcoholic version. "This will be the good stuff," Caleb claimed as if he'd already tasted it. Yeast was added and the blend placed in new wineskins. "Never use old wineskins for fermentation," Caleb emphasized. "In three months, it should be ready. The longer it ages the better it will be."

Once finished, Caleb and Jesus stepped back to admire their work.

"May the process of chemistry begin," an inspired Caleb said.

Caleb resumed help on the family's date farm. Jesus returned to his carpentry work.

While barley and wheat are planted late in the year and harvested in Nisan (spring), grapes are ready for picking in Tammuz (summer). Galilee vineyards matured later than those in warmer climates in the

Jordan valley. As part of the Festival of Harvest, first fruits were celebrated in thanksgiving for God's provision. It was formally known as Shavuot and occurred 50 days after Passover.

Caleb let his wine age slightly longer. In late summer, excited at expectations of a vintage with textbook taste, he invited family and friends to sample the blend created by Jesus and himself. The wineskins were unsealed, a spread of complementary foods provided and the proper prayers said. As might be expected, Josiah, Piram, Thaddeus and other school pals attended the tasting. Even Eli of Nain came over.

The wine was poured, cups lifted to lips and the anticipated nectar of the grapevine splashed on tastebuds.

One by one faces grimaced as if they had just bitten into a rotten lemon, curdled expressions that needed no explanation. Caleb sipped his own wine and coughed in revulsion. He shook his head in disappointment, then covered his face with his hands as if he'd violated the tenth commandment. His partner knew the endeavor flopped before having a sample.

"My recommendation," Josiah approached Jesus with a sour expression, "is that you stay out of the wine-making business."

Chapter 29

NAZARETH, 31AD – Time flew as if being pushed by a giant bellows from the heavens.

News of the carpenter-preacher had become commonplace throughout Galilee and swept beyond to friends and foes and those in between.

I, Peter, went with him to many places, the largest to a hillside near Capernaum. There I saw him feed multitudes from a scant supply of bread and fish offered by a boy.

I was with him when he cast out demons, made the blind see and healed the sick, including my mother-in-law. I witnessed him calming a storm, walk on the Sea of Galilee and fill our nets with fish. I wasn't on all of his missions, but I was there when he raised Jairus' 12-year-old daughter from the dead. Jairus is a Capernaum Synagogue leader.

I was with him when he heard that John the Baptizer had been arrested by Herod Antipas and eventually beheaded. Jesus blamed himself, saying he should have done more to prevent John's death. He said the killing of John was the most horrible thing in his memory. He mourned for many days after disciples entombed John's body.

Most of all I witnessed Jesus' boundless mercy and love. And that, coming from an intemperate, impatient and impulsive person, may be the biggest miracle of all.

Grumbling from Roman authorities, and some Jewish leaders, reached my ears, but I gave it about as much attention as I would a whining competitor who had a bad day fishing. Change is in the wind. Jesus is getting itchy to spread his wings, take his ministry to all of Judea and beyond.

Life, as always, goes on in the fishing villages of Bethsaida and Capernaum. There are days of good catches and times when the fish are hard to find. As you know, after Eden's father died some years ago we moved in with her mother at Capernaum. It wasn't my choice, but Eden felt an obligation to be with her mother. It did save us rent money.

Jesus has been spending more time in the Capernaum region. Ever since that crowd ran him out of his hometown, he doesn't spend much time there. Capernaum is a much bigger place than Nazareth. It's larger than Bethsaida. Capernaum is on the main road between Damascus and Jerusalem, and hence has a huge trading business. More people can mean more business but also more headaches. I prefer quiet places like the sea.

My brother, Andrew, actually knew Jesus before I did. Andrew was a friend of John the Baptizer. John called Jesus the Lamb of God, and invited Andrew to meet him at the Jordan River where John was preaching. Then came the day Andrew and I were preparing our boat for fishing when Jesus comes along, and, as they say the rest is history.

I want to tell you more about that time when Andrew and I first met Jesus. He came into our boat after we had a horrible night of fishing. James and John were in another boat nearby, and nobody was catching anything. Maybe a few scrawny sardines. Fishing was lousy. I used worse words than lousy to describe it. We couldn't remember a more abysmal outing.

Andrew was his usual disgusting, calm self, saying something stupid like the fish had gone on vacation. Not me. I used every cuss word I'd learned in all my years in the business. Holy Moses. I did this for a living. I knew the tricks of every fish and their kin. Nothing worked. We caught absolutely nothing!

Then Jesus says to row out a little further on the sea. Right. As if we didn't already cover every square inch of water. He says to cast out the nets again, as if the blisters on my fingers needed new blisters. Agreeable Andrew nods approval, and so we row out to deeper water and lowered the nets again. After all night of failure!!

You know what happened. The nets overflowed with fish. James and John had to help us with the catch. Sure I was happy. But also angry. Embarrassed. I fish for a living. What does Jesus know about fishing? Nothing, as far as I know. I admit. I was ticked. Of course Andrew and the other two were overjoyed. Okay, so I had a lot to learn about this Jesus.

I think Jesus has been talking about the kingdom of God for 10 years now. They tell me he was a bright boy in Synagogue in Nazareth, knew nearly all the Scriptures. Funny how things work out. You would think all Nazareth would be proud of Jesus, but they chased him out of town. He only goes back to see his mother.

He says he was a fair distance-runner at one time. Jesus talks about his boyhood buddies, Caleb, Josiah and Eli of Nain, especially about that Passover trip when he was 12. And one day he told me about Naomi, really the only girl he ever gave a second look. Of course I heard all about his birth and the family's time in Egypt.

Now we are here, just Jesus and I, sitting under that Sycamore tree outside of Nazareth, his favorite place for praying and meditating.

I had walked over the day before from Capernaum to learn what he planned for his ministry in the coming weeks. Eden's mother was feeling much better, and the fishing was slow. Last night I stayed with one of Andrew's fisherman friends a short distance from Nazareth.

In a way, I dislike invading his private place, but I have questions. His face looks troubled. So, after greetings were exchanged, I asked him straight out what was on his mind. It surprised me when Jesus said he is sometimes lonely. I have come to believe he is the Messiah, the God-man talked about by prophets. How can he be lonely? He has the entire world as his companion. He could snap his fingers to create a dozen friends, command into existence a Synagogue of followers, fashion a multitude of believers.

On the other hand, maybe his life is like fishing. Some days the fish are eager to take your hook, fill the nets like water filled the lands of Noah. Other times it's as dry as the desert. You wait and wait while nothing happens. It's lonely in a boat in those moments.

It's been a peculiar day. The dawn was born angry, full of thunder and lightning. By mid-morning the skies were clear. Jesus' mood was similar. Early in the day he said he sometimes felt deserted. I told him that I would never abandon him as a friend and follower. He responded with this funny smile.

I'm no psychologist but it seems there is something heavy on his mind, a foreboding that has overwhelmed his senses. It's as if someone came to you and predicted an event that would change your life forever. That would keep you awake at night.

An hour later he seemed more relaxed.

"Peter," he said, "I'm nearing the time when my preaching will wind down in Galilee. I must take my ministry to the rest of Judea, especially Jerusalem." He calls me Peter now rather than Simon. I was shocked that day when he said he wanted me to lead his followers and that henceforth he would call me Peter. Me a blusterous fisherman with no formal education.

Jesus told me that Peter means 'rock', in either Greek or Aramaic. I don't recall which. All of us followers are common people. But I was as dazed as a fish out of water when he selected me as leader. Especially his knowing my reputation. He's heard me violate the commandment against swearing. On top of all that, I haven't been in really in good standing with his mother.

"Peter," Jesus asked with a brow bent to the troubled side, "how can I get my message out so that people will be more receptive? I don't want to talk like the prophet Joel about invading armies of locust, or days of darkness, although there certainly will be some. Rather, I want them to freely embrace the mercy of a loving God, imagine the unexplainable joy of eternal life in heaven.

"They see God's wonders around them every day, in their families, their friends and when I heal the sick. Oh, they run and tell friends of the miracles of God when the deaf hear and the blind see. But the next day many expect more miracles. What happened to the faith in God from the day before?"

"Master, you dare ask me such questions?" I responded. "I am a simple man. I know you invited us to be fishers of men, but I'm still puzzled why fish don't bite on certain days. You may as well ask me how people 2,000 years from now will respond to your message. Figuring out people is impossible, and that includes me. I don't understand why you picked me as a disciple and then made me leader of the bunch."

"Peter, I picked you for your unabashed honesty. No one has any difficulty in knowing how you feel, what your opinion is. You have a knack for listening to both sides of an issue, and then stating your position. And I've seen you convince a majority without punches being thrown. You are a sinner and know it. Most important, Peter, you are solid in your faith in God."

"Well, Jesus, my opinion is that many people are faithful to the God of Israel. Some are conveniently faithful, say if it benefits their business or doesn't interfere with something else. Others are like that lost sheep you talk about, so fixed on the present predicament they can't see the future."

"I see your point," he said. "But what more should I say to convince people of the importance of giving thought to the future, to the final kingdom? Human life is brief, a puff of smoke. It saddens me that I am unable to convince some people of that."

"I'll just say this, Jesus. I think you may be too hard on yourself. Perhaps, and I am just throwing this out – I'm no theologian, as you know – you need to think more about the faithful."

"No, no, Peter. As you suggested, it is the lost sheep where we must concentrate our attention. But among the faithful, too, there are those who don't get the full picture. Even some of the disciples don't seem to appreciate that all are welcome at my table, God's table, men and women, rich and poor, the just and unjust. Jews, Greeks, Gentiles and even Romans."

"Do you want me to speak to the group, let them know your feelings?"

"No, Peter. People must come to their own conclusions. Thank you for joining me this morning. I think we're overdue for first meal. I'm hungry."

As we walked up the incline to Nazareth, I wondered about the practical matters of any long mission to the south. I asked him about provisions, water and shelter. How many will be in the party? Who will do what? Do we need scouts? What about security?

"Peter, do you hear the doves singing and the sparrows chirping?" He pointed at the surrounding trees and undergrowth. "They are everywhere and none seem to be worried where the next meal is coming from. They sleep in the open. They fly to the nearest stream for a drink. And while they have their squabbles, most get along just fine. Why shouldn't we?"

"I don't much like thistle seed," I replied, "nor for that matter sour berries. I go for fish, lamb, bread, honey, wine, almonds, olives and most things. Not seeds."

"Peter, we will be fine. We will depend on the generosity of people along the way. I can't say how many will be on the journey. Some disciples may be ill when we leave. Some may bring family members or friends. But you are right in suggesting some planning. Visit with Matthew about any necessary arrangements. Someone suggested that I give a talk in the Capernaum area before we leave. I may do that."

"What will you talk about? The need for repentance? Loving your neighbor? The end of times?"

"I don't know yet. Matthew thinks I should pay tribute to various kinds of people, the holy, the troubled, those who negotiate peace. But I would also like to say something about the importance of following Moses' law, the commandments. And the importance of good example. We'll see."

There is a certain resolution in Jesus' manner, more so today than ever before. He is bent on a destination, almost as if he senses the final days. I can't figure it all out.

"I would like to stop off in Bethany to see my friend Lazarus," Jesus said as we neared Nazareth. "He has been sickly. Have you met him, Peter?"

"No, I haven't."

My immediate concern was not upsetting Jesus' mother. I always felt as if she looked at me like scum on a backwater bay. Jesus claimed I was wrong about that. Nevertheless, I scrubbed well before I left home. Washed my beard twice. Smelled under my arms. I made sure any fish odor was gone. I put on a clean tunic and shoulder shawl, and even combed my scraggily hair this morning. I was careful to keep my bird inkings well covered.

It may be the spiffiest I've looked since Eden and I were married.

"Good morning, Mary," I said with a slight bow upon entering her house. I clasped my hardened hands behind my back. She is still a pretty woman, and her red shawl and scarf set off her rosy cheeks. "It's nice to see you, again. Eden and her mother send their regards."

"Good day to you, Simon, or I should say Peter. Jesus has told me of the name change and that you will lead his followers. I'm sure you will do a good job. I'm pleased to hear Eden's mother is feeling better. Thanks be to God. I expect both of you are hungry. How about some barley bread and honey and we have dried fish."

"It all sounds good to me," I said. "Thanks, Mary for your hospitality."

I must be dreaming. I haven't said one wrong word so far. And she is friendly.

Jesus came in behind me and closed the door.

Mary beamed with satisfaction. After all these years.

He walked to his mother. They embraced. Their eyes met and said a thousand words. They did not talk for some time but continued to gaze at one another. Finally, he spoke.

"Peter and I have been discussing plans to take my ministry beyond Galilee, down along the Jordan River and up to Jerusalem." He turned toward me. "Mother has expressed an interest in coming along. Have you made up your mind, Mother?"

"No, I haven't. From what you tell me, it's a long walk."

"It is that," Jesus said. "However, it will be spread out over many days."

"Well, I have news for both of you," Mary said, as she gathered the bread and honey and placed them on the table. Then came the pomegranates and dried fish and figs. "Before any trip there is going to be a wedding." Jesus shrugged as if it were news to him. I certainly didn't know who she was talking about.

"I have been asked to be a co-hostess at a wedding two weeks from today for Mark and Chana, a lovely couple who Jesus knows," Mary said. Jesus nodded. "Mark's mother is one of my dearest friends. Jesus is invited and so are all his friends, so that would include you, Eden and all the disciples."

"Chana is from Japhia, a town just west of here," Jesus explained to me, "but she used to live in Nazareth. "I assume the ceremony will be in Japhia?" he addressed his mother.

"That's right. And her betrothed comes from a well-off family, so it will be a big affair."

"I guess that's settled then." Jesus said. "We'll be there. If the family is wealthy, they shouldn't run out of wine – like happened at Cana."

Mary gave him a raised-eyebrow look.

Eden and I were at that wedding, too. I knew the story.

"Peter, will you and Eden be at the wedding?" Mary asked.

"I believe I can slip that into my busy schedule," I said. "Eden and I will come, and if I know anything about the group Jesus has selected as followers it's that they like free food and wine. So, I say let's have fun."

I hoped that wasn't too direct and out of line.

Mary looked at me and smiled. She walked over to where I was standing and gave me a hug. Jesus' face produced a big grin.

Then he invited us all to sit and broke the bread.

Printed in the USA
CPSIA information can be obtained
at www.ICGtesting.com
JSHW082110071024
70976JS00001B/1

9 781959 620983